NOUHA JULLIENNE

COPYRIGHT

THE DIÁVOLOS: PART I
NOUHA JULLIENNE

Editing by Jennifer Innamorati
Proofreading by Stevi Mager-Lightfoot
Cover Design and formatting by Melissa Cunningham (To.All.The.Books.I.Love.)

This book is a work of fiction. All characters, places, incidents, and dialogue were created from the author's imagination. Nothing in this story should be constructed as real. Any similarities between persons living or dead are entirely accidental.

COPYRIGHT © NOUHA JULLIENNE ATOUI

All rights reserved. This book and its content are protected by Canadian copyright law. Except as otherwise provided for under Canadian copyright law, this book and its content may not be copied, published, distributed, downloaded or otherwise stored in a retrieval system, transmitted or converted, in any form or by any means, electronic or otherwise, without the prior written permission of the copyright owner.

ISBN: 9798371617224

Trigger Warnings

Graphic violence, gun violence, torture, assault, kidnapping, hostage situation, stalking, decapitation, death, mention of parental and sibling death, mention of child abuse, emotional abuse, verbal abuse, traumatic events, mental health issues (panic attacks, anxiety, PTSD), self-harm, drug manipulation, sexually explicit scenes (nudity, masturbation, dub con, consensual non-consent, knife play, blood play, gun play, sadism/masochism, mild breath play, primal/prey, degradation, impact play, crying kink, orgasm control).

Author's Note

Dear readers,

This story will seriously challenge your notion of what is right and wrong. The protagonists toggle between morally grey and black. They are unpredictable, and there's no telling what they'll do in any given situation. There is little to no discussion or struggle on their part. As a writer, I aim for moral ambiguity, which leads to better character development. The most interesting part of an arc is the moment a character's goal becomes completely opposed to what they want to do, and that's what happens in this novel.

This book is dirty, very kinky, and fun...at times. If you're not a fan of dubcon/CNC, this isn't for you. If you don't enjoy reading about blood, this isn't for you. If you have triggers, please read the warnings on the previous page.

The heroes have no limits, don't care about consequences, and would do anything to get what they want.

The Diávolos is part one of two in the Godfather's of the Night series. It is a triple POV, M/F romance with a slight twist—a

AUTHOR'S NOTE

stalker. This book has very mature themes, including an eleven-year age gap, an obsessed main character, another jealous/possessive one, and a strong-willed heroine. Please read at your discretion.

Playlist

For more songs, open Spotify search and scan this barcode.

Romantic Homicide - d4vd
　Last Night - Russ
　Heaven Angel - THE DRIVER ERA
　Haunt Me - RINI
　The Grey - Bad Omens
　Like I Want You - Giveon
　Trust - Brent Faiyaz
　If you Let Me - Sinéad Harnett, GRADES
　Closer - Nine Inch Nails

just like i do - Loveless
Agree to Disagree - Sleeping with Sirens
I Really Wish I hated You - blink-182
Lonely Day - System of A Down
Decode - Paramore
The Days - anders
Circles - Post Malone
Insecure - Brent Faiyaz
Flowers - Miley Cyrus
Something in the Orange - Zach Bryan
What You Heard - Sonder
All Mine - PLAZA
Freak - Lana Del Rey

Glossary

Diávolos: Devil
Baba: Dad/Father
Mama: Mom/Mother
Louloúdi mou: My flower
Yayá: Grandmother
Papoús: Grandfather
Princesita: Little princess
Carajita: Little girl/Brat
Malákes: Motherfuckers
Engoní: Granddaughter
Kalí douliá, kóri mou: Good job, my daughter.
Ta silipitíria mou: My condolences.
Yié: Son
Vlakas: Stupid
Tha mou kláseis: Suck my dick.
Ánte gamísou: Fuck you.
Kaliméra: Good morning.
Agápi mou: Sweetheart
Lolos: Crazy
Oo theé mou: Oh, my god.
Oo skatá: Oh, shit.
Asteri mou: My star

Christé mou: Jesus Christ
Íne sto ipógio afentikó: He's in the basement, boss.
Kamari mou: My pride
Kalimera afentiko: Good morning, boss.
Moró mou: Babe
Ómorfi: Beautiful
Angeloúdi mou: My little angel
Ti tréhei: What's wrong?
Kripse to korítsi. Tóra: Hide the girl. Now.
Poutánas yos: Son of a bitch.
Fáe skatá karióli: Eat shit, asshole.
Gamoto: Fuck
Ti sto diáolo: What the hell/fuck
Adelfé: Brother
Yia sou moráki: Hey, sexy.
Poutána: Whore
Ton agapás?: Do you love him?
Íne dikiá mou: She's mine.
Zíta mou na se filíso: Ask me to kiss you.
Óhi: No
Glykiá mou: My sweet
Maláka: Asshole
Me kánis na kavlóno: You're making me hard.
Se thélo: I want you.
Ti mou kánis ágele mou?: What do you do to me, my angel?
Piáse to poulí mou: Touch my cock.
Dikiá mou: Mine
Yié mou: My son
Kóri mou: Daughter
Mikrí mou: My little bird
Yiasou: Hello
Noná: Godmother
Me aidiázeis: You disgust me.

Agápi mou: My love
Pes to ónoma mou: Say my name.
Skáse: Shut up.
Tha sou spáso to kefáli sta dio: I will break your head open.
Se misó: I hate you.
Se agapó: I love you.

CONTENTS

Prologue	1
PART I The Revenge	5
PART II The Reveal	185
PART III The Betrayal	343
Epilogue	423
Author's Note	433
Acknowledgments	435

For the people who wear many hats, but struggle to keep them on.
　　　—Nouha Jullienne

Prologue

Fifteen Years Ago

Three men quietly stand a safe distance apart, forming a crescent in the empty space of an abandoned warehouse. The flicker of a yellow lamp, the only source of light other than moonlight, illuminates the dark area around them. The ceaseless sound of water dripping on the concrete echoes throughout the building.

One man, the eldest of the group, sporting a three-piece grey suit to match his hair, breaks the silence. "What did you tell the girl about her mother, Peter?" he asks the youngest.

The similarities between the two are unmistakable. Both are of equal height and stature, but while one's face is wrinkled with age, the other's is still young, the only lines are those between his brows, caused by his incessant frowning. Their eyes have the same shades of green and brown and change color depending on the light around them. Right now, in the dark, they appear light brown.

"That she accidentally died from a head injury," Peter replies. *Not necessarily a lie.*

"Will she be a problem?" the older man questions, crossing his arms at his chest.

"She's eight years old."

"Yeah, but you know kids her age are more curious and fearless than they ought to be."

"Don't worry about her." Peter's eyes glint with annoyance.

"We can always send her away until things calm down," the third man suggests, his tone full of mischief. He is middle-aged, and his unappealing looks match his unpleasant energy. He follows the eldest around like a loyal hound.

Peter knows exactly where he means and that option is out of the question. He might be a hypocrite, but he learned not to mix business with family the hard way.

"Fuck no. You know where those little girls end up. I'm not sending her into the lion's den." He readjusts the peaked lapels of his blue jacket and pulls on the collar of his shirt to give his throat some more room. Despite the large open space, the walls feel like they are closing in on him.

The grey-haired man intervenes, "He's got a point, Peter. She could use some structure now that she has no mother."

"I said no," Peter snaps.

"Then make sure she doesn't end up like her mother."

That hits a nerve. *Her mother.*

Despite the way they got together, and the hate she had felt toward him, Peter had loved the little girl's mother something fierce. Maybe it had been her unstoppable drive to find ways to leave that had him getting more and more attached over the years. As fucked up as that may be, the fact that she hadn't wanted him in the beginning had made him want her even more.

She hated loving him. But that hadn't stopped her from being the Bonnie to his Clyde, until something in her had switched and she'd wanted out. *Really* wanted out.

He'd had no choice.

Either she left and they risked the whole empire crumbling, taking the whole city down with them, or they got rid of her for good. It wasn't a total lie when he'd told the little girl that it was an accident. The main detail he'd left out was that he was the one who had caused it.

"I don't need your advice, *Father*. I know how to run my household," he spits, his pupils contorting with anger.

His father raises his hands in the air and takes a step back. "I'm just looking out for my family and the future Godfather of the Night."

At that exact moment, the three men hear an engine whirring and they notice a white, medium-sized cargo van with tinted windows as it turns the corner. The grey-haired man rubs his hands together and looks at the other two. "Let's see what we got."

The driver exits the vehicle with a clipboard and approaches them for a signature. Peter's father signs off and the driver nods, making his way back to the truck to unlock the back doors.

Eleven.

Peter counts eleven pairs of eyes staring right back at them. Terrified, tear-filled eyes.

This confirms it. There's no fucking way he would send his daughter there.

The little girls, none looking older than ten years old, flinch and clutch each other hard as the hound approaches the bed of the truck. He motions for the others to join him, and the smell of urine invades their nostrils. Peter turns away while the other two examine the girls. When they're done, the grey-haired man closes the doors and gives him one final look, a question in his eyes. Peter shakes his head.

His father taps the side of the van. "Send them to the Sisterhood."

Part 1
The Revenge

"No matter how hard the past is, you can always begin again."
—*Jack Kornfield*

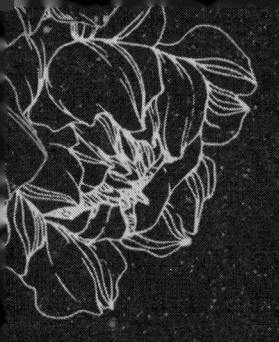

Angelica

*P*urse, *check*. Phone, *check*. Keys, *check*. Pocket knife, *check*.

In the four years I've been living in Antium City, I have never left my place without protection. When I ran away from Cebrene at eighteen, I came to The Big A, and never looked back.

I was tired of the secrets, the lies, and the *death*.

I had my reasons for leaving, but they weren't enough to override the persistent, gnawing feeling that I had done something wrong. We've all felt it. Guilt. That incessant throb in your heart telling you to apologize. My father made sure to teach me the importance of loyalty, obedience, and honor. And there's nothing honorable about leaving your family behind to start a new life. Even though the family in question participates in rather dishonorable things. *Funny, right?*

As a mafia princess, I had to be loyal to my family, obey my father's commands and wishes, and respect my elders. I had never truly understood the extent of what he was involved in, though. He had told me his job consisted in settling disputes in the family and keeping any threats at bay. But every time his shady business associates walked into our house, the way they would eye me from head to toe, even as a little girl, made my skin crawl.

I remember a particular incident when I ran into a middle-aged man halfway up the stairs to my father's office. The curiosity mixed with hunger in his eyes as he looked over me had creeped me out. He was probably thinking of different ways to tear me into pieces and put me back together. The expression on his face had made me stop abruptly.

I had darted away from him, gone back to my room, and slammed the door shut, locking it behind me. With my back against it, I had pushed my twelve-year-old body into the door, as if my small frame could block the big, scary man from busting it down. I closed my eyes and counted to ten. I gasped for air. The clear image of my *mama* appeared before my eyes. Her frail body curled up on the floor at the foot of the bed in her sweat-soaked nightgown, crying into her hands and choking on her sobs. I remember she couldn't inhale as she clutched onto her chest to catch her breath. I faced the same struggle as I pictured one of her panic attacks. I stretched out my arms to her, but she wasn't real. So, I had reached for something—*anything*—that could appease the panic, and my fingers landed on the hair tie around my wrist. I pulled it back and let go, the snap against my skin hard enough to hurt.

That was the day I had my first anxiety attack. I've been wearing an elastic band on my wrist ever since, a coping mechanism I can't do without.

A reminder that I can still feel. That I'm still alive.

My father's presence still looms over me. I don't know which is worse, the constant fear I was in while at home with him, or being here, almost 100 miles away, and feeling like someone's eyes are always on me. It might just be paranoia, or a product of growing up in the mafia, but being the daughter of a prominent Godfather in the Greek mob means there is a constant target on my back.

There are five families who run the streets of Cebrene, the city where I was born: Petrakis, Vasilakis, Mastsouka, Cirillo, who originate from Italy, and us, the Kouvalakis family. We have been predominant in the Greek organized crime syndicate for decades, due to the many ties that my father has with other cities. We have always been known to bring in the most revenue, and we control the entirety of the importing and exporting done at The Port and Cebrene Harbor. My *baba* inherited the business from his father, and my grandfather from his father before that. The Greek mob has connections with the Italian crime families in Cebrene and the Greek ones in Antium City. We own and control a major part of 'The City of Brotherly Love,' alongside the other families. Ironically, there's nothing *brotherly* about a group of men in a pissing contest to see who can rule the city the best. There's definitely no absence of conflict.

A life in the mob was all I'd ever known. And everything I've been working against these past four years.

The only time I miss home is when I think of my two childhood best friends, Aria and Gianis. I don't keep in contact with them as much as I would like to because I worry that I'll be tempted to move back just to be with them. Aria visits me occasionally, but I miss talking to her everyday and listening to her gush about her latest crush. While in high school, we used to see each other daily. We were stuck to each other like glue. Soul sisters in every sense.

But things changed when she turned twenty-one.

Her father is forcing her into a marriage with one of his associates. Unlike me, Aria always believed in finding her true love, but with her upcoming engagement, she has lost hope in her happily ever after. I wish I could be there to support her.

Gianis, my oldest friend, now works for my *baba*. Our families always got along well and never feuded. Damon, his father, is the Godfather of the Night for the Petrakis family. When Gianis turned eighteen, he was expected to join the business, even though he clearly didn't want to. He had always dreamed of being a mixed martial arts fighter and had been training since he was a kid, but was never allowed to pursue it professionally. Despite the potential, Damon had never cared, and used his son's talent as a fighter to do his dirty work. After a heated argument, Gianis had walked out, came to our house for solace, and was taken in by my *baba*, who groomed him into the enforcer he is today. Somehow, my friend preferred working under my father rather than his own. Damon didn't fight his decision.

Gianis has never come to visit though. With all the history and deep family ties between us, I've never asked him why. I always assumed that he had distanced himself because of my *baba*.

The last time I saw him was the day I ran away. Gianis was at my house when I decided I was going to leave and never come back. I had gotten into a massive fight with my father and, as soon as he'd left, I ran upstairs to pack my bags. It was the same dispute we'd had time and time again. I'd had enough of the emotional abuse.

Gianis had overheard the whole argument.

"*You're just like your mother,*" baba spat. "*Never minding your own business. It'll be the death of you too, Angelica.*"

I never understood what his comments about my mother's death meant. Even less what I'd done to deserve such treatment. He knew she was everything to me. Was it because I reminded him of her? Or was it my stubbornness? But her passing wasn't the cause of the rift between us.

Before my *mama* died, it used to be me and her against the

world. I had never paid attention to my father's ways because I had her to protect me. He was rarely around, anyway, constantly away on business trips, or meeting with associates. Though I know my mother was lonely, you'd never have guessed it by the way she always had a smile on her face. She used to say that my happiness was hers, but I was too young to understand what that meant. I never saw the strain in her relationship with my *baba*, because she never let me see that side of him. The cold, heartless, dark side.

Mama made sure I only ever saw the best in him, and I did. But as I grew up, I began to see behind the veil. My mother passed away when I was barely eight years old, so my father had to step up and take care of me. He showed me love by paying extra attention to my silly projects. He would pick me up from school, help me with homework, and had breakfast and dinner with me every day. He was affectionate and never let me go to bed without a goodnight kiss. I thought he was the best *baba* in the world. I loved him deeply. Despite only having one parent, things were good.

Until they weren't.

There's a part of my childhood that I can't seem to remember. A part consumed with darkness, and no matter how hard I try to put the pieces together, I can't. I don't know what happened during that time. It's still a mystery.

I learned very quickly not to question my father. Once I'd start doubting his actions and opinions, he would become cold, withdraw, and emotionally shut down. Even with his own daughter. I was tired of the secrets and the lies.

The night I left, Gianis followed me to my room.

"*Where are you going?*" he asked.

"Away," I replied, not paying him too much attention, too preoccupied with grabbing my things quickly so as to leave without being caught.

"Angelica. You can't just leave."

"Yes. I can," I answered coldly. "I've had enough of this, Gianis."

My best friend had tried to talk me out of it and get me to stay. I knew he didn't want to be left alone to deal with our fathers. But I had to put myself first. As sad as I was to go, I couldn't stay in that house for another minute. When he asked me where I was going, I made him swear not to tell a soul.

"Antium City. That's where I'll go. To my mom's hometown," I finally answered.

I remember my mother telling me stories of her childhood in Upper-Antium. How she had grown up in the nice neighborhood of White Plains with my grandparents. I'm not sure why my family never ventured out to Antium City, but I have a feeling that it was because my father didn't want us to. He was probably scared we wouldn't come back.

My *mama's* parents would come to Cebrene and stay with us a couple of times a year. My parents would put on a show of a united front for each visit. It was the only time I saw them show affection to one another.

I don't remember when or why things changed. From what I could gather, *mama* was unhappy with something *baba* did and it created a fracture that was never healed. She went from a loving, doting wife to a spiteful and hateful one, suffering with mental breakdowns and panic attacks. When it was just us, they never touched, hugged, or kissed. They hardly spoke. I always thought there was something wrong with them, seeing how my friends' parents interacted with each other, but I was too young to realize that evil lurked between them. They went from having a partnership to despising each other right before my eyes.

In the end, only their title remained. Married. Husband and wife, but nothing more.

My *mama* always told me stories of princesses falling in

love, getting married and living happily ever after. I stopped believing in them as I looked at my parents' relationship. I saw nothing worth fighting for.

I don't need love to be happy.

That night, I packed my bags and fished out the money I kept in a small jar under my bed. My father had been contributing to my bank account, but I wasn't sure if he would cut me off once he learned that I'd run away. I looked up the next train to Antium City and left. I said a quick goodbye to Gianis, knowing if I looked at him for too long, I would change my mind.

He watched me with sorrow in his eyes as I walked out the door. "I wish I could come with you."

"I know," *I said, looking down at my feet to avoid his gaze. The guilt for leaving him was gnawing at me.* "I'll call you from my new number when I get there, okay?"

I called Aria as soon as I got down the street and made plans to meet at the mall. I didn't want to explain everything to her on the phone. When I told her that I was leaving the city, she burst out crying and leaped into my arms.

"Angie, what am I going to do without you?" *she asked in between her sobs.*

My heart ached. Saying two goodbyes in one day was not what I had planned when I had woken up that morning. Aria was aware of how it had been at home for me, how strained the relationship with my father had become. She understood why I had to go. We came from the same world. Her father had high expectations of her, much as mine did, but she still had her mother to guide her.

"Come visit me?" *I asked her, and she nodded enthusiastically, wiping away her tears. It was totally like us to make a scene in the middle of a crowded area, so we paid no mind to the people gaping at us crying in each other's arms.*

I then bought a one-way ticket to Antium City, and just like that, I was gone.

When my father got word that I'd left, all hell broke loose. He sent his security detail on a wild goose chase to find me and made multiple calls to my friends to figure out my whereabouts. Gianis sent me a text while I waited for the train to tell me that one of my father's bodyguards had seen me leave the house with my bags. Immediately, my heart leaped into my throat, and I looked around for anyone that could've seen me at the station. I thought I had done a great job sneaking away. *You should know better, Ang.*

Gianis promised he wouldn't tell them where I was going, but I knew they would question him. The dread of being caught had grown in me all day. I had gotten twelve calls from my *baba* before boarding the train and I let them all go to voicemail. He left me three messages, each one nastier than the prior, threatening to cut me off and never speak to me again unless I came home. I ignored them all.

Somehow, the idea of not talking to him anymore brought me relief.

On the train ride to what would become my new home, I shed layers of anxiety. I felt a sense of freedom in the suspension between who I was and who I would become. I started to feel lighter the farther I got from Cebrene.

Once in Antium City, I called my grandparents from a payphone. My *yayá* picked up the call and was surprised to hear my voice. After my mother died, I hadn't been allowed to talk to her. But occasionally, I snuck calls to my grandparents when my father wasn't around to update them on my life and check up on theirs. I'd missed her soft voice and the tenderness only a grandparent could provide.

"Angelica? Louloúdi mou," she said. *My flower.* "How are you? Is everything okay?" she asked.

My eyes filled up with tears hearing her call me her flower, her nickname for me, and I sniffed into the phone. "Yayá, *I'm in*

Antium... I had to get away. I couldn't stay..." I struggled to get the words out.

"Shhhh, it's okay, little one. Come over; your papoús *and I will take care of you."*

I had jumped into my *papoús*'s arms when he greeted me at the door. And just sobbed. I was so happy to see him and be away from my old life. In that moment, I had finally felt free from all my fears, judgment, and expectations. I could live the life I wanted. My grandma made us *tyropita,* Greek cheese pies, and we talked for hours. They didn't ask me what was wrong, why I was crying, or what I was even doing there. This told me that they understood and were ready to accept me, no questions asked, even if it meant facing my father's wrath.

I stayed with my grandparents for several months, while I applied to different colleges. As a mafia princess, I hadn't been allowed to continue my education. My father had intended for me to marry someone who would solidify his partnerships and bear his grandchildren. At the time I left, I was approaching the prime age for marriage.

Thankfully, I got out before I could be tied down. At twenty-three, I'm still single.

I got accepted into Antium City University and moved out of my grandparents' house to an apartment in the Greenwich area to be closer to school. My father still transferred money to my accounts. I didn't want to rely on him, but I wouldn't have been able to support myself while attending college full-time. After everything that had happened between us, I didn't want anything to do with him, but I wouldn't have refused money when I needed it. It's the least he could've done. He had called my grandparents in his quest to find me, and when they confirmed I was there, he didn't press me to come back. Instead, he checked in with them every now and then and kept sending me funds. The switch in his behavior was confusing, given how he was initially threatening me to come home, but I didn't question it.

It's hard for me not to think that he, too, was relieved I was gone.

As I walk to take the subway to the university for the last time, I realize what day it is. It's been four years and we still haven't spoken.

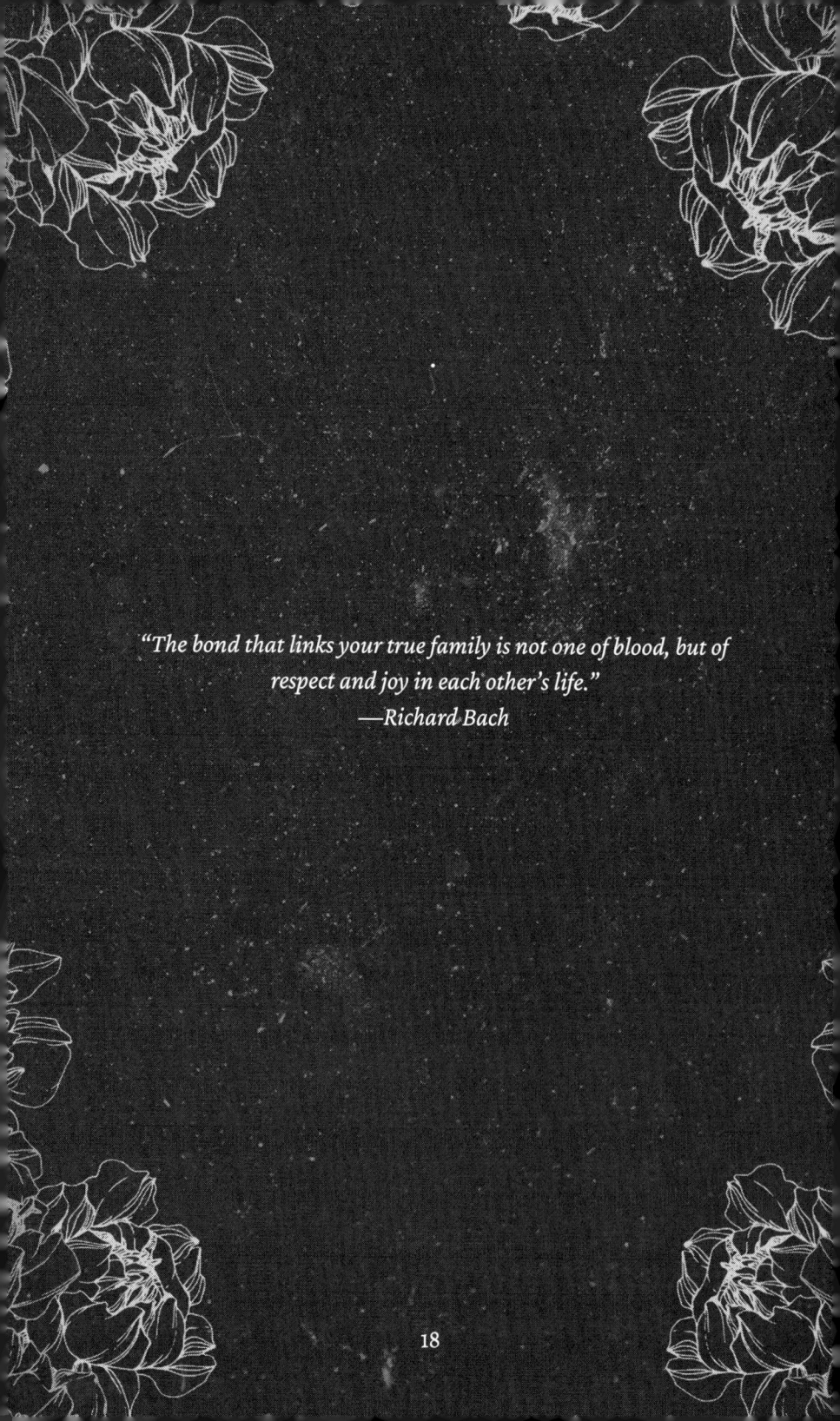

"The bond that links your true family is not one of blood, but of respect and joy in each other's life."
—Richard Bach

Angelica

Being alone in a new city was a welcomed change. I was able to start over and make new friends who knew nothing about who I was or what type of family I came from. I was a different person here.

While at college, I met Amanda, Nicole, and Daniel.

Danny and I studied in the same program, both majoring in Sociology. We met in our intro course and were instantly drawn to each other. He is a sassy, outspoken, and gorgeous man who loves to have a great time. As soon as we were tasked with a group project, Danny pointed at me. We've been inseparable since.

Nicole and Amanda were his long-time best friends. He introduced me to them almost immediately. They accepted me without hesitation, and we soon became a foursome. We do everything together, and crash at each other's apartments after long nights. None of them pry into my life and they love me for who I am.

I'm so happy to feel part of a family. A found family.

We graduated a few days ago and are meeting at the The Watertower Bar in Williamsburg for celebratory drinks. It was Daniel's idea to go out in the 'Burg.' There's a long-standing silent battle between Anzionites and Burganites in Antium

City, the latter thinking that people who live in Anzio are pushy, rude, and boujee, which just so happen to be the exact categories that Danny falls under. He comes from a rich family and has expensive taste, so the girls and I weren't surprised by his choice.

The Watertower is the best place to go in Williamsburg if you want a taste of Anzio.

I take a moment to check my outfit in the mirror. I'm wearing a black, form-fitting, backless jumpsuit, with a plunging neckline that makes the most of my small chest. My highest pointy heels poke out from the bottom of the wide legs. My hair is half-up with two curly strands framing my face, and I painted my face with a soft smokey look to complement my dark brown eyes. I apply some sheer gloss to plump up my lips and finish off with a bit of sparkly body powder on my shoulders and chest to highlight my honey brown skin.

After one final glance at my reflection, I step out of my apartment and strut down the hall to hop in the elevator of my sixteen-story building. I do one last check to see if I have everything with me. I get into the Uber, pull out my phone, and send my friends a text in our group chat.

> Heading out! I'm in my Uber. Can't wait to see your outfits...or lack thereof 😈

AMANDA
> Brat. See you soon!!! Nikki and I are hopping in a cab 🚕

NICOLE
> HA HA. You're a hoe as much as we are...but maybe not as much as Danny.

DANIEL
> Fuck off, Nikki. Don't be jealous I get more guys than all of you combined.

> Touché.

AMANDA
> Hey! Leave me out of this 😈

NICOLE
> @Daniel 🖕

> This is going to be fun! Get ready for the best night out bitches! 😈

I smile as I put my phone away. Our group chat messages are the highlight of my day. Four fiery personalities in one conversation equals a lot of teasing, swearing, and laughs.

The girls are waiting for me at the entrance and they both look gorgeous.

Amanda is wearing a short, emerald, sparkly, strapless dress that brings out her green eyes and her pale skin. Her short brown hair hangs in perfect curls right above her shoulders. Nicole is in a shimmery, sleeveless romper in black with matching wedged heels, her short blond hair swept to the side. Her perfect, pouty lips shine with a dusty nude gloss.

I'm so proud to call these bombshells my friends. I wish Aria were here to celebrate with us, I know she would get along with the girls so well, and Daniel would love her. They met briefly once when she came to visit, and all had great first impressions of each other.

"You can pick your jaw off the ground now, Ang," Nicole teases while Amanda flips her hair off her shoulders with a smirk on her face.

"Sorry, I'll get right to it," I respond as I pretend to reach for the hotel floor. "It's not my fault my best friends look like two of the most expensive hookers waiting to take all my money."

"Who are you kidding? You could never afford us," Amanda jokes.

"When is Danny getting here so I can ignore you both for the rest of the night?" I ask with a hand on my hip, showing them the finger with the other.

I try hard to maintain a humorless facial expression, but we can't contain our giggles and burst out laughing. The doorman lets us in, and we walk to the bar arm in arm. I don't know what the future has in store for us, but being here with two of my best friends makes the unknown seem a little less scary. As long as we have each other, everything will be okay. Since moving to Antium and meeting them, I've not been as stressed and I rarely get panic attacks anymore. I feel like I can finally let go and relax.

The Watertower Bar is at the top of a gigantic water tower and has the most beautiful views of the Antium City skyline from the Burg. It's mid-June, so the weather is warm and breezy, which means we can enjoy the outdoor patio. The hostess brings us to our table, and we order drinks while waiting for Danny. When he arrives, we order another round and let the night begin.

Amanda and I grace the dance floor with our drinks in hand, our bodies twist and twirl as we feel the effects of the alcohol. The DJ is playing early 2000s songs tonight and we're mouthing all the lyrics to 'Baby Boy' by Sean Paul and Beyoncé. Nikki and Danny are at the bar ordering more drinks. A cosmo for Amanda, a spicy margarita for me, a dirty vodka martini for Nikki, and a gin and tonic for Danny. It's Saturday night, so the bar is packed, the music is loud, and I couldn't be happier to be here with these people.

A few handsome men approach us, and we entertain them for a while. They buy us drinks and tell us about their "interesting" lives. Guys always do the most gloating when trying to impress women. I roll my eyes at one of them after he mentions his high-paying job and expensive sports car.

Rule number one: never gloat about how much money you make. Most women don't get off on egotism.

Either way, I don't do one-night stands and I don't date. I always use the excuse of focusing on school and my career. But deep down, I put an X on love a long time ago because of my parents. It gets lonely sometimes, but you can still feel alone even if you have someone. It's life's cruelest irony.

After a break from the dance floor and some much needed fresh air, we walk back toward our table. Tonight has been perfect. I'm tipsy and in a good headspace. I'm with my favorite people, and I'm having a great time. Danny leaves us to go chat with the cute male bartender. I catch Nikki eyeing him at the bar a few times and I notice a glimpse of something in her eyes. I can't figure out if it's jealousy, possessiveness, or just plain judgment.

As we navigate through the throng of partiers, I take in my surroundings. I like to prowl ordinary places, people-watch, and observe them interact. I'd sometimes rather go unnoticed and fade into the crowd than be the center of attention.

As I scan the bar, my gaze lands on a tall and bulky man staring at me, studying me from the tip of my toes to the curls on my head. The hairs on the back of my neck stand up and I duck my head to dislodge his gaze, an attempt to hide from his stare. When his light green eyes reach mine, he looks away. *Weird.* I shift my weight from one heel to the other, trying to brush off the unease as I take a seat next to Nikki.

She yells over the music, "Have you seen that guy?" She gestures her head toward the man. "He's been staring at you for a little while now. You should go talk to him," she says with a wink while she pokes the side of my boob.

"No, thank you," I quickly dismiss the idea and swat Nikki's hand away. I don't know who he is, but I wouldn't touch him with a ten-foot pole. The intense way he was studying me made me feel nervous and uncomfortable.

Danny suddenly appears at my side and says, "You're no fun. You need to loosen up, babe." He sits across from Amanda and continues, "You're beautiful and you deserve to get laid." Nikki and Amanda animatedly bob their heads in agreement.

He might be right, but I don't need sex badly enough to sleep with someone who gives me the creeps.

"I get enough love from you cuddling me at night, *Danny boy*," I retort, mischievously.

Daniel flicks my arm. "*Coquine,*" he says, and I choke with laughter. *Naughty.*

Not to say I've been celibate, but I pick my conquests

wisely and never get attached. The last person I had sex with was a guy I met at the campus library while studying for finals. We both happened to be there at the same time on numerous occasions. One day, he approached me and stuck a post-it note with his number right on top of my Globalization & Human Rights textbook. 'Adrian 212-290-8583' was written on the yellow piece of paper. I texted him later that evening and we had a short fling during the last month of school. Our time ran its course, and we both parted ways amicably after graduating.

I'm zapped back to reality by Nikki pinching the sensitive area behind my bicep. "Bitch!" I yell to her as I rub the spot with my hand. I look back at where the stranger was standing but he's gone. My body slumps back on the chair and I let out a pent-up breath. He stayed in the same corner the whole night, sneaking looks at me various times, but never made a move. I tried to ignore him, though his body language seemed to scream stranger danger and I couldn't shake off the unease I felt by his presence.

We stay at The Watertower until three a.m. and leave the bar drunk. Daniel informs us he's staying longer to go home with the cute bartender. Amanda and I high-five him. Nikki's face turns a bright shade of red and she simply turns around without even acknowledging him. We stumble down to the hotel lobby and hop into a taxi. We spend the whole ride taking drunk selfies and laughing in the back seat. Building memories to last forever.

The cab comes to a halt at the entrance of my building. I give my friends each a kiss on the cheek and throw a twenty-dollar bill at them despite their protests right before slamming the door behind me. I shoot an apologetic smile to the driver for the disruption and blow them more kisses over my shoulder as I walk away. I hurry inside and call the elevator to go up to the sixth floor. The lobby is empty at this time of the night. My building doesn't have a doorman or concierge, so it's chillingly quiet.

The elevator bell dings, and I step in, slumping against the mirrors. I'm so intoxicated and tired, and my feet hurt so badly. *Stupid heels.* I'm so tempted to take them off and walk to my apartment barefoot.

I stare at my reflection in the mirror. I look like a sweaty and drunken mess. My smokey makeup is now blurred all over my lids, my lip gloss smeared all around my mouth, and my hair is frizzy from the humidity. Despite the way I look and feel, I'm happy. It might be the liquor talking, but I'll soak in every ounce of happiness I can get.

The elevator stops on my floor, and I dig into my purse to find my keys. Not paying attention to where I am, I trip on my own feet and let out a quiet giggle while leaning onto the wall in the hallway to steady myself. It feels like I'm on a tightrope with no experience or a balance stick. My fingers finally make contact with the cool metal when I approach my apartment and I fumble with the keys as I try to unlock the door. After what feels like five long minutes, the key enters the bolt and I realize the door is unlocked. *Shit.*

Frozen in place, I hear my heart pounding in my chest fast and hard. *I must've just forgotten to lock it.* I leave the keys in the door, not wanting the jingle to make any more noise, and I slowly inch the door open to poke my head inside.

"Every pawn is a potential queen." —*James Mason*

Angelica

"Hello?" I whisper out into the dark. I hear no response and no sound. I briefly sigh in relief. It's not like an intruder would casually reply to my greeting, anyway.

The door creaks when I push it open. The darkness on the other side prevents me from seeing anything. I tiptoe into the apartment, leaving the door ajar in case I need to make a run for it.

It's okay. You're safe. You are home and no one is here. You're just overly cautious because of who you are. I keep repeating to myself, even though the feeling of dread gets stronger and stronger.

I turn on my phone's flashlight, tear off my heels, leaving them haphazardly on the mat by the front door, and set my things down on the kitchen counter. I point the light in every direction and turn in circles as I scan the room for possible threats. My drunkenness is doing the opposite of what it should as my stress levels increase. Sensing no immediate danger, my shoulders relax. I pull out the keys from the lock and click the door shut behind me. *See, Ang? No danger. Just an oversight.* I desperately want to get out of this jumpsuit, so I saunter down the hallway toward my bedroom. I reach for the zipper, when a sense of apprehensiveness invades my body and almost knocks me over. The hairs on the back of my neck prickle, and I stop dead in my tracks. It feels as if my feet are welded to the floor, but as adrenaline surges through my body, my fight or flight instincts kicks in.

Someone grabs me from behind, cupping my mouth with their hand to muffle any screams. I holler anyway, fear overtaking me, but the noise is drowned out by the assailant's grip. I begin to hyperventilate, and my skin breaks out into a sweat. I can't breathe, everything is moving too quickly around me. I'm suddenly dragged back to the living room, but I thrash against my captor, my legs jerking from side to side, as I try to fight my way out of their hold. Frenzied, disjointed thoughts run through my mind as it zips from one idea to the next, my eyes flickering from side to side in search of an escape route. *No. This can't be happening.* If I could just reach for the pocketknife in my purse.

I attempt to twist my body around when strong arms lift me off my feet and I'm thrown onto the couch with force. Before I'm able to scream or run, realization dawns on me as I recognize the person's face.

It's the man from the club. The guy who kept staring at me. The one who averted his gaze when I looked at him.

I shriek and he rushes at me to stifle my scream with a pillow. I throw my arms up to grab onto him, my nails scratching his arms on contact. I violently kick him with my feet, but he's too strong and his weight is suffocating me. *I am not going out like this. I can't.*

I won't allow myself to die at the hands of a stranger right at the beginning of the next chapter of my life.

I gasp out, "Stop. Please." My voice is muffled against the pillow, but my attacker keeps it glued to my face. Air is being taken from my lungs and I struggle to breathe. My eyes slowly drift shut and I fight to stay alert. *Stay awake, Angelica. Do. Not. Give. In.*

"If you don't stop wriggling, you're going to make my dick hard," my attacker says while laughing. The repulsive sound rings in my eardrum.

I stop moving, the more energy I waste, the more I'll sink into a deep sleep and pass out. I can't let panic win and deprive myself of strength. The man notices I've stilled and eases his hold on the pillow.

"Good. No need to make this harder than it should be, Angelica," he says. "You're quite brave for a girl your size."

My eyes open wide at the sound of my name. The world crumbles around me as my terror multiplies, and I wonder how on earth he knows who I am. I thought this was a burglary attempt gone wrong, but I have no doubt now it has something to do with my father. I can't even shake in fear. I'm in total paralysis thinking about what this stranger could want from me.

"I'm going to remove the pillow, but if you scream or try to run, things will get a lot worse," he threatens. "Am I clear?"

I nod my head and he throws the pillow to the side. I gasp loudly, hungry for air, and I try to calm the massive panic attack threatening to surface. I feel like a fish out of water as I struggle to catch my breath, tears stinging my eyes.

I realize that somehow, during the struggle, he managed to drug me because I feel dizzy. My eyes are so heavy. I can't seem to keep them open no matter how hard I try, but I manage to look up at him. "Who are you and what do you want from me?" I croak.

"It's not you we want something from, it's your father," he says, hovering over me. It's the last thing I hear before I slip into unconsciousness.

When I wake up, a surge of pain goes straight to my head; I'm not sure if it's a hangover or whatever the guy used to sedate me, maybe a combination of both. I struggle to pry my eyes open, but from what I can see, I'm no longer in my apartment. *How did he get me out of there unseen?*

My hands are bound behind my back to an uncomfortable wooden chair. I try to wriggle myself off with no success. Panic starts rising, but I will myself to stay calm. If there's anything that I've learned from being a mobster's daughter, it's that these people thrive off fear. I will not give them that satisfaction.

My eyes open wide enough to take in my surroundings and I notice I'm in the middle of a large, furnished office, with a mahogany desk and leather chairs, though none of it seems familiar. *Where am I?*

I squeeze my eyes shut and pray that this is all just a dream. That I'm going to wake up from this terrible nightmare. My instinct is to snap the hair tie around my wrist to check if this is real, to calm my anxiety, but I can't reach it with my hands tied. Regardless of how many times I blink, I'm still in this office, bound to this chair. I shift in my seat, but the only thing I achieve is inching my chair forward and chafing my wrists. I wince in pain as I start to feel the soreness in the rest of my body. *My body.*

A rush of terror hits me as I realize I don't remember anything after losing consciousness. I look down and exhale in momentary relief seeing that my clothes are untouched.

I hear footsteps approaching and I instinctively squirm on the chair as panic creeps back in. The office door swings open.

A tall, tanned man walks in, flanked by two others, one of which I recognize as the guy who assaulted and kidnapped me yesterday. *Was it yesterday? God knows how long I've been here.*

I quickly run my gaze over them, but I let my stare linger on my attacker, wishing I could throw darts at his face. My heart races in my chest as I take in the sheer size of the three men in front of me.

What appears to be the leader of the group walks over to me and effortlessly turns my chair to face his desk as he leans against it, crossing his legs and staring at me, not one ounce of emotion in his steely eyes. I turn my face away and will my legs to stop shaking. If I weren't in this situation, I'd even think him handsome, with his perfectly coiffed hair, thin goatee, and slightly pointed nose. He looks like the spitting image of Wilmer Valderrama. *Seriously, Ang? You've just been kidnapped.*

"You're probably wondering why you're tied up to a chair," he says. *No shit, Sherlock.* "I wouldn't have taken such drastic measures, but Luis told me you're a *feisty* one," he adds with a dry chuckle.

My assailant laughs as he grabs his crotch in response. Bile rises up my throat.

"See, my issue isn't with you, Angelica," he says. "But when my men found out that Peter's daughter was living among us, I couldn't pass up the opportunity."

"It's too bad it took us this long," he adds. "I'm surprised he even let you out of his sight after the incident many years ago." *What the hell is he talking about?*

Seeing I have no intention to talk, he continues. "Your father and I have been in a silent war for quite some time now, but he won't let up." He uncrosses his legs and leans closer, as if to tell me a secret. "If he won't stop trying to take over my part of Antium City, I will *make* him," he says in a threatening tone, and I shiver. "If he thinks he can bring his dirty business into my city, he has another thing coming." *Great. I'm being used as a pawn.*

I roll my eyes. If he truly believes my *baba* will stop his plans on my account, *he* has another thing coming. "Good luck," I say. "My father doesn't give enough of a shit about me to care that I've been taken."

The man moves even closer, only a few inches away from my face, and rubs his thumb over my lips with a smirk plastered on his face. I yank my head away in disgust, but he quickly grabs onto my chin, turning my head back to face him, and laughs. He looks up at my attacker. "You weren't wrong about her feistiness." Luis shrugs his shoulders and I let out a scoff. *This is ridiculous.*

"Your father might not give a shit, but I know someone else who does. I'm sure he'll be persuasive enough to get your father to care," he replies.

I twist my head and a look of puzzlement crosses my face. *Gianis?*

"Well, this will be fun," he says with a chuckle and lets go of my face with a jerk. I still feel the pressure of his fingers on my jaw. He walks around his desk and slams both hands on the tabletop, making me jump in my seat. I'm trying not to show my fear, but the unknown is making it hard for me to stay calm.

"Are you hungry? Do you need Advil?" he questions, amused. "I heard you had quite a drunken night out, and mixed with the chloroform, you must be hungover as shit." He chuckles wickedly.

"*Go to hell,*" I seethe. "I'm not eating your food. Let me go, *now*. I'll kill you with my bare hands if someone else doesn't get to you first," I yell, as I try to escape out of the hold I'm in. I'm being ballsy, but I'm sick of being here. I doubt my father will run to save me, so I'll have to find a way to break free on my own. I'm not a violent person, but I won't be afraid to fight my way out of here.

He gives a sniff of disapproval, and runs a hand through his short, dark hair. His pissed off expression turns amused as his top lip slowly lifts on one side, a menacing smile that does nothing but irritate me further. He swings his head back and lets out a roar of laughter. "*You?* A precious mafia princess. Hurt *me?*" He cracks up again, and it only makes me angrier, my fear snuffed out for the moment. "Did you hear that, boys? She's going to kill me." The two other men join him, and they laugh in unison. *I can't believe this.*

"I'd love to see you try, *princesita*. It might make for a fun time," he replies. "But I can't have you croak on my watch, little girl." He grabs his phone out of the inside pocket of his suit jacket and dials a number on speakerphone. After three rings, a woman picks up.

"Yes, Hendrick?" she answers.

"Please bring some food for our guest. And some pills for her hangover." He hangs up the phone before she has the chance to respond.

I can't believe the audacity of this man. "First of all, who are you calling '*little girl*'? Second, I said I don't want your food," I spit.

"You're acting like a child," he replies bluntly.

I glare at him with my mouth wide open. "Screw you, *Hendrick*," I drag out his name. "Let. Me. Go."

He looks at me, and his brows lift in surprise and anger. He walks around the desk and puts his hands on the arms of my chair. He gets close to my face and says, "You listen to me closely, *little girl*. You might be a sight for sore eyes, but I've had enough of you running that pretty mouth."

He pulls out a pocketknife from his back pocket and flicks it open with one hand. I flinch, and the right side of his mouth slowly rises in amusement. He holds the blade up to my cheek and presses firmly, poking at my skin. My breath hitches, but I don't take my eyes off him. I don't want him to sense my fear.

"I can't lie," Hendrick says, now petting my face with the knife. I close my eyes and subtly try to move away. "The urge to carve my initials on your pretty face and see the blood run down your cheeks is making my dick twitch, Angelica. But I can't send you back damaged. I would never hear the end of it." He rolls his eyes and waves the weapon around.

He summons one of the guys with a gesture and gives him the knife. I don't have the guts to turn and look, so I squeeze my eyes shut, bracing myself to feel the blade meet my flesh. Instead, Hendrick takes his weight off my chair and someone tugs at my arms to cut through the ropes holding my hands together. I rub my wrists as soon as they're free. My fingers instinctively search for my elastic band. Even though the skin is sore, I pull on it to find relief. Something familiar to keep me grounded in my state of panic.

"You're worth more to me alive than dead," Hendrick says, as if he could read my mind. "So, you better keep your words to a minimum. You wouldn't want me to fill your mouth with something other than food." He winks at me, and I can't stop myself as I spit in his face. I don't give a shit if he hurts me, I can't let them think I'm a weak, little girl waiting for her *baba* to save her. I can be strong, capable, and vicious when I need to be.

Luis and the other man take a step forward, but Hendrick puts his hand up to stop them. He reaches for the handkerchief resting in the jetted pocket of his suit and wipes his face. I keep my eyes on him, my breathing heavy.

"Tread carefully, *carajita*," he says under his breath, "because I won't let another instance like this happen without punishment." He puts the square of thin fabric down on the desk and continues. "You're going to eat the food and shut the fuck up until I get in touch with your father. Trust me, I don't want to keep you here longer than I must."

He walks out of the office and his men follow. I let out a sigh of relief before I realize I'm still stuck to the chair by my ankles.

Luis comes back a little while later with food, water, and a couple of Advils. I take the pills and eat my food grudgingly, only doing so to keep my strength up in case I need to defend myself. I ask Luis to untie my legs to go to the bathroom, but he hesitates. So, I threaten to pee my pants, and he changes his mind.

I'm sure Hendrick wouldn't want his office to reek of urine.

"No funny business," he says, pointing his gun toward the bathroom door. To any other person, the gun might be frightening, but I've had my share of experiences around weapons. I know how to manipulate one comfortably. If only I could find a way to grab the gun while he's distracted. But if my plan goes south, I'm screwed and risk getting hurt.

After relieving myself, I promise Luis I'll be good, and he doesn't tie me back to the chair, making it clear that he'll be right outside the door.

I sigh. There's no other way out of this room, unless I feel like jumping to my own death.

The day passes, and once the sun goes down, I wait for someone to come back. My mind is reeling with questions I don't have answers to, and the memory of what Hendrick said about my father disturbs me. I occupy myself by walking in circles around the desk and pulling out random books from the shelves, reading the first passages and then putting them back.

Being stuck in here, not able to contact anyone to tell them I'm okay, is torture. I wonder if my friends are worried. They're the only ones who might give enough of a shit to notice I'm missing. I look around the room, but of course, there's no phone or computer in sight. I search for my cell, but it's nowhere to be found either. I'm assuming Luis took it last night. I sigh into my palms and let out a muffled scream. "Get me out of here!" I yell through tear-filled eyes. I'm tired, hungry, and I need a shower. Soon enough, I'll go crazy from staring at these walls.

A while later, Hendrick walks in the office with a smile plastered on his face. "Guess what, *carajita*? It's your lucky day." The door opens wider and Gianis walks in behind him, followed by Luis.

Gianis.

My lips start quivering and I let out a loud sob. I can't move. I'm unable to make my legs go to him.

"Your father agreed to my terms and your knight in shining armor has arrived to take you home." Hendrick points to Gianis. He came all the way from Cebrene to get me. He looks impassive, but the glimmer of concern in his eyes tells me otherwise. He must have been worried sick. Gianis has always kept a hard shell around himself to hide his true feelings. Only I was able to pierce through it over the years.

I take a good look at my best friend, who I haven't seen in four years, and I begin to wonder how I could have let so much time go by without having him by my side. The exhaustion, mixed with the guilt, makes my knees feel weak, and my gaze falls to the floor.

Gianis stalks over to me. When he reaches me, I wrap my arms around his waist, and let my body melt into his. I squeeze him hard, my sobs escaping me like a waterfall.

"Angie," he says softly, as he pulls back to look over me for any injuries. We hug again and he whispers, "Let's go home."

"I missed you," I say into his shirt. He kisses the top of my head and replies, "Me too, Angie. Me too."

If it wasn't for Hendrick clearing his throat to interrupt us, I don't know how long we would've stayed in an embrace. Gianis unhooks my arms from around his waist and asks me to wait outside as he walks up to Hendrick. Before stepping out of the office, I glance back and see him whisper something to my captor. I don't know what's being exchanged, but they nod at each other before he joins me in the hallway. Usually, I'd pry for information, but I'm just relieved to be free and can't wait to get the hell out of here.

⚜

Gianis and I make our way out of the building as I shake and cry inconsolably. All the bottled-up emotions I've been keeping at bay burst out as the adrenaline seeps out of my body. I can't believe he's here.

He came for me.

He gently places me into the passenger seat of his car, laying a sweater on top of me. I thank him and use the sleeve to wipe my tears. He starts the car, but doesn't move, and turns to me.

"Ang, I'm sorry this happened to you. You should've never been involved," he says as he drags his hand through his hair. "When your father received the call from that piece of shit, I left right away." He lets out a huge breath and continues, "I wouldn't have let anything happen to you." He's rambling now. "I would've killed them if they hurt you, Angie. I'm—"

I cut him off mid-sentence. "I know, G. I don't know what I did to deserve a friend like you. Thank you for coming for me," I say.

He winces at the word friend but smooths out his expression quickly and gives me a soft smile.

We drive back to my apartment, but I stop when I get to the front door. The memories from last night come rushing through my mind, and I have to close my eyes to steady my breathing. Gianis stops right behind me and caresses both of my arms.

"It's going to be okay, Ang. I'm right here. No one is going to hurt you now," he promises, and I believe him. He takes my hand and walks in first, leading me. He swears as he notices my coffee table displaced and pillows on the floor. A piece of cloth is sitting next to one of the cushions and he picks it up. "*Malákes,*" he swears. "They fucking drugged you."

I stand next to him as tears threaten to fall down my face again. A few hours ago, I was in this room, fighting for my life. The scene is triggering my anxiety and I have to walk away. My legs wobble and Gianis grabs me before I fall. He lifts me up in both arms, my weight barely affecting him, and carries me to the bedroom. When my butt touches the mattress, I cover my face with my hands, embarrassed by my reaction. Gianis has always known about my anxiety troubles. He even knows about my self-harm habit. But I've never broken down like this in front of him. He kneels in front of me as he pries my fingers off my eyes and interlaces our hands.

"Angelica, you have to come back to Cebrene with me. I can't leave you here unprotected."

I was expecting this. I know that it's no longer safe for me here, especially after what Hendrick said. But leaving the life I've built here—*my* life—and my friends, is the last thing I want to do. As much as I miss Aria and Gianis, I don't want to go back to Cebrene and face my father.

Although, a small part of me wants to find out the truth. Why my parents' relationship failed, why my mother died, what happened to me to trigger such unpleasantly familiar feelings during my kidnapping, and what business my father is trying to bring to Antium City.

"I know," I reply hopelessly, not able to say anything else. I'm completely defeated.

I pull out a suitcase and a few bags from my closet and start packing enough clothes to last me until I'm able to get a truck here to move all my things. I keep my face turned away from Gianis so he doesn't notice the tears rolling down my cheeks. My heart wants to believe this is temporary, that I'll be able to come back, but I know better. This is the end of my life here.

Gianis hears me sniffle and grabs my arm.

"Hey, *hey*," he says softly. "Don't cry, Giegie. I know this isn't ideal, and I don't expect you to be thrilled about it, but at least you'll have Aria. You'll have me. And I'll have *you*. I'd be a liar if I didn't admit it makes me happy."

The dam of tears finally bursts, and I cry. Gianis lifts my cocooned body and sits on the edge of the bed, perching me on his lap, and I cry some more as the emotions of the day flood out of me. He doesn't let go, holding me tight until I'm drained.

After a couple of hours, Gianis loads up his car, and I take a final look at my building before hopping in. He pulls out my phone from his back pocket, and hands it back to me. "Hendrick gave it to me before I was allowed into the office."

I nod and turn it on. A stream of notifications pop up on the screen from the girls and Danny. I debate sending a text back, but how am I supposed to explain this disappearing act to them?

They have no idea what I come from.

I open the group chat and type a message, ignoring all the unread ones since last night.

. . .

Me: I have a family emergency back in Cebrene and will be staying there for a little while. I'll explain soon. I had fun last night. I'm hungover as shit! Love you xx

I immediately turn off my phone, knowing I'll receive an influx of messages and calls I'm not mentally capable of dealing with right now. I rest my head back on the seat and close my eyes.

Gianis drives off, and we start our journey back home. *Home.*

Antium City has been my home for the past four years.

Now, I'm going back to my own personal hell.

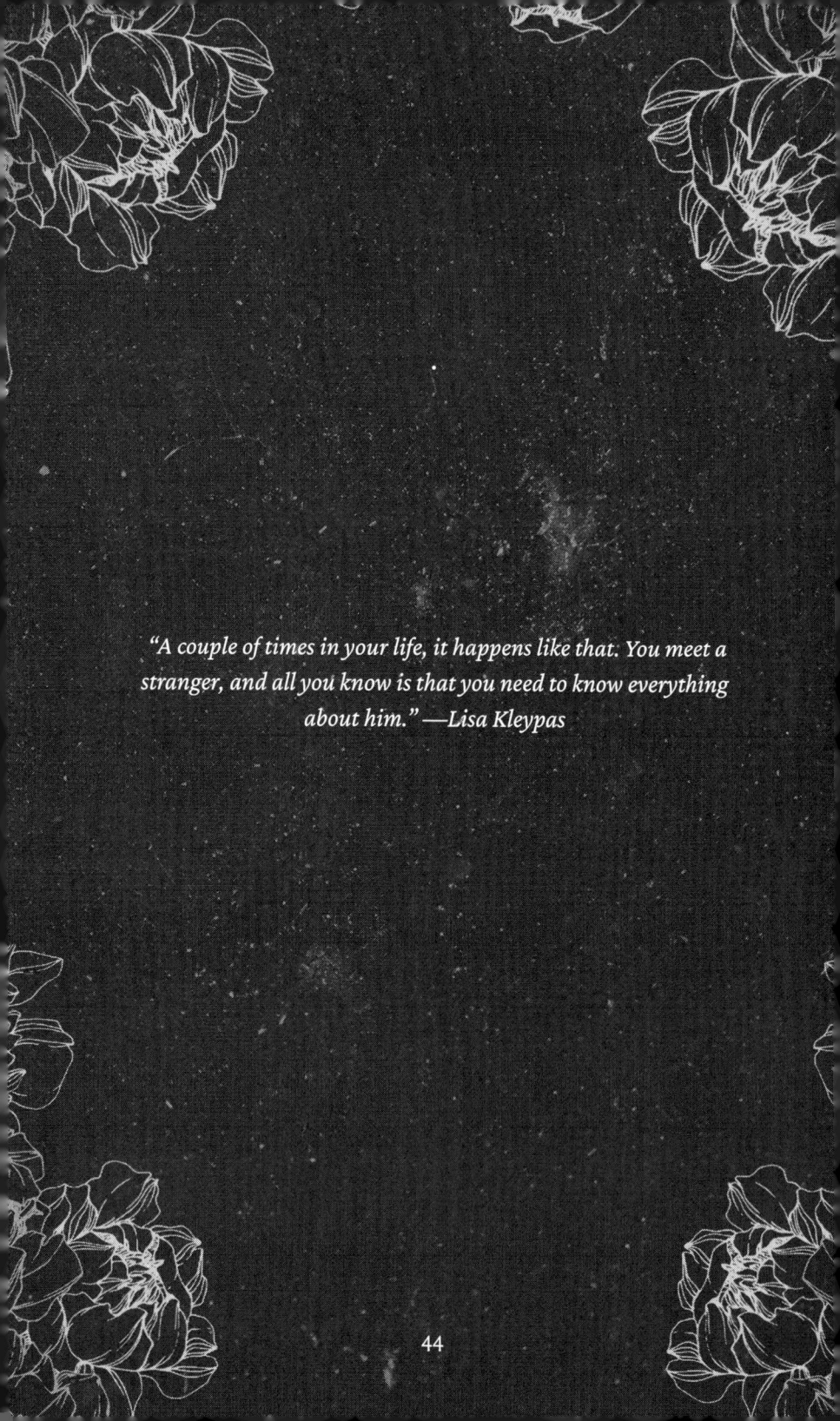

"A couple of times in your life, it happens like that. You meet a stranger, and all you know is that you need to know everything about him." —Lisa Kleypas

Angelica

Three weeks later

It's Thursday, and I'm getting ready to go to the shooting range. It's funny how this is the only consistent thing in my life since I moved back to Antium. I never used to train before; I didn't need to. *Or so I thought.*

I moved out of my childhood home four years ago because I craved normality. Now, everything triggers memories of a time when I was always being watched. I couldn't even be in my own home without the worry of getting involved in affairs I did not care to know or witness. I wished for a life where my *baba* and his cronies didn't surround me. I didn't want the life of a mafia princess then, and I still don't.

After losing my mother, I leaned on my father for love and support. When I was a young child, I thought he was loving. But that wasn't reality. He was the furthest thing from what a loving man should be. I came to know who he really was through whispered conversations behind closed doors, with my ear pressed tightly at the crack. I became more aware of what he did and what kind of person he was—cold and calculated. I was privy to information that not many people knew, simply because I lived in his house. He conducted shady business, and he murdered people. He never came right out and told me, but between the eavesdropping and what Aria would tell me about her father, it was obvious. After going back and forth with information, we figured out that my *baba* was a Godfather, and that hers was his second-in-command. We still didn't understand what it meant to be in the mafia, but we knew they did unspeakable things.

This is when everything started to unravel. Once I pieced together who he really was, I couldn't help but wonder if he had ever really been honest with me. He lied and killed for a living. He clearly was capable of anything, with no regard to the consequences. Which led me to thoughts of my mother. He never told me the details of what had happened to her, so I started looking into her death. I would sneak into his office when he wasn't around, looking for any information about her untimely demise. I searched every drawer, filing cabinet, and every book in his library, savagely tearing his office apart, only to put everything back the way it was so that no one would notice. I would get so angry when I couldn't find anything, and it just fueled my rage. It made me want to dig deeper. I asked him questions that he didn't want to answer, which made him treat me differently. He told me that if I was so interested in his affairs, he would make sure I was involved in them.

And that was a promise he kept.

From then on, he started punishing me for my curiosity. He made me sit in meetings where he would execute people for doing or saying anything against him. He brought me along when he conducted business and made me watch as he and his goons would tear fingernails off men one by one, take hammers to their knees, or cut off digits to extract information, prove a point, or heck, just for fun. I saw things no twelve-year-old girl ever should.

One dreadful night, I convinced him to let me stay in the car while he met with some of his partners. It was late, and we were in the parking lot of an abandoned property. I could barely see a thing through the darkness other than a yellow flickering light inside the building. I squinted and could see my father standing with three other men, engaged in conversation.

I wasn't paying attention to my surroundings when I heard the car door open on the driver's side. A large man wearing a ski mask climbed into the car.

I panicked.

The keys were still in the ignition, so I threw myself over the middle console to remove them. He grabbed my hair and pulled. I started to scream, hoping my father would come running. He didn't, and I was left to fend for myself.

In the midst of all the chaos, I remembered he always left a gun in the glove compartment, so I reached over with my free hand. The man was too preoccupied with trying to take the keys away from me to notice. I had never fired a weapon but had seen my father and his men do it many times before. I cocked the gun, praying that it was loaded, aimed it at my attacker's head, and fired.

The sound was deafening in the small space, and my eardrums felt as if they were going to explode. The man's grasp on my hair loosened as he went limp. I shot up from my seat and glued myself to the door. There was blood splattered everywhere, including on my face and clothes. Shivers racked my body as I waited for someone to come find me.

I had *killed* someone. I'd felt his soul exit his body as his head hung over the steering wheel. One moment I was fighting for my life, the next I had taken one. I couldn't believe it. Even though it was in self-defense, I was disgusted with myself for being capable of such a horrific act.

Turns out, I was more like my father than I thought.

I lifted my bloodied hands to my face and sobbed, the adrenaline seeping out of me and its withdrawal making me disoriented. What had I done?

No one was coming to help me. I reached over to the door handle and let myself out of the car, walking unsteadily to where my father was so deep in conversation, he hadn't even noticed his daughter had almost been abducted. Someone saw me, and said something, causing him to turn. His face showed no emotion, no worry, no concern, no fear. As I got closer, I recognized one of the men as my grandfather.

"What happened, engoní?" My grandfather asked, his tone flat.

"A man tried to drive away with me in the car," I stuttered, my lips quivering. "I–I killed him," I whispered. I had done something wrong, but I didn't regret why I'd done it. The attacker was going to kidnap me, and God knows what else.

That incident confirmed my moral code. In the moment, I realized there was a difference between knowing what is right and doing what you have to do to survive.

My father simply smirked. *Smirked.*

"Kalí douliá, kóri mou," *he said. Good job, my daughter.*

I stood there, helpless, in front of my *papoús,* and two strange men, while soaked in another man's blood and brain matter. I didn't know if I would ever be clean again, and he was...*proud?*

I had almost been snatched away. I could've *died,* and he hadn't even flinched at the thought.

"As a Kouvalakis, *you must learn to defend yourself,* engoní. *Your father won't always be there to protect you,"* my grandfather added.

Then, it clicked. It was all planned. A twisted initiation into the family.

From that day on, I began to carry a knife with me, knowing I was my sole protector.

Standing in my living room now, I look down at my wrist, pull on the hair tie I always wear around it with all my might, and I let it go. The sting makes me hiss loudly. I do it again, and again, and again, until little bubbles of blood form under my skin. *Inhale. Exhale. You're not that helpless girl anymore.*

"Shit." I sigh as I glance down at my wrist. I'd rather not draw attention to this habit, but I don't have time to conceal the damage. Thankfully, there's not much lighting at the shooting range, and no one usually gets close enough to me to notice.

What doesn't kill you gives you a lot of unhealthy coping mechanisms, and this one is mine. Feeling physical pain numbs the mental anguish I feel inside.

I grab my hair and tie it into a messy bun, leaving the marks of my self-harm exposed. I walk over to the mirror in my living room and check my reflection. I catch a glimpse of a piece of paper on my dining room table behind me, and butterflies flutter in my stomach.

Since my return, things have been *different*. I seem to have gained a secret admirer. *More like a stalker.*

A week after settling into my new home, I started finding random notes and gifts around the house. When I saw the first one, a perfectly wrapped tray of *loukoumades*, little bite-sized fluffy, sweet, honey balls—*the Greek version of donuts*—with a little note that said, 'Welcome home, sweetheart,' I thought it was from my father.

Until I found another note, and another one, and another. Every day, I find a poem or gift from my 'admirer.' As much as I should be terrified that someone is breaking into my house, especially after what happened a few weeks ago in Antium, I'm not. Oddly, the little surprises that my stalker leaves me are... comforting. *Not concerning at all, Angelica.*

At a time when I am most vulnerable, his notes make me feel important and safe, as if someone is watching over me.

My stalker could be a psychopath plotting the perfect plan to murder me. I might be crazy for thinking this, but I enjoy the thrill. This secret is just for me. It's mine to keep. And so far, it's been harmless. It could very well escalate, but it's *my* danger. The attention I craved my entire life is now in my hands, and I wouldn't dare tell anyone and ruin this feeling. Everything I've ever done has either been overseen or controlled by my father. Even when I was in the Big A, my safety relied on him, and I didn't even know it. This new 'development' makes me feel like I have something to call *my own. My* stalker. *Do I sound like a lunatic? Yes. Do I care? Not so much.*

I shake off the thoughts of my admirer and send Gianis a brief message to say I'm ready to be picked up, and I put my phone down on the dining room table. Several minutes later, I hear his obnoxious sports car pull up in the driveway. I grab my things and head to the door.

We arrive at the opening of the alley of the shooting range, and I swing the car door open to get out. Gianis tells me he will be back to pick me up in an hour, which is strange given that he always waits around for me. But I shrug and tell him that I'll see him later. He watches me walk down the narrow passageway before I disappear behind the door.

THE DIÁVOLOS

The smell of gunpowder is heavy in the air, and I can hear the faint sound of bullets ricocheting off the walls through my protective earmuffs. The scent triggers my senses, and I instantly feel at peace. It reminds me that, here, I'm in control, even if it's just for a little while. I've been coming to this shooting range a few evenings a week since I moved to the area three weeks ago. Thursday nights have been my favorite so far as it's the least busy day of the week. It wasn't easy to find, but I discovered Sharp Shooters after a little research and some asking around. It's located downtown, in the heart of Cebrene Heights, about a twenty-five-minute ride from my place in the suburbs. I desperately needed to find a place to release tension and forget about my worries, especially after the experience in Antium. I still have to look over my shoulder when I'm out, and I don't leave my house that much anymore.

I grasp my handgun firmly, making sure to keep a space between my thumb and trigger finger to help with the recoil of the semi-automatic glock as I shoot. I use my other hand to cover the rest of the grip, with my fingers pointed down at a forty-five-degree angle. The sensation of the weapon in my hand feels like a weighted blanket covering my body, my nervous system feels more relaxed, less anxious. When I shoot at the range, it's exhilarating; my adrenaline spikes, creating a surge of energy in my body. Like a runner's high, a brief state of euphoria.

In a matter of seconds, my eyes land on the moving target, and I pull the trigger. The sheet flies back as my forearm absorbs the recoil. I hit exactly where I aimed. *X marks the spot.* A wave of satisfaction runs through me at the sight.

I unload the gun, put it down, and take off my protective gear. I notice Henry from the corner of my eye, staring at me from the front desk with a wide grin. "Spying on me, are you?" I ask, jokingly.

"I always feel bad for the targets when you walk in here," he says with a chuckle.

Henry is the owner of the range. We hit it off instantly the first time I came. He's a tall, gentle, older man with hair as white as Clint Eastwood's and has owned this establishment for decades. The patrons of this place are a little *sus*, but Henry is always warm and welcoming. The first time I walked in, he was surprised that someone like me knew how to handle a firearm.

I learned how to shoot a gun at a young age, a little *too* young, if you ask me. But when your father is a mob boss, you need to learn how to defend yourself. I had no choice but to prepare for the eventuality I would need to use a deadly weapon against someone.

If you'd ask me to use a gun outside of a controlled area, I would probably hesitate. I don't have the same thirst for blood that others in my surroundings have. Although, given recent events, like being *kidnapped*, I should maybe work on carrying something other than a pocketknife with me. I don't feel safe anymore. *Not that I ever really did before.*

"Practice makes perfect," I say, winking at Henry. "What are you still doing here, old man? Isn't it past your bedtime?" I tease as I clean the glock to give it back to him.

He laughs loudly. "I'm leaving right after this, young lady. Done already?"

"Just taking a little break, Hen," I reply with a smile.

He stores the handgun in its case and hands me my target sheets. I'm not the type to keep them as souvenirs, so I crumple the large pieces of paper and throw them in the recycling bin on my way to the washroom, waving goodbye to Henry in case he's gone by the time I get back.

The darkness of the hallway engulfs me, but I feel a sense of tranquility. I find comfort in the dark. Maybe that's the introvert in me, but too much stimulation makes my senses go into overdrive. I walk through the narrow, poorly lit corridor as I look down at my phone. I'm so engrossed in my thoughts I don't notice where I'm headed, and I bump into a wall. My phone goes flying and I let out a little shriek of surprise as I fall back a few steps. The 'wall' I bumped into bends down to pick it up. I'm about to apologize when I stop and stare at the tall, dark-haired man standing before me. When his eyes reach my face, a glint of surprise flashes across his face. It's subtle, and I almost miss it, but I catch it right before his expression goes serious and impassive again.

"You shouldn't text and walk," the man— *not a wall*—says, his tone unimpressed.

I can't stop myself from gaping at him as he looks down at me from his towering height. *Holy hell.* I tilt my head farther back to get a better view. The dim glow above us casts his features in shadow. Hints of a strong jaw covered by stubble and high cheekbones. His presence wraps around me like velvet. Despite the partial absence of light, I'm still able to conclude that he's one of the most gorgeous men I've ever laid eyes on. Even though I'm burning with embarrassment, I can't seem to break contact from his piercing eyes. I close my mouth and feel myself blushing. Hopefully the lack of light is my saving grace. *Get it together, Ang.*

"I'm sorry. I wasn't paying attention. Thank you...for picking up my phone," I stutter.

His annoyed demeanor seems to dissipate slightly as he takes me in, his gaze traveling the length of my body. His face softens and my breath hitches. His eyes inch back to mine, caressing my every curve along the way. My body heats like it's being kissed by the golden sun.

He pauses on the redness of my exposed wrist, and I see his lips twitch, his face twisting into something that resembles anger, and then morphs into understanding. Not pity. I couldn't take pity. I immediately cover my wrist with my hand, feeling self-conscious that he noticed my self-inflicted injury. In any other circumstance, I wouldn't care. But the intensity of his stare makes me feel bad and guilty for hurting myself. It's as if I don't want to disappoint him. I lower my gaze to the floor and scurry away after another muttered apology. I curse myself for even caring about what a stranger might think about my bad habit.

Who is he? I've never seen him before. I make a mental note to ask Henry, but he's probably gone for the night. I'm a little disappointed I won't find out who this mystery man is tonight. This stranger made me feel so many emotions at once just by looking at me. I've never felt so bare, as if he could see right through me.

I shake off the feelings left from our little run in and continue down the hall to the restroom. When I get back into the shooting range area, I give my name to one of the employees behind the counter, and she grabs my equipment out of my designated locker. She hands me a semi-automatic and I scrunch my face, confused.

"Um, sorry, I don't shoot with rifles. I use the glock 19 or any other 9mm caliber you have available. I was using one a few minutes ago," I explain, slightly irritated.

"Sorry, hun, but that man," she points behind me, "took the last handgun."

I turn around. *Go figure.* The gorgeous man from before looks over at me and smirks, a knowing glint in his eye. *What an ass.* Forget all those warm, buzzing feelings he gave me. This is going to be an interesting night.

"Fine. I'll take this one," I sigh loudly in exasperation. Having to use a different gun gives me a bit of anxiety.

I walk to an empty station and notice he is two rows down.

I shake my head in annoyance. Between the rifle and the human wall made completely out of muscle that almost took me out earlier, I'm not sure tonight is my night.

I'm not comfortable shooting rifles, but I'm already here and can't leave until Gianis picks me up. So, I put on my big girl pants and prepare to shoot. I slip on my protective gear, straighten my safety goggles, and place the earmuffs over my ears, effectively canceling out most of the background noise. I draw in a deep breath, lift the gun, and rest it on my shoulder. I place my legs in a widened stance, my left side facing the target.

Rifles are a lot bigger than handguns and require much more precision and technique to use accurately. I know I can handle it, but something about this is making me nervous. I try to shoot once, and the drawback almost kicks me off my feet. I miss the target by a longshot. I let out a defeated sigh as I prepare to aim again. Suddenly, I feel a strong presence behind me and all the air I'd already let out gets sucked back into my lungs. It's *him*. I fight the urge to turn around and acknowledge him.

He smells like...cedarwood and mint, with a hint of musk. I was too flustered during our run-in, in the hallway to focus on his scent. It reminds me of a cabin escape in autumn. I briefly close my eyes as I inhale his smell, and I slightly angle my head to face him. It's as if something inside of me awakens.

I feel him lift one side of my earmuffs slowly, as if giving me the time to stop him. When I don't make a move, he brushes the hair out of my face, tucking the strands behind my ear. I freeze in place. I shouldn't let him put his hands on me, but I don't want him to stop. The sensation of his fingers on my skin sends a flutter down my body. He leans in, a bit too close for comfort for any other complete stranger, and whispers, "Do you mind?"

The warmth of his breath gives me goosebumps and the hairs on the back of my neck raise in response. I must be sick. I've never met this man in my life, yet my body is reacting as if he's capable of touching my soul, awakening feelings I didn't know were dormant.

"What?" I respond, disoriented.

"Do you mind if I help you? You seem nervous," he asks as he points to the rifle.

I hesitate before answering. My brain is overworked, unable to keep up with what's going on. It feels as if I have whiplash. "Uh, sure, I guess," I reply, absent-mindedly. My mind is racing. I couldn't keep a coherent thought in my brain right now if my life depended on it. *What is happening to me?*

The man moves closer. So close, my back is almost flush with the front of his body. He extends both of his arms, grabs the rifle, and places it correctly on my right shoulder. His body surrounds me, and it makes me feel so cocooned, sheltered from the world, comforted, safe.

His fingers tap the side of my right hip, and I see his foot trying to make a wedge between my feet. I widen my stance a bit and he pushes my legs open even farther. Once I'm steady, he squeezes the side of my left hip and tugs me into his body. My ass is glued to his crotch, and I can feel the outline of his length. It's not fully erect, but it's hard enough for me to feel it through the layers of clothing. *Oh, God.*

The most gorgeous stranger in existence is standing right behind me with his legs in between mine. This feels so inappropriate…ly *good*. My heart is fluttering, and I'm not sure if it's because of the adrenaline or his presence, or both.

He takes my right hand and sets it on the pistol grip, grazing my injured wrist with his thumb ever-so-slightly, and delicately places my fingers in a "V" next to the trigger. The feeling of his calloused palm sends a shiver down my spine, as my mind goes straight to an image of him running his hands down my bare skin. I want this stranger to touch me all over. He puts his lips to my ear, and I get another whiff of his scent. It makes me dizzy.

"You can breathe now," he says, playfully.

I was holding my breath this whole time. I take a deep inhale in, and exhale. Right before he puts the earmuff back on my ear, he takes my left hand in his, and puts it on the fore stock, midway down the length of the rifle, and says, "Shoot."

With him still pressed against me, I bring the rifle close to my head and push my cheek firmly into the stock. I keep my head straight and squeeze the trigger, causing the weapon to fire. The discharge of the gun surprises me with its force. But his body helps absorb the recoil, and his hands grip my hips to steady me. After a moment, I put the rifle down on the counter. My heart is racing, and my breaths are harsh. Electricity courses through my veins. I feel invincible.

I peek at the target paper. A perfect shot. I turn around to face him as I take off my protective glasses. He gently tugs at a strand of loose curls hanging out of my bun and smiles. And, God, does his smile take me to a place I've never been. His eyes soften, the hazel in his irises piercing right through me. I feel a sense of pride in myself. I never thought I would be confident enough to handle such a big firearm, but this stranger swooped in and helped me conquer my insecurity. He stares at me with intent, his eyes gleaming with something like...awe. I shy away from the intensity, my gaze dropping to the floor, and I see that his hands are still holding onto my waist.

"Good girl, Angelica," he says under his breath, and my body stills. *How does he know my name?*

He squeezes my hip, lets it go slowly, and backs away from me without breaking his gaze. I feel the absence of his body instantly.

"Wait! I didn't even get your name," I call out.

As he moves back to his station, he briefly stops in his tracks, and I sense hesitation before he responds.

"Evan." He grabs his bag and walks out of the range.

Something tells me this isn't the last time I'll see him.

Secret admirer. A stalker with stationery.

Angelica

Thirty minutes later, I push the door of Sharp Shooters open, and walk out into the dark alley, the only light a streetlamp several feet away. I breathe in the cool air and turn to my right, where Gianis is waiting to take me home. My father thinks I need to be followed everywhere I go now that I've moved back. I was in Antium City for years with no protection and he never seemed to care where I was or what I did. Now, he insists Gianis accompany me whenever I go out at night. Although I don't totally agree with this demand, walking through an alley in the streets of Downtown Cebrene at this time of day isn't safe for anyone. As much as I love my independence, a small part of me is thankful to have a lethal enforcer by my side.

"Ang," Gianis says, as he pushes himself off the side of the building.

"Hey, G, thanks for coming back for me." I still wonder why he didn't wait for me. But if there's one thing I know about him, it's that he is very secretive with respect to his whereabouts. I debate asking if the name Evan sounds familiar to him, but I refrain from it. He knows everyone of importance in the city, and I'm sure he's aware of every single person who walks in and out of the range, given I've been going for weeks.

He's only stepped foot in the establishment once, but I guess it was enough for him to vet the place. He wouldn't risk sending me into the line of danger.

He nods at my response. For once, I know Gianis is okay with my father's methods regarding me. He's been obsessive about my safety ever since the kidnapping. He barely leaves my side and constantly checks on me. He doesn't let me go anywhere alone, unless it's with Aria. I wouldn't be surprised if he planted a tracker on me. But I'm thankful for his concern. If it weren't for him, I wouldn't ever leave my house. There are three things that make me feel safe now. Shooting, Gianis, and my admirer.

We walk the rest of the way to his car parked on the side of the road and I look up at Gianis' six-foot-four, chiseled frame. The dim light of the streetlamps shines on his face, making his sculpted cheekbones and sharp jawline more prominent. His long legs walk in glorious strides and his charcoal grey-fitted suit jacket flaps in the wind, exposing his handgun tucked into the side of his pants. He is *beautiful*. We've grown even closer over the last few weeks, and it reminds me of when we were young. We've been around each other ever since I was little, and although I have never been *in* love with him, I did grow attached. We used to play together all the time as kids—me following him around everywhere—and when we both grew as teenagers, he started looking at me differently. He still looks at me the same way now, but I've always been too scared to give in. He's the first boy I ever loved. He's family, and I would never do anything to jeopardize our friendship.

We shared our first kiss when I was fifteen and he was nineteen. It was my first time kissing a boy, so I didn't know what to expect. I wasn't a prude or anything, but I was one of the only girls left in my grade that hadn't even gotten to first base. All the boys were scared to approach me because of

Gianis. I used to be the one following him around, but the roles reversed, and no boy felt comfortable talking to me.

I don't blame them. Even as a young adult, G was big, tall, and intimidating.

It took a while to convince him to pop my kissing cherry, but he finally conceded, agreeing that he would rather be my first than let some 'horn-dog' teenager slobber all over me. That got a loud "ew" from me, and I debated whether I wanted to be kissed after all.

Gianis was a lot more experienced, having already been with girls, but he was gentle, and showed me how to pucker my lips and tilt my head. It was the opposite of slobbery, and I wondered why it took me so long to ask him to teach me.

It wasn't the only time our lips touched, but we never passed first base. Everyone thought we would start dating eventually, but I was never interested in taking our relationship to the next level.

Eventually, we decided to stop whatever we were doing, in case my father caught wind of it. He trusted Gianis, but I'm sure he wouldn't have been happy to find out that he was sticking his tongue down my throat whenever he got the chance.

"Are you okay?" he asks, his brows furrowed, and I'm brought back to the present.

I snap my head forward and look straight ahead. "Yeah, why?" I answer, shaking off the thoughts of his lips on mine.

He raises an eyebrow. "You were staring at me."

"Sorry, I was...daydreaming?" *Good one, Ang.*

"You don't seem so sure of that," he chuckles softly.

I give him a little wink. "I was just thinking about how I don't need a chaperone." Not exactly true, but he doesn't need to know that.

He shakes his head and lets out a little sigh. "You know I didn't *choose* to be your glorified babysitter, right?"

I roll my eyes at him as we reach our ride. For once, he's not driving one of his obnoxious sports cars. I open the door and slip into the passenger seat of the sedan, and he heads toward my place.

When Gianis pulls up to my house, I get out of the car and shut the door without saying goodbye. He's used to my attitude by now and doesn't think twice before backing out of the driveway. I can't help my bitterness. Ever since I moved back to Cebrene, I have been in a terrible mood, but I know Gianis understands. He always does.

"Pssht, so much for protection," I mumble, noticing he didn't even wait for me to get inside before driving away.

My father wanted me to have two bodyguards, but I fought him tooth and nail. Gianis suggested installing a top-of-the-line security system that contacts him as soon as the alarm is triggered, and he reluctantly agreed. I'd convinced myself I was free of my father's hold in Antium, but it feels like I'm almost back to square one now. I guess this arrangement is better than nothing.

I didn't choose to live in this specific house, but I had to compromise with my father when I came back from The Big A. If I wanted to live on my own, I had to live in *his* part of the city, in a house *he* owned, where he would be able to ensure my protection.

I step in, disable the alarm, and lock the door behind me. I set my things down on a chair in the family room and make my way down the long and wide hallway, passing the powder room, office, guest bedroom, and the main living room. This place is unnecessarily big for one person with three more bedrooms upstairs and a home theater in the basement. The sensor lights turn on as I walk through the corridor toward the kitchen located at the back of the house.

I'm starving given that I skipped dinner to go to the range. I don't normally forget to eat, but my mind has been distracted with the move, the fragile state of my safety, and my newfound secret admirer. I open the fridge and the first thing I see is a white box with a sticky note on the top. I rip it off and read it out loud. *I'll take care of you*, it says.

I drop the piece of paper as if it's a hot potato, and my instinct is to look around the room. I squint my eyes to peer outside the patio doors, but it's too dark, and I see no movement. My house is surrounded by sensor lights. I'd obviously be alerted if someone was on the property. But somehow, this intruder has found a way around my security system, and I don't know if I should be concerned or impressed.

I open the cardboard container and find a whole cheesecake. My favorite. I dig in and smile, the weight of the day melting away. All thanks to an unknown person who chose me as the target of their undivided attention.

> "They've promised that dreams can come true - but forgot to mention that nightmares are dreams, too."
> —Oscar Wilde

Evander

I leave the shooting range and let out a huge sigh of relief. I sling my bag over my shoulder and lift the hood of my sweatshirt over my head as I walk down the alley. My two bodyguards, Sebastian and Gregory, stayed behind to not bring any attention to me. I have to keep a low profile. It's never a good idea for a high-ranking member of the mob to be seen alone and vulnerable.

I wasn't expecting Angelica to be at Sharp Shooters at the same time I was. I knew she came here a few nights a week, always on Thursdays, but I didn't think I'd run into her. I was only supposed to pop in, talk to the owner, and head out. But when our bodies collided in the hallway, I couldn't help but feel a crackle of electricity pass between us. Her hair was in a messy bun, and it brushed against my face as I picked up her phone from the floor. The fresh aroma of rose and peony, mixed with a hint of sweet cocoa hits my nose, taunting me to pull on the loose strands that were poking out.

I hadn't realized how much taller than her I was until I looked down and saw her big brown eyes gaping up at me. She may have been small in stature, but her mere presence loomed over me. I trembled with the need to feel her body against mine, to connect with her soul. It had almost knocked me off my fucking feet. *Literally.*

She is even more gorgeous up close, her beauty *suffocating*, blazing with a fire even the devil couldn't handle. I couldn't keep my eyes off her. I'm positive she caught me staring. I wish I cared. As my eyes were traveling along her body, they'd landed on a scar on the inner part of her right wrist. My eyes had lingered for a fraction of a second too long and she must have noticed as she quickly covered it with her hand. Seeing her hurt didn't sit well with me, even if it seemed to be self-inflicted. I want to find out who or what caused her to need to feel pain to cope and make them pay. *Why do you even care, Evan? She's the enemy's daughter,* I remind myself.

I can't get the feeling of her body pressed up against my chest out of my mind. The way her small frame fit perfectly in mine. I was simply going to exchange a few words with her and introduce myself, just enough to pique her curiosity and leave her wanting more. I wasn't going to stay and use the facilities, but when I realized she was uncomfortable with the idea of shooting a rifle, I felt drawn to help her. *Let's be honest, what the fuck was I thinking? There was no way I could keep my hands off her.*

It was my fault there were not any handguns left for her to shoot after all.

She froze when I stood behind her, her body's reaction to my touch making my dick twitch. I hope she could feel it lengthening under my pants. She was wearing one of those low-cut tank tops that gave me a full view of her cleavage from my towering height and my eyes kept drifting there. The air was thick with tension between us as I'd parted her legs. I wanted to slip my fingers down her tight as sin leggings to feel the warmth of her pussy.

The way her hand had gripped the forestock had me

picturing how it would look wrapped around my cock. She followed all my instructions without saying a word, and her obedience made me wonder how submissive she would be in bed. I ought to punch myself for even thinking this way. But I never claimed to be a good man.

Which is how I end up stroking my cock in the dark corner of the alley, thinking of Angelica. I suddenly snap back to reality. I shouldn't be doing this, not in response to *her*. My enemy's fucking *daughter*. Anyone could walk by and see me right now, but there's no use trying to stop. I continue touching myself at the reminder of her body against mine. And I come so hard I think I might pass out.

***

Three weeks earlier

"Goddamn," I say out loud as I open the door to the small gym in my building and I'm hit in the face with freezing cold air.

Summer has begun, and the Cebrene heat is already suffocating. My building always overdoes it with the AC. I walk to the back of the gym, passing walls covered with floor-to-ceiling mirrors, and set my bag down near the lockers.

It's five a.m. *The early bird gets the worm*, as they say. I can't be bothered to be surrounded by people. I'm more comfortable alone with my thoughts.

I connect my wireless headphones to my phone and press play on my current workout playlist before putting it in my pocket. The sound of 'Popstar' by DJ Khaled featuring Drake starts playing loudly in my ears and I focus on my workout.

Forty-five minutes later I'm still going strong. I take off my sweat-drenched shirt, throw it to the side and lie back on the bench to start working on my incline press. I place my hands on the bar and as I lift the rack up, I try not to think about the pressure I've been under these past weeks. I'm tired and overworked but I don't let those feelings cloud my focus. I release a puff of air and slowly lower the bar to my chest, then press it back up again, over and over, only stopping when I can't feel my arms. I keep pushing myself to the limit, as it's the only thing that will stop my thoughts from overwhelming me. I grunt, sweat dripping down my forehead and chest all the way down to the ripples in my abdomen, and I wipe away the dampness with a towel.

Even though I stay up late most nights, I can't sleep more than a few hours at a time. Working all day, taking calls and meetings, and going to the club afterwards to check on my crew, I usually don't get home until one or two in the morning. Sometimes later, if a woman is lucky enough to grab my attention. Then there are the nights where my sleep is interrupted by nightmares.

However, I don't let fatigue stop me.

I wasn't raised to be a little bitch complaining about being tired and taking naps. My uncle, Ignatius, always taught me that success isn't an accident. It's hard work, perseverance, and sacrifice. So, if I have to forgo a few hours of sleep per night to be successful, I'll do it.

But this morning, I'm struggling to stay awake.

Last night, I was at my club with Dion, Xander, and my uncle. The drinks were flowing and the ladies were flocking. I welcomed the distraction and indulged in way too much alcohol and pussy.

My uncle has been coming down on me to maintain our business relationships and meet with his many partners. I don't normally play this part with the big dogs; I prefer to wait in the shadows for orders to punish or kill. But lately, my uncle has been occupied and distant. He's been quiet about his whereabouts and who he talks to, which is out of the ordinary. I have a hunch he's mixed in something he doesn't want me to be involved in. I know better than to question him, but whatever he's doing can't be good news. I'm sure I'll find out when the time is right.

On top of all the work I have to do for my club and warehouse, now I have to deal with my uncle's cranky, man-child associates. He's probably forcing this on me because I'll soon take over the family business, but *fuck*, I'd rather deal with a nursery full of newborns than have to put up with overgrown trigger-happy babies.

Ignatius doesn't like dealing with violence himself, so when he wants to send a message, or teach a lesson, that's where I come into play. *The Diávolos. The Devil.*

I didn't get that nickname for nothing. I'm ruthless as fuck and I'm not scared to eliminate our enemies, even if it means getting my hands dirty.

I was what people would describe as a 'troubled' kid. My uncle found a way for me to channel my temper, use it as a weapon. Over the years, I developed a taste for punishment as Ignatius let me take my anger out on his enemies, allowing me to connect to the evil within me. I became a different person when I tapped into my rage. I knew I was fractured, but this was how I made peace with myself. By becoming the devil himself when I needed to protect my family. They say, *'to know your inner demon is to know yourself,'* and I can tell you it's true.

Yesterday, I had to pay a visit to one of the warehouses my uncle owns. He got word that some of the guys were messing up the shipment schedule, which ultimately caused a delay with one of the trucks. In the arms trade, every minute counts, and sending out a delivery late could potentially create a domino effect of problems that neither my uncle nor I want to deal with.

The workers immediately sensed trouble the moment Xander and I had walked in, looking at each other frantically or scurrying away to hide. We could hear their frightened whispers. It's never good news when the *Diávolos* comes around unannounced. I hadn't been sent to murder these men, but I called on the ones who were disrupting the schedule. All three had knelt before me, a few feet away, while Xander aimed a gun to their heads. The goal wasn't to shoot to kill, but if one of them tried to make a run for it, a bullet would've been sent right through their kneecaps.

I took off my jacket, rolled up my sleeves, and approached them. They were trembling, begging, and sniveling for their lives. I squatted down to analyze them, I could smell their fear. *I fucking love it when they cower in terror at my mercy.* One cried, the other prayed to God, and the third pissed himself. *I fucking hate when they piss themselves.*

I beat the fuck out of them in front of everyone.

"This ought to teach you all to pay more attention to your fucking jobs," I casually stated to no one in particular. Xander handed me a rag to clean my bloodied hands and we walked out of the warehouse.

I still somehow had pent-up energy to release. That rarely happens, usually exacting punishment gives me total satisfaction, so we went to the club right after to help me blow off some steam. By steam, I mean find some hot girl and bury myself deep inside her pussy. I don't sleep around as often as I used to, but things have been stressful at work.

At the club, a pretty, young brunette kept hovering near me. The smell of her perfume mixed with her subtle advances made my cock twitch in my pants. She had looked over at me, smiling, her eyes hazy. She was clearly drunk, and I *never* take advantage of women in that state. So, I grabbed the drink from her hand, put my arm around her waist, and pinned her back against me. Her ass pressed onto my groin, and I couldn't help but let out a grunt at the feeling. She giggled, and I moved a strand of hair from the side of her face to whisper, *"If you want me to fuck you tonight, you better stop drinking. I'm going to need you to be sober to take my dick."*

Her whole body froze, but within a second, she turned to me and crashed her lips on mine. Our tongues swirled for a few seconds, the taste of whiskey and tequila mixing together, before I realized my mistake and pulled my mouth away.

"No kissing," I grunted.

The girl's face turned pink with embarrassment, and I thought of turning her ass cheeks the same color. In my heart, I felt nothing. All the feelings were gathered in my cock, right where I needed them to be.

I never bring women to my penthouse, so I took her to my office on the second floor of the nightclub at the end of the night and had my way with her on one of the loveseats.

I have a bedroom to crash in on late nights, but I rarely ever use it. Especially not for one-night stands. I'll never share a bed with a woman. I don't do cuddles or sleepovers. It makes me uncomfortable, and I don't want them getting the wrong idea.

Though I always make sure to leave the women I fuck satisfied. I make my intentions clear before engaging in anything sexual, which is another reason why the woman must be sober.

After the brunette left my office, I took off. Regardless of the time, I always make the trek back home. I didn't get to bed until three a.m. *Tired* is the understatement of the year today.

At least I got to bust a nut.

I finish my workout and slip my t-shirt back on before

grabbing my gym bag. I walk out the door and head to the penthouse elevators when my phone rings. I don't check the caller ID before I pick up, knowing exactly who would call me this early.

"Dion," I state, waiting for his witty reply, but it never comes. I only hear silence on the other end. "*Dion,*" I repeat. "What's going on?"

I halt mid-walk in the lobby and see Jude, the concierge, from the corner of my eye. He waves hello and I nod back, still waiting for Dion to say something. I call the elevator and he finally breaks his silence. "Ignatius is dead."

Time stands still. I can hear the loud pounding of my heartbeat in my ears. The elevator door opens, and I step inside, hoping no one will follow me in. I quickly punch in the code to the penthouse level. It's still early, so most of the tenants of the building haven't even started their day. I clench my fist and punch the wall.

The rage inside of me bubbles up and I can't let out a word. It feels as if my whole world is caving in as I try to process the news of the death of the man who raised and loved me like a son.

Dion interrupts my spiraling. "*Ta silipitíria mou,* Evan." *My condolences.*

"What happened?" I ask. I slide down the elevator wall with my head in my hand. It feels like my heart is going to burst out of my mouth.

"After he left the club last night, he was followed home and shot as he was getting out of his car. Edna found him sprawled on the ground this morning with several gunshot wounds, one to the head," Dion's voice cracks. Ignatius was like a father to him, too.

I'm suddenly brought back to my seventh birthday, a year after my parents' and sister's deaths. I begged my uncle not to throw me a party. I was a recluse, not a normal boy. I didn't have any friends and I didn't care to make any. I couldn't fit in at school. I didn't even get bullied. I was just there. Alone and quiet. I was the weird kid, but no one messed with me. There was this *anger* laying dormant inside of me, you could see it through my eyes. My teachers tried to help me integrate, but I never cooperated. Eventually, they just left me alone until my uncle pulled me out to be homeschooled the year prior.

On the day of my celebration, I recognized all the children Ignatius had invited from my old school. But there was one kid I had never noticed before. He was smaller, with dark hair and light blue eyes. We stared at each other for a moment without blinking. I could see through his darkness, and he could see through mine. I could tell he was just like me. Quiet, angry, sad. I wondered what had happened to him.

My uncle brought him over to me. *"Yié, this is Dion,"* he said. *"I want you to take care of him, Evan."*

The kid just stood there, unmoving. I nodded and walked away. The other children were playing outside in the inflatable structures, and some were in the pool, but I couldn't be bothered with any of it. I went upstairs to lock myself in my room, but I could hear footsteps trailing behind me. I knew it was Dion. I had no doubt he would follow me. I opened the door to my bedroom and we both stepped inside.

He broke the silence first. *"My parents are dead,"* he stated.

I nodded again as I reached into a drawer, pulled out two Gameboys and handed him one. We sat there, me on the bed and Dion on the floor, and played games for hours in complete silence. It was the most peace I had felt in the company of another person apart from my uncle. I didn't feel like I had to try to be his friend, he just was.

Ignatius kept bringing Dion around after that. Every day, after dinner and homework, Dion would barge into my room and we would play video games until it was time for him to go. Eventually, he moved in with us. Turns out his situation was worse than I thought.

We became brothers and my uncle became a father-figure for us both. He knew exactly what we needed and how to raise us. He loved us, cared for us, and trained us to be the best men we could be, given the circumstances. We'd be nothing without him. It feels like another piece of my heart has broken. I don't know if I have anymore to spare.

"They must've used a silencer, because Edna didn't hear anything," Dion adds, snapping me out of my stupor. "When she realized he wasn't in his bed this morning..." He lets out a heavy sigh and continues, "She went to check if his car was parked in the driveway from the window and saw a pool of blood." *Fuck.*

My mind can't grasp this information. I run my hand down my face and stand to exit the elevator. Poor Edna. She has been my uncle's housekeeper for as long as I can remember. They were great friends, so this loss must be hard for her.

I rub my forehead, feeling a strong headache creeping in. My exhaustion settles as a hangover looms over me.

"Why the fuck was he alone? Where were his guards?" I ask. Now, I'm furious.

"Phil and Elias weren't around. He had told them to go straight home after the club, but they rushed over as soon as Edna called them."

They should be punished for not being with my uncle. They should never take no for an answer, even if he begs them to leave. "They know better than to leave him vulnerable."

"I know, brother. I went over with Xander and checked the security footage. We caught a glimpse of the men inside the car and recognized them as Peter Kouvalakis' men."

"Gianis?" I ask.

"No, it wasn't him. Jurian wasn't there either. He sent his lower soldiers to do the dirty work," he confirms.

"I'm going to fucking kill Peter and take everything he's ever cared for," I seethe.

My family had a rivalry with the Kouvalakis family, so my mind went straight to them. Peter had always caused trouble, trying and failing to infiltrate our ranks, but it had never been enough of a conflict for them to kill each other. My uncle used to catch informants creeping around our turf and establishments trying to fish for information, and it never ended well for the spies. I would know, because he would send the *Diávolos* to end them. Killing is in my nature and I excel at it.

I step into the grand entrance of my penthouse and kick off my running shoes, heading straight for my office. Peter and Ignatius have had issues for decades, but they were still able to put their differences aside to live peacefully. For him to kill my uncle now, after so many years, for no apparent reason, doesn't sit well with me. There must be something he hasn't told me, and I'm going to find out.

"I need all the information you can gather. His intentions, his next moves, who those men were. *Everything*, Dion."

"Already on it, Boss," Dion responds without hesitation. "We were able to find one of his soldiers and I forced him into giving me details."

Knowing Dion, that means *torture* him into giving up the information. I'm not the only one with a thirst for blood.

Now that my uncle is dead, I will be called upon to take over for the Vasilakis family as their Godfather of the Night. Shit is about to get real. I've been preparing for this my whole life, but now that it's all happening so suddenly, I realize just how unprepared I am. I was meant to acquire the business next year, when I turned thirty-five and my uncle retired, but it seems God had other plans.

Ignatius raised me since I was six years old. He was the only father-figure in my life from that point on and took care of me like I was his own. He didn't have children, so I was his pride and joy. He never expected to become the Godfather of the Vasilakis family. But when my parents died, he took over for my father and took me in. At the time, I didn't fully comprehend what my father did for a living. He never wanted to involve me at such a young age, and I didn't blame him. I would not have understood.

As I grew older, my uncle started involving me in the family business and I gained more responsibility. I even opened my own nightclub next to one of our warehouses where we conducted business. I eventually inherited that, too. Although I was part of the Vasilakis clan, no one knew I was the son of Georgios and Catherine Vasilakis, or that Ignatius was my uncle. He decided to keep those details a secret to protect me and make sure no one could target me. I tried to convince him that I was an adult and could take care of myself, but he was overprotective and didn't want to risk my safety. He said it was better that no one knew who I was. It would instill fear in them, and when the time came for me to take over the reins, my reputation would withstand the pushback. Everyone outside of Dion and Xander think I'm simply my uncle's second-in-command. A trustworthy family friend. Nobody from the outside knows that the heir to the business would actually be the true successor. And that's something my uncle always prepared me for. To be a Godfather of Night.

"And there's something else I thought you should know," he continues. "Peter has a daughter, Angelica Hera Kouvalakis. She's twenty-three. She recently graduated from Antium U and just moved back from Antium City a few days ago. She ran away from home four years ago to get away from her father but is back because Hendrick kidnapped and released her to Gianis in exchange for Peter's agreement to stop trying to take over his turf."

I scoff at the last bit of information. Peter has been relentless about invading Puerto Rican territory in Anzio, the Upper East side of Antium. They finally found his weak spot, I guess. *And now I know it too.*

"Thanks, D. Call me if you find anything else." I hang up the phone and throw it across the room. The sound of the phone ricocheting off the floor reaches my ears. My vision goes blank, and I feel fury. It promises death to whoever did this to him.

My plan begins to unfold.

Angelica doesn't know who I am yet, but I'm going to find her and make her wish she never met me.

"Traitors are more dangerous than enemies."
—Velupillai Prabhakaran

Evander

Present

In the days following the news, I couldn't process it all. I went about my week, business as usual, like it was any other normal time in the ranks of the mob. Dion and Xander kept asking me if I was okay and tried to convince me to stay home and grieve. But all I could do was drink *ouzo* and plot vengeance. *Again, a normal day.*

On the fourth day after my uncle's passing, I met Dion at Xander's family restaurant. I couldn't wait to get more information on my target. I kept repeating her name and it rolled off my tongue like butter. *Angelica Hera Kouvalakis.* Too bad her last name made me want to gut the insides of her father with my bare hands.

I tasked my men and the group of hackers I employ to dig up as much as they could find on Peter's precious daughter. As the new Godfather, there's no way I had time to do it myself. I'm too preoccupied with getting my uncle's affairs in order and meeting with our associates to make sure the transition happens smoothly. I'm too fucking swamped with shit to do.

Xander followed her around for a couple days to take pictures and footage of her ins and outs. When he showed me a photo of Angelica, my jaw had nearly dropped. It revealed a fresh-faced, freckled young woman at the front door of a house, in the early morning hours, wearing a long blue summer dress that hugged her body in all the right places. I stared at her toned legs and her round ass that swallowed the fabric whole. As Xan flipped through the images, I caught a glimpse of her dark eyes before she hid them under her large sunglasses. Her light brown skin shone in the sun. *Fuck me.*

Seeing photos of Angelica was one thing, but the real her was another mindfuck. I wanted to fucking taste everything under her clothes and memorize every curve of her body. She looked gorgeous. *Snap out of it, Evan.* She's too young, barely an adult. And I don't have time to lust over a woman eleven years younger than me and who only four years ago ran away from 'daddy,' probably because he didn't get her the Prada bag she wanted. I hate her family, her father, and I should hate everything she stands for. I can't let her beauty distract me from the fact that she is the daughter of the man responsible for the death of my uncle.

I grunt, feeling discomfort in my crotch. I'm not supposed to want her. She's supposed to be a means to an end. A way of achieving my goal. I need to focus this energy on finding a way to use her against Peter.

This will be a lot harder than I thought.

I get in my car and head to the club to meet Dion.

I acquired Academia several years ago, when my uncle

approached me about the importance of having my own business to be responsible for, something to call my own. A venture I could use to both give me experience commanding a following as a boss, diversify my portfolio, and give me a location to do legitimate business.

At the time, I was in my mid-twenties and thought a club would be the best way to go. I spent most of my free time drinking with the boys, so I figured it would only make sense to have my own bar. The nightclub scene will always thrive, and it brings in a decent profit on the side of my other pursuits. It's also the best way to launder money.

Dion texted me while I was at the shooting range to tell me one of our men was caught stealing. I never shy away from these situations, but I hate when it's one of my men. *Too bad. I'll have to punish him, anyway.*

I reply right before driving off.

Me: Take him to my office. I want to have a conversation with him, man to man.

One of my attendants is waiting at the entrance when I arrive. There's always someone on guard to make sure the property doesn't get broken into and robbed. This is a sketchy area of Old Cebrene, but it makes for a cool experience for the club goers who want a grungy, dark vibe.

"Leon," I holler, as I throw him my keys. "Where is he?" I ask, my tone filled with fury.

He catches them and replies with a chuckle, "Right where you want him, boss." He knows exactly who I'm referring to. He throws his unfinished cigarette on the ground and proceeds to move my car to the private lot in the back of the property.

I head to my office right away. I barge through the doors, past Seb and Greg, and they follow me inside to stand guard. Dion and Xander are next to the piece of shit seated comfortably in a chair in front of my desk. He has no idea why he's here, but I'm sure his guilt is eating him alive, and the anticipation of seeing the look of shock on his face when he finds out tickles me in all the right places. The loud noise of the door startles him, and he turns to me. I smile, a vicious, Joker-type grin, and the man cowers away. *It's that fucking easy.*

I sit at my desk and take off my suit jacket, laying it on the table.

Dion briefed me on how Cyrus, the traitor in question, stole out of the money bags we use to store cash in our safes. The bastard thought he was slick, sneaking behind the bar while no one was around. His act was caught by the security cameras.

"You're probably wondering why I've called a meeting at this time," I say, my tone casual as I fiddle with a pen. Cyrus looks at me with a hesitant smile and replies, uncertainty in his voice, "What can I do for you, Boss?"

I look at him straight in the eyes for a moment and he turns his face away. He's terrified. I've got him exactly where I want him. He might be dumb as fuck for stealing from me, but he can't be stupid enough to think I don't know. I don't usually like to play games, but this is one I don't mind. Toying with a man's emotions until he shrinks in fear. Until he feels small and insignificant. That's when I crush him until he's nothing but dust in the wind.

"Let's go for a drive," I reply as I push myself off my chair. I grab my jacket and walk out the door. Xander stays back to keep an eye on the club. It'll be filled with partiers in a couple hours, and I need him to watch over the place while I step

THE DIÁVOLOS

away. My guards follow me out while Dion ushers Cyrus out of his seat, who looks like he's seen a fucking ghost.

My hands shake with excitement. It's been several days since I've had the opportunity to release my anger on a poor soul. The rage lives inside me, unable to escape from its confinement.

I shoot Leon a text on my way down and tell him to get our ride ready. As soon as we step outside, a town car pulls up and I climb into the back seat. Cyrus slips in next to me, followed by Dion. He's now sandwiched between two of the most ruthless men in the city. Seb takes the driver's seat and Greg sits next to him. Cyrus has four enemies in the car and no escape.

We drive off, and Seb circles around the Old Cebrene while we deal with the situation. We've done this before, so he knows the drill. Cyrus's demeanor has greatly changed from relaxed to horrified. He's shaking like a leaf, sweat riddles his brows, and his breaths are coming out of his mouth in short pants. It's time to get this show on the road.

"Now, Cyrus, tell me why you felt like you could steal from me?" I ask without warning. He immediately straightens his posture and clears his throat to swallow a harsh gulp. I sniff, my tone nonchalant, and continue, "I was told you were caught going through our safe. Did you really think no one would find out?"

Without giving him a chance to answer, I add, "You do know what happens to men who steal from the Vasilakis clan, don't you? I didn't get my reputation for nothing."

"I'm so sorry, Boss. I didn't—"

"Shut the fuck up, Cyrus," I snarl. I look over at Dion and he lets out a snort. While I'm serious and lethal, Dion has a sadistic sense of humor, and I don't know which is worse.

But Cyrus doesn't stop rambling. "*Please.* Please, don't hurt me! I didn't mean to steal. I just needed some extra cash and didn't think I could ask for it. *Please.* I'm desperate. He said they would kill my family," he spits out in one breath.

"Who the fuck is *'he'?*" I ask as I reach back into the waistband of my pants to pull out my gun. In a matter of seconds, I unlock it and point it to his temple.

"I–I don't know. Some man approached me asking to spy on you..." he pauses to catch his breath. "And dig up dirt on Ignatius. Said he would pay me for it. *But*–but I refused, I swear and then he threatened to kill my family," he sobs. "I thought I could pay him off instead."

Who the fuck could be sniffing around for information about me? Has Peter finally come knocking? I hold the glock up to his neck, pressing firmly enough to dent his skin. "What kind of information, Cyrus?" My mind is spinning with unanswered questions. *What the fuck was my uncle hiding?*

"I don't know! He didn't tell me! I refused before he got the chance to explain," he says frantically.

I tilt my head to the side. "See, I believe you. But what I don't understand is why you thought stealing from me would solve your problem," I say, already bored with this conversation. "But you're right, I wouldn't have given you the money."

I cock the weapon and bring it to the middle of Cyrus's forehead. *"No,* please. No," he cries. "I told you everything! I don't know anything else. I would never betray you," he rambles.

It's always the same story with weak-minded men. They do something wrong and then try to beg their way out of it. I have no pity for him. If he would've told me or one of the guys, we would've dealt with the situation and ensured that his family came out unscathed, but he decided to take the matter into his own hands instead and fucked himself over.

"I'm going to give you a chance to apologize, Cyrus.

THE DIÁVOLOS

Though, it won't change the outcome of what's about to happen," I tease. *Like I'd ever deny myself some fun.*

"I'm s–s–sorry, Boss," Cyrus replies. Tears run down his face and snot trails over his quivering lips. It's disgusting.

The car comes to a stop at one of our warehouses on the other side of Old Cebrene, and Dion gives me a wary look. The last thing I should do is kill one of my men. It could send a message to outsiders that we are weak. That we don't have our men in check. I have to be stern enough to let my people know not to mess with me without giving the wrong impression to our partners and rivals. If word gets out that an enemy was snooping around our business to get information, or if my men find out that I was robbed by an insider, no one will take me seriously as the new Godfather. But I don't give a shit about what people think of me. I'd rather upkeep my reputation as the *Diávolos* than make nice as a Godfather of the Night. I'm getting really fucking impatient and I just want to get this over with.

"Everyone out, except you," I bark, while eyeing the traitor. The guys get out and I open the window on my side. I grab my gun by the barrel and use the handle to knock Cyrus on the nose. His head dips forward as he clutches his face, hissing loudly in pain. I step out, leave him in the car, and point the gun at his head, shutting one eye to get the perfect shot, and I fire. The bullet flies through the window and straight through his temple. Blood splatters everywhere before Cyrus's body goes limp. Quick and efficient. Easy peasy.

"Get rid of him," I command as I walk toward the parking lot at the back of the warehouse to get into a different vehicle. Sebastian and Gregory are probably going to take the town car to an abandoned yard and burn it. We have plenty of other cars where it came from.

"What the fuck were you thinking, Evander?" Dion asks as

he follows me to the building. He never calls me by my full name unless he's actually angry. "Why would you do something so stupid? How the hell are we going to get information about whoever was snooping around if our main source is *dead*?"

"Dion, you're my brother, but watch your fucking mouth," I respond without turning to look at him. "I did what had to be done. He stole from me. No one steals from the *Diávolos* and gets away with it."

"You could've killed him *after* we got the information, *vlakas*. You're acting like an angry teenager," he scoffs.

"*Tha mou kláseis*, Dion." *Suck my dick*. "I know what I'm doing."

"No. I think you don't, Evan. I don't know what's going on with you, but you're losing your touch. The *Diávolos* is calculated. *This?* Was not calculated at all," Dion argues.

I slow down. I turn around to face my brother. I have to remind myself he's just looking out for me. But I have the urge to punch him right in the fucking nose. And I do. I launch myself at him and my fist lands right on his pretty boy face. Dion's head flies back, he lets out a loud grunt right before striking me back on the side of my jaw. Blood projects out of my mouth, so I spit to get rid of the pool of metallic liquid. He knows better than to provoke me. I'm hot-headed and impulsive when I have pent up anger. I don't give a shit who's in the way. It has to come out one way or another.

"*Poutánas yos*," I seethe as I tackle him to the ground. Dion's body lands on the concrete with a loud thud as he swings his fists at my face. I grab onto his wrist, place my elbow right on his sternum, applying pressure. He yells out in pain before he throws me off him. When we were young, we fought all the time. Once we got comfortable enough to let our emotions out in front of each other, we'd argue and fight until we saw blood. Ignatius or one of his men had to intervene to stop us. Too much volatility in one house, my uncle would claim. This reminds me of those times.

We both stand up within seconds and come face-to-face like two characters from a video game, walking in a slow circle. Our fists hover in the air as we plan our next move. *So dramatic.* We both have intense fight training, but when we get into a brawl, our coaching flies out the window and we become show-offs. Dion charges at me first and puts his arms around my neck, putting me in a headlock. Air gets caught in my lungs as my breaths come out shallow. "*Ánte gamísou,*" I croak. *Fuck you.* "You're dead once I get out of this."

"Keep your threats for the people who deserve it, *Evanaki,*" Dion responds as he tightens his hold around my head. "I'm fighting you as your brother, not your second-in-command. Snap the fuck out of whatever spell you're under and get your shit together. You're distracted and taking out your anger in the wrong ways. I thought you'd be smarter than that, so I'm not letting go until every ounce of rage has seeped out of your body," he continues.

Dion is my brother. I value his opinion. I trust him. If he wants to fight, I'm ready. If he wants to be the one to receive the blunt of my wrath, *let's fucking do this.*

I elbow him in the stomach as hard as I can and swing the fist of that same arm right up into his nose again. He lets go of me and we fall to the ground. I climb on top of him and wail onto his face, a growl escapes his lips with every punch. He takes each one without fighting back and I get frustrated he's just letting me win. "Fight back, asshole," I shout.

He shoves me away, but it's not hard enough to throw me off him, so he bends his legs, lifts his ass off the cement and twists his body. The move is unexpected. *What the hell?* I fly off his waist and land directly on the gravel. *Fuck,* that hurts. My body is going to hate me for this.

"Are you fucking good now?" Dion asks as he gets up. I stay on my back and look up at the night sky as I catch my breath. I never get the opportunity to just stop and stare. I'm always on the move, always plotting. I never have time to just *be.* How ironic is it that I'm contemplating all this while on asphalt, my clothes disheveled, and my face bloodied. My brother might be a grade A dick, but he's got a point. Maybe it wasn't the best idea to kill Cyrus before fleecing him for information. I just have so much energy to release, and so many new emotions, I don't know how to handle it all. And I *never* lose focus. *It's because of her, Evan.*

Dion extends his hand to help me up and I grab onto it. "Thanks, bro."

He nods.

We walk the rest of the way to the lot, limping and in pain, but ten times lighter. It's an unconventional way to deal with your emotions, but when are we ever normal?

I walk into my penthouse hours later.

No one would think anyone lives here if they saw it, it looks like a damn showroom. The interior is tasteful, with neutral and dark colors, and my living room is decorated with the most expensive furniture. The expansive area is filled with a tanned, leather couch that hasn't felt the groove of an ass in ages. Beige and chocolate brown throw pillows sit perfectly on top. A massive sand-colored carpet takes over most of the flooring, topped with a black and brown Oggetti Hanako coffee table that cost seven thousand fucking dollars. I could go on, but I have no clue of anything else that's in this house, as I gave my decorator the greenlight to spend my money however they wanted in a place I will never call *home*.

I don't use any of it.

I can't remember the last time I sat on my couch. I hate being home. When I'm alone, my thoughts start to wander, so I'd rather be on the move.

I look out the window to the familiar scenery of Cebrene Heights. No matter what time it is, the streets are always bustling. The sound of traffic calms me.

I purchased this building in Uptown when I first came into a shit ton of money from closing my first deal. I had always lived in the suburbs of Old Cebrene, where my family's estate and my uncle's property are located. When I started doing business, I was often in the Heights, so it only made sense to live here when the time came for me to move. There are many high rises here, but this building was the tallest. It wasn't even for sale, but when the real estate agent brought me up to the penthouse, I had Xander throw a duffle bag full of money at her feet. It was enough money to afford the whole building and then some. She got on the phone and called the owner. When he heard I was looking to buy the tower, he didn't dare refuse my offer. *The perks of being the Diávolos.*

I needed a place to call my own. My personal kingdom, where I could rule over my territory and have eyes all over the city. I called it the Saintville Tower.

My uncle's house was comfortable, but I needed space. Do you know how awkward it is to bring women to a house full of people? I refused to fuck in my uncle's home. I'd started taking them to my office, but now I'd never take them anywhere else, even though I have my own place now. There's no logical reason, it just is.

I turn back toward the kitchen and look at my stove for the time. 4:27 a.m.

I sigh, knowing all too well I won't be able to sleep. Thankfully, there is a gym in Saintville for times like these. As I walk out of the elevator on the main floor, I catch a glimpse out the entrance doors.

Fuck it. I'm going outside.

I head toward the main entrance where Seb and Greg are stationed. They are my eyes and ears, night and day, except when I run. They explicitly know to leave me alone during that time. Running is the only quiet time I welcome. It's my therapy, and it transcends from my body to my mind and through my soul. It reminds me that even in my weakest moments, I am strong. I exit into the fresh spring air, hoping to shed all the weight from these past few weeks. The brisk wind slaps me in the face as I run full speed down the sidewalk. I take my usual route through Schuylkill Banks. Something about being close to the water clears my head.

I started running when I was a kid, shortly after my family passed away. At first, it was because I didn't know how else to express what I was feeling. Most of the time, it was an attempt to get away from home because I couldn't bear to live in the same house where my parents and sister had been murdered. The memories of that dreadful day kept flashing through my mind every time I entered that room. I would stare blankly at the clean spot on the floor where my parents' and sister's blood had seeped from their lifeless bodies into the floorboards. You would never be able to tell the room had been the scene of such a horrific mass murder.

I avoided that room like the plague, but the memories still haunted my mind. I couldn't escape it. I thought running away from home would solve my problems, but no matter how far I got, the images were still there.

So, I started running, not to get away, but to stay alive. It's hard to feel miserable when you're on the move. Instead of using drugs and alcohol as a coping mechanism, I let my natural endorphins keep my emotions in check. *But that doesn't stop me from going on a binge every once in a while.*

I jog half the trail and back, eighteen miles, and I feel like I could still run a fucking marathon. As soon as I get back to my penthouse, I decide to cook a big breakfast, to keep my mind from wandering too much. I can't be idle for too long without drowning in my own thoughts. Two egg whites with chicken sausage, and a side of oatmeal with bananas and honey. I don't necessarily like eating clean, but I know my way around the kitchen, so my healthy meals aren't so bad. But right now, I wish I could devour a huge plate of pancakes drenched in syrup. *If you thought only women ate their feelings, you were wrong.*

An hour later, I hop in the shower and stand motionless for several minutes under the scalding water. My mind has calmed from the effects of my nightmare, but something even worse happens.

I start thinking about Angelica and my dick springs to life. *Why am I thinking of her in my most vulnerable moment?*

I'm a lost cause at this point. Apparently, the first time wasn't enough to get her out of my system. I need to focus on my plan to get back at her family and be the new Godfather. I have no time to lust over a random girl, especially if she's the object of my revenge.

I want to throw a fist into the tile. But I opt to fist my cock instead.

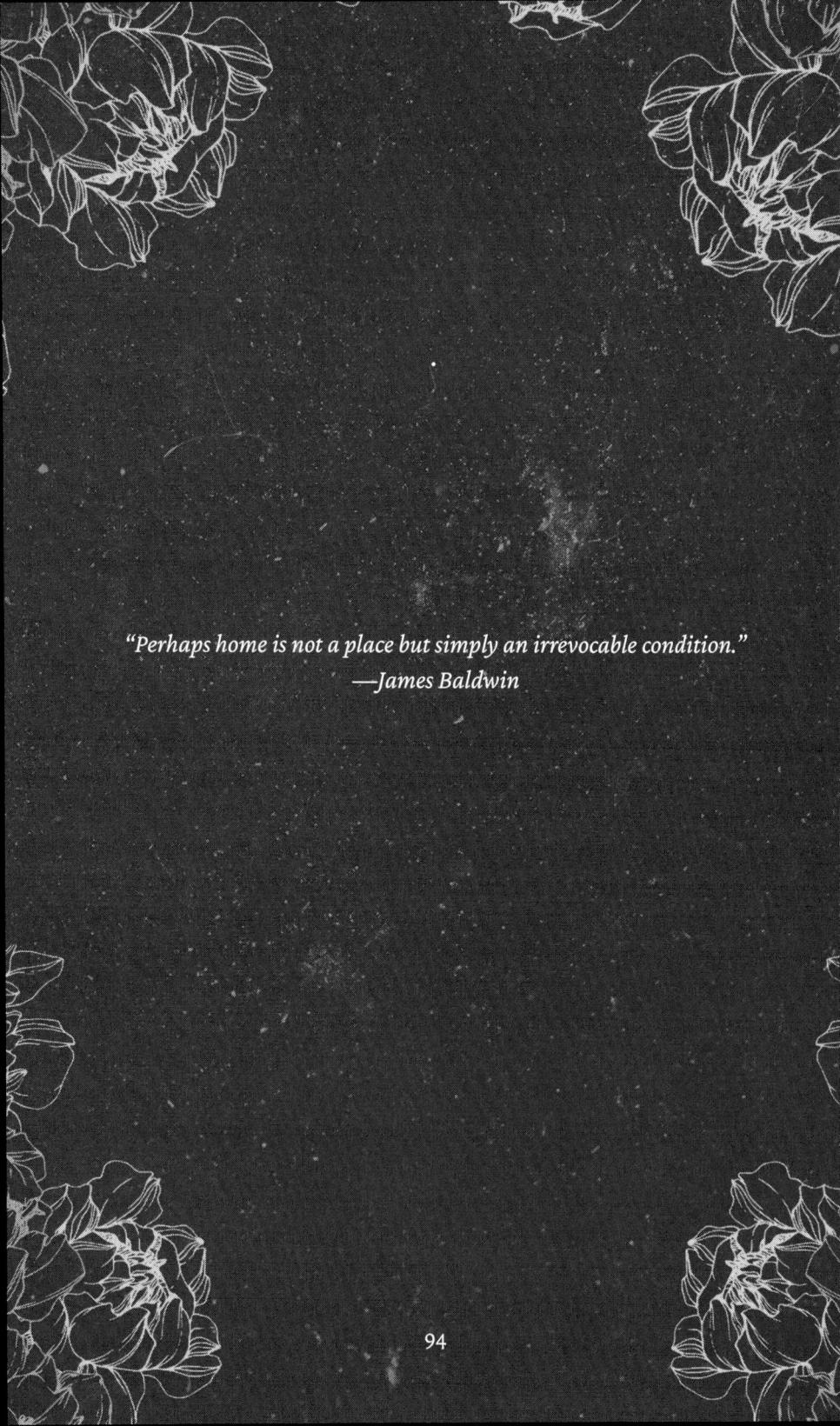

"Perhaps home is not a place but simply an irrevocable condition."
—*James Baldwin*

Angelica

It's Tuesday morning. I snooze my alarm too many times to count.

I groggily reach for my phone and turn off the godforsaken ringing. 8:55 a.m. I groan. *Great.* I'm going to miss yoga class.

I roll onto my back and stare at the ceiling, rubbing my eyes to get rid of the tiredness. My left hand reaches across the bed for the remote and I press the button that opens my bedroom curtains. *Such luxury.*

I snort at the thought and sit up in my king size bed. Everything in this house is too big, including this bed. It's lush and comfortable. And lonely. I'm getting tired of sleeping alone.

I grab my phone once again to check for any missed calls or messages. I see several texts from Aria.

8:01 a.m

Kaliméra Giegie!!! It's almost yoga time. Do you need me to pick you up?

8:11 a.m.

Are you still sleeping? Class is in less than an hour!

8:15 a.m

Hello???

8:37 a.m

Angelica, you better show up to this class!!!

8:59 a.m

You better have a good reason for flopping 😡

Ah, *shit*. The last text comes in just as I'm reading the other ones. I'm not going to hear the end of this, even though it was unintentional. Aria hates when I flake on plans. I click on the text box.

> 9:00 a.m
> I'M SORRY!!! Don't kill me. I overslept.

9:01 a.m
Too late. You're already dead to me.

> 9:02 a.m
> Meet me at BB's after class. I'll buy you a cinnamon roll. Come on.

9:02 a.m
Make it two and I might consider it.

I laugh. It feels good to see my best friend regularly again. After all, she's one of the only positives of being back in Cebrene. Aria is a prickly pear, tough and thorny on the outside but soft and sweet on the inside. I'll never not give her what she wants. I put my phone down on the nightstand and slowly ease myself off the bed, squinting at the bright, shining sun peaking through the large floor-to-ceiling windows.

I notice some movement outside, so I squint to get a better look. My heart pounds against the wall of my chest. What if it's *him*? Approaching the glass with caution, I tuck my body behind the drawn curtains and inspect the area. My bedroom window doesn't face the street, but I have an indirect view of it at a certain angle. There's nothing and no one in sight, but I could swear I saw a shadow move among the trees below. I've felt *his* presence before but have never caught him in the act. The thought of catching a glimpse of someone 'real' creates an awareness that tingles along my skin.

I walk to the bathroom and stop in front of the full-length mirror leaning against the wall. I take one quick look at my disheveled, almost black curly hair and sigh. Today is going to be unfulfilling, as usual. With no school, no work, and barely any distractions, my life seems pointless.

My bathroom is also covered by windows, but I don't care if anyone can see me. I let my slip dress fall to the floor and head to the shower. Clearing my thoughts is almost impossible these days, but I let the strong pressure of the water hit my skin as I turn my back and close my eyes. I focus on the sting to numb my mind.

Forty minutes later, I'm ready to meet Aria. The yoga studio and café are only a few blocks away, close enough to walk to. It's a warm and sunny day, so I decide to wear a long, clingy sundress with wedges.

On my way out, I grab my keys, sunglasses, purse, and I

make sure that my pocketknife is lodged into one of the slits. *Old habits die hard.*

Ready to go, I open the door and step out into the sunshine. And that's when I see it.

A vase of white peonies waiting on my doorstep with a little note. *To my favorite flower.*

At first, I'm confused as to why the delivery person didn't knock on the door. As I bend down to grab the note, I recognize the messy, cursive writing with gaps between the words and the letters.

> *Just like your favorite flower,*
> *It will take years before you bloom.*
> *And once you do,*
> *I look forward to a lifetime of you.*

My heart skips a beat and I look around, searching for my secret admirer. But he's already gone. He must've been the shadow I noticed earlier. A small part of me is disappointed I missed him. I'm also almost angry he had the audacity to come around while I was defenseless and alone in my home. But the other part of me doesn't want this to end.

🏛️

Aria's class ends right as I arrive at the studio.

I shoot her a quick text to let her know I'm downstairs. She replies a couple minutes later and tells me to wait for her at the café. As I look both ways before crossing the street, my senses go on alert. I slowly turn, expecting to see someone, but I'm met with nothing other than a feeling of *knowing*. Ever since I was kidnapped and moved back here, I've been on guard. It's as if my vision is sharper, my hearing keener, and my focus intensified.

I always feel like somebody's watching me and my gut says it's *him*.

I shake off the heavy suspicion and continue walking to the coffee shop.

I still remember when Aria used to come to my house with her *baba* when she was little, clinging to his legs and hiding her face. He would bring her over when he had meetings with my father. She was two years younger than me and so shy. I tried playing with her many times, but she never warmed up to me until she was about four years old and started pre-kindergarten. On her first day of school, she saw me in the hallway and her eyes lit up. For the first time ever, she gave me a hug.

I haven't been able to get rid of her since.

We've always had each other's backs throughout the years. Whether I was mending her broken heart or whether she was comforting me after an argument with my *baba*. No matter what, we could count on each other, and I would hurt anyone who hurts her.

I walk into the Black Bean Café, a quaint coffee bar always packed with an eclectic mix of people, with divine cinnamon rolls, lattes, and cheesecakes to die for. My mouth salivates just thinking about it. It's right next to the town square in the suburbs of the Port of Cebrene, a little area filled with an indie bookstore, small shops, a yoga studio, and a few restaurants.

I don't have a car, since my *baba* thinks it's 'safer' for me to be driven whenever I need to go into the city, so it's convenient that this area is within walking distance. It's got everything I need and the basic bitch in me rejoices at the hipness of this part of town.

Not allowing me to get my driver's license is just another way for my father to keep a leash tied 'around my neck. At twenty-three years old, having to still depend on him financially is beyond frustrating. He says it's not a good look for the daughter of a Godfather of the Night to be amongst the *working people*. They might think that we need money, and my father would never risk his reputation. That's why he never wanted me to continue my education or work. When I moved to Antium, he eventually let me be, probably because I was far enough from home and prying eyes. But there's something different in the air this time. He's been extra protective and worried for my safety. I haven't felt my father's concern in years. I want to blame Hendrick and his people for the change in his behavior, but there's something else. I can taste it.

Aria walks into the café moments later with a huge grin on her face, and I know she has already forgiven me for missing class. She immediately prances over to me, swinging her arms side to side. *She's such a dork.*

I brace myself for the impact of her small body as she slams into me, giving me the tightest hug. Aria is shorter than me, measuring a whopping five–foot-two, whereas I'm five-foot-six. Her usually wavy long blond hair is slicked into a ponytail, and she is still wearing her workout gear. Her face looks flawless. She doesn't look like someone who just did an hour of hot yoga.

"I hate how pretty you are," I murmur as I squeeze her back. She laughs as we let each other go. *Gosh, I missed her.* Since I got back, she insists that we see each other almost every day to 'catch up on lost time.'

We talk about my adjustment to life back in Cebrene, my friends back in The Big A, my future plans, and her upcoming marriage. Gianis shows up halfway through our conversation —we'd texted him earlier to come meet us, but he said he had some stuff to sort out first. He sits down with us, and for a moment, it almost feels like old times, when we were younger. We stay at the coffee shop for a while, until Aria looks at the time and realizes she has to meet her father for lunch. We all hug goodbye, and I start dreading the fact that I have to visit my *baba*, too.

"An obsession is a way for damaged people to damage themselves more." —*Mark Barrowcliffe*

Unknown

*L*ast night, she got dropped off at home by someone who didn't even wait for her to enter the house before driving off. I initially thought he could be a new boyfriend or a fling, which sparked uncontrollable fury inside me, but she didn't linger, hurrying to the door without a glance back. When the car passed mine, I was able to get a closer look and recognized the man in the driver's seat as Gianis Petrakis. Peter Kouvalakis' most trusted enforcer.

From what I know, regardless of the rumors, there is no relationship between the two. Nonetheless, seeing them so close and comfortable with each other makes me want to chop off his head and bury him where no one will ever find his body. *And I know just the place.*

I left soon after she went inside, only to return this morning to wait for her to leave so I could follow her. But not before leaving a bouquet of her favorite blooms at her door. Peonies. The beauty of this flower could never compare to hers. I'm dying to know if she's as soft as its petals. If her smell is sweet and rosy or citrusy and spicy. I want to uncover her like a sprouting peony, expose her many layers, and just like everything I touch, break and sully her until she's filthy. I'll burn the whole world down until she's mine and mine alone.

When I'd figured out where she lived, I drove to her house and found no one in sight and no cars parked around the property. I was able to search the area with ease, finding every point of entry. I couldn't believe Peter would leave his daughter unprotected after she was kidnapped by an enemy. But I'm not foolish enough to think he doesn't have eyes in the sky. I hacked into her security system and linked it to my phone.

I pull out my device, search for yesterday's feed, and I erase the footage of me creeping up to her bedroom. I had to climb the side of the house to get access to her window. Thankfully, I'm fit enough to scale a wall. I do the same with the one from this morning, when I walked up to her doorstep. Then, I send a text to my main hacker to override the data and make sure it's not recoverable.

I've made a habit of coming here at night. I watch her, my heavenly woman, the brightest angel in the sky. Stars can't shine without darkness, and in the darkness is when I'm most at ease.

But right now, I am at her house in the early hours of the morning. I can't get enough. I'm obsessed.

It's not a sweet, tender kind of obsession. It's dark, twisted, and full of passion.

And when passion meets inspiration, an obsession is born. It's maddening. I want to do every depraved thing my mind can possibly imagine to her. Rip her to shreds, uncover her inner demons, and piece her back together in a way that will leave her too damaged for anyone else, but *perfect* for me.

I sense a darkness in her, one she tries very hard to conceal and it draws me closer. Her sweet smile and doe eyes might fool others, but I see right through the façade.

I want to unravel her and uncover her darkest secrets.

I want to possess her, make her mine, be her savior, even if she might feel like I'm her captor.

I started leaving breadcrumbs for her to find. Tokens of my obsession. And there's one waiting for her right now outside her door.

I try to shake every goddamned thought of undressing her out of my head as I watch her notice the flowers. Her face contorts into a confused expression, but it smooths out once she picks up the note. My angel has come to expect these little presents. Sometimes I leave her notes, other times I surprise her with gifts, and instead of being scared, she accepts them.

She reopens her front door and gently sets the vase of white peonies on the entry table, but not before putting the note in her purse.

She steps back outside with her head up, shoulders back, and her perfect breasts covered by a cascade of dark curls, as she starts her journey down the road with a slight pep in her step. I was worried my gifts would scare her, but they seem to be giving her confidence instead. Her man-melting stride turns the head of everyone she passes. Her effect is dizzying. I can't help but notice how in touch with, and in control of her body she is. It's a fucking turn on. I parked on her street two houses down, hoping to get a good view, and I sure did.

Once she's a couple blocks down the road, I follow, slowly trailing her into the city center, where a cluster of restaurants and shops are located.

She stops in front of the yoga studio, pulls out her phone and types a quick message. She lingers there a few moments, then starts walking toward a small coffee shop. Could she be going on a date? I would really hate for someone to interfere with my plan and force me to do something I have way too much experience doing. Although, I wouldn't be against ripping the head off my competition and using his head as a hockey puck. *That's fucking dark. Even for me.*

As she's about to cross the road, she abruptly stops and

turns around, as if to analyze her surroundings. She looks concerned and her gaze is pointed right at me. *Shit.*

I duck low enough to be hidden, but still high enough to see through my car window. She turns around and continues walking. She didn't see me, but did she feel me watching her? Though I almost got caught, I feel proud of my angel's intuition. She sensed me. *What a good girl.*

In the past weeks, I've learned so much about her. The amount of milk she puts in her coffee. The way she paces around her living room when she's restless. The sound of her voice when she hums her favorite tunes while doing her hair. Her hobbies and pastimes. The places she visits. The coffee shops and restaurants she dines at. But most importantly, I've memorized her body language. At this moment, she's on edge, and that makes my cock throb with anticipation.

I might live in the shadows, but I know everything that happens in Cebrene. The ins and outs, who comes and goes. Most of the time, I could care less about who steps foot into the metropolis as long as they don't fuck with me. But as soon as I heard that the mysterious daughter of one of the Godfathers was coming back to town, I had to see it for myself. Curiosity got the best of me, if you will. A lot of shit happens in the underbelly of Cebrene, but nothing has caught my interest as much as she has. And let's be real. I need a fucking distraction.

Angelica Kouvalakis will succumb to me. I will have her forever. She *will* be mine.

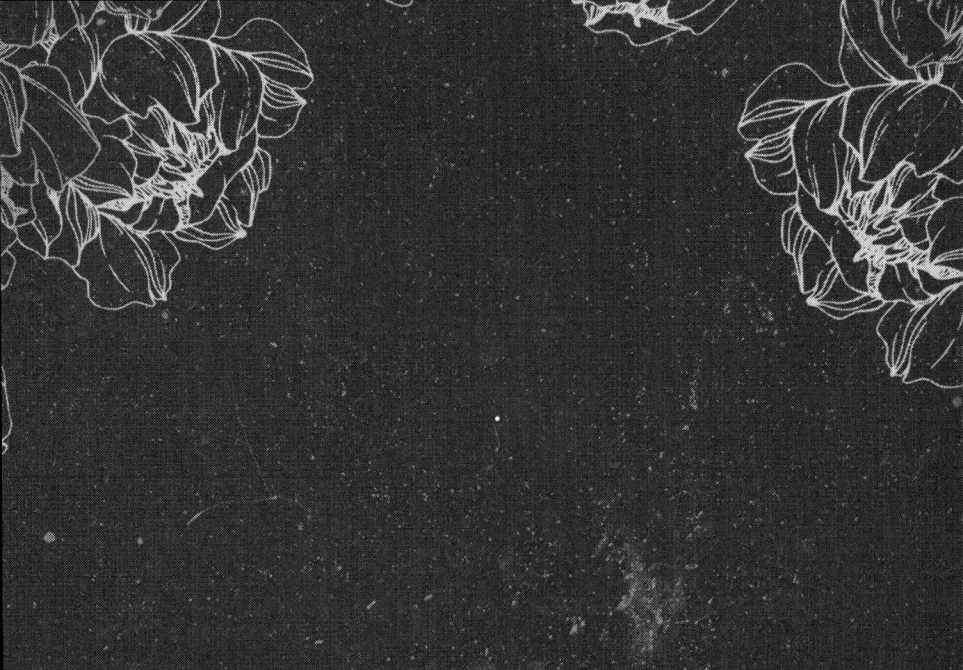

"Give me a muse and I will spend our forever painting her with words." —Atticus

Angelica

I'm greeted by an armed guard as I approach my father's door, and I squint my eyes in confusion. His soldiers are usually only stationed at the entrance of the gate and scattered around the property. This can only mean he's expecting trouble.

The guard moves away from the doorway and gives me a curt nod as I enter the house. The housekeeper is visible from the hallway, busying herself in the kitchen, probably making refreshments for my father and me. She sees me and gives me a warm smile.

Eldora has always been kind to me. She has been around since before I was born and practically raised me after my *mama* died. Sadly, I have more memories of her than I do my own mother.

I walk up to her at the counter and give her a big hug that she returns eagerly. "It's always good to see you, *agápi mou*. You don't come over enough."

"I know, I know." I sigh and bow my head, ashamed. "I'm sorry, Eldora. It's not you. It's...you know." I bite my lip nervously, hoping she will understand.

"Angelica," she says tenderly. She brings both her hands up

to rest on my cheeks. "You don't have to explain. I understand and I'm not mad at you. I just miss you is all."

I tilt my head sideways and rest my cheek on her palm and close my eyes. Eldora has always been my calm before *and* after the storm.

"Where's my *baba?*' I ask.

"He's in his office. He'll be down soon," she responds. "Sit." She gestures to one of the stools tucked under the kitchen island. "I'll make you some coffee."

I oblige and wait for my father to come down after he's done with whatever he's doing. I thank God he hasn't shown any interest in involving me in his business since I came back. I was worried we would slip right back into the same routine, but he's left me alone. I couldn't be more grateful. I want to believe that he finally understands I don't want anything to do with his affairs, but he might have something bigger in mind. And the latter scares the hell out of me.

Eldora hands me a mug of hot java and I bring it up to my nose. Sitting here with her reminds me of simpler times when I was a little girl. I would come down to watch her make our meals, and bake for us and our guests. The whole house would smell like fresh Greek Christmas cookies, the scent of oranges and honey, infused with a blend of spices, invading the air. She taught me how to cook, and it quickly became my stress relief. When I was upset, I would go to the kitchen and make something just to get away from my thoughts. Eldora found me here covered in flour many times, and instead of reprimanding me for messing up her kitchen, she would join me. She's always had a soft spot for me, and I've caught her looking at me with an emotion I could never quite name. Sometimes she'd look almost pained, and I wondered what kind of secrets she kept and if they ate her inside.

I turn around to look outside and decide to wait for my

father on the patio. It's a beautiful day. I might as well soak up some sun before my mood turns sour. My phone vibrates in my purse, and I pull it out to a message from an unknown number. I open up the text box and the message simply says 'Angelica.'

I focus on the digits and try to figure out if I recognize the number when a shadow appears in front of me. I turn back to find my father standing behind me. "*Baba*," I say, startled. I drop my phone in my purse as he sits down on one of the chairs next to me. We both look out to the gleaming water in the pool, and we don't say a word to each other for a few moments. *This is awkward.*

"I need you to attend a charity function for me next Sunday. It's a masquerade ball. Bring a date. Someone with *class*." He looks at me as he says the last part, and I know exactly who he's referring to.

Of course, the first thing he says to me in over a week is an order, but I have no energy to argue today. "Okay," I simply respond.

Eldora walks out to the backyard with a large tray in her hands and I get up to help her carry it to the table. I glance down at the dessert platter and notice the mini cheesecakes I love. I look at her and she winks. She knew I would be a ball of nerves meeting with my father and that cheesecake would at least make my belly happy. God bless her. I immediately dig into the moist cake. She tops off my coffee and pours a fresh cup for my father.

We spend the rest of the time talking about the charity ball. Or my *baba* spends the rest of the time talking *at* me about the event while I half listen. The organization is in honor of the Mouths2Feed Foundation. They raise money for malnourished children in third-world countries. Instead of just dumping loads of food to the families, they supply them with the tools and knowledge to grow and harvest their own fruits, vegetables, and wheat in a sustainable and efficient way. It is a worthy cause that I can get behind, which makes going to the event a lot more tolerable. But I have to buy a new dress. I'll text Aria to see if she's free to go shopping with me.

Our conversation is interrupted by a cell phone ringing and my father walks back inside to pick up the call. He probably doesn't want me to hear his conversation, which makes me even more curious about it. But I take the opportunity to dig mine out of my purse and reopen the anonymous text. Still not recognizing the number at all, I type out a reply.

Me: Who is this?

A few moments later, I receive a response.

Unknown: Your guardian angel.

What the hell?

Me: That's…cryptic. Sounds more like the devil is at my doorstep.

As soon as I hit send, realization dawns on me and my body stills. *Could it be?* There's only one person that comes to mind.

Unknown: The devil was once an angel too, Angelica.

I reply immediately.

Me: Are you here to write down my sins?

I fight the impulse to tell him I know who he is. I want to see how the conversation plays out.

I nervously look back at the patio door to see if my father is back, but he's nowhere in sight. He must've gone up to his office. *Surprise, surprise.*

Unknown: Indeed. Your sins are mine to uncover. Not even holy water can help you now. A hundred men couldn't keep me away. I've come to burn your walls down.

I can't help myself.

Me: Are you my secret admirer?

Unknown: Check inside your purse.

My heart starts palpitating and my palms are sweaty. I knew it was him. I wondered how long it would take for him to reach out to me and now he's *texting* me. I should feel uneasy, freaked out, panicked even, thinking about how close he's gotten to me to be able to put something in my purse. But instead, it excites me... And now, I'm concerned for my sanity.

I dig into my bag and find a small note folded in half that I hadn't noticed this morning.

Je serai poète et toi poésie.
Me: What does it mean?
Unknown: "I'll be a poet, and you'll be poetry." It's part of a poem written by the French poet François Coppée, about beauty and inspiration. And you, my angel, are my muse.

I don't exactly understand what he means, but it doesn't stop me from feeling a rush of warmth in my stomach. No one is here to see me, but I still bite down on my lower lip to try and hide my smile. I don't know who my stalker is, and if I'm being honest, the way I feel toward him is reckless and overwhelming. He's a stranger, yet the sense of familiarity I get when I find his notes, as if I can sense his presence even when he's not there, turns my denial into acceptance, my chaos into order, and my confusion into clarity.

Is it possible to fall for someone you don't know? *We all start as strangers.*

I don't respond to his text; I can't find the proper words to say. Even though he states he's no saint, I change his number to 'Guardian Angel' in my contacts.

My thoughts are interrupted by the faint sound of my father's conversation as he slowly reappears in the doorway.

"I don't care if the new *Godfather*," he says in a mocking tone, "is dangerous. I'm prepared for him. All I need to know is that you have the situation under control, Philip. He can't find out what his boss was involved in prior to his death. It'll blow up in each one of our faces. I didn't eliminate one problem to create another. Do you understand?"

At that, he hangs up the phone and rejoins me outside. *That explains the guards*, I tell myself. He's talking to Aria's father, and knowing them, they're up to no good. He doesn't sound too concerned, but whatever he's dealing with has him worried about his safety.

"Is everything okay, *baba*?" I ask. He grumbles a non-response, dismissing me quickly, and I'm starting to get slightly irritated that he keeps his business completely hidden from me now. I understand I've been away for years in a desperate attempt to get away from the mob life, but he's pushed me so far away, I'm lost in translation. I no longer have a purpose and I feel like a floater in this family. If I want answers, I'll have to get them myself, and what better place to get some than at the charity ball. If my father won't tell me what's going on, I'll do my own investigating by schmoozing information out of the guests at the event. I'm not the most talkative person, but I can be charming at times, and I'll use that to my advantage.

I shove my phone in the back pocket of my jeans. The last thing I want is for him to ask me who I'm texting. How do I explain to him that I'm talking to a stranger who has been stalking me? Not that I can ever tell anyone the truth. They'll think I've lost my mind.

I'm itching to leave my father's side, so I'm relieved when he says he has to cut our visit short to take care of business.

We say our goodbyes and I hang around the back, sipping on what's left of my coffee. I grab my phone again. I don't normally show immediate interest in men who show interest in me, dismissing them the first moment I can, but with him, something feels different. I can tell that he's not like the others. *He's a stalker, duh.*

I don't know if that's a good or bad thing. *Definitely a bad thing, Angie.*

It's been twenty-five minutes since his last message, so I type out a response.

Me: Why me?

Bold, Angie.

But he doesn't respond at all, which slightly irritates me. He could at least tell me what his intentions are. I exit his conversation and open my chat with Aria.

Me: I just heard an interesting bit of conversation between our babas...

She replies almost instantly.

Aria: Spill???

Me: Do you know if anyone could be targeting my family? My father seemed upset and was talking to yours on the phone about a new 'Godfather.'

Aria: Not that I know. I haven't heard anything. My baba has been more on guard recently, though. But you know he never tells me stuff about his 'business.'

Of course not. It's not like our fathers keep us in the loop. But Aria is the greatest snoop of all time, so if she hasn't heard anything about a new Godfather, then they really must be keeping whatever they're dealing with quiet. I decide to forget about what I heard for now.

Me: Are you busy? Let's go shopping. I have other news.

Aria: When and where?

Me: Now. Can you pick me up from my baba's?

Aria: On my way!

I go back inside to say goodbye to Eldora, and I promise to visit more often. Aria pulls up fifteen minutes later and we head to The Gallery at East Market in the Fashion District at the Harbor, where many designer stores are located. If I'm going to a high-class charity ball, I need to look and play the part.

On the way there, I tell Aria everything about my first encounter with Evan and my secret admirer. I didn't intend to spill the beans so soon, but I feel like a kettle about to explode. If I can trust anyone with this news, it's my best friend. She goes berserk.

"*Angelica Hera Kouvalakis.* How dare you not tell me about them 'til now!" she exclaims.

"I'm sorry! I probably won't ever see or talk to Evan again, so I brushed off the whole encounter. And I didn't know how to bring up that I have a weird relationship with a *stalker* without sounding crazy." If I'm being honest, I haven't been able to stop thinking about Evan since yesterday, and I truly wonder if I'll ever see him again. The feel of his breath on my neck still taints my skin. My guardian angel has taken over the other part of my brain, and I can't find it in me to be scared.

I definitely sound like a crazy person.

"So, you're telling me that you physically ran into a man of steel at the shooting range, who proceeded to teach you how to shoot a rifle, standing right behind you, all up close and personal, and called you a *good girl?*"

"Yes."

"And you have a secret admirer who's been stalking you ever since you moved back, writing you poetry, and leaving you gifts around your home?"

I bite the corner of my lip, embarrassed, before I reply, "Yes."

"WHAT THE ACTUAL FUCK, ANGIE?" she screams as she slaps her hand over her mouth. The car swerves.

"Keep your eyes on the road, *lolos*. You're going to make us crash!" I screech.

"Sorry, sorry. But *wow*. You're being serious."

"Yes." I can't seem to say anything else. I look down at my clasped hands resting on my lap, afraid of what Aria is going to say next.

"*Oo theé mou.*" Oh my god. "You went from being single to having TWO love interests? What happened to my prude bitch?" she jokes.

"First of all," I say and flip her the bird. "Second, I haven't seen or heard from Evan since our encounter. We didn't even exchange contact info, and the conversation with my anonymous admirer kind of ended abruptly. I don't know if I should message him again. I don't want to seem desperate." I look down at the phone in my hands and ponder.

"*First of all*, how do you know it's a 'he'?" she asks, wiggling her brows. "Second, since when do you care? You never give guys the time of day." She doesn't look at me, but I can see from her profile that she's trying to give me THE look. The one she gives me when she wants to kick my ass, even though she's a tiny, little thing.

A giggle escapes my mouth. She's not wrong. Either way, the thought of *anyone* being this obsessed with me gives me tingles all over my body. It's so wrong to feel this way, but I can't help myself. *Let your mommy and daddy issues shine through, girl.*

"You're right. I don't. And I shouldn't care about what *they* think." Even though there's a chance my guardian angel could be of the same sex, I'm somehow convinced it's a man.

"That's the spirit!" Aria says.

"But he's a stalker, Ri. What if I make him angry and he decides to come into my house and murder me? Then you'll have my blood on your hands!"

"I'll take my chances," she says, smirking, and I smack her shoulder. "No, but in all seriousness, you're right, Giegie. You need to be careful. As much as I think this adventure is exciting, there's still a risk and you've got to keep your wits about you."

I agree. I might feel a sense of peace when I think about my stalker, but this person's behavior is still concerning. I have to stay alert.

We pull up to the valet parking of the shopping strip and Aria gives her keys to the leering attendant. As she's about to drop them in his palm, the young man winks at her and grabs her wrist. Aria whips her hand back. The look of disgust on her face is enough to make any man fold. He looks nervous now, his bravado gone, as she walks right up to him and points her finger to his chest, looking up at him, and I swear there's steam coming out of her ears.

"If you want to live to see another day, I suggest keeping your nasty, skeletal hands away from me, or I'll stick those fingers where the sun don't shine, capiche?" she spits, venom lacing her tone.

He staggers back, shocked that such a tiny thing could be so terrifying, and I can't help but laugh out loud. Aria is a badass. She comes from the Kastellanos family, and they're known to have short fuses and a tendency for violence. I would not mess with her. And it's not because she has a father, brother, and cousins who will fuck you up if you even look at her the wrong way, but because she would kill you herself.

"Alright, Ri. I think he got the point, right?" I ask him as I grab her by the shoulders to pull her away. I nudge my head toward him for a response, and he nods his head enthusiastically. "Good. Now, park her car and make sure you're not here when we get back. Just friendly advice, don't make it turn into a threat," I add, smiling my most vicious smile. Where Aria is loud and explosive, I'm silent and deadly. We're the perfect combination.

We step out onto the sidewalk, and when we look at each other, we burst out laughing. We're always on the same page. Terrorizing pervy men is our specialty. You wouldn't want to get on our bad side.

We walk to the door of Saks Fifth Avenue, and I decide it's time to send my guardian angel a follow-up message.

Me: So? Why me?

As I walk into the department store, I put my phone back in my purse, dropping it like a hot potato, and it vibrates even before it has even fallen to the bottom of my Louis Vuitton bag.

Guardian Angel: Why not you? You became my muse the moment you walked into my life. You're my biggest distraction and will probably be my downfall, but I will drag you into the darkness with me.

My heart flutters from the beauty of his words, both in eagerness and fear. He renders me speechless. I wonder how someone can make my heart beat faster and slower at the same time. My dopamine levels are going crazy.

Me: What if I don't want to follow you into the dark?

I really don't recognize myself right now. I'm never this upfront and sassy with a stranger, or with men, especially ones who might try to suffocate me in my sleep. But Aria motivated me—*and potentially steered me directly into the arms of death*—to get to the bottom of this.

Guardian Angel: You always have a choice, angel. But don't underestimate the allure of darkness. Yours is drawn to mine. And we will drown in it together.

My breath stutters in surprise. I'm not an open book, yet he can see right through me. I've always felt a shadow looming over me, haunting me with the secrets and memories I can't remember. I've tried my hardest to ignore the black hole in my mind. I've learned to live my life without the answers I felt I would never receive. The darkness within me is *my* secret to keep. I've tried so hard to conceal the damage that has been done to my soul, and for him to waltz into my life and declare that I'm doomed to the deepest pit of hell makes me angry. If he thinks he can drag me down with him, he's sorely mistaken.

Me: I'm not going anywhere with you.

Guardian Angel: Play innocent all you want, Angelica. You're a spirited woman, but you're also damaged. I'm interested in what you have to hide.

I sneer. What an arrogant bastard. I want to keep defending myself, but it's impossible to defeat someone who has such a way with words. I decide it's best to end the conversation here, but texting him feels almost as normal as texting Aria or my friends back in Antium City. As if we've known each other for years. It's unfamiliar territory and I don't know how to feel, but I do know I'm looking forward to the next time I get to talk to him again.

I spend the entire shopping trip thinking about our conversation while trying on dress after dress. Aria chooses most of them as I go in and out of the changing room, modeling each one. She makes three stacks: yeses, nos, and maybes. She hollers 'woot woot,' and whistles at every dress she likes, smacking my ass as I re-enter the room to change, shakes her head and gags at the ones she hates, and shrugs at the ones she's unsure about, tossing each dress in its respective pile.

After what feels like days, we finally find the holy grail of dresses. I can't help but admire myself in the mirror.

"This is the one," Aria says.

It's a RASARIO, crystal-embellished, black, spaghetti strap, floor-length tulle gown with a mermaid hem. The dress hugs every curve on my body perfectly and the crystals twinkle like a starry night sky. The scalloped neckline accentuates my small chest, and the plunging back leaves barely anything to the imagination. It's classy, yet sexy. Now, all I need is the perfect mask to complete the look. I grab my phone to take a picture of myself in the mirror, and I notice a new text.

Guardian Angel: You look perfect in that dress.

Shocked and confused, I run back into the changing room, leaving a puzzled Aria behind, and I lean my back on the door and close my eyes.

He's watching me.

Just like that, I realize I'm never going to be alone again.

"He watched her every move and when she left the room, his eyes allowed her reluctantly to go."
—Maya Angelou

Unknown

Yesterday afternoon, eyes focused on my screens, I watched Angelica climb into an armored Toyota Land Cruiser that picked her up from her place. Her face was marred with a frown, and she walked with a slight slump in her back, looking defeated. I didn't bother to follow, assuming she was going to meet her father.

The tracker I installed on her phone in the dead of night, while she was asleep, alerted me that she went to his house. So, I hacked into his security system and sent the feed to my computer. I spotted her around the property, sitting on the patio alone, looking uncomfortable. I left a note in her purse when I snuck into her place last night, but I figured I could surprise her in another way.

I had an uncontrollable urge to put a smile on her face.

Finding her number was child's play. I wasn't sure how to start the chat, so I simply wrote her name. Her response came several minutes later, and it was blunt, but once she knew it was me, I could tell she lowered her guard. Every message I sent had me impatiently waiting for her reply and constantly checking my phone to see if a notification popped up. I looked like a fucking lovesick puppy.

Watching her while she texted me was thrilling, and her

feistiness made me hard. I love challenges. The thought of forcing Angelica to give herself to me has my dick trying to break through the zipper of my jeans.

I knew my angel would figure out it was me sooner than later. But she trusted me too quickly. I mean her no harm, or at least nothing she wouldn't enjoy, but I can't help but think she's a bit too naive to let a stranger into her life without any hesitation. Much less a stranger, who is undoubtedly stalking her and breaking into her house. A part of me is pleased that she trusts *me*, but the other part wonders if she lets other men into her life just as easily. My blood boils at the thought.

I was aware of this week's charity event—like I said, I know everything that happens in Cebrene, even if it's for the prestige members of society only—and knew her father wouldn't attend. I figured he would ask her to go on his behalf, and my assumptions were right. I got to watch her find the most perfect dress, and *God*, do I want to rip it right off her. Little does she know, she will be wearing it just for me. I need to add my own personal touch, so I plan to leave her a note and gift. I know she'll like them both.

Tailing her to the party will be too risky. *It's a masquerade party, maybe I could still go...*

I can't seem to get her out of my mind. I've spent the last 72 hours with my eyes glued to her every move. I followed her home and watched her until every light inside was turned off. I wondered what she did all alone in that big house, how she looked naked in the shower, what she wore to sleep, if she touched herself at night.

The impulse to break in and watch her do those things is overwhelming, but I don't want to invade her privacy more than I already am. I want her to know I'm there, and to *want* me to watch her. I want Angelica *willing* to show me the most sacred parts of her. And she will.

My favorite distraction.

Evander

It's about 11:30 p.m. when people start rolling into Academia. I flick my wrist to adjust my watch, and smooth down the lapels of my suit.

I don't usually come down to the club on weeknights, but I have to keep a closer eye on things for a little while, especially after the Cyrus ordeal. If I'm being honest, Angelica has been a mental distraction keeping me away from work. I can't fucking stop thinking about her. There aren't enough hours in the day or night for how much I'd happily think about her—or for the things I'd do to her, which is why I let Xander and my men do all the background digging so I can focus on my new role.

I'm making an appearance tonight to check on the club and staff. Dion and Xander are going to meet me here to talk and have a few drinks.

I'm grateful. Business is booming, and the club is always packed, from Monday to Sunday. It's one of the only clubs in Cebrene that operates seven nights a week.

When we first opened, it was only from Thursdays to Sundays, but after throwing events on random days of the week and seeing how successful they were, we decided to try operating on weeknights. It's been profitable ever since.

The lineup outside is lengthening and the noise inside is

getting louder. My bar staff confirmed that they are fully equipped, and I talked to my bouncers to check that they have everything handled.

The general manager, Elias, is talking to one of the bartenders near the back door. He sees me and nods, understanding that I want to talk to him. He cuts his conversation short and walks over to me.

"Eli," I say, extending my hand to shake his. "Is everything ready for the night?"

"Yes, sir. We're all set," he replies.

I nod. "Make sure to man the doors a little extra from now on. I want all the bouncers on high alert. I've already spoken to them, but keep an eye out for any unwanted guests."

Eli acknowledges my request and I dismiss him.

Ever since taking over for my uncle, the threats against me have escalated. It's only a matter of time before there'll be a target on my back. No one fucks with the *Diávolos*, but it doesn't mean they won't try. I'd love to see it, though.

A brave man is one who can look the devil in the eye and not quiver. But no one truly understands what it is to face the devil until they do.

I head upstairs to my office and make a few calls to check on my associates. A not-so-friendly reminder that I'm the new Godfather, and I'm here to stay. I might not be as physically present these days, but I will never let them forget who's boss. I still haven't publicly announced the takeover, but those who need to know who I am already do. It's customary to throw a party when a new heir is ordained, but that won't happen until I complete my plan. I have to solidify my relationship with Angelica and steal her away from right under her father's nose.

The goal is for her to fall for me. Once I start introducing myself into her life, she won't know what hit her, and she won't be able to deny me. I'll manipulate her into going against her father. From what I know, their relationship is already strained, so I assume it won't be that hard. Once she's under my spell, I will marry her and rule the entire East of Cebrene. The Port and Cebrene Harbour will be mine, and I will be able to control half of the city. I will destroy her father's empire from the inside out, take over his territory, and kill him. There will be some backlash, especially from my side, but I don't give a fuck. They will listen to their boss, and if they don't, they will suffer the consequences.

Only then will we celebrate, not only to announce myself as the new Godfather, but to declare the union of the Vasilakis and Kouvalakis families.

After making my rounds, I go back downstairs and settle in the VIP section at the back. Seb and Greg follow me and perch themselves at the side of the booth. Dion and Xander join me several minutes later, back from a visit to our warehouses to check up on our workers. I ask Julieta, one of the servers, to bring us a bottle of *ouzo*. She comes back moments later and pours me a glass on the rocks. I take a sip of the alcohol as I look around, and my eyes drift over the dance floor and fall on someone familiar.

Angelica.

Dion starts talking about God knows what, but I can't focus on anything but her. He's updating me on our affairs and his voice is muffled, not only from the blaring music, but from my laser focus on the girl who has stolen every ounce of my attention.

She's standing at the bar with Aria Kastellanos, her best friend since kindergarten, and daughter of Peter's second-in-command, Philip.

A couple other women join them, and a bunch of douchebags surround them like hyenas. Angelica is smiling and laughing. One of the guys hands her a shot and she doesn't hesitate to pound it back, her face twisting at the taste of the alcohol. Her body seems loose and fluid, and I notice her shoulders subtly moving to the sound of the music, her eyes closed, a provocative smile on her lips. Is she *drunk*?

The group heads to the dance floor, screaming at the top of their lungs to what seems to be their favorite song. I take a good look at Angelica. She's wearing black, knee-high boots; a short, red leather skirt with a slit on the side, showing off her delectable thigh; and a black, plunge-neck, cropped blouse tied right under her breasts, her pebbled nipples poking through the fabric. I can see little beads of sweat forming on her chest from where I sit, and I want to lick the skin from her neck all the way down to the folds in between her legs. *No, Evan. Fuck.*

I run my hand across my mouth and lean forward, putting my elbows on my knees as I watch her every move.

The more I see Angelica, the more my mind screams at me to stay away from her. I worry I'll want to keep her for myself and not just use her. Every time she rocks her hips, I feel my cock throb. I have to hold myself back from going to her when all I want to do is drag her to my office upstairs, lift up her skirt, push her panties to the side, and fuck her brains out on my desk with those boots on. She has somehow found her way into my head and it's fucking me up.

Dion snaps me out of my daydream. "Bro, what is up with you right now? You look like you're about to pounce on some prey."

"It's Angelica," I say dryly.

"*Oo skatá.*" *Oh, shit,* is all Dion manages to say. He looks straight ahead and sees her with her friends, his eyes lingering a couple seconds longer on her blonde friend.

"Did you know she would be here?" he asks.

I shake my head.

I refuse to acknowledge the way I feel. Again, I must remind myself that I cannot fall for her. I wish I could fuck her out of my system, but that would do the complete opposite. If I get inside her, I know nothing would be the same.

There is one major problem, though. The whole purpose of this plan is to get her to marry me, and if she does, I'll *have* to fuck her. I don't even trust myself to wait until then. *There's no way out of this.*

I take another sip of my drink and turn my attention back to Angelica. A guy approaches her from behind and whispers in her ear. I feel anger churning in my chest. Damn it. Every man is a threat to me and my plan. If anyone gets in the way of my revenge, I will have to get rid of them, and I don't care if I leave a trail of blood behind. I have a one-track mind when it comes to Angelica. Procure the goods by any means necessary.

She smiles and presses herself against him, thrusting her hips back into his crotch. My jaw clenches so hard my bones feel like they're about to shatter. I squeeze my hand around my glass, picturing it's his throat. Whatever has been holding me back from going to her now hangs by a fucking thread.

At that same moment, she turns around and we lock eyes.

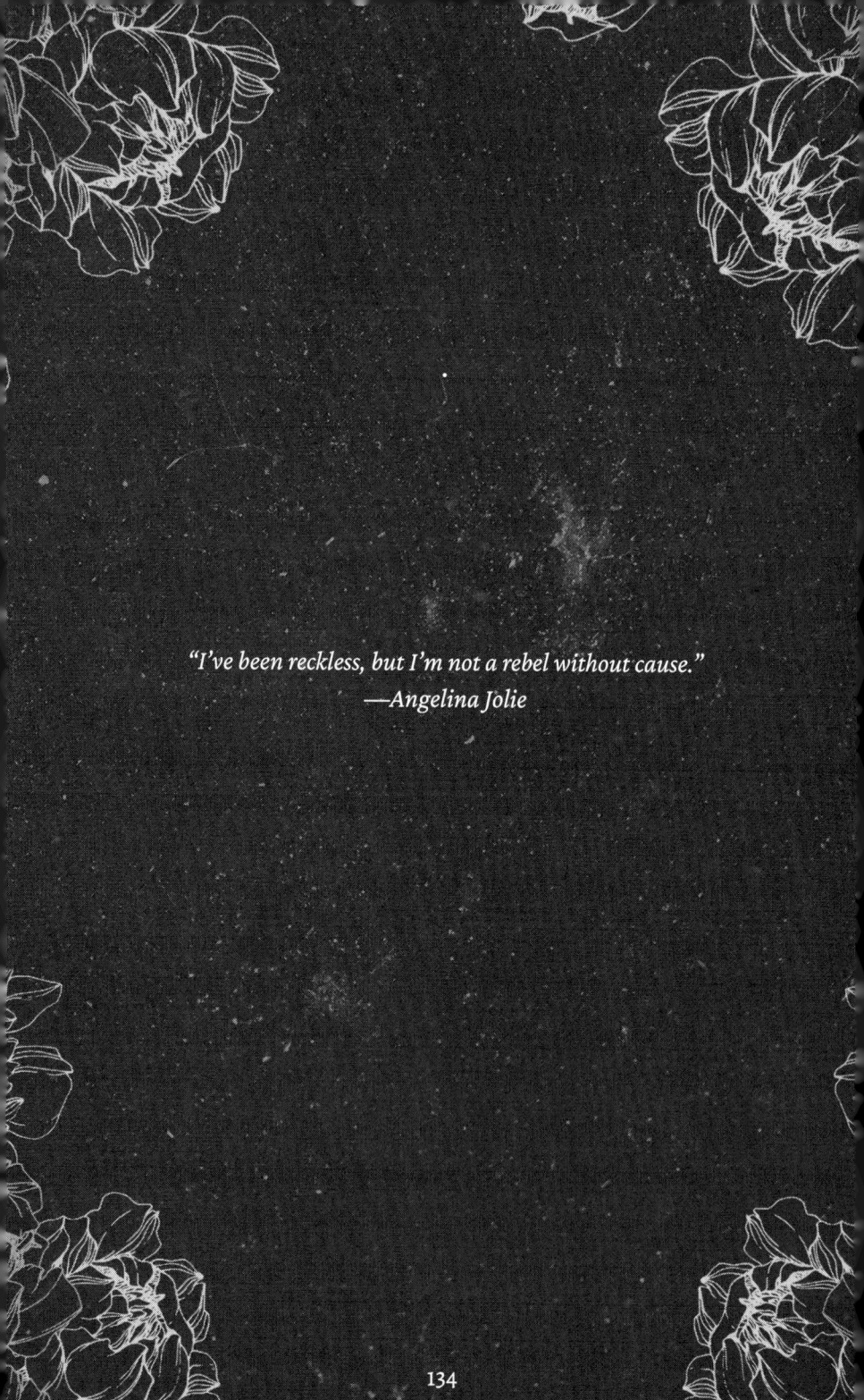

"I've been reckless, but I'm not a rebel without cause."
—*Angelina Jolie*

Angelica

I am in a state of euphoria.
    I feel *good*. My insides are tingly and the lights in the club are so dizzying, it seems like the whole world is spinning.

    For a couple hours now, I've been drinking and dancing at Academia, the city's hottest nightclub, with Aria, her friend Cassie, and a few other girls from high school. This area of old Cebrene is controlled by the Vasilakis family, although I'm not sure who runs this place. When I left, I was too young to go out and drink. This is only my second time here, and even though Aria and I come from another territory, this club attracts a mixed crowd, from the upper classes of Cebrene Heights to the common people from the Lower District. It's a prestigious club, but once you walk through the door, there's no hierarchy; it's simply a blend of people having fun. Even on a Monday, the lineup is around the block, and there's almost no way of getting in unless you know someone. Thankfully, my notorious best friend knows one of the bouncers and he graciously let us skip the line. How could he deny entrance to Aria's untameable sex appeal and the crew of four equally drop-dead gorgeous women with her?

    Squeezing our way through the crowd, we headed straight

to the bar to order drinks. We're not the type of women who schmooze men into paying our tab, but if the offer is extended, we won't refuse. The drinks are flowing, and we're surrounded by a group of men who offer to buy us shots. Whatever it was they ordered was kind of gross, but a free drink is a free drink. We can barely hear ourselves over the loud hip hop beat, but it doesn't stop us from talking, or yelling, to each other. Our favorite club anthem comes on and we can't help but fangirl and scream as we head back to the dance floor.

The music takes over my body and I move to the rhythm. A cute guy approaches me and asks for a dance. He's average height, well-built, and blonde. *Meh.* I start dancing against him, turning my hips in circles. I face him and notice a man watching me from a booth at the back of the club, but I can't make out his features. I feel his gaze burning a hole through my body, and then it hits me. *Evan.* I've only seen him once, but it's impossible to forget that face.

We lock eyes and I completely stop moving. His eyes darken, and he's clenching his glass so hard his knuckles whiten. Evan doesn't look away and I start to feel flustered.

Someone taps my shoulder and I turn to find a man standing behind me. I feel a jerk on my arm from Aria.

"Is this guy bothering you, Angelica?" Aria asks from my side, staring at the guy who is now in front of us.

"Who's this feisty, little one?" he asks, smirking.

"The name's Aria. Who the hell are you and what do you want?" she spits.

I still haven't said a word. When Aria decides to attack, no one can stop her.

The stranger's face changes from surprise to interest. They lock eyes. "You can call me Dion, *asteri mou,*" he says, with a huge grin on his face. Aria opens her mouth, but nothing comes out. She stands down. *Woah, what the hell just happened?*

He turns to me and leans into my ear. "Evan wants to talk to you. Come over to our table," he states, more an order than an invitation. He backs away and glances at Aria. "Bring your friend."

Aria watches him intently as he walks away and brings her hand to her mouth, looking nervous.

I couldn't have chosen a worse time to be drunk. Aria somehow convinced me to drink on a Wednesday. *A Wednesday! Who am I?* I hesitated at first, but when I thought about all the tension I've been feeling, I just wanted and needed to let loose. So drinking was a necessary evil. I was tipsy even before we left our friend Cassie's apartment.

I face Aria and she quickly realizes from my expression that I am unwell.

"What's wrong, Ang?"

"It's him. It's *Evan*. He's sitting *right* there, staring at me, and he wants us to join them," I say panicked, feeling a sudden rush of heat.

Ever since Aria found out about Evan and my stalker, she's been harassing me for developments every chance she can. She's been unable to contain her excitement. I haven't had any more news to tell her about Evan, but she still can't believe I'm entangled with two strangers, including my *stalker*.

"Oh. My. God! What are we waiting for?" she squeals.

She grabs my arm and drags me to the table where Evan, Dion, and another man are sitting. As we get closer to the booth, Evan's burning gaze strips me of each piece of my clothing, and I start feeling so...*horny*. Why do I feel like I'm on drugs when he's around?

"Hey, fellas, you called?" Aria purrs, going into total flirt mode as usual.

Evan puts his glass down in front of him and sits back against the plush bench, his right arm on the backrest. He's wearing a three-piece, fitted, grey suit and his defined muscles stretch the fabric. There's no doubt he takes great care of his body. His presence and posture ooze power and sex. I'm attracted to him, and I know I won't be able to control my feelings or actions in my haze. Suddenly, my nervousness disappears. This might be my only opportunity to act on this attraction. Who knows when I'll see him again. It's not the best idea I've had, but it's now or never.

I don't give anyone time to respond before I slip onto the couch next to Evan, placing my hand on his thigh, and a surge of energy travels through me. It could be the alcohol, but the way his eyes dart to my hand, causing him to shift in his seat, tells me he felt it too. I let my hand travel up his thigh, and he abruptly grabs my hand to stop it from going any further.

"You're drunk," he spits.

"Maybe a little bit. Do you not want me to touch you?" I ask, confused. He was eyeing me like a predator who had spotted the most delicious meal, and now he's rejecting me.

"I'd rather you not when you're like *this*," he gestures toward me, his face showing distaste. Disapproval.

"What do you mean '*this*'?" I ask, frustrated. I'm absolutely stunned. My advances have never been rejected before.

"Like I said, you're drunk."

He turns his attention away from me and looks out toward the dance floor. That sounds more like an excuse to me. I'm not even drunk and he's making me feel bad for letting loose and having some fun. The last thing I want is for Evan to burst my bubble.

"You're allowed to stare at me and make me feel bad for having a good time, but I'm not allowed to touch you because I'm a bit *tipsy*. Are you kidding me? If you're not attracted to me, just say so," I squeal.

"You're being immature, Angelica," he says without turning his face to me.

"You know what? Fuck you," I spit out, feeling humiliated.

I get up and head to the dance floor, leaving the guys and Aria behind, who is too busy talking to Dion to even notice. I don't need them to have fun. I look around for Cassie and the other girls, but I can't spot them.

I start dancing, running my hands from my neck all the way down my body as I keep my eyes trained on Evan. He's looking at me with what appears to be insatiable hunger in his eyes. After all, he is the hunter and I'm the prey in this scenario. I ignore him and turn around and let the music carry me away.

His rejection made me angry. He managed to hurt my ego. Just because I don't usually mess with guys doesn't mean I don't want to feel wanted.

I see a man walking toward me from the corner of my eye, not the same guy from earlier, and I try to hide the smirk on my face. I'll show Evan what he's missing. I don't know why I'm putting on a show, but the urge to be petty is strong, and I can't stop myself.

The man comes up behind me and brings my body closer to his by grabbing onto my hips. His palm is flat against my waist, and I press my backside onto his dick, letting my head rest on his chest. I lift my arm to hook it around his neck and I start grinding against him as I look at Evan again, taunting him. I can see his jaw tick from here. The man's hands travel up my stomach and over my breasts and he gives one a little squeeze. Normally, I'd draw the line before this point, but this is just too damn perfect. If Evan doesn't want me to touch him, I know plenty of men who would. I turn to face my dancing partner and I let my hands stroke his chest. I fake a moan to give him the green light to continue exploring and his other hand cups me between the legs, over my skirt. I slightly jerk away from him, but not enough for Evan to notice I'm not liking it. The whole point is for him to get jealous.

In one swift movement, Evan gets up from his seat and whispers something to the two men standing behind him. One of them reaches for his ear and speaks into the earpiece. Evan doesn't waste another second to shove through the sea of bodies toward me. His eyes are engulfed with flames. When he reaches us, he forcefully pushes the man away from me. The music is pounding in my head and throughout my body, and people are becoming blurry. I have to blink a few times to clear my vision. My drunkenness suddenly hits me like a ton of bricks.

"Keep your hands off her, motherfucker," Evan seethes. The guy staggers back, his eyes wide with fear as he backs away quickly. Two bouncers grab him from behind before he can scurry away, and he tries to fight their hold, his legs swinging as he yells, "What the fuck, man? Let me go! I don't even know this chick. We were just dancing, man!"

"Well, it's your unlucky day, son of a bitch. You decided to dance with the wrong fucking girl," Evan responds, his eyes darkening by the second. I can't seem to move at all. I just stare at the scene unrolling in front of me. My eyes bounce from Evan to the guy hanging off the doormen's arms and I'm suddenly really scared for this man's life. I don't want the blood of an innocent bystander on my hands. It's as if all the alcohol has suddenly seeped out of my body and I sober up, fast.

Right as I'm about to touch Evan's arm, the music stops and all the clubgoers 'aw' and 'boo' over the disruption. He clenches his fists, and his eyebrows lower. I can no longer see his blacked-out eyes through the narrow slits. His lips curl inward as he seethes the next three words with a deadly venom, "Everybody. Out. Now."

My body shivers and the blood drains out of my body at the sound of his voice. The crowd scatters like mice and the two security guards holding up my dance partner drag him away. SHIT. Where are they taking him? I look around for Aria and spot her at the table being held back by Dion and Xander. She tries to fight Dion, but he's too big and overpowers her just by wrapping his arm around her waist. He lifts her up in the air like a sack of potatoes, throws her over his shoulder, and takes her to the stairs as she screams and thrashes against his back.

Evan cleared the whole goddamn club because of *me*? *What the hell did you do, Ang?*

It's just me and Evan on the dance floor now. I turn back to him and he's staring at me. His eyes burn as he sinks his hand into my hair, grabbing a fistful, and pulls my head back hard. He cups my jaw with his other hand and brings my face closer to his. Our mouths are almost touching, and I can feel the heat of his breath on my lips.

"Is this what you want, Angelica?" he asks, hissing the words through his teeth. "You wanted us to touch?"

He pulls harder, nearly ripping the hair out of my head. My knees buckle, but he holds me up with an arm around my waist. The pain is enough to block any words from coming out of my mouth.

"Don't underestimate what I'm capable of," he adds. "I'm taking you home, right fucking now. And we'll deal with your little experiment later."

He lets go of me, grabs my arm, and guides me off the dance floor toward the back door.

"W–wait! I have to tell Aria I'm leaving."

"Don't worry, Dion will let her know. She'll be fine."

We step outside, at the back of the club. He takes his keys

out of his pocket and unlocks a black Tesla. "Get in," he orders as he walks to the passenger side door to open it for me.

I walk toward the car, but I start tipping sideways. I'm so dizzy and I almost feel sick. I shouldn't have drunk so much. I never take shots. *What was I thinking?* Evan runs over to me and catches me right before I fall.

"*Christé mou.* How much did you have to drink tonight?"

"Too much. *Burp.*" *Oh, God.* This is getting worse by the minute.

He places his arms behind my legs and back, hoists me up and takes me to the car, carefully sitting me down in the passenger seat. The inside smells like him. Cedarwood, mint, and musk. It immediately gives me butterflies. *Or maybe I'm just about to throw up.* He sits in the driver's seat and backs out of the parking lot.

I settle into the deep, red leather seat and turn to look at Evan. His jaw is clenched. I just want to reach out and touch the stubble on his chin. Everything about him is attractive. Even the way he holds the steering wheel. He notices me staring at him, but he keeps his eyes on the road. I extend my left arm and start climbing my fingers up his bicep until I reach the nape of his neck, and I glide a finger down the side. He lets out a low growl.

"Angelica," he says sternly, sounding like a professor reprimanding his student.

"Yes, sir?" I reply.

He grips the steering wheel tighter and lets out a long breath.

"What do you want?" he growls.

"Touch me," I say, breathlessly.

"I don't want to touch you when you're drunk, Angelica."

I inch my skirt up just enough to show the edge of my thong that is slicked with wetness, and I hear Evan say, "Fuck."

He loses all restraint and reaches over, running a finger over my underwear. The feeling makes me shift in my seat and my hips buck forward pleading for him to give me more. He still has his eyes on the road, his demeanor unaffected. How is he so relaxed when I feel like I'm about to detonate?

He starts rubbing my clit over the fabric. I moan shamelessly and start swaying my hips against his hand. I want more. But he takes his hand away.

"Evan, please."

A deep rumble escapes his lips. He hurriedly slides my thong to the side and presses on my clit with his thumb, circling it with the perfect amount of pressure, and I moan loudly. This feels so good and it's exactly what I need.

"Fuck, you're so wet," he says.

He slowly eases his fingers down my opening. He spreads me open and slides his middle finger inside, causing me to jolt. He slides another one in, and I relax as his digits work through me.

"That's it," he says as he screws me with his hand. His praising words bring me even more pleasure. "Open wider. Let me see if you can take a third finger like the good girl you are."

I do as I'm told, and he slowly eases in a third one, making my body stiffen from the fullness. The feeling is so intense, heightened by the alcohol I drank. Evan fingering me in his car is the last possible scenario I would've pictured for tonight, but I'm not complaining. *God, I'm* really *not complaining.*

"Watch what I'm doing to you," he orders as he keeps fucking me with his fingers at a hard and steady pace. I look down to watch his digits slide in and out of me. The pleasure intensifies every passing second and I can feel my orgasm rising. My moans get louder and more frantic. He doesn't stop, willing me to explode right there in his car, all over his leather seat.

"Come for me. I want you to come all over my hand, Angelica."

He briefly takes out his fingers, trails my wetness up to my clit and starts rubbing it with his thumb. He shoves them back inside while his palm works my clit, and that's all it takes for my body to shudder and my orgasm to roll through me. I feel myself go rigid and my insides clench on his hand, begging for more. He doesn't stop moving his hand until the tension eases and my breathing is steady again.

As I come back down to earth, I realize the car is at a complete stop in my driveway. I don't know how long we've been here or how we even got here. I never gave him my address. But his fingers had me in such a state of euphoria, I didn't notice where we were going. He looks at me through hooded eyes and thick lashes, and my head lolls in his direction. He lifts his hand to my mouth, running his still moist thumb across my bottom lip. I can smell my orgasm on his fingers. I catch his thumb with my mouth and suck on it, tasting myself. His breathing becomes ragged, his chest heaving up and down. I shouldn't, but I invite him in, expecting him to say yes.

He thinks it over for a moment and runs a hand over his face. But he shakes his head.

"If you let me in your house, I won't be able to stop myself from fucking you as soon as we step inside, and then again on every solid surface I can find. And it won't be gentle or passionate. It would be fueled by anger, and brutally hard. And you're...not sober. I don't want our first time to be like this."

I feel a mixture of confusion, disappointment, and endearment at his response. I'm a little embarrassed for coming on so strong. I'm never this forward and I don't know what in the world has gotten into me. I want to blame the alcohol again, but it's him. He manages to rid me of all decency, and I want to do things I never in my wildest dreams imagined I'd be capable of. Like asking a guy into my house to have sex with me right after he made me come in his car.

This is reckless.

As I'm getting out of the car, Evan calls my name and grabs my wrist to stop me from stepping out.

"Next time you put on a show like you did at the club, make sure that it's for my fucking eyes only. Or I'll kill every single man who looks your way and punish you for being a brat," he threatens.

I stop breathing for a second. The threat does the opposite of what it should do, and the deep pang of arousal is back, like it never left. He lets go of my wrist, and I close my eyes and sigh. *Screw him and his stupid threat.* I roll my eyes and show him the finger as I step out of the car. He scoffs and I notice a smirk curling the side of his lips. I walk to my front steps and, as soon as I enter the house, put my back against the door and sink to the floor.

So many thoughts are swimming through my head, but there's only one that stands out.

I can't help but focus on three words he said: *our first time.*

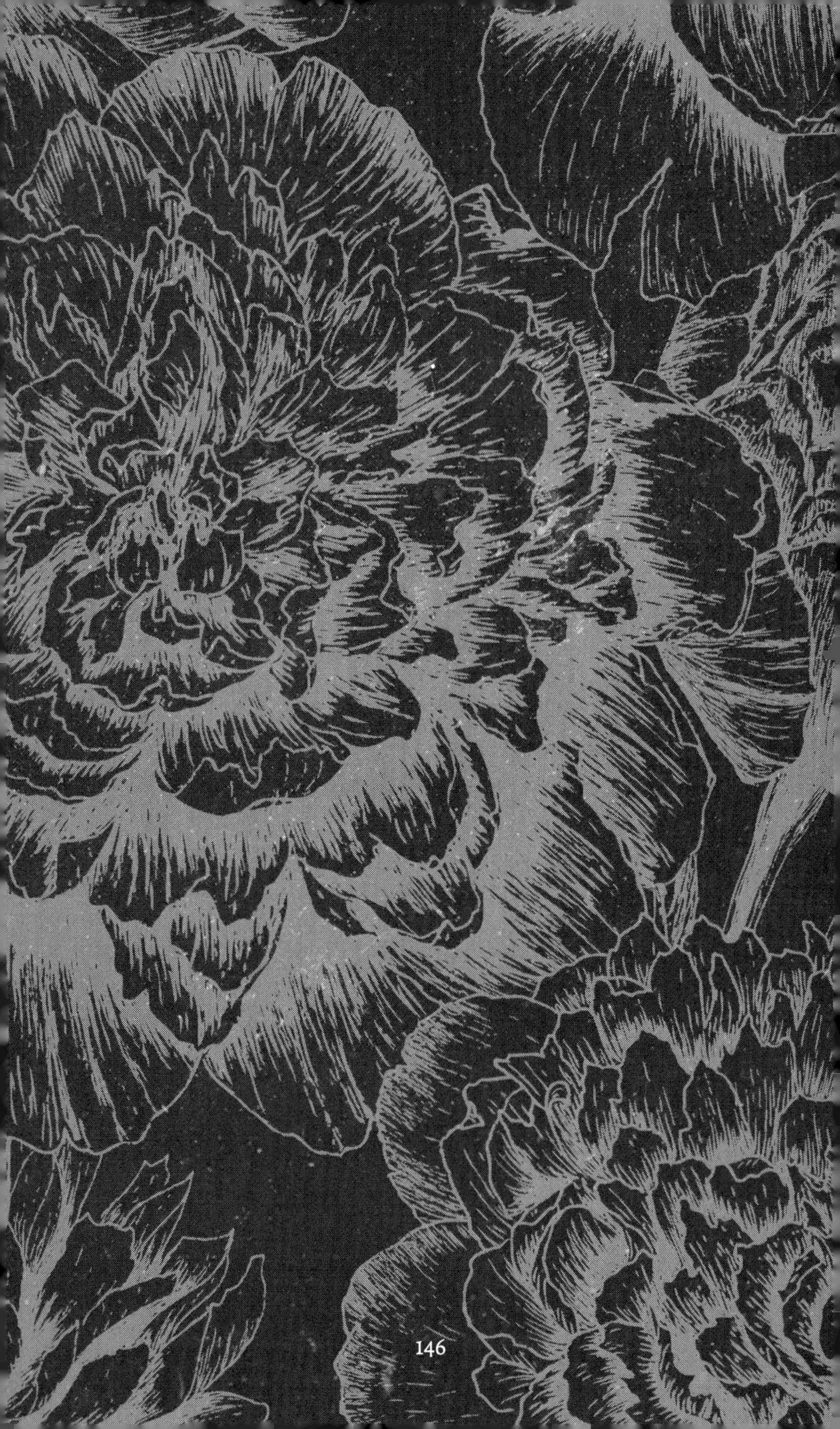

Unknown

N o one touches what's *mine. He will pay for this.*

"There's always going to be that one person in your life that you can't walk away from even if you know you have to." —*Anonymous*

Evander

I've just dropped Angelica home, and I'm itching to get rid of the mix of anger and arousal I feel inside. I had to keep my frustration toward the man she was dancing with in check while driving, and Angelica did a great job of providing a distraction. I don't know whether I want to go home and fist my dick or punch someone square in the face. That woman drives me fucking crazy and it only makes me want her more. She challenges me, keeps me on my toes, and soon enough, she's going to bring me to my knees. I don't get on my knees for no one, but I wouldn't hesitate to kneel for her. She has me in a goddamn chokehold.

Some fucker put his nasty hands on her and he's going to pay. I don't care if she led him on. She doesn't know it yet, but she's been claimed, even if it's just a means to an end. And that prick is never going to touch another woman again after I'm done with him. He's probably chained to a chair in the basement, and I can't wait to take out my anger on him. I call Xander and the phone rings through the Bluetooth in my car.

He answers in his deep, monotone voice. I'd usually call Dion but he's probably still busy with Aria. I tasked him to take care of her. I can only hope he's staying out of trouble. She's a Kastellanos, one of the Kouvalakis family's closest allies. If anyone catches wind of his involvement with her, we'll have another problem on our hands.

"*Pou íne o paliomalákas?*" *Where's the piece of shit?* I ask.

"*Íne sto ipógio afentikó.*" *He's in the basement, boss.*

I laugh inwardly. I can't wait to face the fucker who thought he could play with what's mine. He was probably imagining the countless ways he'd fuck her as she grinded on him, and I am going to eradicate his brain for even having those thoughts. He won't know what hit him. There's nothing scarier than facing a man brimming with hostility, a vortex of anger swirling inside him. Let's see how he reacts to the presence of the *Diávolos*.

Once I arrive back at the club, I make my way inside, turning left immediately, and I walk through the door that says 'Employees Only.' It opens onto a stairwell that leads straight down to the basement, where we conduct our more unsavory business.

As I reach the bottom, I pull out my phone and input a series of codes to unlock the other set of doors. It clicks open and I enter the dark room. We only come down here when we need to interrogate someone or carry out a punishment. The entire basement is made of soundproof concrete. It can also be discreetly accessed from the outside by a side door.

Dion and Xander stand next to the man from the club, tied to the ceiling by his wrists. His feet barely touch the ground and he's already beaten and bruised, saliva trickling down his chin. His hair is matted with sweat and blood. Bruises have begun to form all over his body. Blood slowly drips down his hands from the surface wounds inflicted. *Drip, drip, drip.* The metallic scent is ripe in the air, but it is about to increase tenfold.

The men give me a nod as I approach with nonchalance. I crack my knuckles and when I stand facing him, I slam my fist

THE DIÁVOLOS

into his stomach, which causes him to stagger back and let out a loud 'oomph.' His head falls forward, chin to chest, as he tries to catch his breath. I grab him by the jaw and lift his head back up. He is visibly shaking and can't seem to get any words out. The rush of adrenaline that floods into my system as a result is addictive.

I walk to the far side of the basement where a table lined with various *toys* stands against the wall, and I grab a meat tenderizer, running my fingers down the side of the handle as I walk back toward the guy from the club. His whole body stiffens when he sees what I'm carrying.

Just like an animal stalking its prey, following its quarry stealthily until it is time to pounce, I walk around the man tied to the ceiling.

"What's your name?" I ask. I circle around him again. I can smell his fear.

He doesn't reply and simply stares at me with tears rolling down his blood-stained face. I chuckle. *Okay, time to play.* I motion for Dion to throw a bucket of ice-cold water in his face. The man tenses up from the cold and starts sobbing hysterically.

"My name is Josh! It's Josh," he cries.

I smile wickedly. Some people prefer not to know their victim's name, to not feel any guilt when they hurt them, but it's the opposite for me. I like to address you by your name before I kill you.

I walk around Josh to grab a chair and I kick it toward him, hitting the back of his legs. His body slings forward and I use the knife to cut the rope that was holding his arms up and slam him down on the seat. Xander walks up to him and ties his ankles to the legs of the chair. At the same time, Dion fetches the table from the other end of the room and slides it in front of Josh.

"Put your hands flat on the table," I order. He lets out a whimper but doesn't make a move. My already thin patience dissipates entirely. "Put. Your. Fucking. Hands. On. The. Table. Now," I spit.

Josh reluctantly obeys and closes his eyes. The smell of urine invades my nostrils and I spit in his face in disgust. The fucker pissed his pants. Dion and Xander let out a muffled laugh and stand behind me.

I lift the meat tenderizer and slam it down hard, crushing Josh's right hand. A scream of agony comes out of his mouth. Blood splatters all over me and the table. I lift the tool and smash his hand again, severing it from his wrist. Amputating an appendage is nothing like you see in the movies. It's much more gruesome. *No one fucks with me.*

Josh's head hangs limp and he's slowly losing consciousness. Probably from blood loss. The limb is fucking spraying like a sprinkler. I pull out my gun from the back of my pants and aim it at his head.

I shoot.

"That's for putting your hands on my girl, motherfucker." *She's not your girl, Evan,* the voice in my head reminds me. I ignore it.

Dion hands me a towel to wipe the blood off my face.

"Get him the fuck out of here," I bark to the guys. I turn around and go back upstairs to my office so I can change out of these bloodied clothes.

I make my way to the top floor of the nightclub using the elevator hidden below the stairwell in the basement. The door slides shut after I input the code.

Sebastian and Gregory stand at the entrance of my office. I nod in their direction and they don't even flinch at the sight of the blood on my clothing. *Just another day in the life of a mobster.*

I enter my office and head straight to the bathroom I had installed in my office for instances exactly like these.

I lean onto the sink and take a deep breath, looking at myself in the mirror. Some days I feel like a monster capable of destruction, a human with no moral code who simply exists to bring pain to others. I wonder again if life would've been any different had my parents still been alive. Would I have ended up this way? The memory of my dead family instantly creates guilt, images flashing before my eyes. I'm angry. Why couldn't I have been old enough to fight for them, protect them? My little sister. *Thea.* She was only four years old, helpless, and naive. And I failed her. I let her slip away from me when my father asked me to protect her.

I grip the edge of the sink harder, attempting to calm the jerky movements of my arms from the aftershocks of the earthquake that is my life. My heart feels as if it has been ruptured, like the ground after seismic waves. Like a tsunami washing over coastlines, my lungs are flooded by the absurd amount of pain in my body. I can't breathe. My past, present, and future, all of it is too much to bear. I'm on the edge of losing it. I'm either going to collapse or suffer an outburst. But I will myself to regain composure. A psychogenic blackout from anxiety, or intermittent explosive disorder? Take your fucking pick.

When I was a kid, the repercussions of witnessing the murder of my family were enough to trigger a potion of emotional responses. My uncle sent me to many psychiatrists, and they all said the same thing. *Your nephew has childhood trauma that will develop into PTSD.* They prescribed meds to help me cope, but my uncle refused, having other plans to help me.

I might look like a normal, functioning human on the outside, but on the inside, I'm a fucking monster waiting to be unleashed. With a low tolerance for frustration and inappropriate anger outbursts, I'm scared to let Angelica near me during one of my episodes, when I feel like I can't control my actions. I would never want to hurt her.

When I've calmed down enough to rip off my clothes, I step under the scalding water and scrub the blood and dirt off my body until it hurts.

Once I'm done trying to shed my skin off like a snake, I dry myself with a towel, dropping it on the counter before going over to the walk-in closet to get dressed. I slip on grey jogging pants and a loose white t-shirt and sit on the edge of the bed in the bedroom adjoining my office. I let my body fall back onto the mattress. Feeling the effects of the day, I crash.

I hear the faint sound of glass breaking and footsteps getting closer and closer to my room. They sound frantic but quiet enough to go unnoticed. I hear my mama *whispering on the other side of the door, but I can't understand what she's saying. I stir under the covers and sit up in my bed, clutching onto my Spider-man blanket.*

"Mama?" I call out in a whisper. I can hear her talking to someone, my baba, *I presume, and she's crying now. I don't like when* mama *cries. It makes me sad, and I want to give her a hug.*

She walks into my room followed by my baba *and sits on the side of the bed. She grabs me tightly and her tears seep into my pajamas. My t-shirt is wet, but I couldn't care less. My* mama *is crying, and I want to make her feel better. I kiss her cheek and the salty taste of her tears invades my mouth.*

"Mama, why are you crying?" I ask. My baba *sits next to her, rubbing her shoulder, and looking back at the door every few seconds.*

"Sshh, Kamári mou, everything is going to be alright. I need you to listen to me, okay? We don't have much time," baba *says to me urgently.*

I nod and he leans closer.

"You remember that little crawl space I showed you when we

were playing hide and seek? Under the staircase, behind the library?" I nod. "Okay, I need you to run there quietly with your little sister and hide. No matter what, I need you both to stay in there until me or mama come and get you. Do you understand, Evanaki?"

I nod for the third time. "I'm scared, baba." Tears start rolling down my cheeks. Mama is still holding me in her arms, and it feels like this is goodbye. "Are there bad people here to take you?" I ask, confused. My mother chokes on a sob and covers her mouth to muffle the sound of her cries.

"It's okay to be scared, Kamári mou, just remember that your mama and baba are always with you. You are strong," mama says, and I squeeze her.

We hear muffled voices coming from the back of the house. It sounds like two or maybe three men. My parents quickly usher me out of the room, and I run down the stairs holding onto mama's hand, while my baba heads in the other direction toward my sister's room. My mama takes me to the library shelf under the staircase and pushes the cabinet door that opens onto a crawl space. Baba arrives with my sister, and my eyes widen when I see he's holding a gun.

"Baba, who are these men? Are they going to hurt us?" I ask him.

"No one will hurt you, my son. Just stay hidden, like I told you, and don't make a sound. Everything will be okay, I promise."

They kiss my sister and me and tell us they love us. My baba bends down to help my sister into the cabinet just as someone grabs my mama by her nightgown and shoves her to the floor. My little sister yells out for our mother and tries to reach over to her. I hold her back by her legs, begging her in a whisper to stay inside with me. Baba draws his gun and yells at the men to leave my mother alone. My sister claws at the floor to get out of my hold, screaming at the top of her lungs. Her legs are wriggling so much that I lose my grip and she crawls away too fast for me to catch her. My baba kicks the door to the cabinet shut before they notice me, and I sit in the little crawl space with my legs tucked into my chest.

No, no, no, no, no. Even though I'm squeezing my eyes shut as tight as possible, I can't stop the tears from rapidly flowing down my cheeks. I hear my mama and sister scream and my hand flies to my mouth as I try to muffle the sound of my cry. I start rocking my body back and forth, hoping the movement will ease the upsetting feeling in my tummy. I hug my chest, pretending that it's my mama's arms cradling me. I hear the voices of the men get closer and my baba shouts at my mama to take my sister and run. And then I hear gunshots.

Three. And my whole world crumbles.

My eyes snap open. It takes me a few seconds to realize where I am. I'm still at the office and it's dark, so I know it's not morning yet. I rub my face with trembling hands.

My heart is racing as I struggle to take a full breath. If I had any tears left, this is when they would come out flowing. I'm covered with sweat, so I rip my t-shirt off and sit up to reach for the bottle of water on the nightstand. I drink half of it in one breath, but I need something stronger.

I don't have nightmares often and I never usually remember my dreams, except for this one. The constant reminder of how I failed. The fucking sound of those three gunshots plagues me, but it's the silence that followed that haunts me.

That's why I can't live on the Vasilakis estate. Not because my family was killed in that house, but because it's so fucking quiet. I can't stand it. I need the sound of the city surrounding me to make me feel less alone.

When I think of the fear I felt in that moment, my heart breaks all over again for six-year-old me.

I later learned that my *baba* had called my uncle when he

first heard the intruders entering the house and told him we were under attack. He'd also informed him where my sister and I would be hiding, just in case anything was to happen to him and my *mama*. Flashing back to that horrible day, I remember hearing a familiar voice call my name after what felt like days of being trapped in the small space.

A minute later, the door to the cabinet had opened and there stood my uncle, looking like all the blood had been drained out of his body. He carried me out of the crawl space and held me tight, making sure to not let me see the bloodshed of my dead family.

"They will all suffer for this. I will protect you from now on, *Kamári mou*," he said.

He fulfilled that promise until his last breath.

My heartbeat finally starts slowing down, the adrenaline rush leaving my body. I get out of bed and head into the office area. I open the liquor cabinet, pull out a bottle of *ouzo*, and pour myself a glass. I don't even bother adding ice and swallow the liquid in one swig.

The burn is a welcome feeling right now.

I wake up some hours later, still in my office. I don't remember how and when I got back to bed, but I drank enough *ouzo* to tranquilize a horse. It's early as hell, but that doesn't stop me from drowning in my own thoughts. I've barely dragged myself out of bed and I'm already thinking of going back to Angelica. I should just call the whole fucking plan off. I'm failing miserably.

The events from last night flood my mind and I close my

eyes, rubbing my temples, as if that will erase the memories. But nothing happens. I open my eyes and still see Angelica in all her intoxicated and aroused glory, begging me to touch her and make her come. I have rules and one of them is to not fuck drunk women, *especially* drunk Angelica. Last night, I struggled between listening to my cock or my brain, both giving me different opinions. It was either break my own rule and give Angelica what she desired or stand my ground and follow my carefully devised revenge plan. It's been getting harder and harder to abstain from her, so I gave in. I didn't fuck her, but I still made her come all over my fingers. *That doesn't count as breaking the rules, right?* Doing it again is all I can think about.

Something about Angelica coming onto me last night pissed me off. Was she only flirting with danger because she was intoxicated? It might've been harsh to reject her so ruthlessly, but I don't care, she was drunk, despite what she claimed. I don't have the energy to deal with childish acts, and her tantrum last night proved my point. She's too young for me.

Although I wasn't impressed by her behavior, it didn't stop my dick from twitching in my pants. I saw the way her eyes wandered over my body. When her hand landed on my thigh, I felt something travel through me. I had flinched ever-so-slightly, but she jerked as if she'd been hit by a lightning bolt.

She tried to make me jealous, and *God, help me,* she succeeded. The anger that had coursed through me when she was grinding on that guy was enough for me to lose all my self-control.

In a moment of weakness, I rushed over and claimed her in front of everyone. He's lucky I wanted to avoid any bloodshed in my own club because I was *this* close to pulling out my gun, aiming it right between his legs and pulling the motherfucking trigger.

I'm a bad man. Not someone soft with *feelings*. But Angelica is definitely turning me into one.

Vulnerability is the last thing I want her to see in me.

I don't love anymore. The last time I let myself feel love, my heart was left on the floor, ripped out of my body. I never want to feel the pain I felt when the people I cared for the most passed away. So, I must keep Angelica out of my head and my feelings at bay long enough to complete the plan and get justice for my uncle's death the only way I know how. *Revenge.*

I'm supposed to have a business meeting with Dion today, so I grab my phone and dial his number to coordinate a time.

"*Kalimera afentiko,*" Dion snickers. *Good morning, boss.* Despite us both being fully Greek and fluent in the language, Dion embraces the culture more than I do.

"You know you don't have to call me boss, right?"

"I know, but you hate it. So, I'm going to keep doing it." He laughs.

Ever since becoming the Godfather and promoting Dion to my second-in-command, he has been having way too much fun calling me 'boss.' It feels awkward to be called that by someone I've known my whole life.

"Whatever, prick. When can you be at the office?"

"ASAP. But I have to go home, shower, and change first," he replies.

I take the phone off my ear to check the time. It's eight in the morning. I'm assuming he never made it home last night.

"What happened with Aria after the club?" I ask. He hesitates to reply. "Please tell me you didn't spend the night with her," I add.

Dion muffles a laugh. "Something like that. You know I like them feisty, but this girl...she's different. I can't explain it. She's got me all fucked up." His voice lowers toward the end as if he's just realizing *how* fucked he is.

I know that feeling all too well.

If he found out how I'm starting to feel about Angelica, he would think I'm a fucking idiot. He knows how much my uncle meant to me, to us, and how important this revenge is. He would be disappointed if I let feelings get in the way. But at the same time, Dion thinks with his dick most of the time, so he wouldn't judge me.

I'm not actually surprised he took Aria home last night. I should've known what I was throwing her into when I asked him to watch over her.

"Well, from what I could tell last night, she's a firecracker. It's about time you found a girl who can keep up with your nonsense," I chuckle.

"Yeah...but her situation is complicated, to say the least. I don't know if I'll see her again," he says, sounding disappointed.

"What's her deal?" I ask.

"She's getting engaged."

I don't know how to respond to that, but Dion fills the silence after a few moments. "It's an arranged marriage her father set up with one of his associates. She doesn't even know him."

Fuck. That sucks.

Soon enough, Angelica will be in a similar position with me, but hopefully she won't be too against it. And even if she is, she won't have a choice in the matter.

It's such an outdated practice, but in our world, arranged marriages tend to be the go-to for mending broken affiliations and creating new alliances. My uncle dodged that bullet because he was never set to be heir, so he married his wife out of love. They had a happy marriage up until she died of heart failure when I was a teen. My aunt was a great woman who took care of me as her own, too. I miss her dearly. They never had kids, and after she passed, everyone tried to convince him to remarry a younger woman and have children, but he refused. He claimed it was too late for him.

As the new Godfather, I'll be expected to get married and have heirs of my own.

But no one will expect me to marry the enemy's daughter.

"Not like you to mope over a girl, *Dionaki*. But if you do see her again, keep what you tell her to a minimum. She's Angelica's best friend, and I will kill you if she figures out who we are." *I'm such a hypocrite.* I'm the one who has been putting us most at risk by failing at staying away from her.

"Yes, boss," he says, and I scoff at the title. "What's going on with the Kouvalakis girl, anyway? You seemed to be two seconds away from catching fire last night. I've never seen you that worked up over anything."

He's right. I never let anything affect my composure, but with Angelica, I can't seem to control what I'm feeling, and I fucking lost it. Dion deserves the truth.

"She's all up in my head, bro. I can't stand it," I say as I pace around my kitchen. "I can't think straight. I'm supposed to be *using* her, not *courting* her," I add, running a hand through my hair.

Dion laughs. "I told you not to get attached, *Evanaki*. How the hell are you going to handle this now?" he asks.

"Fuck if I know. Meet me at the office at 10," I say, and I hang up. I rub my forehead and I look at the time again.

Not even thirty minutes after I made the decision to bar myself of all feelings, I'm thinking of ways to see her.

A flash of her face while I touched her pops into my head, her head back, eyes closed with her mouth slightly agape as I worked her to release, knuckles deep in her pussy.

I'm a bastard, and I don't even care.

I need to see her again.

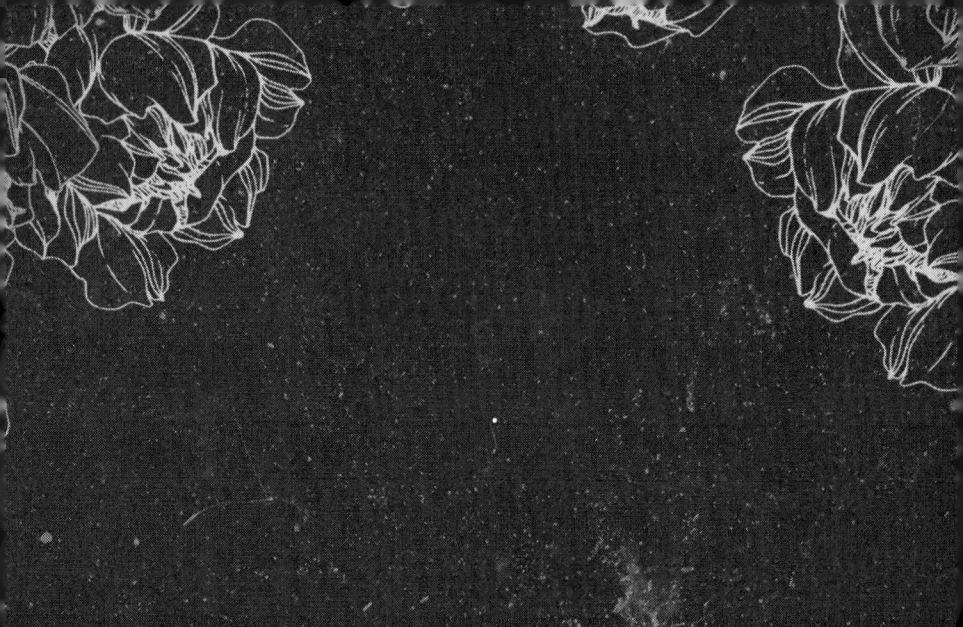

"What we have once enjoyed we can never lose. All that we love deeply becomes a part of us."
—Helen Keller

Angelica

I wake up with a pounding headache, nursing the biggest hangover, but it's nothing a little quiet time and stretching can't fix.

Sadly, Aria can't make it to yoga today. She texted me something about 'not feeling well.' I wonder if she's hungover from last night, too. I left the club much earlier than her, and she sent me a message around two in the morning confirming she was alive and well. I'll have to check up on her later.

Yesterday was a whirlwind.

I can't wrap my head around what happened on the drive home. I never actively pursue relationships, and neither do I fool around with someone I barely know. But all my inhibitions flew out the window when I saw Evan again. I can't help but feel the need to be around him and be touched by him. I don't know when I'll see him again, but his words still linger in my head. *Our first time.*

If he'd accepted my offer to come in last night, I would've lost all control over my body and let him have his way with me. The thought alone sends flutters between my legs.

I shake my head, trying to get rid of those ridiculous thoughts, and I distract myself by getting ready to head over to the yoga studio. As usual, I'll stop by the Black Bean after class to grab a coffee. I plan to call Aria to ask if she wants to meet me there. As I grab my phone to dial her number, I realize my guardian angel hasn't texted me since Tuesday. The last message he sent me was a comment on the dress I bought for the charity ball. I never responded. I was thrown off balance. Was he hiding in the store like a creep? Did he hack into the surveillance cameras? I knew he watched me while I was at home, but I had no idea he was *following* me. *As if one is better than the other,* I scoff.

I have the urge to text him, but I don't want to get too comfortable. After all, he is a stalker, and as much as I enjoy his attention, I can't let myself be too vulnerable. And now that Evan has entered my life, I'm not sure how to handle this situation. For all I know, the man stalking me could turn on Evan and hurt him. Who knows to what extent my secret admirer will go to show his devotion to me.

I settle on not texting him, and I dial my best friend's number instead.

"Hi Angie," she says, her voice still sleepy.

"You never sleep in. What the hell happened last night?" I ask, my tone full of worry.

"Ugh, long story. I'll tell you later. How was your ride home?" I swear I can hear the wiggle of her eyebrows through the phone. *That's my Aria.*

"It was...eventful. But I'll tell you later," I reply, mimicking her response.

"I'm rolling my eyes at you so hard," she says.

"I would expect nothing less," I retort with a giggle.

"Evan is a very intense guy. Not a man of many words, I must say."

"I can confirm that," I respond through a laugh. "Come meet me at our spot for a coffee after my class and I'll give you all the juicy details."

"You know I hate saying no to you, Ang, but I'm exhausted. I need a couple more hours of sleep. Raincheck?"

"Of course, *Arioula*. Call me later, okay?"

We say goodbye and hang up.

Something's up and I'm going to question her about it later, whether she likes it or not. I wonder if it has to do with her arranged marriage. I hate that she has to give herself to a man she doesn't know or love. She always brushes me off when I ask her about it, acting like she doesn't care, but I know Aria, and this isn't her ideal scenario by any means.

I make it to class at a reasonable time, and I allow myself time to relax and shake away all thoughts of yesterday with deep breaths and deep stretches.

Yoga was a very welcomed distraction, and I leave the studio feeling lighter. I needed to get rid of the lingering feelings of my actions toward Evan yesterday, more specifically the embarrassment. I'm never that impulsive. Or horny. And now, I'm confused. What happens now? Do I act as if it never happened? I don't even have a way of reaching him. I still know nothing about him, and the more I think about him, the more I wonder about his life. The whole club emptied last night at the snap of his finger, and I question how he has that much power. Could he be involved with the Vasilakis family?

I guess I'll have to wait and see what happens.

I make my way out of the studio at the same time as Emily, the instructor, and I thank her for the wonderful class. We briefly chat about our plans for the day as we exit the building. We part ways, and I turn around to head to the coffee shop when I hit something solid. I *really* need to become more aware of my surroundings. The collision causes me to take a few steps back, and I look up to see—*you've got to be kidding me*—Evan.

"Are you going to make a habit of running into me?" he asks with an amused smirk.

"I see you've got jokes this morning. Maybe I wouldn't run into you if you weren't everywhere I go," I say dryly, rolling my eyes at him.

"I thought the only time I'd get to see your eyes roll back was when my fingers were deep inside of you," he replies with a smirk.

I blink, and I immediately turn fifty shades of red. Evan laughs at my reaction.

"I should've known that would be the first thing you'd bring up, asshole."

Evan laughs again and the sound is music to my ears. I've lost my damn mind.

"Of course," he says. "How could I not bring it up? It was quite...memorable."

"I doubt I'm the first woman you've pleasured in your car."

His face turns serious, and he looks at me straight in the eyes. "You are."

I don't believe him for one second. The hottest man I've ever seen claims I'm the first woman he's ever touched in his car. *Right.*

"Anyway." I change the topic. "What are you doing around here? I've never seen you in the area."

"You've just never noticed me." He shrugs. Impossible. Evan is the opposite of unnoticeable.

"I was just headed to the coffee shop, so I guess I'll see you later," I say, awkwardly.

Evan tilts his head to the side, as if to get a better look at me, and squints his eyes. It's like he's trying to read me, and it makes me feel exposed. I shift uncomfortably on my feet.

"I'll walk with you. I could use a coffee, too," he finally says.

Shit. I was not prepared to see Evan the day after my little lapse in judgment. I don't regret what happened, but I'm still embarrassed by my behavior.

He turns around and walks in the direction of the café, but I stay put.

He looks back at me and sighs, an annoyed expression on his face. "Walk, Angelica."

I follow him hesitantly, like a puppy being commanded by its master. *I am clearly not okay.*

As we get to the entrance, he opens the door to let me in. I walk inside and see my favorite barista, Anna, at the coffee bar. She smiles at me and asks if I want the usual. I nod and Evan says, "Make that two."

I turn my head toward him. "You don't even know what my order is."

He reaches into his back pocket to pull out his credit card and casually responds, "Double-shot espresso, half-sweet, vanilla latte with oat milk. Extra hot with a sprinkle of cinnamon."

He gives Anna his card as I stare at him dumbfounded.

"How the hell do you know my exact coffee order?" I ask him, stunned.

"You shouldn't be surprised, *moró mou*. I know *everything*, and whatever I don't, I'll find out soon enough," he states. *Run for the hills, Angelica. Now.* But guess who stays put, staring at this tower of a man.

"I don't even know what to say." Truly, I'm speechless.

"Don't get your panties in a bunch, Angelica. I just do my homework."

"You're a creep," I say under my breath.

"Do you need a reminder of what this creep can do to you if you keep running your mouth?"

I'm melting faster than a glacier as my temperature rises. I'm having a hard time containing my reaction. How can I go from wanting to run away from this man, to wanting to run *toward* him. I see Evan's lips trying to muffle a smile. Global warming has nothing on him.

"I already know all the ways I'm going to touch you, hurt you, until you squirm and beg me to stop," he whispers as he moves closer, invading my space in the middle of the coffee shop. He takes a strand of curls and twirls it around his finger, tugging it gently. "You're at my mercy, Angelica. Remember that when you try to disobey or disrespect me." His words hit me like a head-on collision, and the force of them is a powerful caress along my body. I struggle to close my mouth from the shock, let alone formulate a response. Thankfully, Anna calls us over to get our order and he swiftly releases the thin lock of hair, leaving me standing in an imaginary puddle of water caused by the overflow of wetness between my legs.

He walks up to the counter, and I take the opportunity to gawk at him. He is tall, *very* tall, built, and lean. Strands of his disheveled wavy brown hair fall perfectly on his forehead. The stubble around his face gives off a rugged look. He's wearing deep blue trousers and a white buttoned-down shirt with the sleeves rolled up, showing a trail of tattoos that start at his fingers and go up his arms. The first few buttons are unbuttoned forming a 'V' at his chest. I can see a peak of the Greek wreath inked on his collarbone through the opening and under the fabric. And those damn rings he wears make me want to have the imprints stamped on my ass.

He is perfect. I hate that he makes me feel like I can't control myself.

He grabs our drinks, and hands me my coffee as we settle

at a table. I bring the mug up to my nose and sniff the lovely aroma of coffee, vanilla, and cinnamon.

After getting comfortable, we engage in conversation, and by that, I mean Evan asking me loads of questions while he listens. He succeeds in getting me to talk about my time in Antium City and I see him watch the way each word slips out of my mouth, his eyes laser-focused on my lips.

The trance he seems to be in gets interrupted as soon as he hears me say the name 'Danny.' He snaps his head up.

"Who the fuck is Danny?" he asks.

I blink at him and laugh. *Is he jealous?* "Settle down, cowboy. Daniel is one of my best friends from college."

"Does he have a dick?"

I stare at him, amused and maybe a little puzzled, as he scowls at me, pushing me to answer the question. "Uh, yes?" I reply.

"Then, you can't be friends with him," Evan states.

"Says who?" I ask incredulously.

"Says me."

"And who are you exactly, Evan?"

"Someone to be obeyed, Angelica." I want to tempt him further, ask him what he means by that, but no coherent words seem to formulate in my brain. I had a feeling Evan was slightly out of his mind, but he sounds straight up deranged right now.

"You've got to be kidding?" I finally muster. He laughs out loud and the booming sound reminds me of happiness. I wish he would do it more often.

"Of course, I am," he says with a wink. I don't believe him for a second. I roll my eyes at him and he grabs hold of my chin with his hand. The feeling of his fingers on my skin makes me forget everything else except his presence.

"*Ómorfi.*" *Beautiful,* he murmurs as he looks over my face.

His piercing eyes set me on fire. He lets go of my face, and I lower my gaze to hide my shyness. I get so nervous when I'm around him.

I want to know what he does for work, so I ask him about his business endeavors to distract me from the way my body is reacting to him. He gives me a vague answer about helping with his uncle's business and brushes me off almost instantly, so I decide not to pry or push it any further.

He encourages me to keep talking by asking about my family. I reveal that my mother passed away when I was young. I don't usually talk about such intimate details of my life, but something compels me to share that part of me with him.

When I talk to him, I feel comfortable, like I don't have to hide.

To my surprise, he reveals that both his parents and younger sister are deceased too. He seems to be taken back by his own admission. He stutters and breaks off what he was saying. I give him a soft, encouraging smile, and he carries on. He doesn't disclose how they passed away, but I can respect that. Talking about a traumatic and painful memory is never easy. It's best for me not to pry.

"I'm so sorry for your loss, Evan. I had no idea. I mean— How could I have known? But I'm sorry. I know it's tough." I'm rambling, but I was not expecting us to have shared trauma. No one truly knows how it feels to lose a family member unless they have lost one too.

"Don't apologize. I'm sorry for your loss too, Angelica," he says, and I can see the sadness in his eyes. His parents must have meant the world to him, like how my mother meant everything to me.

"I miss my mom every day," I whisper, sorrow consuming me. I lower my gaze and look at the coffee mug in my hands.

He scoots his chair closer to mine and rests his palm on my thigh. A charge of electricity hits me as it always does when he touches me. This time, I notice a change in his behavior. He straightens and leans into me, closing the space between us.

"The people we love never truly leave us when they pass. There are things in here," he points to my temple, "and here," he points to my heart, "that death can't take away from you. As long as you have memories and love, you have never truly lost."

He looks at me through soft eyes, and my heart skips a beat. No one has ever spoken to me this way about the grief I've felt and still feel over my mother's death. I can't help but be thankful for him at this moment.

"Thank you...for telling me that," is the only thing I manage to say.

He grabs my hand and squeezes it. Some moments don't need words, and right now, I don't mind the silence.

He lets go of me a few seconds later. "You're coming to work with me today."

"Is it 'bring your daughter to work' day?" I tease.

He laughs. "I realize how that might have sounded, but no. I'm not ready to let you go, and I have to work, so you're tagging along."

I don't know what his intentions are, I truly don't understand how I even feel, but the thought of spending the day with him sounds extremely appealing.

"Sure. I have nowhere else to be." I shrug. *Keep it casual, Angie.*

"Good. Let's go then. Dion will be waiting for me at the office."

"What do you do there all day, anyway?" I ask, taking another opportunity to pry about his work. This time, he gives me more of an answer.

"Well, if you must know, I go over my day with Dion. He tells me when and where my meetings are, I head down to the club and check how things are going with the manager, I meet with my bookkeeper to make sure that finances are in check... Am I boring you, yet?" He winks, and I roll my eyes again in response.

"So, Dion is basically a glorified personal assistant," I say, trying to suppress a laugh.

Evan snickers, seemingly surprising himself. "I guess you could call him that, but never say it to his face. Actually, please do. I want to see his reaction."

I briefly met Dion at the club yesterday. If I remember correctly, Aria left with him. There was another man with him I didn't get the chance to talk to, because Evan hauled me off the dance floor quicker than lightning.

I wonder if Dion might know what's going on with her. If he did something to her, I'm going to kill him.

"You just got an angry look on your face. Please tell me you're not planning on hurting anyone?" Evan asks.

"I might." I give him a big smile.

After we've finished our coffees and taken our dirty dishes up to the bar for Anna, we head out.

We walk the short distance to his car, and he opens the passenger side door to let me in. I don't know what to make of him inviting me to his office, but I'm looking forward to seeing him in his element.

Flashbacks flicker through my mind of what happened after the club last night. I'm reminded of the way Evan's hand slid up my skirt and expertly touched my throbbing center, teasing me just the right amount and riding me to a climax. I slightly sink in my seat, my cheeks flushing as I think about how I threw myself at him. *Embarrassing is an understatement.*

"What are you thinking about? Evan asks, sounding intrigued.

He doesn't turn his gaze away from the road. His posture is relaxed, his left arm resting on the side of the door, hand on the steering wheel, his other on the gear stick. I want to touch it, hold it. I take a long time to respond, but he doesn't rush me.

"Don't be embarrassed about last night," he says.

I'm surprised he figured out what exactly was on my mind. Then again, he knows everything apparently.

"How did you know that's what I was thinking about?"

"I can see it in your face, and you're literally shrinking in your seat," he notes, amused.

I am mortified and this is not helping. *At all.* I cover my face with my hands and shake my head. Evan laughs.

I glare at him. "I'm glad my humiliation is amusing to you."

"I can't help myself." He shrugs. "You look cute when you're embarrassed."

"*Cute?* Please. This is beyond embarrassing. I was basically throwing myself at you. I blame it on the alcohol."

"Uh huh," Evan replies. "The 'alcohol'," he says, making a quotation mark with one hand. "A drunk tongue is an honest one. And I thought you said you weren't drunk." He takes his eyes off the road for a second to wink at me.

"Yes. The *alcohol*." I cross my arms and pout. I'm not helping my case by acting like a big baby, but I really need this conversation to be over with.

Thankfully, at that moment, Evan pulls into the nightclub's parking lot. We get out of the car and enter through the same door we exited last night. The club is lit up, bright and empty, no bartenders or bouncers in sight, which makes the place look strange. We walk through the space, past the bar and dance floor, as we head toward the main entrance. It's silent for the most part, but I can hear faint voices coming from outside. The main door opens, and a short, tanned man walks in, flicking his cigarette outside at the last second. He nods in Evan's direction and smiles when he notices me.

"Hey, boss, who do we have here?" he asks, now nodding his head my way. Evan scoffs at his attempt to flirt with me and shakes his head.

"Leon, this is Angelica." He gestures toward me. "Angelica, this is Leon, my attendant. His main job is to man the door and stay out of trouble, which seems to be a lot to ask sometimes."

Leon lets out a deep chuckle as Evan slaps him on the shoulder. I smile at the interaction. Evan seems to have a good relationship with his employees, which makes me wonder how many sides this gigantic, tough man has. The more I'm around him, the more I feel I'll get to see the man he doesn't show to others.

"Hi, Leon, nice to meet you," I say, grinning.

Evan puts his hand on the small of my back and leads me toward the rounded staircase between the main entrance and dance floor.

We're greeted by two other men standing outside of Evan's office and they approach us to shake his hand. They're both tall and bulky. One is blond, the other has black hair, and they are both tatted all the way up to their necks.

"Sebastian, Gregory, this is Angelica. She will be spending some time with me today," he says, pointing at the blonde man first. "Make sure no unnecessary distractions come our way."

The men acknowledge me and nod as they move to let us into his office. I step in ahead of Evan and I'm immediately taken aback by the immensity of the space. The right side of the room is covered by a library filled with books. There is a large oak desk at the further end of the room with two brown leather loveseats facing each other in front of it. To the left there are two doors and a mini bar flanked with expensive alcohol and glasses. Art hangs on all the walls. I could stay here for hours going through every art piece and book.

"Make yourself comfortable," he says as he points to the couches. "Are you hungry? I can ask Pete to bring us something."

I'm too preoccupied looking around the room, wide-eyed, to acknowledge his question. Is it possible to have this much money just from owning a club? I don't know what his uncle's business is, but it looks like Evan lives a pretty lavish lifestyle. He leans on the edge of his desk and crosses his legs as he stares at me.

"I'm going to take that as a yes." He grabs his phone out of his back pocket and types out a quick message.

I don't argue. I haven't eaten anything all day.

"Sorry. This office is impressive," I say. "Are all of these books yours?"

He glances at the library and a look of sorrow flashes across his face. He walks toward the shelves and grabs a book. "Yes. They belonged to my parents. I brought them here when I bought the club. I spend most of my time here, so I didn't bother moving them to my place."

These books obviously have sentimental value to him. My heart sinks in my chest at the thought of him having lost his family so young. I want to touch him and tell him it's okay to be sad.

"It brings me peace to be around them, knowing I still have a piece of my parents with me. My mother used to read poems to me as bedtime stories." He shows me the book he pulled out,

The Complete Poems of Emily Dickinson. He opens it up on a dog-eared page and recites the prose out loud.

> **"Hope" is the thing with feathers –**
> **That perches in the soul –**
> **And sings the tune without the words –**
> **And never stops – at all –**
> **And sweetest – in the Gale – is heard –**
> **And sore must be the storm –**
> **That could abash the little Bird**
> **That kept so many warm –**
> **I've heard it in the chillest land –**
> **And on the strangest Sea –**
> **Yet – never – in Extremity,**
> **It asked a crumb – of me.**

"I always come back to this one when I find myself losing hope. It was her favorite."

The poem jolts my memories, and a dark, faceless stranger pops into my head. My stalker, the epitome of darkness, the reason for my ultimate demise. I haven't heard from him in a little while, and I can't help but wonder if he's moved on.

I shake out those thoughts. *Not the time.*

"That's beautiful, Evan." I take a few steps closer to him. "I'm sure your mother and father are always looking down on you, protecting you." He slightly flinches at the mention of his parents.

"Thank you," he says. He looks at me for a moment, burning intensity in his eyes, but quickly turns his gaze to the two doors on the other side of the room. "Let's continue the tour."

He takes me to the first door and into a large bedroom with a king size bed, covered with light grey bedding, and a large mirror set in front of it. The walls and furniture are dark, the only light coming from the chandelier hanging above the bed.

There are two other doors in the bedroom that Evan explains lead to a walk-in closet and bathroom.

I can't help but think about the many girls he has probably brought up here. How easy it must be to convince a girl to go home with him when 'home' is right upstairs. I shake the bitterness away as I face Evan.

"Do you sleep here often?" I ask, trying to sound innocent.

"Not really. Only if I have business to tend to and it runs late. I prefer sleeping at my penthouse."

Business. In a club filled with drunk women probably throwing themselves at him. I don't realize I'm drowning in an unjustified fit of jealousy until I notice Evan smirking from the corner of my eye.

"I always sleep here alone, if that's what you're wondering, *angeloúdi mou.*" *My little angel.*

I tense up and immediately go on the defensive. "No. Why would I care about that? That's your business," I blurt out.

"Then why did it look like you saw red as soon as you walked into the room and found a bed?"

"I just wasn't expecting it, that's all." I turn around and pretend to study a piece of art on the wall in an attempt to avoid Evan's gaze.

He lets out an amused breath and I hear him pad toward me. Next thing I know, he is right behind me, a mere inch away from my back, completely dominating the space around my body. I hold my breath and don't move as he lowers his head down to my ear.

"I think you might be jealous, Angelica," he whispers slowly before tsk-tsking. "I think you're wondering how many girls I bring up here from the club."

I try to let out a breath so I can respond and deny what I know is the truth, but he leans in lower and brushes his lips against my ear. My entire body shudders and my nipples stiffen under my shirt. He runs his hands down my arms agonizingly slowly and continues to speak.

"You want to know how many women I've fucked here." A statement rather than a question.

No point in denying my curiosity now. My breathing becomes uneven, and I swallow hard as he keeps running his hands up and down my skin. Goosebumps erupt all over my body. I want to press my back into him but resist the temptation. I close my eyes and tilt my head back onto his chest. I can hear his heartbeat quickening.

"How many?" I ask, softly.

He caresses my arms right down to my forearms and then grips my hips, bringing my body flush to his. "You're the first woman I've ever brought in here. No one has touched this bed other than me." His words are laced with heat.

He turns me around abruptly and the air gets stuck in my lungs as he backs me up against the wall and presses his body onto mine. I feel the hardness of his length nudging my lower abdomen. He lifts my head by my chin, and we lock eyes. My vision goes hazy as he leans closer, and it feels as if he has stolen my breath.

"Believe it or not, I don't make a habit of fucking random women," he says onto my lips. "And you are most definitely *not* random. But I didn't bring you here today to fuck you."

His forwardness causes a throbbing ache between my legs. I'd like to think I wouldn't let him touch me so easily while sober, but in my current state, I don't know if I could stop him even if I wanted to.

He grazes my lips again and I part them, our breaths now intertwined. I expect him to kiss me, but he lingers at my mouth, panting heavily, and we don't say another word. Evan seems to hesitate, as if struggling with our closeness. We've never come this close to kissing, and I want it more than ever. I let out a deep exhale right onto his mouth and he licks his lips. I want to lean in so badly, but I refrain, not wanting to worsen his uncertainty. If we kiss, it will take whatever is happening between us to another level I'm not sure either of us is prepared for.

Just when he seems to lean in even further, we hear a faint knock at the door, and it brings us back to reality. Maybe it's for the best. I need to keep a good head on my shoulders, I should be vigilant. And with Evan affecting the chemicals in my brain, I can't think straight.

"That must be Leon," Evan says, backing away from me as he regains his composure. I stay glued to the wall, my face and neck flushed.

After a moment, he smiles and extends his hand to me. "Let's eat."

> "A Scout is never taken by surprise; he knows exactly what to do when anything unexpected happens." —Robert Baden-Powell

Unknown

*I*t's 7:15 pm on Sunday. Angelica should be leaving for the gala any minute. As I lift my eyes from my watch, she opens her front door. *Right on time.*

She looks gorgeous in the black, sparkly gown I watched her buy. It hugs her in all the right places, gripping her so well it's sinful. Her curly black hair is half up with two strands framing her face on each side. I can see her lips glistening from here, and I want to...

The sound of a car approaching interrupts my thoughts. A black-on-black Phantom pulls into her driveway. I crease my brows to get a look at who is in the car, but I don't recognize the person through the tinted windows. A man in an expensive-looking suit steps out and walks around to the passenger side. *What the fuck?* I didn't expect her to be going to the ball with a *date.*

She gives him a coy smile from her porch and walks over to him, placing her hand in his palm so he can lead her to the car. He places a kiss on her knuckles and his lips linger on her skin longer than necessary before he opens her door. She effortlessly slips into the seat, and he helps gather her dress before going back around to get in. There is too long of a pause before they drive off. *Fucking tinted windows. If he is touching her...* I feel the blood boiling under my skin. Their encounter looks a bit too comfortable. Who the fuck is that guy and why is she taking him to the gala?

I look to my side and stare at the full-face mask I bought just in case I decided to follow her. I brought my tuxedo for this reason, too. Fuck it. It's too risky, but Angelica is *mine*.

My plans have changed. I'm going to the fucking charity ball.

Part 11

The Reveal

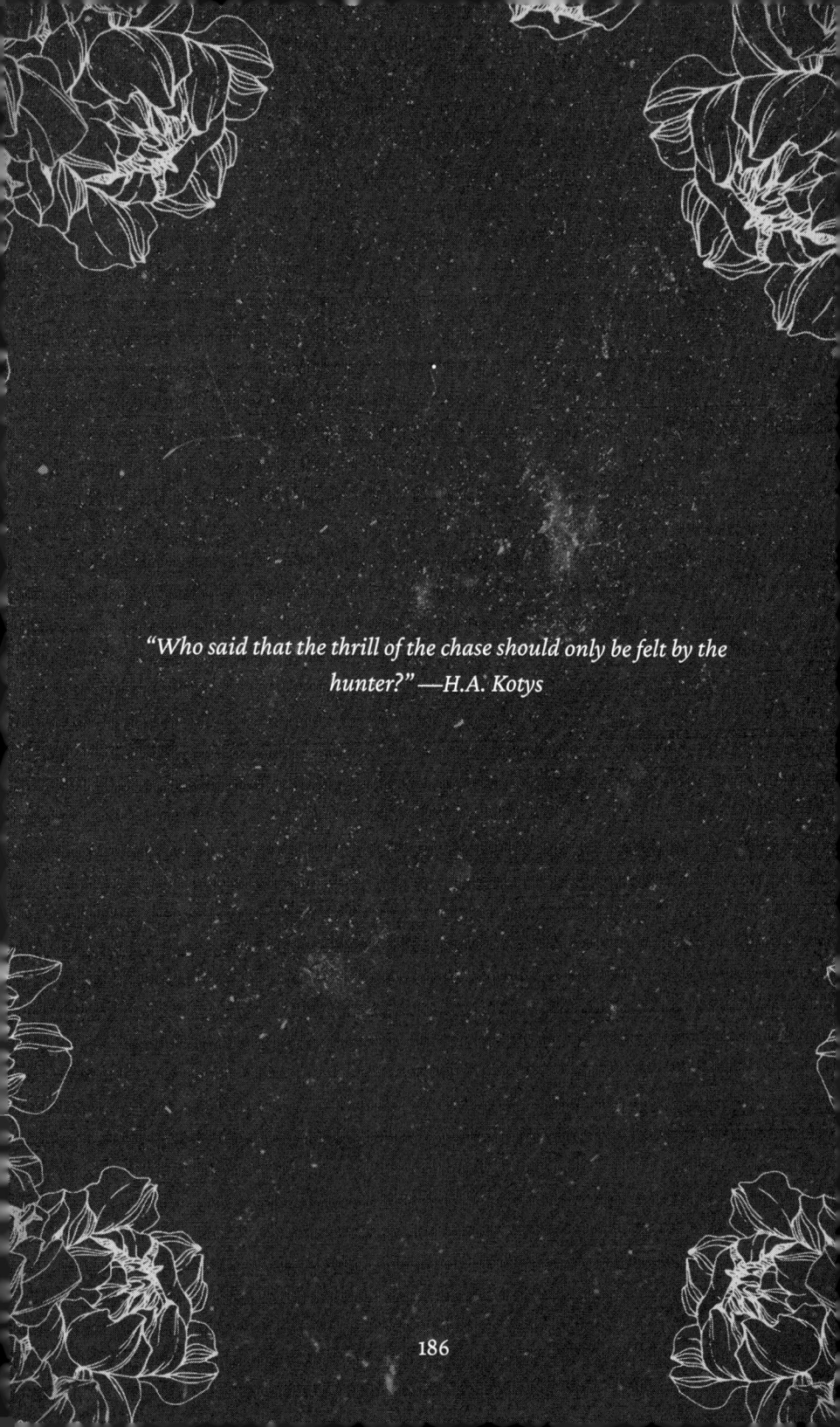

"Who said that the thrill of the chase should only be felt by the hunter?" —H.A. Kotys

Angelica

I felt nervous as I waited for Niko to pick me up. I asked him to be my date for tonight's charity event. I haven't seen him since I left Cebrene. My *baba* always had me attend these types of functions on his behalf even as a teenager. Now that I'm back in town, he didn't hesitate to throw me back to the wolves. He loves to show off and pretend he cares about the welfare of others. Donating to a big charity every year is the perfect way to showcase he's just as successful as his rich counterparts.

I only agree to attend these events because I'm a huge believer in charity work and I love helping others, especially children. Even though I know it's all for show, the money still goes to disadvantaged families and that's all that matters.

Although I dread having to socialize and put on a fake smile all night, I'm going to take the opportunity to find information on whatever is happening with my father. People of that social standing are tight-lipped most of the time, but with a few drinks, they might loosen up enough to let some information slip. I need to know who this new Godfather is that my father was referring to.

I was forced to come back to Cebrene because of my *baba*'s ventures. I deserve to know what brought me back, get rid of it, and go back to Antium City. I miss the freedom, my life, my friends, my grandparents. But I can't leave until the threat toward me has been extinguished.

I stepped out earlier today to find a mask for the ball but came back empty-handed. Finding the perfect one this last minute is almost impossible, so I decided to borrow one from Aria. She's been to masquerade parties before and has an enormous selection.

When I got back, there was a note and a small, black jewelry box wrapped with a red satin bow waiting for me on my bed. My heart fluttered with excitement. He knows I'm going to a masquerade party. Does this mean he'll be there too?

For days, I had anticipated when and where I'd find my next gift from him. Under the letter was a beautiful, stark white, lace mask, with the most intricate detailing, shaped like angel wings. The little tokens my guardian leaves me are what keeps me going. They are a reminder that he's watching me, keeping me safe. Mostly from the things that hurt me on the inside.

It's the smallest things that take up the most room in your heart.

When I unfolded the note, I found a poem written inside.

I want to be the sun,
The first thing you see when you rise.
The glow that touches your skin.
The sparkle in your eye.
And when you are lost,
I want to be the light that guides you.
Even within my darkness.

I'd unwrapped the gift and inside the velvet box sat a pair of diamond teardrop earrings. I had gasped at how beautiful they were. In the sunlight, the sparkle had reflected rainbows around me like a prism. They must have cost a fortune. Why would he spend so much money on me when we are still strangers?

We are nothing to each other, but it's the kind of nothing that means everything.

***

A little while later, Niko and I are in his car on our way to the venue, located in the Heights, the most 'neutral' territory in the city. The ride is quiet. He attempts to break the silence with small talk, but the conversation is fragmented and awkward. My arms are crossed, and my body language is tense. I've never been this uncomfortable around him, and I know it has to do with a certain someone.

Niko has been around my family for almost as long as Gianis. They were best friends, which meant wherever G was, Niko was. He doesn't work for us, but he's always been my *baba*'s first pick as my future husband. I was barely legal, and he would talk about us getting married. It never happened, as we broke up a year before I moved away. It's not that I don't find Niko attractive or worthy, I just don't see the point. I'm not in love with him and the marriage would only benefit our fathers.

We dated for several months during my junior year of high school. He was cute and quiet, and definitely not like the other guys. I was drawn to him for the simple fact that he was different. We lost our virginity to each other, but our relationship didn't last long after that. If our families had found out we'd had premarital sex, my head would've been on a chopping block, or we would've been married at eighteen. Thankfully, Niko never told anyone. He never bragged. Not even to Gianis, who secretly loathed seeing us together.

Either way, I prefer the friendship we have now. I still feel the tenderness he's always had toward me.

I knew he would jump at the opportunity to go to the charity ball with me. He probably knows nothing is going to come of this, but he still agreed to come. I think a part of him still hangs on to a sliver of hope that I'll marry him one day. I have no doubt he would treat me with the utmost respect, but out of spite toward my father, I refuse to tie myself down to him, or anyone. *Call me petty.*

I fiddle with my dress, nervous at the thought of my secret admirer finding out I'm going on a date with another man. I don't owe him anything but, for some reason, I feel uneasy. I know he's always watching. Then, there's Evan. I've spent a lot of time with him recently, and my attachment to him is growing. As much as I try to shove all thoughts of him away, it's useless. His face always comes to the forefront of my mind. I don't know how to handle my feelings. He seems to be equally interested in me, but I don't want to get my hopes up. I barely know him. The bonds I have with both men are so different, but so alike at the same time. I have no idea who one of them is, but the tingles that travel through my body and land right in the pit of my stomach when I get his gifts and read his poems make me feel like he truly sees me, knows me. A rush of adrenaline courses through my veins when I think of him watching me.

The other is mysterious, and I feel like he may be hiding his true self from me. I yearn to peel away his many layers. I want to uncover him and learn everything there is to know. His touch, feel, and smell are branded on my skin. My core flutters just at the thought of him.

The two are a perfect match for me. I wish I could blend them together and call them both mine.

I push those thoughts aside and focus on my date. We catch up during the ride, talk about his family, his work, and he tells me about the horses he's been betting on. Several minutes later, we arrive at the venue, where a valet attendant waits for us at the entrance. Niko gets out of the car and rushes to my side to help me out of my seat, then we walk into the building holding hands.

The Ballroom At the Ben is beautifully decorated. The folks at the Mouths2Feed Foundation really outdid themselves this year. I can't help but stare at the gorgeous gardenias and baby's breath covering the balconies looking over the hall. The beautiful golden chiavari chairs are covered with magnificent bows. The stunning backdrop of flowers behind the dais is sure to be a crowd pleaser. Wealthy people want to see that their money will be well-spent and appreciated before they donate hundreds of thousands of dollars.

We find our table and take a seat. My father paid a hefty price for our tickets, so we are seated near the front stage in the VIP section. The guests are all in ball gowns and tuxedos. Even though everyone is wearing masquerade masks, I can recognize most people. The individuals at our table are long-time friends of my family, so no one looks twice at the sight of Niko and I arriving together. I make my rounds and indulge each of them with polite conversation. After all, that's what my father sent me here to do, kiss ass and look better than everyone else doing it. Given this event is mainly attended by high-profile mobsters and business moguls, we are acquainted with most of the guests. It's a fairly small pool of individuals. Plus, being the only daughter of a well-known mafia boss guarantees that everyone knows your name.

I start planning my next moves and look around to see who I'll interrogate first. My eyes narrow in on Mrs. Cirillo. Her husband, Homer, is the Godfather of the Cirillo family, and they control the Lower District. *Bingo.* She loves to dish the dirt and gets really chatty when she's had one drink too many. When I was younger, I'd always hear stories of the rumors Gloria would spread around the city. She was everyone's personal gossip channel. Hopefully she's kept up with the same habits while I was away. I'll wait until she's slightly intoxicated, and I'll make my move.

A jazz band plays in the background while people mingle, have drinks, and schmooze. Niko and I decide to go to the bar to escape the loud noise. He grabs my hand and holds on tight as we wind our way through the crowd. I feel a presence to my right and notice from the corner of my eye someone staring directly at me. I let go of Niko, but he keeps walking, not bothered by the empty void left by my hand. I turn back and see a man wearing a full ornate black mask with devil horns. Unlike everyone else, his entire face is covered, which means he sticks out like a sore thumb, but nobody else seems to notice him. He's hidden, but I can still see the intensity of his eyes through the gaps in the mask. He's at the opposite end of the ballroom, leaning against a cocktail table, drink in hand, absently participating in a conversation with two other men I don't recognize, but his eyes remain laser-focused on *me.*

I can't help but mumble out loud, "Who is that?"

The way his gaze never leaves me fills my body with a sense of familiarity, but I can't point out why. I take a long look at him from head to toe and it's impossible to ignore how delectable this stranger looks in a tuxedo. When I lock eyes with him again, I feel a tightness in my throat and I try to swallow, keeping my eyes on the way the suit hugs his tall and muscular frame. His bow tie is snug at his throat and his Adam's apple bobs underneath. I shudder at the sight. *Who is he?*

I shake my head to get rid of the sudden heat I feel creeping up my skin. For some godforsaken reason, I feel guilty for having these thoughts because of some deranged man who has made it his life's mission to stalk me, and because of Evan, who simply waltzed into my life and turned it upside down.

The distraction causes me to trip over my dress and I stumble into Niko's back. I dismiss his concern and quickly gather myself to continue following him to the bar. As we approach the bartender at the back of the ballroom, I can still feel the stranger's eyes on me, and I look back at him.

Despite still being in the middle of a conversation, he doesn't take his gaze off me for a second. There is a fire brewing behind his eyes. He only moves to take sips of his drink. His eyes seem to pierce the depths of my soul. I feel like I recognize the unique color of his irises. My bones rattle at the hunger in them and the way he looks at me through his dark, thick lashes, but I feel myself getting hot and bothered. *What is wrong with me?* I jerk my head back toward the bartender and order a double gin, neat.

I need something strong if I'm going to survive tonight.

For a while, I focus on my date. Niko is a gentleman and initiates most of our conversations, while taking care of me and ensuring I always have a drink in hand, with sips of water in between. He leans close to my ear to ask if I'm comfortable or if I need anything, gently touching my arms whenever he wants to get my attention. I try so hard to ignore the stranger's presence, but I catch myself looking over at him on multiple occasions, making eye contact each time. He doesn't flinch.

As time goes by, I start feeling more guilty for being here

with Niko. *But why? Is it because of Evan? Or my guardian angel?* Either option is preposterous. I'm single. Yet, I feel bad for being here with a friend, because a man I've never met is looking at me like he's about to claim me as a prize, and the two other men I daydream about, I don't actually owe anything to, and they aren't even here.

I'm annoyed with myself for turning what I expected to be an already pitiful night into something full of misery. I've lost focus. I'm supposed to get information out of Mrs. Cirillo in the hopes of uncovering my father's operation, but instead, I'm here, drowning in my drink like a coward. The masked stranger threw me off my game and ruined my plans. All he's done is stare at me all evening without uttering a word. What is his problem? I need to figure out who he is.

Frustration starts bubbling inside of me amid my conversation with Niko, and I spill some of my drink on my dress as I try to take a sip with shaky hands. I reach over the bar to grab a napkin and the spaghetti strap of my dress slips off my shoulder. Niko reaches for the tissue first.

"May I?" he asks, and I nod. He dabs the serviette on the corner of my lips to wipe off the droplets of liquid and then gently pats my chest to clean up the spill. Heat rises to my cheeks. When he's done cleaning me up, he sweeps his hand up my arm and places my strap back on my shoulder. *Nope. That's it.* If I turn any redder or get any hotter, I'll probably burst into flames. I need to exit this situation now. The awareness of being watched while Niko touches me is eating at my skin. I excuse myself and make haste, *away* from him.

I walk through the large crowd to the ladies room. I just need a moment alone without Niko's hands on me, the masked stranger's eyes following me, and the thoughts of Evan and my stalker plaguing me. I can't think straight right now.

I walk into the bathroom and rest my hands on the counter

on each side of the sink, and I let my head fall between my shoulders. I release a large pent-up breath just as the door swings open, startling me when it hits the wall. I whirl around and the man who's been eyeing me all night marches in. I stare up at him with wide eyes.

"What the hell? Are you crazy? You just barged into the woman's washroom like a Neanderthal!" I yell. "And you almost scared me to death!"

"You should be scared, Angelica," he murmurs dangerously. His voice is low, full of bass, like the deep thunder of a storm. I don't recognize it, it shakes me to the core, but I'm not afraid.

"And I don't give a fuck. If anyone is in here, they can leave." His chest visibly expands with each breath. Why is *he* angry right now?

No one emerges from the stalls, and I relax my shoulders. I wouldn't want anyone hearing this exchange and taletelling.

"Can I help you? It's not polite to follow people into the bathroom, especially after having stared at them for hours," I state, crossing my arms in front of my chest. I have no idea who this person is, and he's definitely right, I *should* be scared. But right now, there are loads of other emotions that are threatening to seep out of my body like lava.

His body language screams rage. Pure, wild, and unfiltered anger.

"You can help me by telling me who the fuck you came with," he spits, his voice muffled from the mask. "I'm in here because you seem to be on a *date*." His whole body trembles. Now that he's closer, I narrow in on his eyes to see if I can recognize him. His entire face is covered, but I can see that the bottom of his jawline is absent of any stubble or hair. I take a good look at his darkened pupils, and they not only show anger, but something like anguish and pain. They tell a haunting story I want to hear over and over again. There's something so oddly familiar about them, but I can't put my finger on it.

"Why do you even care?" I ask. "I don't even know who you are, so I don't owe you an explanation. I've been here for over an hour, and you've been staring at me the whole time like a psychopath!" The pitch in my voice increases with each word.

He slams his left fist onto the counter, and I try to hide my flinch.

"Who the *fuck* is he, Angelica? Are you fucking him?"

I wonder why none of this is scaring me. Why isn't *he* scaring me?

"No. I'm not *fucking* him. Not that it's any of your business."

He closes in on me fast and backs me into the corner. He places his hands on the wall on each side of my head, trapping me between him and the concrete. "What do you want from me?" I ask, my heartbeat racing a mile a second. I'm now beginning to feel maybe slightly scared of him, but I can't help the different kinds of tension building in my body.

His anger doesn't subside, and his piercing eyes turn dark, empty. He seems to be fighting an inner battle, his breaths labored and short. He bows his head, and I can sense his struggle. For some unknown reason, I want to help him take away the pain. The only thing I manage to do is lift my hands and cup the back of his neck, letting my fingers gently caress his skin. *What the hell are you doing, Ang?* I've truly lost my mind. But it doesn't stop my hands from exploring what's uncovered. The movements of his chest visibly slow down and he lifts his head to look at me. For a moment, I think I caught a glimmer of surprise in his eyes.

"Do not question me right now. You don't know what I'm capable of," he says under his breath.

I reach for my purse and grab my pocketknife. As much as I'm confused about the situation and how my body is reacting, I need something to keep me safe.

He stops my hand mid-air, and right before he snatches it out of my hand, he lets out a deep rumble from his throat. "I should use this little knife to scrape the skin he touched right off your shoulders," he seethes, his voice calm but deadly. I gasp as he steps closer. "Burn the straps off your dress so he doesn't have an excuse to put his unworthy fingers on you," he continues, breathing right into my ear. The heat from it travels straight to my core. "If I see him touching you one more time, I won't hesitate to stab him in the neck with *your* knife, right there in front of everyone. So, you either tell whoever he is to get the fuck out, or you make up an excuse to leave. In any case, you're leaving here without him tonight, Angelica. You can decide how."

Who does he think he is? This *stranger* is acting like a possessive alpha-wolf about to mark his chosen female to keep the other males away. Who I date and sleep with is none of his concern. I'm not his. I don't even know him. My mind is reeling, the effects of this encounter are like massive waves crashing through my brain. It hurts, everything hurts. I clench the sides of my head, bending forward and I let out a whimper.

"You do *not* have the right to control me!" I shout. He backs away as I launch myself at him, reaching for his mask. I need to uncover his face. I'll go crazy if I'm stuck in this bathroom with him for another minute without knowing who he is. He extends his arms out to stop me from coming any closer and I start clawing at his face. "Who are you?" I scream, I don't even care if anyone hears me. I try to reach for him again, but he's too strong and blocks every blow. "Take off your mask!" I yell.

As if realizing I won't stop trying to unmask him, he grabs

my hands, forces them to the side of my body, and turns me around so my back is against his front. His arms are wrapped around me so tightly, I can't move. I stop thrashing, it's no use. Once I relax into his hold, every part of me fits into his frame like a puzzle. Again, I'm hit with that same sense of familiarity. I shove those thoughts away. *You've never met him, Angie. You'd remember.*

"I'm not taking the mask off, Angelica. And I don't care if you think I have no right to tell you what to do. You will obey me, even if it's the last thing you want. If that makes me a villain, then so fucking be it. You're *mine*," his deep voice vibrates through my body, and I momentarily drown in it.

I roll my shoulders back and let out a dry laugh. "*Yours?*" I ask.

"You're wearing *my* earrings, sunshine. I knew they'd complement your dress perfectly," he purrs into my ear.

He squeezes me tightly before letting go. I slump forward and clutch onto the wall. I can't breathe. The shock I feel right now is unbearable. I turn to face him, and I press my back into the concrete. My heart is beating beyond measure. I might throw up.

I'm standing in front of my *stalker*. My guardian angel. My secret admirer. The man who has been watching me this whole time. I try to pull on the hair tie at my wrist and realize I left it at home. *Goddamn black-tie dress codes.*

He grabs my arm and looks at the marks on my skin. "Why do you hurt yourself, Angelica?"

He asks with concern. I don't reply. I've never had to explain myself about this habit. He runs the pad of this thumb across the jagged scars, and it sends flutters to my stomach.

"Tell me who caused you to start doing this," he growls. I try to yank my arm away, but he holds on tighter. "Answer me," he seethes. "I need to know who to fucking slaughter for this."

The threat, albeit not to me, sends a chill down my spine. I wholeheartedly believe he would make someone pay. The thought increases my anxiety by a few notches, and I continue panicking. This is too much.

"Breathe, Angelica," he orders.

I try to bring myself back from my state of shock by inhaling two shallow breaths and exhaling slowly. I eventually calm down.

"That's my girl," he praises in an almost soothing voice.

"You're a psycho," I breathe out, sounding raspy.

"I beg to differ, my angel. That's not how you've felt about me every time I've watched you open my notes and gifts," he sneers.

"Fuck you," I seethe.

I storm out of the bathroom and make my way back to Niko at the bar, in disbelief over what just happened. I just met my stalker and I still have no clue who he is. I can't think straight from the obscene amount of anger I feel coursing through my body. I have to calm myself, so I take more labored breaths.

I don't want to risk Niko's life, so I think of an excuse to get rid of him. As I approach the bar, I put a hand on my stomach. *Oh my god, I can't believe I'm actually doing this.*

"Niko, I'm sorry, but I have to leave. I'm suddenly not feeling well." I twist my face in pain.

"Did something happen? I can take you home if you'd like," he asks with concern in his voice, making me feel even guiltier.

I want to punch myself in the face for lying to him. Obviously, he cares. *I'm an asshole.*

"No, nothing happened. It's just...cramps. Don't worry, I can take a cab home. You stay and enjoy the night for the both of us. My father paid a lot of money for these seats, I wouldn't want them both to go to waste." I give him an awkward smile.

Worry creases his eyes. "Are you sure? I don't mind leaving."

I shake my head and he reluctantly agrees to let me leave alone. I really don't deserve a friend like him. Any girl would be lucky to be on the receiving end of his attentiveness.

I grab my purse and speed walk to the exit. I have no idea where my stalker is, but I don't want to run into him now. I get to the door and push it open, instantly feeling relief from the cool air hitting my face. I close my eyes and take in a deep breath before walking down the street. I don't realize I'm still angry until I start marching down the sidewalk with quick and brisk steps, my fists clenched at my sides. Actually, I'm stomping like a three-year-old throwing a tantrum. All I want to do is get home and into my warm bed. The chill is starting to lower my body temperature.

How can someone I don't know infuriate me this much? His words crawl under my skin, making me want to stab him right in the gut with my 'little knife.'

I belong to no one. I don't want to be claimed. And yet, my stalker calling me *his* made me feel all gooey inside. I felt a tug in my stomach at the words 'you're mine.' I hate it.

A car pulls up next to me and slows down to follow my pace. Knowing who it must be, I ignore it and continue down the road. The passenger window rolls down.

"What are you doing, Angelica?" he asks, his muffled voice oozing with venom. "You seriously don't plan on walking all the way home, do you?"

"Yes, I do. Leave me alone. You got what you wanted," I spit.

The laugh that comes out of his mouth is mocking. "You

have no idea what I want, angel. Let me clue you in, this is not it."

I finally turn my head toward his car, and I halt my steps. He comes to a stop. When I finally look his way, his devilish mask is still on.

"You are despicable. You know that, right?" I cross my arms to hug myself. An act of self-preservation, creating a barrier, a protective or defensive gesture. Whatever you want to call it.

He laughs, again. "You haven't seen my worst, angel. Now, get in the car so I can drive you home."

"No." I stay put on the sidewalk and cock my head to the side in defiance. "I'm not getting in the car with you!"

"Suit yourself. I'll just follow you all the way to your house."

"I'll take a cab," I retort confidently.

"Then I'll follow the cab."

"Why do you want to follow me home? I'm not letting you into my house." After what he pulled tonight, the only way he's seeing the inside of my house again is in his dreams. *So much for feeling comfortable and at ease with my secret admirer.*

"You know damn well I don't need permission to get into your house, sunshine. I just want to make sure you get back safely," he states casually.

I growl in frustration. "Don't call me sunshine," I say with a fake smile on my face.

"I'll call you whatever I want. Get in the car," he orders.

"When did my guardian angel become such an asshole? I don't even recognize you!" I shout, exasperated.

"Oh, yeah? Come tell me about it *inside* the car. Or so help me God, Angelica."

"Or what?" I tempt him.

Whatever he's trying to accomplish with his threat is sending mixed signals to my body and brain. The anger I feel makes me want to disobey him, fear is begging me to bow down, and the adrenaline rush coursing through my veins wants me to run. I might crumble into pieces right here on the sidewalk. I've tried to avoid another authoritative figure in my life after my father's bullshit, but here I am, attracted to my stalker's commanding tone.

He scoffs at my disobedience. "Angelica," he says slowly. His deep voice is curt and laced with anger. "I'm going to count to five, and if you're not in the car, all hell will break loose, I promise you that." The shiver that goes down my spine sends chills to my core and turns me on at the same time.

"One."

My legs buckle a little, and suddenly, I'm no longer cold but hot—*very hot*. A rush of heat invades my body in flashes, and my dress feels too tight, too warm.

"Two."

His voice is so low I can barely hear him count, but the power he radiates hits me right in the gut. I feel the fabric of my panties getting wetter. At this rate, they will be soaked in no time.

"Three."

My heart starts racing. I'm both terrified and excited as I keep my gaze locked with his. Scared of what he's going to do to me, yet exhilarated by the thrill of defying his threat.

"Four."

One more second to decide whether I get in the car, giving him the satisfaction of a win, or whether I run like my life depends on it.

"Five."

I stop breathing for a fraction of a second as I hear a seatbelt being undone.

"Run."

I turn on my heels and sprint. I race down the street, while holding the bottom of my dress in one hand. I pump my legs as fast as I can in stilettos and look back to see the masked stranger catching up to me.

My calves are on fire and my heels hit the cement heavily, causing pain to radiate up my legs. I tear off my heels as I run and clutch them in the same hand I'm using to hold my dress. My purse slips off my shoulder and I struggle to keep it on.

A thin layer of sweat covers the nape of my neck and a bead trickles down my back as I try to outrun my stalker. It's so dark I can barely see ahead of me. The sound of my feet slapping the asphalt and my ragged breaths is the only noise on the street. I feel like my legs and lungs are going to explode any minute.

I spot a small copse of trees up ahead, so I head toward them, hoping to outrun him. My foot nearly slips on the grass as I glance behind me, but I continue through the wooded area. I can hear his footfalls getting closer. He is only a few feet away. I become frantic, my steps pounding in time with my heartbeat, fast, *too fast*.

Suddenly, everything becomes a blur as I'm tackled to the ground face first, strong arms breaking my fall.

His body is on top of mine, crushing me as I struggle against him, my breaths coming in short gasps. The cool air bites into my lungs and I can feel the movements of his chest on my back, up and down, as he catches his breath. But other than that, he seems unphased by our little sprint.

"You can't outrun a hunter, Angelica. I enjoy the chase," he says wickedly.

"Let me go," I spit, my eyes shutting tight in fear.

He turns me on my back and pins my wrists to the ground above my head with one hand. "I told you not to go against my word, and you did, knowing very well there would be consequences."

He presses his masked cheek on mine, and the coldness of

it sends shivers down my spine. I squirm under him to get out of his hold. I manage to release my arms and I throw them into the air, clawing at my stalker's face to remove his veil. I dig my fingers into his chin, scratching him with my nails. To stop me from moving, he places one of his palms around my neck and holds it there with enough pressure to stunt my breathing and I gag. I scrape at his arms to loosen his grip, but he's relentless. My legs start flailing as panic sets in.

"Please. I can barely breathe," I plead.

"That's the best part," he says into my ear. "Knowing that your fragile life is in my hands is part of the thrill. That if I were to put a little more weight on your chest or squeeze your throat a little harder, I could drain the life right out of you."

"You're an animal!" I choke out. My eyes are filled with tears, but my face isn't the only thing that is wet...*and we both know it.*

I can't move and risk suffocating. The lack of oxygen is going straight to my head, down to my stomach, right to my center. I can't make sense of the effect he's having on my body.

He laughs, wildly, and it sounds primal, raw. "I know you feel the same way. This excites you. I can smell your arousal from here," he whispers into my ear, and my breath stutters. He pushes the fabric of my dress up my legs and lets his fingers trail up my inner thigh.

"No, don't. Let me go," I beg breathlessly. He's two seconds away from forcing himself on me. My mind is on overdrive. I'm panicking. I don't want him to touch me, but my body says otherwise. I don't know who to trust. Mind over matter? Tell that to my throbbing vagina.

He reaches my panties and pushes his thumb right on my clit over the silk. My entire body jolts as if I've been hit with a wave of electricity.

"Stop," I plead. But my voice isn't convincing. Deep down, I want this, but I know it's wrong. *So* wrong.

"Beg," he commands, as he lifts himself off me to allow some air to flow more easily through my chest, but he keeps his finger right on my sweet spot. He squeezes my throat a little tighter. Before I'm able to say anything, he removes his thumb, pushes my panties to the side and dips his fingers right into my opening.

He's cast a spell on me. The intensity of this moment and the unfiltered, uninhibited emotions he's pulling out of me are frightening, but I want more. *Ang, he's forcing himself on you. Get a fucking grip.*

"Please. Please, stop. Let me breathe," I beg, my voice starting to sound ragged. Truth is, we both know I don't really want him to stop.

He doesn't let up and keeps his digits buried deep inside of me. I have the carnal urge to grind against his hand, but my brain keeps telling me this is insane, that I shouldn't want this. I let out a loud snarl of frustration and that only seems to egg him on. Something pokes at my leg, and I realize his dick is pressed right against my thigh, and it's hardening by the second. *Fuck, fuck, fuck.*

He removes his fingers and I sigh in relief. But he slams them right back inside and fingers me with brute force. I lose it.

I kick my legs up, not caring if I die from exhaustion and suffocation, and I attempt to knee him in the balls. Everything I'm doing only encourages him to keep going. This is turning him on. He's sick. *But so are you, Ang,* my mind responds. I squeeze my eyes shut and pray for my inner demons to stay away.

"I'm going to crack you open, Angelica. Leave you bare."

I'm undoubtedly sick because, instead of being repulsed,

my body is reacting differently, and I have no control over it as I feel the build-up of my orgasm. Waves of pleasure hit me, and I focus on them as they get heavier and more intense. It feels heavenly, and the tingle in my lower abdomen gets stronger.

"That's my good girl," he growls as he focuses on my g-spot.

"Oh my god. *Oh my god*," I moan. I stare at him deep in the eyes and there's an unmistakable eagerness in them. He wants to please me, make me come, and it's turning me into a pile of mush.

"Come for me, Angelica. And only then will I let you go. But if you try to run again, I will catch you, and I won't have mercy on you next time. Never play games with the devil."

"Okay," I croak from under him, and then I climax so hard, it hurts.

When I've come back down to earth and the tingle between my legs has lessened, he lets go of my neck, and I scramble off the ground. My stalker gets up in one swift movement like the most sinful-looking dark angel to ever exist.

"Get in the car, Angelica," he commands.

I start walking as he picks up my purse and heels off the grass, staying behind me in case I decide to run off again. *Who says chivalry is dead.*

This time, I don't run.

I slide into the passenger seat, handing my life over to my guardian angel...the devil.

> "Never run from a predator. Even the most behaved of them will have a hard time restraining themselves from chasing after a prey."
> —Patricia Briggs

Unknown

Angelica is stubborn as hell.

But I won't lie and say I didn't enjoy the chase and the adrenaline high I got from seeing her struggle.

I knew she would run. I could see the indecision in her eyes, and I hoped she would try. She doesn't know I'm a runner, a hunter, a predator, and she is my prey. I'm relentless when I want something, and she is the unlucky person caught in the middle of my seductive dance of life and death. They say there's something profound about the relationship between predator and prey. Angelica was withering like a wilting rose under my hold, and then the sweet smell of her arousal traveled up to my nose and triggered an undeniable need to consume her. And I did. *Sort of.* I gave her a taste of what it would be to feel me inside her.

She *physically* fought me. She scratched the sides of my face and I hope I keep the scars forever.

My cock is still throbbing at the thought of her precious life being in my hands.

I finally convinced her to get in my car after she decided to tempt her fate, and she's now sitting next to me, frowning and crying silently. I want to reach over, squeeze her cheeks, and bite her pouty lips until she stops sulking. But I need to let her go through the process of accepting her new reality.

At first, I hadn't recognized the man she was with, but when I saw her walk into the ballroom with him on her arm, I almost charged him like a bull. You would've thought he was a damn matador waving a red cape. I wanted to gouge his eyes out and cut each finger off his dirty fucking hands for touching Angelica. He was looking at her like she was the most beautiful thing he'd ever seen, and although I agree, the thought of him doing something about it made me burn up inside.

I'm aware of her history with Niko. I thoroughly dug up her past. If someone even breathes Angelica's way, I'll know about it. They dated in high school, and he took her virginity. If it were up to him, he would make her his wife. I heard of her father's plan to arrange their marriage before she left the city. I'm not sure if that's still his intention, but it's the last thing I would ever let happen. Which is why I had to put an end to whatever fucking fantasy Niko had in his head by accompanying her to the ball.

It was time for her to meet her *secret admirer*.

Before I realized what I was doing, I'd pushed my way through the crowd of wealthy assholes and followed Angelica right into the women's restroom. I know she isn't dating Niko anymore, but seeing him touching her arms, rubbing her back, and whispering in her ear like a lover over and over made me go apeshit.

I needed to know that she was no longer sleeping with him, and if she still had any feelings for him. The only reason he is still alive is because he's not fucking with what belongs to me.

In the midst of my jealousy, I called her mine. I saw the look of confusion on her face, and for a fraction of a second, her features softened. But her anger resurfaced faster than a speeding bullet.

I don't give a shit if she's mad at me. She needs to know no other man is allowed to touch her now that I'm in the picture, whether she likes it or not. And by wearing the earrings *I* bought her, it's clear that she subconsciously knows I own her.

She just hasn't admitted it yet.

Before driving off, I reach in the back seat and grab a black scarf. Angelica notices the piece of fabric in my hands and her body freezes. "What–what are you planning on doing with that?" she asks, warily.

I play with the silk between my fingers. Her fear fuels me. I want more. "Close your eyes," I order.

She shakes her head. "No, please," she begs. It's getting harder to deny her. The more she begs, the more I want to give her everything she desires. She might be the one at my mercy now, but she doesn't know the lengths I would go for her. It's immeasurable.

"Turn around and close your eyes, Angelica. I'm not going to ask again."

She obliges and I tie the scarf around her eyes. I can't take my mask off until she's blinded. It's not time for her to find out my identity just yet. Plus, where I'm taking her is a surprise.

"Give me your hands," I demand once I'm content with the placement of the covering. She doesn't argue this time and I tie her wrists together with a piece of rope that I pull out of the glove compartment. I can't risk her taking the scarf off while I'm driving. Though, I wish I were tying her up to my bed right now. *Soon enough.*

A little whimper escapes her lips when she realizes she has no way of escaping.

"*Shhhh*, my angel. You're safe with me," I whisper, as I let the back of my hand trace the outlines of her face. She slightly flinches at the touch.

"Where are we going?" she asks, her voice sounding defeated.

"Home." Little does she know; she's coming home with me.

I park my car in the underground parking, and I help Angelica out of the car. Her black gown is covered in dirt and grass, courtesy of her little attempt to escape. But she still looks heavenly. I bend down and slip her stilettos back on because I'm fucking Prince Charming and she is my Cinderella. *Who says I can't be a gentleman?*

I grab her wrists and yank her out of the passenger seat, bringing her flush to my chest. Her sweet rose and peony scent clings to my nose and tears are still flowing down her cheeks.

"You look beautiful when you cry for me, *angeloúdi mou*," I say. Angelica stills before jerking her hands out of mine.

She tries to push me away, and I can't help but smile at her feistiness.

"What did you just call me?" she asks, her tone distraught.

Before she even notices how close I am, I press myself to her. She immediately steps back and her body tenses, goosebumps exploding all over her skin.

"My little angel," I reply, murmuring the words into her neck. "And you better not shove me away again."

"Why do you torment me?" Angelica retorts in a shaky voice. She turns away and I grab her by the arms.

"Because I love seeing how much you want me," I whisper in her hair.

"I don't want you," she breathes.

"Try to convince me otherwise, sweetheart, because your mind and body aren't on the same page." I let the back of my fingers trail down her arms slowly and her breath stutters to a stop. "I see the way your body calls out for me." My hands slip away, but she says nothing.

A car turns into the parking lot, so I lead her to the side and urge her to walk. "Come on." I grab her by the wrist and pull her behind me toward the door.

We walk into the building and the concierge greets us without lifting his eyes. *Smart man. What you don't know won't hurt you.* We hurry into the elevator. Surprisingly, Angelica is being cooperative. I think it might be out of fear. I like that. When we walk into my apartment, she stands at the entrance, unmoving. I guide her to my bedroom and place her at the edge of the bed. "Sit."

"Or what?" she taunts. *There's my firecracker.* My dick twitches at her snarkiness.

"Do you really want to do this again, angel? Did you not learn your lesson earlier? You won't get very far this time," I reply, teasingly.

Angelica sits down, reluctantly. "Who are you?" she asks under her breath. I don't respond. "I'm sick of you trying to control me. You have no power over me," she cries out as she tries to wiggle her hands out of the rope. I catch them and hold on to her wrists.

"Keep telling yourself that if it makes you feel better, my angel. You might not know who I am, but I know exactly who *you* are. And I know *what* you are. That's all that matters," I say bluntly.

"If you're so sure about yourself, then *what* am I?" she argues, and I can almost feel the heat of her anger through her skin. *Good.*

"Mine," I growl, and I let go.

This renders her speechless. She thinks I don't know her, but I do. I know everything there is to know about Angelica's life, but what I'm dying to find out is what makes her truly angry, what makes her churn inside. What makes her smile. What scares her and what turns her on. *Everything.*

"Angelica Hera Kouvalakis. No siblings. You suffered a great loss as a child. The relationship with your father is strained, so you moved away four years ago to start a new life. You went to college at Antium City U and studied Sociology. You're close to your maternal grandparents and your childhood best friends' names are Aria and Gianis. You have history with him, but you never dated. You've had one serious relationship when you were seventeen, with the dickwad I stole you away from earlier. You do hot yoga once a week and you go to the shooting range a few times a week, but Thursdays are your favorite days. You love coffee and cheesecake. You have scars on your wrist hidden by an elastic band you rarely take off..."

Angelica's jaw tightens as I mention all the things I know about her. "Should I keep going, angel?"

She stays silent, so I continue.

"Your three best friends in Antium might not know the truth of who you are and where you come from, but I do." I approach her cautiously so as not to scare her, given her eyes are still covered. She begins to turn her face, sensing me getting closer, but I grab onto her chin before she can move away from me.

"Like I said, I know you. When I want something, I do my research. You might not feel it yet, Angelica, but you're mine and that's something you're going to have to make peace with." I let my fingers caress her cheeks, and I rub her bottom lip with my thumb. "And if you can't, too fucking bad."

Angelica's body language is angry, but her face relaxes into my hold, anyway. Whether she likes it or not, she knows I'm going to get my way and she can't do anything about it.

"There's nothing this world can do to get in the way of my obsession with you," I add.

"What do you want from me?" she asks, tears seeping through the black, silky fabric covering her eyes. A drop travels down her face and I swipe it away. More tears follow and I wish I could take the fear away. Angelica believes I'm out to hurt her. I once was. But when I saw her true colors, or the lack thereof, her darkness consumed me, drew me in, hooked me. She'll realize soon that I'm not the true enemy.

"Everything," I respond as I bend down to lick a stream of salty liquid rolling down her face, making her gasp.

"I have nothing to give."

"You have exactly what I need," I retort.

"And what is it that I have, *stalker*?"

"Your life."

Angelica's mouth opens and closes a few times as she tries to come up with words, but I don't need her to say anything. Sooner or later, she will understand that her life is mine to keep.

I need her for more than I initially planned. She somehow fills the void I didn't know I had.

I want to fucking own her, body and soul. I can't think straight from the physical pull I feel toward her. I've been watching her for weeks, but being this close to her is a game-changer. The sense of familiarity and comfort when she's near messes with my head. I know I shouldn't let my feelings get in the way, but it's too late.

She doesn't know who I truly am. She doesn't even know my full name. Or that I'm going to use her and break her apart. Take the pieces of her life, the shattered bits, and assemble her back together like a puzzle.

Selfishly, I want her all to myself.

I untie the knot of her blindfold and let the scarf fall down her face. It takes a few seconds for her eyes to adjust to the bright light, and when they do, I watch as her whole world turns black again.

"Many of us crucify ourselves between two thieves - regret for the past and fear of the future."
—Fulton Oursler

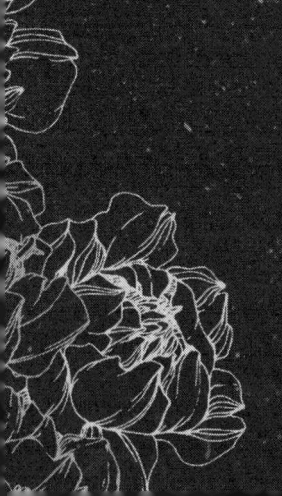

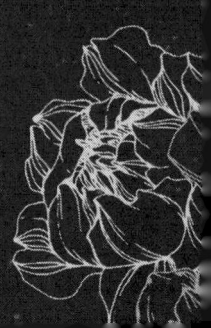

Angelica

*W*hat the hell just happened?

I slowly open my eyes and stare at an unfamiliar ceiling. How did I end up on my back when what felt like seconds ago, I was sitting and conscious? My brain is in a fog as the memories take their own sweet time to re-appear. When I finally remember, panic sets in.

No amount of adrenaline in the world could have roused me enough to stay conscious after I saw my stalker's face. I'd felt a deep gut sickness, a feeling of impending doom, like my body would die from the inside. Now that I'm awake, I still feel like I'm dying at the thought of who I saw when the cloth fell away. I didn't want to believe it, but when he'd called me '*angeloúdi mou,*' bile had risen to the back of my throat. I vividly remembered only one other person calling me that endearment in Greek, but my brain still tried to ignore the link.

Evan. My stalker. Same fucking person.

I feel violated. Evan knew *exactly* who I was when we met at the range, yet he pretended he didn't. I feel like a complete idiot, but I try to give myself some grace. How could I have guessed they were the same person? It's not like our interactions gave anything away. *He knew your name.* I'm so naive.

I'm confused and I don't know how to feel. Now, it makes sense that Evan had an effect on me, as if my subconscious knew he was my secret admirer, the stranger I had been forming a bond with for weeks.

At the masquerade ball, my body remembered him, but I didn't give it a second thought. I recognized the feeling of him pressed against me, the familiarity. The way he softly caressed my skin. The huskiness in his voice when he said, 'you're mine.' His scent. How could I have not realized it was him?

I was so caught up in *him* that I ignored all the signs. I feel like a fool.

"Angelica," a deep voice says from my side. I whip my head toward it and see Evan kneeling by the bed with a glass of water. I jerk my eyes back to the ceiling and squeeze them shut so hard. *No, no, no.*

I feel a slight weight on the bed as Evan sits next to me. He touches my arm and I jolt away from him, crawling backwards toward the headboard. I need to put space between us now before my panic escalates. But it's too late. I inhale sharp breaths, but I can't keep up, as if there's a massive boulder on my chest flattening my lungs. I pant loudly and clutch onto the sheets under me. Tears threaten to fall. I blink a few times and the drops roll down my cheeks. I turn my gaze toward Evan and he's still sitting next to me, unmoving, with a concerned but hard look on his face.

"Angelica," he murmurs again. He hesitantly moves his hand toward me and rests it on my knee. This time, I don't flinch. I can't focus on anything else but my erratic breathing as I struggle to catch my breath. My heart is beating so fast, it feels like it will explode out of my body. I clench my dress and whimper. *Help me.*

"Drink this," Evan commands as he shoves the glass of water in my face. "Please," he adds.

Despite the panic, I still shoot him a death stare. "I'm not taking anything from you," I seethe. "I'd rather die."

Evan looks as if he's seeing red and it reminds me of what happened at Academia. His self-control is slipping. I want to escape before this situation turns sour, but I can't think straight, and my body feels like it's deflating. If I don't calm down soon, I'll lose consciousness again.

Evan puts the cup down on the nightstand and buries his face in his hands, letting out a loud growl as he runs his fingers through his hair. "I fucking did this. This is all my fault," he says angrily.

I'm able to snap out of my panic for a moment. "Yes, it is. How dare you toy with my emotions like a doll? I'm a human being, Evan. Not some prize," I snap, finally regaining control of my anxiety attack through my anger.

I'm relieved to finally know the identity of the person who has been leaving me gifts and notes for weeks. But how can I ignore that he pretended to be two different people? What is his endgame?

"*Angeloúdi mou*," he starts, grabbing onto my fingers, and my breath hitches for a second, but he doesn't stop talking, his eyes steady on mine. "When I first saw you, I had the strongest desire to touch you. Your entire existence called to me, and I knew I had to find out who you were, dig deep into your life, and figure out all the details that make you who you are. I still have a way to go, but what I've learned so far has affected me so much, I can barely function. Just the feeling of your hand sends signals to parts of my body I don't want awakened. Mainly my heart. They go straight to my chest and thoughts, clouding my judgment. But as much as I want to stop them, I can't make myself do it."

All the things he's mentioned, I feel too. I'm terrified and unsure about what the future holds, but a part of me refuses to let go of my feelings for him. Although I know I should be running for the hills, I stay seated exactly where I am, hand in hand with Evan. The stranger I met at the range and my stalker morphing into one. The intensity of my current emotions makes no sense to me. How can I go from barring off love and relationships, to being involved with someone so deeply I don't know if I'll ever make it out. I need time to figure this out.

I break my silence. "I want to go home, please."

I expect pushback, but Evan simply nods. "I'll take you. I just need to make a stop first."

"her,
because she
makes life poetry,
she turns every bit
of it into art"
—butterflies rising

Evander

Angelica gives me her hand, and I lead her out of the bedroom. I take a good look at her appearance, and she seems to still be in shock. I don't blame her. I knew she wouldn't take the news lightly. I blame myself for letting the situation get out of hand. It was stupid of me to allow her to think me and her 'guardian angel' weren't the same person, but what started as a simple plan to get information on my target turned into an obsession.

I didn't know that my pawn—the main piece I needed to complete my plan successfully, the person I would use for my own advantage—would be someone like *her*. I keep reminding myself that she's Peter's daughter. She's tied to the man who took my uncle's life so unapologetically. In our world, people kill and torture each other more often than necessary. I'm one of those people. But my uncle is where I draw the line. Losing men is always hard, but losing family is harder.

But that changes nothing. I still want Angelica. I have a crazy fixation on owning her and making her mine for good. I'm royally fucked.

Now that she knows it's me, we can work on getting her to accept it. I shake my head. *You've gone soft, Evan*, my mind tells me. I almost *kissed* her. That's how much she's affecting me.

But seeing her have a panic attack right in front of me made me feel like a piece of shit for being the cause. For a moment, my rationality came back to me, and I seriously considered toning it down a bit. *Maybe I can convince her to want me?* No. I don't care if she tries to push me away. She will be mine. I can't imagine what she'll do when she ultimately finds out the truth of my plan. But that's for another day. *One step at a time.*

We walk into the kitchen, and suddenly, I'm hungry, and not for food. I'm starving for the woman in front of me, looking like a whole goddamn meal. Her cheeks are stained with tears, and mascara is smudged around her eyes and runs down her face. Her dress has grass stains all over. Her hair is a jumbled mess. But still, when she's around me, all I want to do is rip her fucking clothes off and tie her to my bed.

This is the closest I've ever been to wanting a relationship. I'm not supposed to *want* this. I have to stay clear-minded, yet I can't help myself. My destiny doomed me with this very predicament.

I need her to fall in love with me for my plan to work, but I can't allow myself to fall for her. My feelings have to stay out of this. But I find myself wanting to do things to make her happy. I should be focusing on my plan, but I can't take my eyes off her to concentrate on anything else.

I don't date. I don't fall in love.

I fuck and move on.

Even that I don't do often.

Her presence brings waves of joy that wash my burdens away until I only see her, my muse, the ink to my pen, the pen to my paper, the words to my page. I want to bathe in her essence.

Angelica glances around my penthouse while I drown in my thoughts, and the look of awe and innocence on her face makes me want to bend her over the kitchen counter and pound into her mercilessly. I'm craving to be inside her. My cock awakens and I grunt as I try to wriggle it away without being noticed. I need to get us out of here before I fuck her. Once again, I remind myself this is not the way I want our first time to be.

"Let's go." I motion to the door.

"Where are we, anyway?" she asks under her breath.

"Home. *My* home," I specify.

"Oh. Am I the first woman you've brought here too, then?" she asks, her tone snarky. Immediately, I notice her wince at the question. It seems to have slipped out of her mouth before she had the chance to stop it. I snigger internally. She'll warm up to me in no time.

"Yes, you are," I reply matter-of-factly. *Soon, this will be your home, too.*

I wasn't ready to end the night. I knew I wouldn't get a word out of her if I dropped her home, so I took her to my office at Academia in the hopes of continuing our conversation.

Angelica spent the entire drive looking out the window, her fingers interlaced on her lap. Her chest visibly expanded with every breath. She was no longer experiencing a panic attack, but I could tell her state was fragile. Yet, my angel is strong. She will fight me, I expect her to. But deep down, she knows she can't deny me, she will let me have her.

Within five minutes of arriving, a loud commotion breaks out outside my office door, and Dion barges in with Xander right behind him, both looking distressed. I recognize the expression on Dion's face. Trouble is looming. I jump out of my chair and grab the gun I keep hidden in my desk drawer. I quickly check that it's loaded and remove the safety before I slip it into the waistband of my pants. Angelica's facial expression changes when she sees me pull out the weapon, but I ignore it.

"Dion, Xander. *Ti tréhei?*" I ask. *What's wrong?*

"There are people outside," Dion responds.

"We can't tell who they are yet, but it's trouble, boss," Xander adds.

Shit. I've been expecting pushback, waiting for someone to strike. But this is the worst possible timing.

"*Kripse to korítsi. Tóra,*" I order. *Hide the girl. Now.*

I turn to Angelica. "Angelica, listen to me. Dion and Xander are going to take you downstairs, and I need you to stay there. Don't come back up until one of us gets you. Can you do that for me? Please," I plead.

She looks at me with a stunned expression on her face, but I don't have time to explain. She's trembling and I can tell she's worried.

"It'll be okay," I assure her. "I don't know who they are or what they want, but I'll deal with it. I just need you to stay safe, just in case." I try to reason with her. She's no stranger to peril and has been in threatening circumstances over the course of her life. I know she understands the potential severity of the situation, but I can't jeopardize her safety.

Her gaze lingers on me, reading the plea in my eyes, and she nods. Dion and Xander gesture for her to follow them and they disappear down the side stairwell. Seb and Greg walk into the office seconds later, freeing their weapons from their holsters. We head down to meet our guests in the lobby.

When we reach the bottom of the stairs, three men are standing next to the bar. Leon is behind it, pouring glasses of *ouzo*. I recognize Jurian, one of Peter Kouvalakis' cronies.

I curse under my breath as I approach them. Dion finally appears with Xander in tow, and I look back at them. My second-in-command slightly nods his head, a silent confirmation that Angelica is safe. If her father's goons see her, it would start a war, and my plan would be ruined.

I can't risk losing her.

The goal is to find out what they want and get them the fuck out of here as soon as possible. The boys and I cautiously walk toward them, prepared for any of them to make a move.

"To what do I owe this pleasure? I knew I had the best ouzo in town, but I would've expected a call first," I sneer, looking at the two other men I don't recognize. "Where's your other half, Jurian? Did you leave Gianis at home?" Jurian scoffs and puts his drink down on the bar. "I'm surprised he isn't here to do your boss's bidding, since he's the enforcer, and not you," I add, knowing the hidden insult would throw him off his game.

"Fuck off, Evander," Jurian spits, clearly holding back from responding further to my jab.

"What are you doing in Old Cebrene, Jurian? You're on my territory. That's pretty fucking ballsy if you ask me. I could put a bullet in your head right now and not bat an eyelash, especially after what your boss did to my uncle. So, I suggest you tell me what the fuck you want before I kill all of you."

Jurian picks his glass back up and raises it, snickering, and the two others follow. "We were in the area. Thought we'd drop in," he says, casually.

I ought to kill the son of a bitch for coming all the way here to taunt me. I know what he's doing. He wants to get a reaction out of me and push me to make the first move to retaliate. That would open the door for Peter and his men to wage war on us. There's no fucking way I'm letting that happen. Peter already decided his fate when he killed my uncle, but I'm getting back at him on *my* terms. It would've been easier for us to strike back right after Ignatius's murder, but it would've caused too much bloodshed. Silent but lethal is my tactic. *Slow and steady wins the race.*

Dion asks Leon to pour three more glasses of ouzo. He hands them to us, and I point to one of the VIP booths. "Well then, let's take advantage of this time together, shall we?" I say, begrudgingly.

We walk toward the booth, aware of who is next to us and who is not, and we take a seat. I need to know what Jurian wants so I can send him on his way and get back to Angelica.

He clears his throat and ends the silence. "I heard you're taking over for Ignatius." He takes a swig of his drink, studying me.

"You heard correctly," I reply, and take a sip of my own drink.

"I guess it turned out good for you now that the whole Vasilakis clan is dead, huh?"

I frown, my temples pounding from my rage. "What the fuck did you say?"

I bang my glass down on the table and stand up from my seat. Everyone else at the table rises, too, hands on their weapons. Jurian stays seated and laughs.

"Looks like I hit a nerve."

"Keep the Vasilakis name out of your fucking mouth, *poutánas yos.*" *Son of a bitch.*

"Why do you care? You benefited from their demise," he says.

"Ignatius was like family to me, and I will not let you slander his name." Though I'm seeing red, this all confirms that the other families still don't know I'm blood-related to my uncle. *Good.* My nostrils flare as I look at him. "Now, tell me what you want and get the *fuck* out of here."

Jurian sets his finished glass on the table and rises from his chair. "I just wanted to see an old friend."

"*Fáe skatá karióli.* Don't patronize me." *Eat shit, asshole.*

Jurian swings his head back and lets out a loud, menacing laugh. "You were Ignatius's pet, Evander, and that's all you'll ever be. No one in this world is going to take you seriously, especially not Peter. His plans are too big and important to let a minion like you ruin them."

My rage passes the point of no return, and I reach back to grab my gun. Dion tries to stop me, but I'm too angry to listen. I pull it out of my waistband, cock it, and the other men do the same as I square up to Jurian, pointing the gun to the middle of his forehead, too fast for him to even make a move. His two companions are rendered helpless by Dion and Xander pointing their weapons at them from behind me.

"I will not lose a second of sleep if I let this bullet fly, so don't fuck with me, Jurian."

I press the gun into his skin hard enough that he stumbles backwards.

"I came here to inform you that Peter won't let you get in the way of years of work. Ignatius was nothing but an annoying gnat that had to be dealt with, and I would highly suggest not to follow in his footsteps, because change is coming," Jurian seethes.

"I don't give a fuck about what he has planned, and I'm certainly not going to stand down. So, tell your boss that if he has a problem with me, he can deal with it himself. Stay the fuck off my turf. I'm done with this conversation."

I put my weapon back in my waistband and turn my back on him to walk away when I hear another gun cock.

I don't have time to make a move before I hear Dion yell at me to take cover. I quickly turn around to see Jurian pointing his gun at me. "I warned you," he says.

Jurian pulls the trigger and the gun fires. The deafening sound of shots echoes around me, and I reach for my weapon to fight back. The next second, I'm tackled to the ground by Xander, and a pool of blood starts forming under our bodies. I slowly realize I've been shot, but I don't know where.

As the adrenaline starts to dissipate, pain explodes in my shoulder.

The pulse in my gushing wound is intense. The pain is excruciating, and my breaths become erratic. I'm soaked in sweat and numb everywhere but my shoulder.

Xander is still laying on top of me and I can feel his labored breaths, but he doesn't move. Dion runs over to us with Seb and Greg, and they slowly slip him off me and he groans in pain.

"*GAMOTO*. They've both been shot!" Dion yells. "Leon, call Dr. Pappas. NOW."

I try to get up and I grimace in pain. I only manage to turn my head toward Xander and see him lying next to me with his eyes closed. *Fuck.*

Jurian and his companions are nowhere to be found.

If Peter wants a war, he's going to get one now. No fucking holds barred.

But there's no way I'm sacrificing Angelica.

"The girl," I croak.

Right at that moment, I see Angelica burst out of the stairwell door, panting like she was running for her life. She looks around the room, her eyes wide, and her face goes stark white with shock when we lock eyes.

"Trust is like blood pressure. It's silent, vital to good health, and if abused it can be deadly."
—Frank Sonnenberg

Angelica

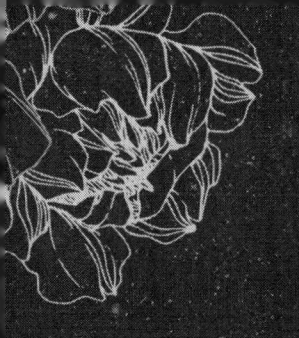

When Evan asked me to wait in the basement while he dealt with whoever was downstairs, I pictured the worst. My father used to send me to my room when he had unexpected guests and it always ended in a bloodbath.

Dion and Xander escort me into the elevator, and I can't bring myself to say a word.

The tension is so thick, it feels like there's a fourth person in the small space.

Dion looks legitimately worried, his body rocking from side to side. Xander stands behind me, still as a statue. He was the other man seated with Evan when I first came to the club that night, but I hadn't properly met him until now. I wish it were in different circumstances.

We arrive at the bottom floor and the doors open. It's dark and humid, and I hesitate before I step out. I feel the light touch of a hand on my back, and I turn to Dion.

"It'll be okay," he says, gently. I walk out of the lift and the door closes behind me.

The radio silence in the basement is eerie. It's oddly clean down here. It smells like bleach and laundry detergent. I walk around the space with my arms crossed over my chest, feeling a chill down my spine. There's nothing here except a table and chair. The ceiling is riddled with pipes, and I notice chains and a rope hanging from one of the larger ones in the middle of the room. I walk up to the chains, and I wonder what kind of activities happen down here that require shackles. After walking in circles a few times, I take a seat at the table and wait.

I don't know how long it's been, having left my phone in the office upstairs, but I'm startled out of my confused state by the sound of commotion coming from upstairs. I hear a loud bang, but the sound is muffled, and within a couple seconds, multiple gunshots go off, and I immediately go into panic mode.

Evan is up there, and he could be hurt.

The gunshots cease and silence invades the space again. He specifically asked me to stay down here until someone comes back. But what if he's injured? What if he's *dead*?

Oh, hell.

I run to the elevator we used to come down here and push the call button frantically, but nothing happens. The light goes red, but I hear no hint of it moving. That's when I notice it's controlled by a keypad. *Damn it*, I don't have the code.

I turn around, looking for another exit, and see a door tucked in the corner of the room. I rush to it and desperately pull on the handle, pleading to God to let me out of this dungeon. On the fourth pull, the door cracks open and I jerk it with all my power.

I sprint up the stairs and burst out of the door on the main floor.

I'm in total paralysis as I drink in the sight before me. I watch the scene unfold as though it's happening in slow-motion.

There is blood everywhere.

Sebastian and Gregory are walking around, checking the main area with their guns out, ready to fire at any given moment if a threat appears. Tables are flipped upside down and chairs are scattered on the floor. Trails of blood lead from one of the booths to the entrance. Leon is at the bar making a phone call.

There is no sight of Evan or Xander.

Dion is hunched over something on the floor, but I can't see who or what is lying there, until he moves to look back at me and I see Evan on the floor, surrounded by blood, his face pale.

I gasp as my hand flies to my chest. My heart feels like it's about to stop and my world feels like it's crumbling. *No, no, no, no.*

This can't be happening. He cannot die. I didn't even have the chance to get to know him, enjoy him, be a part of his life. To fully get angry at him for what he did. I'm still hurt and distraught by the news of him pretending to be two different people, for having barged into my life so selfishly. He acted on his own accord and didn't care how it would affect me. As much as I enjoyed the attention from him as my stalker, it doesn't excuse his behavior. He still deceived me. So, yes, I'm mad. But do I want him to die? No. I'm not ready for whatever this is between us to end.

And if anyone were to kill him, it should be me. I deserve it.

An explosion of adrenaline bursts within me and I run toward him, despite the warnings for me to stay away. I ignore them all and I sink to my knees in front of Evan.

"Oh my god." I scan his body to see where he has been

injured and see a large bullet wound in his chest near his left shoulder. "*No.*" My hands tremble as I savagely tear off the top part of my dress and place it over the wound, pressing down hard to stop the bleeding.

"Somebody call an ambulance!" I scream.

Xander is lying on his stomach next to Evan, his back covered with blood. I can't see where his injuries start and end.

"What the fuck happened?" I shout to no one in particular, and I can feel anger bubbling inside of me.

Evan's eyes flicker. He's close to losing consciousness. *Fuck.*

"Whoever did this won't get away with it," I whisper, the rage seeping through my words. He squeezes my hand and tries to speak, but I stop him by putting my finger up to his mouth. "I need you to save your energy to stay alive. I'm not letting you leave me."

Leon walks over and informs us that the doctor is on his way.

"Doctor?" I ask. I turn to Dion. "They need to go to a *hospital*. They are bleeding out, for God's sake!" I shout, my tone clearly frantic.

"We can't go to a hospital, Angelica. Do you know what they'll do once they find out they've been shot? They'll call the police and start a whole investigation, and that's the last thing Evan needs."

I don't break eye contact with Dion. When my father used to tell his men not to go to the hospital, it usually meant that some shady shit was involved. I can't help but wonder what Evan has gotten himself into. First, he brought me back to Academia, a club in the heart of Old Cebrene, an area controlled by the Vasilakis family. Could he be involved with them? Second, he behaved like he owned the place. Third, the basement looked like a torture dungeon. There's something he's not telling me, and I need to get to the bottom of it fast.

My life might be in danger, and I already have enough on my plate from dealing with my father's wrongdoings. I'm not letting anything come between me and my freedom again. For now, though, there's only one thing that matters, and it's making sure Evan comes out alive.

I nod and turn my attention back to Evan, who is drifting in and out of sleep and I grab his face. "Evan, please. Stay awake. Keep your eyes on me," I plead. "The doctor will be here soon."

I give instructions to Leon to keep Xander awake. He looks in much worse condition than Evan. It looks like he jumped in front of Evan to protect him. It would be heartbreaking if he didn't make it.

Dion comes back with two wet rags and hands one to Leon and me. I run the cloth over Evan's forehead, and he tries to smile. His mouth barely rises, but it makes me forget that my heart is bleeding.

I might not know what to call this thing between us, but my heart seems to know, and I can't let him die in my arms.

A few minutes later, the doctor arrives with two helpers, and they immediately get to work setting up IVs and laying out all the equipment to start operating on the men.

They carefully place Evan and Xander on separate tables, give them some anesthetic, and start meticulously extracting the bullets from the wounds.

I sit at a table far enough to not interfere, but close enough that I can keep an eye on Evan. After a couple moments, it dawns on me that half of my top is missing, and my bra is exposed. I timidly cover myself with my arms.

I don't know how I managed to do it, probably out of sheer panic, but I tore the top half of my dress almost to shreds to use on Evan, leaving me almost topless. I want to hide under a rock. I'm half-naked, while surrounded by strangers. Dion sees me fidgeting in my seat and joins me at the table.

"Here." He takes off his suit jacket and tosses it at me.

"Thanks," I say, avoiding all eye contact.

"Let's agree not to remind Evan that I let you strip in front of us to save his life." He chuckles nervously, playing with the collar of his shirt.

"It won't end well for you, huh?" I say, as I teasingly nudge his shoulder with mine.

"Nope. He'll hunt me down and gouge my eyes out."

"At least you've just confirmed he's seven shades of crazy with everyone, and not only with me," I state.

Dion shakes his head. "You've seen nothing yet, which is why I need you to do me this solid."

"Your secret is safe with me." I mime zipping my mouth shut, locking it, and throwing away the key.

He laughs and I suddenly remember how defeated Aria sounded the last time I spoke to her. He was the last person to see her, so I figure he might know something.

"Hey, did something happen with Aria when we were here a few nights ago?" I ask, innocently.

Dion awkwardly shifts in his seat. "Um, no. We stayed for a little while longer. Then, I took her home. Why?"

He's acting suspicious. They're both being secretive about that night, so there must be something they're not telling me. "No reason. I spoke to her recently, and she seemed a little spaced out."

"Well, nothing bad happened on my watch," Dion confirms.

I nod and decide not to push the matter. I wrap Dion's jacket tighter around my body and debate what to do or say next when he interrupts my thoughts.

"You know he'll be fine, right? He's bounced back from worse." I can't imagine anything worse than being in a gunfight and getting shot. What has Evan been up to?

"I hope so," I reply.

I'm not ready to lose him.

After removing the bullet lodged in Evan's shoulder, they moved him up to the bedroom in his office and hooked him up to IVs for hydration and morphine for the pain.

He's been passed out for a few hours, but the doctor said he should recover fairly quickly. I'm exhausted, but I don't want to leave Evan's side.

There were only fragments of the bullet left in his shoulder since it flew out the other side when he was shot, and it miraculously didn't damage anything important, or puncture an artery. Xander's recovery will take much longer, since he took the brunt of the attack, but he's stable and should be back to himself with most of his mobility in a few months. When the doctor told us, a flood of relief washed through me, and Dion's face lit up. I couldn't imagine having to tell Evan that his friend succumbed to his injuries trying to save him.

The doctor will stay on the premises until Evan wakes up, and Dion will be here too. But I still can't make myself go home.

I get off the couch in his office and go to the bedroom door. Even though Evan is attached to monitors, I still check up on him occasionally to make sure he's still breathing. Despite the state he's in, he looks so peaceful lying on his back, fast asleep.

Something tells me to enter the room, so I walk in on tiptoes, careful not to make a sound, and I gently lie on the bed next to him.

The feeling of the plush mattress under me and the steady

beeping of Evan's vitals on the machine lull me to sleep. I hear faint noises in the background, but my body is exhausted and I'm not able to wake up.

My eyes snap open and I realize I'd fallen asleep in Evan's bed while watching over him. I blink my eyes a few times to clear up my sight and they're met with someone's stare. Evan is still in bed next to me, but he's awake and looking right at me.

"Hi, angel," he says softly.

I slowly sit up and pat my hair down to get rid of any stray strands that might've gotten frizzy during my nap and straighten out my shirt. Evan doesn't take his eyes off me for a second and my body starts to heat, color rising to my cheeks.

He does a once-over of what I'm wearing, and I remember I have his clothes on. Dion told me to look in Evan's closet, so I grabbed a pair of joggers and a t-shirt. I haven't showered yet, but I needed to get out of that torn and soiled dress.

"I'm sorry. I should've asked first, but my dress was filthy." He smirks and lowers his gaze but doesn't respond. "I didn't mean to fall asleep. I came in to check on you and—"

"You stayed," he states, cutting me off mid-sentence.

"Of course, I did. I couldn't leave you like this. I wanted to make sure you were okay."

"I'm sorry you had to witness that. The club is usually a safe place. I would've never brought you here if I knew there would be a threat." The words come out strained, and I know he's in pain, in more ways than one.

"I've seen worse, Evan. I was just... When I saw you laying

on the floor, soaked in blood, I thought you were going to die," I say faintly.

Evan smiles. "No, sweetheart. I'm not leaving you, yet. We're just getting started."

An hour later, Evan finally convinces me to leave his side, claiming it wouldn't do him any good if I don't get some proper sleep and food. He orders Dion to take me home, causing a whole other ordeal, because he didn't want to leave Evan's side either. But the boss always gets what he wants. Evan pleads his case: he doesn't trust anyone else other than his brother and second-in-command to get me home safely.

"Please, trust me, *angeloúdi mou*. I'll be okay," he says.

I do trust him, and it feels like an odd concept right now. So much has happened in so little time, I'm sure it'll be a lot to handle once I make sense of it all. But there's one thing I confidently felt the second I met Evan. Security. I even recognized the same feeling when he was stalking me. I felt safe, and that's not an emotion that usually comes easily for me. My brain believes that most people are out to betray me, but my heart wants to believe that Evan wouldn't deceive me again. Now that he's come clean about who he truly is, we can start on a clean slate. It's been a short time, but I'm ready to put myself on the line.

I really hope it doesn't backfire on me.

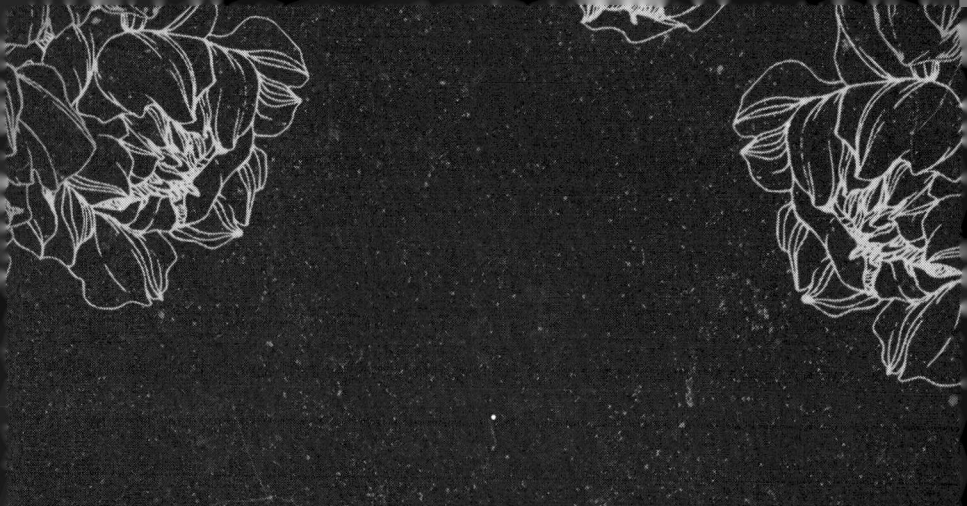

"Always wear a smile because you never know who is watching."
—Gracie Gold

Angelica

It's been twenty-one days since I last saw Evan. And it's been twenty-one days of texting back and forth, all day and night.

He messages me when he wakes up, up until he goes to bed, and keeps me updated on his injury. Two days after the shooting, he was cleared to move back into his penthouse to continue healing. That same day, I came home to a bouquet of peonies and a poem that filled my chest with butterflies.

> There's something about feeling
> devoid of someone.
> There's something about feeling
> devoid of someone.
> No matter how much you try,
> the hole doesn't fill.
> Nothing compares
> to the real thing.
> You.

I'd missed being on the receiving end of these love tokens.

Since finding out it had been him all along, the absence of his gifts and attention was even stronger. The lack of a presence looming in the shadows created an emptiness. For the first time, it felt lonely not having a ghost around me.

I was ready to scold him for not following the doctor's orders, but he assured me that he'd sent someone else to leave the flowers. The need to see him increased as he filled my screen with the most meaningful words, leaving me weak, but filling me with power.

Evan: My bed here doesn't smell like you. Amidst all the chaos, that was the only thing keeping me sane.

I vividly remember falling asleep next to him while he slept off the sedation and waking up to his piercing hazel eyes boring into my soul. I could see pain, confusion, and awe. His eyes spoke a thousand words, revealing what his tongue could never express. It felt like I'd caught something I wasn't supposed to see, but instead of turning away, I stared back. I can still feel his lingering gaze on my skin.

I need to see him, but I don't want to impact his recovery with my presence.

Through our many conversations, I learned that it's hard for him to sit still and not be productive. He's had to delegate his workload to Dion until he's able to go back to work, and that quickly turned him into a helicopter boss. Dion soon had enough of the micromanaging and threatened to block his number. I couldn't help but laugh.

I lie in bed restless, thinking of what has happened in the past three weeks, as every moment runs through my mind, repeatedly. Ever since uncovering Evan's true identity, I've had a hard time coming to terms with him being both my stalker and the man I fell in lust with at the shooting range.

You care about him. I finally admit to myself.

But does he? It might just be an infatuation, and like everything new, the allure could fade when it's no longer exciting. I shouldn't run into the arms of obsession if it'll eventually wither away.

Evan's life is still a huge mystery. I've never heard of him, and I don't know which family he comes from, but if he was ever involved in the mafia, I'd like to think I would've known.

Then again, I was gone for four years and cut all ties with my father. Before I moved away to Antium City, I was checked out and only going through the daily motions. I barely left the house, other than to accompany my father around, and I was never privy to conversations.

My mind goes back to the night of the gala. All I can think about is the way Evan looked at me from across the ballroom, and I feel a mixture of frustration and lust. Frustration, because he had no right to accuse me of doing something wrong by being there with someone else. Lust, because the sensation of his gaze on my skin still sends ripples of excitement through my body.

Those same feelings had surfaced when I saw him at Academia, and he'd pierced my soul with his claiming gaze. That look had set me on fire, and I knew I didn't want to be touched by any other man in the club that night, or ever again, for that matter.

He'd looked at me like I was his. His eyes had feasted on my every move, and I couldn't help but feel desired. I wanted him to stop watching me, but at the same time, I'd loved the way his eyes had devoured me with such greediness. The tension between us was too much then, and it's too much now as I lie in bed alone.

My phone rings and snaps me out of my daze. I hastily grab it and see Evan's name on the screen.

Speaking of the devil.

I let it ring once more before I swipe to answer, my voice low and husky. "Hi."

"Angelica," he replies, his voice smooth like butter. "Am I interrupting something?" he asks.

"No...I'm just lying in bed."

"Hmm...thinking of me, I hope," he flirts.

"Just a little. But don't get too excited," I flirt back.

"I wanted to hear your voice."

"Oh... Well, I wanted to hear yours, too," I whisper.

"Have a good night, *angeloúdi mou*," he says, right before hanging up, and I'm left speechless. *That's it?*

Evan isn't a man of many words, but his intensity makes my insides scream. I can feel the blood rushing through my veins from the strength of my beating heart. I get up and take a lukewarm shower, hoping to cool myself off. Fresh and clean, I change into a slip dress and lie back in bed.

All thoughts of him start to resurface. *Oh, for god's sake.*

I can't get away from him. I think about the way he eyed me up in the ballroom, the fire in his eyes when he noticed Niko touching me and whispering in my ear. The same blaze that had erupted when I'd danced with the stranger at the club. Both times, his gaze had followed my lips every time I spoke or took a sip of my drink. It still boggles my mind that the resemblance didn't click immediately.

I can't help but close my eyes and my body hums to the thought of him.

My fingers lift to my neck, and I caress my skin. I gently slide them down my body, over my hardening nipples visible through the silk of my dress. I stop at my right breast and squeeze it, wishing it was Evan touching me.

My other hand slowly travels up my thigh, releasing shivers through me. I picture his tattooed hands all over me, touching me in all the right places, and heat rushes through my body, sending an ache right to my swollen bundle of nerves.

More.

My hand goes to the edge of my panties, and I can feel the dampness through the fabric. With my right hand still caressing my breasts, I push my thong to the side and touch my clit. I instantly moan.

Needing to release the pressure, I open my legs wider and work my finger in circles over the little bud. I picture Evan hovering over me, using his hands instead of mine, and the pleasure intensifies.

I need more.

My fingers slide down to my opening and I drag the wetness up my folds. I close my eyes and imagine him whispering in my ear, "Show me how you like it, angel."

The thought alone is enough for me to ease my index and middle fingers inside of me. I gasp as I work my digits in and out, removing them to slide my arousal over my center, and I use my thumb to draw circles on it. The idea of Evan touching me only sends more ripples of pleasure through my body. "Oh, god, yes. *Yes.*"

I don't even care that I'm being obnoxiously loud. I live alone and this tension needs to be released. *Badly.*

My hips start moving to the rhythm of my fingers as the husky voice in my head whispers, "Good girl. Fuck your fingers for me." This tips me off the edge, and my breaths become ragged. The tension is bubbling inside me, and I'm ready to explode. My moans get louder as my orgasm overwhelms me. Release hits me, and I call out his name. "Evan." I shudder as I wind down from the wave of pleasure, gently removing my fingers. I rest my arms alongside my body and breathe through the aftermath of my climax.

Suddenly, a penetrating gaze tickles my senses. My head

whips around, and I jerk up on the bed. Evan is standing at the entrance of my bedroom, leaning against the door, his injured arm crossed at his chest in a sling. I draw in a breath and clutch my chest.

"Evan!" I shout. "*Ti sto diáolo?*" *What the hell?* "How long have you been standing there?" I ask, frantically, my face turning several shades of red. Did he see everything? Did he hear me moaning out his name? *Oh my god.*

"Long enough to see the grand finale," he says through a smirk, pushing himself off the door. "Do you always call out my name when you come, angel?"

I should feel panicked that he's here, but I get a whiff of his woodsy and minty smoke scent as he walks over to me, and it puts me at ease.

"No." I shift uncomfortably as I make my way off the bed. I need to get out of this compromising position as quickly as possible. I barely make it to the edge when Evan appears right in front of me. I gasp at his speed.

"Don't move," he orders as he grabs the hand I used to pleasure myself. He shoves my fingers in his mouth and pops them out, making a sound of satisfaction as he tastes my juices. My eyes widen.

"You taste so fucking good, *kitten.*" *Oh, god.*

"With your wide, innocent eyes, and the way you purr when you call out my name. So soft and sweet," he says as he pinches my chin gently, using the tip of his thumb to rub my bottom lip. "Like a cat, you are sacred and should be worshiped. But I see the viciousness inside you, and I can't wait to see the lioness you become when you are cornered."

I shudder. This man has a way with words that can make your insides turn into a pile of mush. Evan is a Big Bad Wolf, but I am not afraid of him. He doesn't drag me down or weaken me, he fills me with a rush of so much feeling, reminding me I'm alive.

His gaze meets mine before his eyes travel down my body. He stops at my chest, where my hardened nipples poke through my slip dress. I blush and lift my arm to hide my breasts, but he grabs my wrist and stops it midair.

"Don't you ever hide from me, Angelica. Let me stare. I love watching you."

Such a double entendre. I wonder how much he's seen while stalking me. The thought of someone's eyes on me didn't bother me before, so it shouldn't now, but I can't help feeling annoyed at how he decided to impose on my life and now force himself into my home like he owns the place. Like he owns *me*.

I pull out of his grip and cross my arms over my chest. I raise my eyebrows. "You're supposed to be at home resting, Evan."

"I've done enough healing for a fucking lifetime. And I do what I please," he says, raising his eyebrows in return.

"Right." I let out a huff of air. "You didn't have to sneak up on me like that. It's an invasion of privacy," I say, angrily.

He grabs a handful of my hair and runs his fingers all the way down the strands. His hand travels to the side of my face, and he grazes his thumb over my cheek, sending tingles down my body. Then, he tips my head back and wraps his palm around my neck.

"You need to accept that you're just as messed up as me, angel. You enjoy this torment. You yearn to be watched, pursued, and captured. You want me to destroy you in every possible way. And I *will*. As soon as you stop playing games," he answers, his grip on me tighter.

I gulp and let out a soft whimper. He is so close to me, I can barely stand it.

"I *needed* to see you, so I came. Three long weeks without seeing your beautiful face was torture."

He tightens his hold again and I feel my heartbeat pulse in my throat. "No injury could keep me away from you any longer." His very presence steals the air from my lungs.

"You should've never seen me in that private moment. You don't have the right to see me like that," I argue weakly as I try to shuffle backward. He catches my ankle, pulls me down the bed, and I yelp. "Evan!"

My butt is at the edge, and he hovers over my body with one arm, speaking softly into my ear. "How do I not have the right to see you touch yourself when it's my name you're calling, *angeloúdi mou?*"

In one movement, he lays his weight on top of me and starts grinding his crotch between my legs. I immediately lift my hips to meet his thrusts and curse at myself for reacting so quickly to his every touch. The closeness is almost unbearable.

His forehead is nearly touching mine and his scent fills my nose. The hardness of his length grazes my center. Swift aftershocks rock my body from my recent orgasm as he hits my sweet spot.

"All the lights were turned off, so I thought you were sleeping. Little did I know, you were awake. *Very much* awake. Screaming *my* name."

He buries his face in my neck, his breath teasing the skin, and he laughs sinfully. I blink. He's got a point, but I'm still bothered by his arrogance. Still angry that he thinks he can get away with everything.

Several seconds go by before I muster up a response, and as I open my mouth to speak, he suddenly gets off the bed. He closes his eyes, and I can sense his struggle as he inhales harshly. Had he stayed on top of me any longer, he would've likely been deep inside me any moment, yet he continues to hold himself back. As much as I want to indulge my urges, it might be best this way.

I sit up, already feeling the absence of his weight.

"I wanted to witness your beauty. Be reminded of your smell. Feel your skin."

He sighs heavily, almost in defeat, like he just admitted something to himself. He's allowing his vulnerability to poke through his tough exterior, and it makes my heart flutter. It takes courage to reveal your heart.

He bends over and rests his head on mine for an instant, then presses his lips to my forehead, giving me the softest kiss. He pulls away, hesitantly, and walks out of my bedroom, glancing back at me as he disappears in the hallway. He marches down the stairs, and I hear him leave through the front door.

Unable to move, I stare at my ceiling. I want to push him away, but the pull I feel toward him is unstoppable.

I close my eyes and eventually drift off to sleep, Evan showing up once again, in my dreams.

"No matter how much cats fight, there always seem to be plenty of kittens." —*Abraham Lincoln*

Evander

*F*uck.

It took everything in me to leave Angelica last night. She was even more beautiful than when I had last seen three weeks ago.

I feel this magnetic pull toward her that's almost impossible to ignore. I can't stop thinking of the moment I woke up from surgery after the shooting and saw her lying in bed next to me. She was asleep, her forehead slightly creased, as if in concern. I'd reached over, wincing from the pain, and caressed her soft skin. The thought of waking up to her every morning didn't seem so far-fetched anymore. She had stayed and taken care of me, and Dion confirmed that she hadn't wanted to leave my side at all. I had to force her to go home. I don't know what I would have done if she'd been found by her father's men. They wouldn't have hurt her, but my identity would've been leaked prematurely, and all my progress ruined. Our trust broken.

Once she finds out who I really am, I might lose her for good. I'm not ready for that to happen yet.

I wish I could say that the thought of failing my uncle bothers me more than the thought of losing her.

But it doesn't.

When she left my side, her lingering sweet, flowery scent made my dick hard and brought me peace at the same time. I need her in my life at my worst moments, even more than the best ones, and that speaks volumes.

Allowing myself to let her into a fraction of my life ended with me getting shot, my whole life flashing before my eyes. The look on Angelica's face when she saw me lying on the floor, covered in blood, is a moment I will never forget. She was panicking, and I didn't have the strength to reassure her that everything was going to be okay.

I knew then that I had to do everything in my power to keep her safe. Protect her.

I'm mad at myself for putting her at risk. I've kept her away for three weeks, terrified to endanger her again. We were so close to being caught because of my recklessness. I should never have brought her back to the club.

I constantly find myself gravitating toward her and it pisses me the fuck off. I wanted to play it safe and not get attached, but my heart and mind are at odds, creating a train wreck waiting to happen.

My plan was supposed to be simple. Watch her for a couple weeks to learn the ins and outs of her life, meet her, get her to fall in love with me. *Easy, right?*

A three-step plan that keeps throwing curve balls at me.

Even though we'd been texting since I was put on bed rest to recover, seeing her name pop up on my phone wasn't enough anymore. I had to see her and appease the ache in my chest.

As I make my way back to my car, I'm reminded of the first night I'd seen her in person after the incident. It had been twenty-one agonizing days without her. There was no way I could keep myself from driving to her house the minute Dr. Pappas removed my bed rest order. I shouldn't have been driving with only one arm, but fuck if I would've stayed home knowing that Angelica was only a short distance away.

Except, I had not anticipated her touching herself and screaming my name. I don't really know what I expected by sneaking into her house, but it definitely wasn't *that*.

My guess was that she would be sleeping, but she was...*awake*. I quietly entered the house from the back door and heard moaning. *Her* moans.

I immediately thought the worst, picturing her getting touched by another man, and my fists clenched so hard that my nails dug into my skin, leaving red half-moons on my palms.

The sweet sound lured me from her kitchen to the entrance of her bedroom, where I stood at the door, leaning on the frame. She didn't notice me, and the idea of her touching herself while I watched was enough for my dick to twitch under my jeans. I was in awe.

My angel. She looked delicate, yet wild and free. Our dynamic is like that of a cat and its master. She might be my kitten, but I don't own her, she owns *me*.

And she will never stop fighting me. *I like that.*

I soaked in the sight of her small, athletic body, nipples poking under the slip, the hem lifted slightly above her hips.

Angelica's fingers worked her clit, and then drove in and out of her pussy. I had to hold myself back from replacing her tiny hand with my throbbing cock. I wanted to be the one pleasuring Angelica so badly, but I needed to see how she wanted it, what she enjoyed. I couldn't give in to the temptation to rip the straps off the nightgown she wore and tie them around her neck like a collar I could pull as I pounded my dick into her from behind. *A dream that must become reality.*

And then, she yelled *my* name.

She thinks of me when I'm not around, and the satisfaction

of knowing that I consume her thoughts and her body when she is alone is gratifying as hell.

When she had finally realized I was standing at her bedroom door, she hadn't cowered or screamed. She merely flinched, her urge to run away apparent, but she knew there was nowhere to go.

I can see the constant battle in her mind between 'I need to get away from him' and 'how can I get closer,' and it's bringing me to the edge of losing control.

On my drive to meet Dion at Xander's restaurant, my attention keeps wandering back to Angelica and I try to suppress the thoughts. I can't allow myself to fall for a girl I'm trying to con into marrying me. The last thing I need is to start feeling guilty for wanting to avenge my uncle's death.

I should be focused on my family's business, leading my men, and getting revenge.

Everything I've done since I was a little boy was for my family, and I can't stop now. *I won't.*

I could tell Angelica the truth, but she will never agree to marry me if she finds out that I've been toying with her emotions and stringing her along in a plan to use her.

She's a feisty woman, who doesn't take shit from anyone. So, I doubt that would end well for me.

Dion is waiting for me at the door of the restaurant when I pull up to the entrance. I'm planning to go by the warehouse to oversee the arrival of one of the shipments, and I know Dion is going to throw a fit when I tell him. He has been acting like an overprotective parent ever since I got shot and hasn't let me do any work this past week. I asked him to take me to our meetings today so that I didn't have to attend by phone, and he refused.

I won't take no for an answer tonight, though. I have to be there to make sure we receive our delivery. In fear of being targeted again, I've been laying low, but I can't miss this business transaction.

The Vasilakis family doesn't sell drugs. We deal in arms trafficking, and the import and export of several of the most dangerous weapons in the world. Our clients are mainly criminal enterprises, but I'm trying to secure bigger agreements, and this meeting is worth almost three hundred million dollars.

If all goes well, my organization will be discreetly supplying guns and ammunition to the army.

Not only will this make my family and its people richer, but it will also allow me to control more of the streets and have leverage over my rivals, especially Peter.

As I walk around my car to meet my second-in-command, he bows his head and smiles, but it doesn't reach his eyes. He turns around and leads me inside to a private area near the back door. Before I get the chance to question him, Dion speaks.

"It's Aria's engagement party next week," he states.

Dion seems to be having a hard time accepting that Aria is getting engaged. I don't know what happened between them on the night of the club, but he's been a sad puppy ever since.

"I'm sorry to hear that, *Dionaki*."

He doesn't acknowledge me. Greek men are proud, and we pretend to be strong even when we don't feel it, so I know Dion is putting on a front.

"You know we're going to be expected to attend the party, right?" he asks, ignoring my sympathy.

"Oh, fuck," I reply. How did I not think about this before?

"Yeah. '*Oh, fuck.*' How are you gonna explain *that* to your missus?"

I completely forgot I would have to be at the engagement party on behalf of the Vasilakis family, now that I'm the new Godfather.

I can't tell Angelica now. She'd never speak to me again.

"I have to come up with an excuse and you're going to help me find it," I order. Dion swears under his breath. "Before that, we have to figure out what to do about Jurian and Peter," I continue.

I'd had no intention of starting a full-on battle with the Kouvalakis clan, but Peter had other ideas. Jurian didn't come to my club by his own will. Not only did Peter have my uncle murdered, he also tried to kill me, and could have potentially hurt his daughter in the crossfire, had she not been hiding. I wanted to be fully healed before my next move, but as time passes, I get angrier.

I want to personally slit their throats and hang their severed heads on my mantle like prized possessions. A fitting decoration for my very cold house.

I know Peter is hiding something. Jurian mentioned a 'plan.' It's up to me to figure out what it is. And once I do, I'm going to end them.

"I've been doing some digging using the information Cyrus gave us, and I think I got a lead," Dion says. "Xander had started sniffing around, but I had to take over..." He puts his head down and my jaw clenches at the thought of my brother, not from the same mother and father, but chosen, who selflessly risked his life to save mine. Dion had waited until I was fully conscious and stable to tell me that Xander was in critical condition, knowing I would turn the whole place upside down, injured or not. That didn't stop me from trying to extricate the

THE DIÁVOLOS

IVs out of my veins and unplug the machines to rush to his side. Dr. Pappas and Dion had to hold me down until I calmed down. I still have the bruises where I tried to force the needles out of my skin.

Fortunately, Xander made it out alive, but his recovery will be much longer than mine, since his injuries were more than flesh wounds. His back was riddled with bullet holes, like a target sheet. Some bullets damaged bones and hit organs. One of his kidneys had to be removed. It's a miracle he's alive.

I grab onto Dion's shoulder. "How's he doing?" I ask.

I haven't seen him since the day of the shooting. He's been recovering at the hospital, while I've been on bed rest at home.

"He's good, but the stubborn bastard keeps asking about you, as if he's not riddled with holes, like a block of Swiss cheese," he jokes.

"Do you expect anything different from Xan? The mammoth cares more for others than himself."

Dion laughs and agrees. I'll have to pay him a visit now that I'm able to move around.

I revert to the lead they found. "Follow it and get back to me. Whatever it is, I want you to oversee it. Do what you gotta do to find out the truth," I say, and Dion nods.

While I was stuck in my penthouse recovering, I went over computer files and physical documents that Dion had brought me from my uncle's office, looking for something—*anything*—that would lead me to the bigger picture. In my research, I stumbled across a name. The Sisterhood.

It was the title of a file on my uncle's computer, hidden deeply within other folders. When I clicked on it, it was empty. It didn't make sense that there was nothing there. He must have wiped the folder clean before his impending death, like he saw it coming.

I know my way around the dark web, so I pulled up search

tools, looking for anything pertaining to the Sisterhood. It was a dead end, until I discovered a forum that had several posts from usernames I did not recognize from the underground world.

Throughout the forum, there were comments from users, who I assume were men, asking how to get access to the Sisterhood. From what I could gather, it's a secret society that only allows access by referral. I got a bad feeling about it, and it's been gnawing at me ever since.

The last entry was posted a month before my uncle was killed, by someone with the username '2young4you,' and it only contained an attachment.

When I opened the document, I felt sick to my stomach.

It was pages and pages of names. Girls' names. With their date of birth, height, eye and hair color, weight, where they were from, along with medical records. I skimmed through the list and saw that none of the girls were over thirteen years old.

The document looked like school records dating back to fifteen years ago, and I couldn't push down the queasiness I felt. *What the fuck?*

I immediately saved the file and sent it to Dion, asking him to get in contact with our hackers. We employ a trio of men who take care of all our hacking needs. Xander is the computer genius between the three of us, so he oversees their work. They are masterminds at what they do, so I knew that they would find something.

"Did the guys find anything about the 'Sisterhood'?" I ask Dion.

Dion's face turns grim. "They did," he says, lowering his voice. "And you're not going to like it."

I straighten, bracing myself for the bad news.

"All those girls had gone missing from their homes. They

were brought there from Greece, stolen from their parents, and given to the Sisterhood. Whatever it is, it's evil, *adelfé*."

I let out an exasperated breath and rub the nape of my neck. I was expecting something terrible, but this is disgusting, even for someone like me, who toggles between morally black and grey.

"Were there any missing persons reports for the children?" I ask.

"Hundreds, but some of the girls had nothing to trace them back to their parents."

"Where are they now?"

The list was posted a little over a month ago, so some of the girls are still part of this organization, whatever it is.

"We don't know yet. The guys are trying to locate where they are being hidden. They found a list of donors and women who worked there. They seem to all be nuns."

"Hence why they're called the Sisterhood," I gather.

Dion nods. "There's more," he says, nervously, and I get a sinking feeling in my gut.

"What?" I ask.

"Marco went through every single entry and found a girl registered fifteen years ago by the name of Hera Kouvalakis."

A roar starts in my ears at the mention of that name. *It can't be.*

"How old was she?" I ask, my voice coming out hoarse.

"Eight," Dion replies.

Fuck.

Hera Kouvalakis can only be one person: Angelica. Angelica Hera Kouvalakis.

She was eight years old when her mother died. This can't be a coincidence.

Does she even remember any of this? She has never even

brought up being part of the Sisterhood, and nothing we've dug up on her shows that she was involved.

She either remembers and doesn't want to talk about it or she somehow blocked it out of her mind. I can't be the one to tell her any of this, but she must remember *something*. What if she was hurt there? Is that where she developed her self-harm habit? The thought of my angel being mistreated as a child fills me with a fierce rage. How could her father allow her to be taken there? Whoever is responsible for this demonic child abuse ring will pay for this dearly. I will not rest until I find and kill everyone involved. Even if that means bringing hell to Cebrene.

My uncle must have been involved to some extent. It makes me sick to think he could've been implicated in the mistreatment of young girls. He always taught me the importance of never hurting women and children, so none of this makes sense.

My mind is reeling.

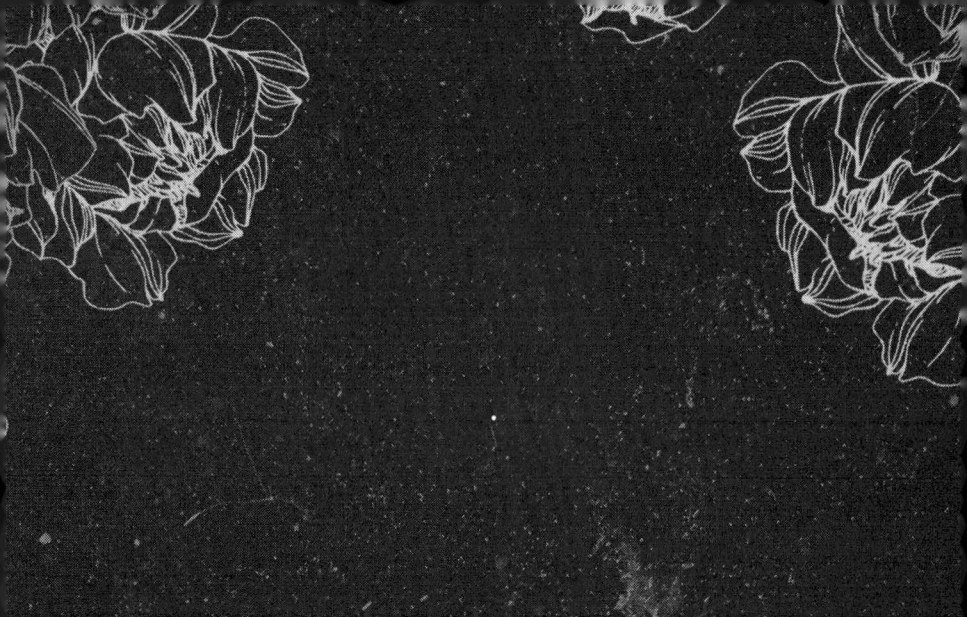

"Bad circumstances have a way of ruining things that would otherwise be pleasant."
—Lemony Snicket

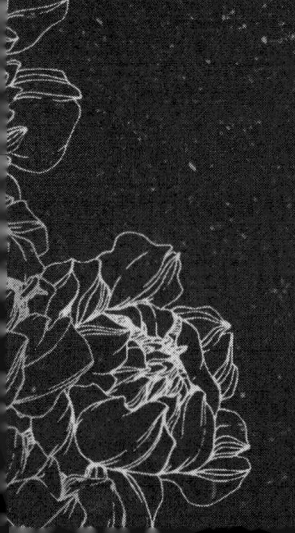

Angelica

I still haven't seen Aria since the night at the club and I'm worried about her.

Since I've been back to Cebrene, it's unusual for us to go this long without seeing each other, and I'm starting to think something might be wrong. She's been avoiding my calls and barely replying to my texts, which makes me think the worst. So, I decide to pay her a little visit.

I haven't left my place in days, too preoccupied with drowning in my own thoughts about Evan and what it all means. means. He hasn't been to the house lately either, which leaves a sore spot in my chest. Maybe I'll come back to a surprise if I leave. Wishful thinking. Who knew I could miss my stalker's obsessive attention. I also have to catch Aria up on all things Evan before she loses her mind, again. She may be small, but she's mighty fierce, and you don't want to get on her bad side.

Aria's family estate is a short walk away, so I don't bother asking anyone for a ride. I smile at the cameras at the front gates of the property, and they open. I walk down the long driveway to the entrance, and I hear commotion on the other side of the door, the sound of footsteps speeding toward it. Aria's brother, Dimitri, swings it open, and I'm greeted by a flirty smile. Dimo is younger than us, only eighteen years old, but he's much taller than both of us and jacked. I always wonder what kids eat these days.

He leans into the door and crosses his legs. "Angie, I wasn't expecting company today," he purrs.

You'd think this guy is a cat in heat with the amount of purring he does. Is this what boys are like these days? I don't remember them being so obnoxious when I was that age.

"You are insufferable, Dimo." I push him out of the way. "Where's your sister?"

He laughs. "I gotta shoot my shot when I can, babe," he says, shrugging his shoulders. "She's up in her room. Good luck getting her out."

I don't waste another second and run up the stairs, straight to Aria's room. I carelessly swing the door open and startle her with my grand entrance. She jumps off her bed and clutches her chest.

"Jesus Christ, Angelica. You scared the shit out of me!" she cries out.

"Glad to see you're alive," I say dryly, crossing my arms.

Aria sits back down on her bed and covers herself with her blanket. "What are you doing here?" she asks.

"Saving you from yourself, apparently. What's going on, Ari? You've been avoiding me."

She sighs and throws herself back on the mattress, her gaze pointed at the ceiling. "I don't know, Ang. I'm lost. My whole life is being taken away from me," she says in a voice that's barely audible.

I lie down next to her and grab her hand, intertwining our fingers.

"I can't begin to imagine how you feel, but staying locked up in your room isn't going to help, *Arioula*." I exhale and turn to face her. "You know you don't have to deal with this alone, right?"

She looks at me and I see tears welling in her eyes. "I don't want to get married to him, Ang. I don't know him. He's a stranger. And I'll have to live with him, sleep in the same bed, have *sex* with him." She gags at that last part.

I want to go downstairs and yell at her parents for allowing their daughter to be used like this. I count myself lucky for managing to avoid an arranged marriage this long. I was able to escape and get away from all the expectations, but Aria didn't stand a chance. I don't know how to help her, but I won't rest until we stop this.

"We have to find a way out of it," I reply.

"How, Ang? My engagement party is next week."

I push my head back, stunned. Next week? No wonder she's cooped up in her room.

"*How*? Your engagement was just announced. What's the rush?" I ask.

"That's what I said! But our parents want us married by the end of the year."

"That's six months from now, Aria!" I exclaim.

The tears that were threatening to fall out of her eyes finally make an appearance. I grab her little body and hug her tightly.

"We'll find a way to stop this. We just have to," I repeat.

We hold each other for several minutes, while Aria lets out all the tears she's probably been holding in for weeks. I caress her hair, allowing her to empty her emotional tank. After a while, she breaks out of my hold, grabs a tissue to wipe her face, and cracks a tiny smile that I reciprocate.

"How do you feel?" I ask.

"Better," she confirms and gets off the bed. "I can't believe I cried for a whole seven minutes."

I chuckle. "Bad bitches cry, too."

Aria laughs, her voice slightly raspy. "Okay, enough about my depressive life. Tell me more about you. How was your date night with Niko at the charity ball?"

I fill her in on all the activities of the past three weeks and Aria eagerly listens to my every word, her eyes wide.

"Okay...my stalker showed up to the masquerade ball, but catch this. He came with a full mask on, so I had no idea who it was at first. He glared at me for over an hour without saying a word, and then followed me to the women's bathroom, barged in, and ordered me to leave or else he'd kill Niko." Aria gasps and I pause to catch the look on her face.

"Yes, you heard me correctly. I made up a lame excuse and left Niko all by himself. The stalker followed me out, wanting to take me home, but I refused. He wouldn't take no for an answer, so I tried to run away, but he caught me and pinned me to the ground, almost suffocating me. I finally obeyed him and got in the car," I blurt all in one breath. I purposely leave out that he forced me to climax on the grassy floor like an animal. "Then, he blindfolded me and tied me up in the car, drove me to his penthouse, where he finally revealed himself as...Evan."

Aria looks at me, stunned, for several seconds. "Back. It. The. Fuck. Up. Right. Now. WHAT?" she asks in a hushed yell, her mouth gaping open and her eyes wide. "I've been MIA for *way* too long."

I start from the beginning, telling her the story from A-Z, but I spare the details of my orgasm. When I'm finally done, Aria looks at me with a bewildered expression. I've known her a long time and can tell the wheels are turning inside her head.

"I already have enough stories featuring Evan to last me a lifetime. Everything is moving so fast. I don't even know how to feel." Every time I think about him, my heart skips a beat.

"The masked stranger at the ball, the man you met at the shooting range, and your stalker are the *same guy*?" she asks.

"Yes."

"You're fucked, babe."

I chuckle, even though this situation isn't the slightest bit funny. "Whenever he's around, I don't want him to leave, and whenever he's away, I wish he were there." I rub the nape of my neck and continue, "I've never felt like this before. You know I never let guys into my life to this extent..."

"But he's different," she finishes.

I nod. "He's different."

"What are you going to do about it?" Aria wonders.

"I wish I knew." I sigh. "On one hand, I hate that he thinks he has control over me, that he can be possessive and boss me around. I've worked so hard to get away from people who didn't let me do *me*." If anyone can understand what I mean, it's Aria. She knows how much I hate being under my father's thumb. Aria takes my hand in hers to comfort me.

"On the other hand, he makes me feel, Aria. I haven't *felt* in so long, and he has managed to bring out all these emotions after having seen him only a handful of times. He made me laugh and got me to open up. My feelings for him are genuine and that scares me."

"Why are you fighting it, Ang? He makes you happy and you deserve someone who makes you feel things. Hell, he might be unhinged and dangerous, but we've been around men like him our whole lives. The only difference is that his attention is on *you*. But that might be a good thing. Maybe he's the answer to your freedom," she says. "Think about it. It seems like he won't take no for an answer, and he'd do anything to be with you, and you need someone who's willing to fight for you. So, if you truly like him, go for it. He might be the key to finally getting away from your father and the mob once and for all."

"I never thought of it that way," I reply.

"I'm ready to endorse him just because of this conversation, and I haven't even met him." She laughs.

Caring about someone never comes easy for me, especially after my mother's death and losing the loving father I once knew. I've been in a constant state of numbness ever since. I always wondered if something else happened to me when I was younger. I often have this nagging suspicion I'm forgetting events from my past. I dream of my mother and father arguing. I have flashbacks of when I was a little girl, surrounded by others like me, scared and alone in a strange place. I can't figure out if they're just figments of my imagination or if the dreams are conveying real information my brain has chosen to forget. As a child, I'd woken up many nights, screaming or crying, and drenched in sweat. Eldora would come to my side to comfort me.

She tried talking to my father about taking me to therapy, but he'd always brushed off my behavior as me being an 'angsty teenager' and said that I'd 'grow out of it.'

Well, here I am at twenty-three years old, still full of anxiety and angst.

I don't know if my brain will allow me to let Evan in, or if I even want to. I might be making excuses for my concern and worries, but as we stand, Evan is a stranger, and he means nothing to me.

Or that's what I'm trying to convince myself of, at least.

Aria and I get summoned downstairs for brunch. We're greeted by Magdalena, the family's domestic helper. I exchange a few words with her in the little Spanish I know, and she leads us to the family room while the food is placed on the table. Dimo is on the couch playing video games. I run my knuckles through his hair, giving him a little noogie. "Hey, again."

He winces and swats my hand away, and I laugh. He removes one side of his headphones and stares up at me in awe. *"Yia sou moráki." Hey, sexy,* he purrs. I roll my eyes at him.

Aria swiftly smacks him behind the head and he yelps. I cover my mouth with my palm to muffle my laugh.

"What was that for?" he asks her, rubbing the back of his skull as he tries to handle his controller with one hand.

"I told you not to hit on Angie. She's too old for you and she's my best friend. Stop being so gross."

"A little flirting never hurt anybody, Ri. Leave the boy alone," I interject.

"Yeah, Ri. She likes it," Dimo says, with a wink aimed at me. Aria shivers in disgust at the sight.

"You just like the attention, you little *poutána*," she spits at me, her tone serious.

I look at her, my facial expression stoic, and we burst out laughing. I lean into her on the couch, and we lock each other in an embrace. I've missed Aria so much, it's nice to spend time with her, even for a little bit. When we're together like this, we can forget, just for a moment, about all our troubles and worries. Dimo looks at us, dumbfounded.

"You both are so weird," he says and puts his headphones back on, once again focusing on his game.

"So, what are you going to do?" Aria asks me when we're back in her room a while later.

"I don't know. I'm scared to be let down. Everyone I've loved has either left me or betrayed me," I state.

"Not everyone. You have me and Gianis."

Unease spreads in my chest. I haven't spoken to Gianis in weeks. I've been so caught up with Evan that I haven't been returning his calls. He wasn't at my father's the last time I visited. He texted me the following Thursday to ask if I needed a ride to the shooting range, but I didn't go because I was too focused on Evan's recovery.

"You're right. I know I can always count on you both."

"Speaking of G, I haven't seen him in a very long time. I'm starting to get worried about him," Aria expresses.

"Why? What's wrong?" I ask.

"I overheard my *baba* talking to yours on the phone the other day. Apparently, Gianis hasn't shown up at your father's place in several days and no one can get a hold of him."

Crap. That's not good. When Gianis is internally dealing with something, he withdraws from the world and disappears.

"I know where to find him," I state.

She looks at me warily. "Be gentle with him, Ang."

I'm taken aback by her comment. "What do you mean?"

Aria hesitates before she responds. "Haven't you realized it yet?"

I'm confused as to what we're talking about here. I shake my head.

"He loves you, Ang. Like *love*, love. When you left, it tore him apart, and I was the only one here to pick up the pieces. He would never make you feel guilty for anything, your happiness and safety come first for him. He's loved you since the first time you kissed as teenagers. I don't know if he thought he'd get a second chance with you when you moved back, but this isn't easy for him, Angelica. He knows you better than anyone else, and if you've been distant, it's probably eating him alive," Aria admits.

I'm suddenly filled with regret and anguish. I've always had a feeling that Gianis cared for me as more than a friend, but he was never clear about his feelings or intentions, and I preferred to ignore it because he's *Gianis*. My best friend in the entire world. I'd die and kill for him without hesitation, and I love him with my entire being, but I never let my feelings pass the friendship threshold. As a teenager, I would have been over the moon at this news. But over the years, I learned that what I felt for him had turned into something more platonic, brotherly.

I have to speak to him.

An hour later, I get out of Aria's car in front of The Rig. She agreed to drive me when I told her there's nowhere else Gianis would be. When he's upset, he often releases the tension with many, many hours of training.

It takes several seconds for my vision to adjust to the darkness of the gym. It's quiet, with only a few patrons training on bags. I look for Gianis, but I don't see him anywhere. I walk farther into the space and see a man on a bench at the far end. As I get closer, I recognize Gianis' figure. He's sitting with his elbows resting on his legs, his head lowered between his knees.

"Gianis?"

His head jerks up at the sound of my voice. "Angie."

I sit next to him. "Aria told me that my *baba* hasn't heard from you in days. I knew you'd be here."

He nods his head a few times and brings it back down

between his knees. A drop of sweat drips from his face down to the floor and his body glistens with beads of perspiration. The unevenness of his breath fills the silence between us. He's been overexerting himself.

"Where have you been, Angie?" he asks, without lifting his head, and I can hear a lace of bitterness in his words.

His question catches me off guard. Not because I think it's unusual, but because it creates instant guilt. I play with my nails as I try to find the right words to say. I hesitate to tell him that I met someone, not wanting him to ask questions about Evan. I don't want to hurt his feelings. I would never want to break his heart.

"I saw him leave your house the other night," Gianis continues, breaking the silence. My breath gets stuck in my chest.

"What are you talking about?" I ask, trying to play dumb.

"I passed by your place on Thursday night, after you told me you didn't want to go to the shooting range. You know, just to check up on you, because I hadn't heard from you in a while. I wanted to make sure you were okay. You've been...distant," he explains, his head still lowered. My heart cracks.

"I'm sorry for being so absent lately. But I'm here now."

"*Ton agapás?*" *Do you love him?* he asks as he slowly looks up at me.

I stare my friend in the eyes and I can see he's one more blow away from breaking.

"No, I don't," I reply, calmly. *Not yet.*

"Just make sure you know what you're getting into, Ang. Be careful."

I nod, but I'm confused as to what he's talking about. *Be careful?* Does he know something I don't? He leans his body back onto the wall behind the bench and stares at the ceiling, letting out a long exhale.

"What do you mean?" I ask.

"Never mind. Just don't rush into anything. Promise me," he pleads. But it might be too late. I feel as though Evan and I have passed the point of no return. His obsession with me will never allow him to let me go, and the feelings I have toward him only get stronger by the minute. Our so-called relationship has been on fast-forward since the day he laid eyes on me and began stalking me. I can't give Gianis my word, but I can't lie to him either. I don't know what to do.

"Why have you never told me about your feelings?" I ask, my voice a low murmur.

He fiddles with the hem of his gym shorts and lets out a breath. "I didn't think I could," he admits, quietly.

"Gianis, I had the biggest crush on you growing up. You knew it, everyone did. You could've said *something*." I'm almost angry at him. How could he keep this from me all this time? He was aware of my crush. I don't know what the future would've held for us had we acted on our feelings, but we could've at least *tried*.

"I know, Ang. But you were so young, and when I decided to work for your father, I didn't think you would still consider being with me," he explains.

"You couldn't have known that," I respond, tears forming in my eyes.

"I thought I had more time," he whispers, and I can see the sorrow in his expression for something that will never be.

My composure breaks and I cry—*ugly cry*— for what we could've been. It may not have worked in our favor in the end, but now I will be haunted by the what-ifs. I know I would've still been worried about potentially damaging our friendship, but at the time, I would've jumped on the opportunity to be with him.

"I love you, G," I say, reaching for his hand. "You're my best friend. I hate to see you in pain. But I can also see the love you have to give; the love I wish you would've given me years ago." I lift his hand to my cheek and close my eyes, letting the tears fall down my face. "But I'm not the right person for you now. I hope that one day you'll realize I don't deserve to be loved by you and that you'll find your own person."

Gianis stares at me for a long moment, and then simply nods, his silence speaking more than a thousand words. Sometimes it's the best answer.

He cups my face with both hands, and I cry, knowing I just broke him. I broke *us*. He wipes away my tears with his thumbs and leans in to give me a kiss on the forehead. I close my eyes and bask in the moment. After a few seconds, he lets go and lifts himself off the bench. With one last look, he walks back to the boxing ring.

I ripped out a piece of my heart that I will never get back by hurting him, but I needed to let go of the little part of me that still held on to him. We will always be friends, and I will always love him, but I know things will never be the same between us.

"Nice guys finish last." —Leo Durocher

Evander

My men are already at the warehouse, preparing for the shipment, when I arrive with Dion. It took lots of convincing for him to let me tag along, but he ultimately had no choice. I compromised by agreeing to bring Seb and Greg as extra backup. *Not like they weren't going to tag along, anyway; I don't go anywhere without them.*

I feel sorry for whoever Dion marries because he will suffocate her with overbearingness.

A truck backs into the warehouse through the dock door. I give the guys a nod and we slowly place our hands on our guns. I'm still wearing a sling, so I reach for my weapon with my free hand.

The driver gets out of the truck and gives us a small wave. I acknowledge it and ask him to open the doors so we can inspect the merchandise. He obliges and my men proceed to check the cargo boxes. It's the first huge shipment we've received since my uncle passed away, so it's very important for this transaction to go smoothly. This will decide whether we level up and take over the city or get trampled on by the other families who think us weak.

My hand rests on my handgun, while I wait for Dion to emerge from the truck. When he does, he gives me a nod of approval, and I hop into the cargo hold to examine the ammo. The boxes carrying the bullets are sealed shut, so I order Greg to pry one open with a crowbar. I bend down to take a good look, and the faint smell of sulfur hits my nose. Most modern propellants have an acrid bite. I toy with a bullet in my hand to feel the weight and balance of it. Every measure of lead and powder is carefully reproduced to ensure consistent behavior of the bullet through the air. The rounds were sent from Albania, passing through Greece. So, it's important for me to oversee the loading of the ammunition to guarantee quality and legitimacy.

I dislodge my pistol and load it with one hand, aiming to the sky. I shoot, taking note of the way the bullet travels through the air. Satisfied, I call the others to unload the boxes. This deal will be ours, and I'm ready to run the city, with my angel by my side.

My brain can't manage any more interaction, so I leave with every intention of passing by the club to check on things. Instead, I head home and make a stop on the way.

I lean against my car in the parking lot of the gas station near my apartment building. I pull out the pack of cigarettes I just bought from the back pocket of my jeans. I don't usually smoke, but I need some sort of stress release right now.

I fumble with the package, managing to take out a cigarette with one hand. I put it to my lips and light it. I take a long drag and inhale the toxins, blowing out the smoke as I tilt my head back to look at the dark sky.

My thoughts immediately turn to Angelica, and I'm seriously starting to wonder if something is wrong with me. She's always on my mind, images of her face, smile, and body flashing before my eyes. This time, something like worry consumes me because of the new revelations I learned today. I need to get to the bottom of it for my uncle and her. I'm her protector, and if anyone hurts her, they're going to face my wrath, regardless of who they are.

After a few minutes of standing there in silence, I finish the cigarette, flick it on the ground, and get back in my car. I shut the door and grip the steering wheel hard, making my knuckles turn white as memories of her resurface. The feeling of her skin is branded on my fingertips. The smell and taste of her dominate my senses.

When did I lose my mind?

She has no idea what she's getting into. When I first started this whole plan, I had no intention of wanting her. No intention of really calling her mine. I need her to make me *feel*. I crave to steal her breath away and remind her that the only name she will be screaming from now on is mine. She will fall in love with me, be my wife. There's no doubt about that. But my brain can't seem to figure out how to make my plan still work while obsessing over her.

I need to get her out of my system the only way I know how. I have to get rid of this burning obsession. It might open the floodgates to what I've been dreading the most—my feelings—but the incessant urge to claim her consumes me. I'm going to fuck her into oblivion, and hopefully, that will ease my compulsions.

My phone rings and I don't check the caller ID before I pick up, knowing exactly who it would be. I'm surprised it took him this long.

It was only a matter of time.

"Gianis," I answer.

The dreaded day has come.

I gaze at my reflection in the mirror. I clean up nice. I fix my tie and smooth down the jacket of my all-black tailored suit. I shake out my arms to straighten out my sleeves, and a lingering ache settles in my injured shoulder. My gunshot wound has almost completely healed, but the pain is still present and will be for weeks. Today is the first day I get to remove my arm brace and that's cause for celebration.

I glance at my phone on the dresser in my walk-in closet, but there are no notifications. Angelica hasn't texted me. I haven't heard from her all day.

It's been over a week since we last saw each other, but I've been keeping a close eye on her, staying up to date with what she's been doing and where she's been going.

I've been busy catching up on my affairs, having missed so much while I was recovering, and she's been absorbed in Aria's engagement party preparations. So, we haven't seen each other since that night in her room. I can't deny this emptiness I feel. I miss the smell of her hair, the feeling of her skin, and her big doe eyes.

I sent her peonies every day and watched from the security feed as she opened the door and found each bouquet on her porch, the glow on her face obvious. She's aware that I'm watching her. Each time, she'd greet me, not by looking up at the cameras, but by wearing outfits, each one skimpier than the last, exposing her soft cleavage and allowing me to see down her shirt. Or dresses so short I could see the edge of her sweet ass popping out the bottom when she bent over to pick up the vases. She was putting on a show for the devil and she knew it.

She's playing with fire, and soon, she's going to burn.

I put the phone in my pocket and grunt at the wave of disappointment I feel. Dion should be meeting me at my penthouse any moment to head to the engagement party.

Tonight might be the make or break moment of my relationship with Angelica.

Tonight will be the night that Dion sees his girl officially off the market.

Dion and I thought long and hard about what to tell Angelica as my reason for being there, and we couldn't come up with anything of substance. I'll have to let my charm and good luck improvise on the spot. I rub my forehead, already feeling the stress of what's to come. *Fuck, I'm going to regret this.*

I haven't stopped thinking about her. The sound of her voice calling my name as she climaxed still makes my dick hard every time that I think about it.

I take a step back from the mirror, hating the tightness that the thought of her causes in my chest, and I try to focus on my motive.

But it's to no avail, as my longing for her has no limit.

She's my drug and I'm fucking addicted.

I hear my front door open, and I walk into my living room to see Dion reaching for the bottle of *ouzo* in the bar cart.

"I didn't know it was that kind of night," I joke.

Dion doesn't look amused as he grabs two shot glasses out of the cabinet and pours two drinks.

"I've spent the whole day trying to figure out how to avoid tonight and the best I could come up with is to get drunk and pretend I was never there," he says glumly, passing me a shot glass. We clink them together and shoot the *ouzo* back, the burn down our throats making us grimace. Dion grabs the bottle and pours some more.

"You've got it bad, bro," I say.

"You have no fucking idea," he replies.

After the second shot of *ouzo,* I call my driver.

We spend the ride talking about business and the fact that tonight will be my first public appearance as the new Godfather. I just hope that no one mentions my new title around Angelica.

The driver pulls up to the Kastellanos estate and the gates open, allowing us to make the short drive to the entrance of the mansion. Several other cars are being driven away by attendants, and many guests are making their way up the steps to the house.

We head inside through the sea of people, keeping our greetings short and sweet.

Phillip Kastellanos increased his security for tonight. The place is flanked with armed guards. Something tells me this is Peter's doing.

Aria's father, Phillip, has been the Kouvalakis' chief counselor and advisor ever since Peter became Godfather decades ago. I have no doubt they took extra precautions tonight, given I was rumored to show.

After murdering my uncle and trying to kill me, he expects retaliation. He won't get what he's anticipating, especially not tonight. My plan is to lay low, but to also make sure everyone knows that the *Diávolos* doesn't shy away from anything, and if anyone tries to mess with me, I will fuck them up.

We walk around the cocktail area, stopping to talk to some people. Some gawk at us, while others start whispering to each other. I know what they're thinking. *The Diávolos is here.* My reputation runs wild in all parts of Cebrene.

Dion is on edge. A waiter passes by with a tray, and he

grabs two glasses of champagne, his fingers fidgeting on the rims. The fucker is trying to double-fist. I snatch one of the flutes from his hand and gulp the whole drink down in one swig. Tonight is going to be a shit show for both of us.

I see no sign of Angelica yet, but as I turn around, my eyes meet another pair that are shooting daggers at me, full of anger. Gianis. *Here we go.*

I didn't tell anyone about our conversation the other night. If I'm being honest, I was expecting his call.

Angelica's security system was installed by him, so I knew he'd be watching and would recognize me.

Mind you, I wasn't trying to be discreet. I've given up on covering my traces.

It was only a matter of time until he realized who Angelica was spending her time with, and for whom she was casting him aside. I have taken over her body and mind. He's no longer her priority.

I'm not an idiot. I know Gianis loves Angelica. I can tell from the way he carries himself around her. The way he jumps at any and every opportunity to follow her around.

I've been watching her for weeks, but he's been watching her for longer. Before she left Cebrene, while in Antium, and ever since she moved back to town, monitoring her ins and outs with the help of his security system and foot soldiers. I know this because I've been watching him, too.

Anyone who poses a threat to my relationship with Angelica is on my radar. He's not fooling anyone, especially not me.

Our conversation that night only solidified what I already knew.

Gianis stalks over to me, his face an expression of rage and hostility. I turn around and walk to a backdoor that hopefully leads to an outdoor area.

I pass a server handing out drinks and grab a glass, setting my empty champagne flute on the tray. *This one better be stronger than champagne.*

Dion notices me walking away and immediately catches on that someone is following me. He turns and sees Gianis storming after me, and he gives me a warning look. I subtly shake my head at him, a sign to stay back. This is between Gianis and me.

I push the veranda doors open and head to a dark corner, Gianis right on my tail.

"I thought I told you to stay the hell away from Angelica, Evander," he spits as soon as the doors close behind us.

I smile. "I thought I told you to mind your fucking business, Gianis," I snap back, taking a step into his space. "I'm here to celebrate Kastellanos' daughter's engagement, just like you."

I'm trying not to make a scene, but he's getting on my last nerve.

"What the fuck do you want from her?" he asks.

"The same thing you want." *To make her mine.*

Gianis scoffs at my response. "That's bullshit and you know it, Evander," he says, mockingly. "A guy like you can have nothing but ill intentions with a girl like her, *especially* her."

I take a sip of my drink as I eye him from the rim. He's not wrong, but I'll never admit that to him. I can't deny I had a one-track mind when it came to Angelica when this started, but things have changed.

"What do you know about guys like me, Gianis?" I retort, raising an eyebrow.

"I *am* a guy like you," he states.

"Then, you admit you don't deserve her, either," I mock. "No wonder she hasn't loved you back after all these years."

Gianis balls his fists, and the next thing I know, he is

standing mere inches away from me, his face beet red and contorted with rage, holding a knife to my neck. I laugh.

"Do you really think a knife is going to scare me, *vlakas*? I live for this shit."

I avert my gaze from him for a second and scan the area back inside the house to see if Dion is still watching. I notice someone else's stare. Angelica stands behind Dion, frozen in place, her gaze on us.

I can't make out the expression on her face, but it must be of shock as she notices the knife at my throat. She has no idea Gianis and I are acquainted. I can only imagine what she must be thinking.

I turn my attention back to the man about to explode in front of me. He notices Angelica, too, and a flash of worry crosses his face.

"Come on. Don't be a pussy, Gianis. Be a man and slit my throat in front of your girl," I taunt him.

"Watch your fucking mouth, *Vasilakis*," he hisses.

I let out another mocking laugh. *Finally*, someone figured out who I truly am. My uncle did a phenomenal job hiding my true identity. No one else in the city knew my last name. Hell, barely anyone even knows my first name. I always go by the *Diávolos*, whether I'm doing a business deal or severing heads. As Peter's enforcer, it's Gianis' job to know who I am. He's probably known for a while. So, it makes me wonder why he hasn't mentioned it to his boss yet, like he's keeping this bit of information for a rainy day. *What are you planning, Gianis?* Regardless, I know the fucker won't do shit with this information for now.

"Do you think you have leverage by knowing my last name? What are you going to do? Tell her and risk gaining the reputation of a snitch? Come on, Gianis. Don't be an idiot."

"Leave her alone, Evander," he repeats, fury laced in his voice.

No one tells me what to fucking do. I've had enough of pretending I don't want her, that I only need her for my plan. It's time I claim her for good.

"*Íne dikiá mou*, Gianis." *She's mine.* "I think you need to accept that from now on. She'll never be yours, and if you try to stop me, I'll fucking kill you," I seethe.

He presses the knife into my neck and the pressure of the blade on my skin is almost arousing. Angelica is still watching us, and I catch Dion trying to talk her down from coming outside. My dick starts growing in my pants. The combination of his blade threatening to pierce my skin, and the look of terror and confusion on Angelica's face is turning me on. I could easily disarm him, stab him in the gut, and then take my girl, in more ways than one, finally claiming her as mine. But I didn't come here to fuck her or kill Gianis. He's a nuisance, but he's harmless. She'd never forgive me for killing her childhood best friend. Either way, I've got bigger fish to fry than a jealous piece of shit.

"You've already warned me once on the phone, Gianis. I don't take threats lightly. So, if I were you, I would get the fuck out of my face and not do it again. It won't end well for you a third time," I say, angrily, and I step to the side before heading back inside.

I walk by Dion and come face-to-face with Angelica. I whisper to her in passing, trying not to attract any attention. "Take me somewhere private. Now," I demand.

"No," she responds, confidently, her chin lifted in defiance.

My eyes widen. I push my tongue against my bottom lip, pondering. "No? Do you need me to ask nicely, Angelica?" I circle around her. Her body stills, but she doesn't let her gaze follow me. I'm intimidating her.

She doesn't reply, only shakes her head no. "How about we do something fun? Let's play a game," I taunt.

"What's the game?" she asks, nervously.

"Hide. If I find you, I get to make you scream."

"And if you don't?"

"Don't worry. I will."

I move to the bar and order a drink. Angelica is frozen in place, her eyes bulging out of her sockets. Her chest heaves and she squeezes her eyes shut. But a moment later, she ducks through the throng of people and heads toward a door being used by the staff. I wait a few seconds before I follow her. When I emerge on the other side, it's a passageway that leads to the kitchen, lined with various doors. Kitchen and waitstaff walk past me as I look side to side, trying to find Angelica.

I spot her dark hair and the train of her dress disappearing through a door.

When I enter the room, it's small and there's nothing other than a library filled with books and two armchairs. The smell of leather and old books hits my nostrils. The shelves go from the floor to the ceiling and the books look weathered. I walk along one of the walls, letting my fingers trace over the spines of aged books and dust flies in the air. It's silent; only the creaking of my footsteps on the ancient, wooden floors is audible. Where could she be? I'm certain she came in here, but there's no trace of her.

"Angelica," I whisper. There's no response.

I reach the edge of the library and notice a small lever on the side. Old mansions always have secret passages and hidden doors, so this must be one. I lift the handle and part of the shelf disconnects from the rest. I snigger. "I'm going to find you, my little angel," I say out loud.

I pull the secret door open, and I step into an even greater room. My eyes travel around the space. We're in a large conservatory that extends onto a patio overlooking the garden. The floor-to-ceiling, partially glazed windows connect to a glass roof. I can faintly hear the commotion of people coming in and out of the property. Angelica stands in the middle of the room, looking outside. The moonlight shines directly on her, accentuating the shine of her emerald gown. She doesn't turn around to greet me, but I know she senses me.

My heart is pounding in my chest as my mind races with the hundreds of things I want to say and do to her at this very moment. I have the untameable urge to claim her and take her right in this room, branding her with my seed, from the inside out.

She looks different today. Her hair is straight, gone are the wild curls that she usually sports. If I hadn't memorized every curve of her body and all her mannerisms, I wouldn't have recognized her from behind.

I take long strides toward her, and my hand goes straight to her hair, my fingers running through the silky strands. "I win." Her breathing hitches at the contact and I take that as my cue to make a fist and pull her head back to my chest, pressing my body to hers. "Your hair, it's different."

"Your arm, it's better," she replies.

"Yes."

"Why are you here?" she asks, the words breathy.

"I'm here to make you scream."

She smacks her lips in exasperation. "No, Evan. Why are you *here*, at Aria's engagement party?"

"I came to claim what's mine."

"And what's yours, Evan?" There is frustration in her tone.

"You."

Before she can respond, I push her toward the window, keeping her body glued to mine, and I press her face to the glass. She gasps out, "Evan."

Her body squirms against me as she unsuccessfully tries to escape from my hold, using one of her arms to push off the window. Her face is flushed with what seems to be anger and arousal, and I'm hungry for what I know is waiting for me between her legs.

I release her head and quickly grab both of her wrists. My large hands envelop them as I join them at her back. I thrust hard against her ass, pushing her body onto the window. I drop my face to the crook of her neck, and I inhale deeply, running the tip of my nose up and down her skin. The smell of sweet florals and cocoa hits my senses and travels straight to my cock. I nip her earlobe with my teeth.

"You see all of those people down there?" I whisper in her ear, pointing down at the guests arriving at the party. "Soon enough, they will all know who you belong to." I lick her lobe, and a whimper escapes her mouth. The small sound makes my cock respond immediately, tightening my trousers. I grab hold of her shoulders and turn her around in one swift movement, her body still lodged between mine and the window.

Angelica looks into my eyes, her head lifted as she stands tall, chest heaving as she struggles to control her breaths. Although I've stolen the words from her mouth and the air from her lungs, this is an act of defiance. It's turning me the fuck on.

I inch my face closer to hers, causing our mouths to graze. My no kissing rule flies out the window at this very moment. I have to taste her lips.

"*Zíta mou na se filíso*, Angelica." *Ask me to kiss you, Angelica*, I command.

"*Óhi.*" *No.*

I tug at her hair and tilt her head up. "Ask me to kiss you," I order again, my lips lightly scraping hers.

"I don't want to kiss you, Evan. Not until you tell me why you're really here."

I growl at her. "I told you. I'm here to claim you as mine," I reply, my voice filled with lust and frustration.

"I thought I was already yours."

"Now, the whole world will know."

She freezes and her eyes widen. "No, Evan, we can't! You don't understand—," she stutters, but I don't let her finish her sentence.

"I don't give a fuck about any obstacles, *angeloúdi mou*. I get what I want. If anyone comes between us, I will slit their throats and slice their fingers off, gifting them to you as a token of my love. A reminder that no one else can *ever* touch you." Her breath hitches and I continue, "Now, ask me to kiss you, Angelica. I'm not going to say it again."

She gives in after a moment of hesitation. "Kiss me, Evan," she utters, her words laced with intense heat.

I don't waste a second to press my mouth to hers. I spear my hands into her hair and hold her close to deepen the kiss. The tension that has been building over the past couple months snaps. I groan into her mouth, eliciting a moan from her in response. I pull her closer to me, crushing her breasts against my abs, and I thrust my bulge against her again. We pull back to catch our breath and my eyes go straight to her gaping mouth, her lips swollen from our kiss, and I wonder why the fuck it took me so long to do this. I never thought a kiss could feel this right when everything else is so wrong.

I know my eyes must be two pools of obsidian as I stare at her face and body, a burning flame of desire.

I cup her face with my hands and bring her mouth up as I let my tongue explore her closed lips, parting them, begging her to let me in again, and she does. My tongue dives into her mouth and swirls around, tasting her.

"You were made for me, Angelica," I whisper against her mouth. "These lips were created for me to kiss." I press mine on hers. "These nipples, for me to pinch." I flick her breast over the fabric, and she squirms in my arms. "This pussy, for me to fuck." I cup her through her dress. "Every. Fucking. Inch. Of. You. Is. Mine. Do you understand?"

She nods and her breaths harshen as I lift her up, squeezing her soft ass, and I wrap her legs around my waist. "Someone might catch us," she pants.

"Then, let's make it count."

Our tongues dance together, the urgency of our kiss overpowering my senses. In this moment, I realize I was a fool for ever denying myself of Angelica.

I don't know the exact moment in time when I started falling in love with her.

It just happened.

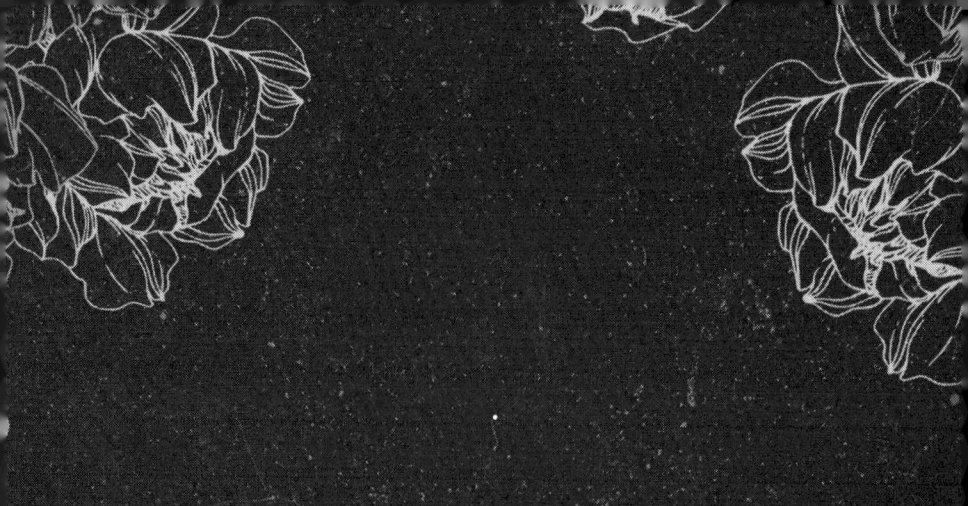

"Patience is bitter, but its fruit is sweet." —*Jean-Jacques Rousseau*

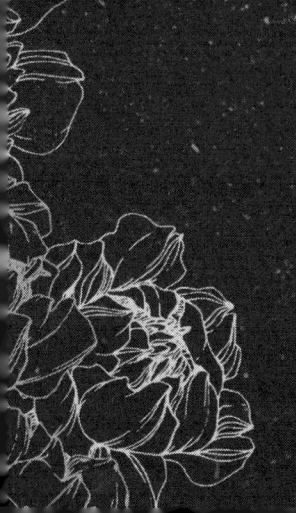

Angelica

Evan's perfect lips crash onto mine, full of hunger, as if he had been depriving himself of his favorite meal for years.

I lift my gown up to accommodate him between my legs as he hoists me up and spreads his large hands on my backside. I wrap my legs around his waist, kissing him back with as much fervor.

Our first kiss. It's better than I would've ever expected. Our lips touch again and it's hard, rough, and deep. I realize at this moment that kissing him has ruined me. Nothing will ever be the same, and I only want more. This is the first time a kiss has caused a churning inside my chest. A deep-rooted feeling of need.

I want to be the last person Evan ever kisses. My body's reaction to him goes against every ounce of common sense in my brain. I know I should be wary of him.

He knows everything about me, but I barely know anything about him. He's keeping things from me, and I don't know whether to be concerned or be patient. The shooting, the withholding of information, the fact that he's here at Aria's engagement party and was talking in private to Gianis, who had a *knife* to his throat.

Good things come to those who wait, but at what cost?

As much as I try to think things through, my attraction to him clouds my judgment. I am like a moth to a flame. He is beautiful, he is darkness, and I'm not afraid of what lies beyond. I want to give my life to him, even if he has the potential to set me on fire.

Evan's hand travels up my back to cup my neck tenderly, and I drown in his kiss. His tongue tastes sweet and spicy, the faint taste of black licorice still lingering from the *ouzo* he must've drank. He twirls his tongue with mine, making me burn inside with desire. A moan escapes my mouth, not caring if anyone can see or hear us, and I press my breasts against him, the plunging neckline of my dress revealing enough skin that I feel the hardness of Evan's unyielding chest through his suit.

He pulls away and we're both breathing heavily.

I'm willing to give him everything, every part of me, regardless of my worries. I am his, but only if he also belongs to me.

"You're mine," I whisper against his mouth.

"For as long as you'll have me, angel."

I press my forehead on his as I grind against his waist, feeling the friction and the hardness of his length at my center. I don't care where we are anymore. I need him.

"Evan. Please," I beg.

His eyes darken, and the intimacy of this moment, with our bodies pressed together, our intentions finally out in the open and our hearts connected, pushes me over the edge.

"Show me how much you want me, *moró mou*," he says.

He sets me down, and I take his hand, placing it under my dress, right against my panties and his fingers instinctively move against the fabric.

"You're fucking soaked, Angelica," he groans.

I muffle a response into his neck, too entranced by the feeling of his fingers as I grind against his hand, and my body aches for more.

"My filthy girl," he says. "Not yet."

He walks me over to the other side of the room and lifts me up onto a tabletop. I rest my forearms behind me and watch him, already breathless. He removes his suit jacket and rolls up his sleeves, exposing his veiny, muscular arms adorned with tattoos. He quickly pushes my panties to the side, and wastes no time burying two digits into me, his hand slamming into my core and sending a wave of pain and pleasure through my body. I yelp at the feeling, but he doesn't stop, only going harder and making my screams louder. I cover my mouth with my hand and try to muffle my sobs while Evan fucks me with his fingers. He jerks my hand away briskly.

"I want to hear you scream. If you hold yourself back, I'll stop," he threatens.

The lewd sound of his hand sliding through my wetness fills the room, and I'm almost embarrassed by how turned on I am. My body starts to quiver, and my breathing turns harsher. "Fuck me, please," I rasp.

The filthiness of my words surprises me, but I'm craving him inside of me. I want to experience the wrath of Evan's desire. He tenses for a moment, but doesn't stop beating my pussy with fervor. I can see the indecision in his eyes, but he doesn't entertain my request.

"We fuck when I say we fuck," he growls.

I let out a loud cry, wanting to be upset at his rejection but unable to focus on much else than his hand. "Listen to you whine like a pathetic, little slut. You're needy for my cock, aren't you, Angelica?" he asks me.

The growl in his voice sends a pang of arousal so deep into my stomach that I'm this close to begging him again, needing

Evan even more now that he's purposely withholding sex from me. He hooks his fingers inside me.

"Show me how desperate you are to come. I want you to squirt all over my hands. I want your juices to drip all the way up my arms and down your legs. I'm walking out into that crowd with your scent on my skin. I want you to think of me every time you take a step and feel how sore your pussy is. Understood?"

Lord have mercy on my soul.

"I've never squirted before."

"I'll make you," he replies confidently. "Lay back and relax," he commands.

He doesn't stop playing with my g-spot as I lay my head down on the table. He spreads my legs wider with his free hand and grunts at the vision in front of him.

"So fucking beautiful and all mine," he grumbles as he bends down between my legs, and then dives for my clit and sucks on it with vigor, causing my back to arch off the table and a loud moan to slip out of my mouth. *Holy shit.*

If I thought Evan's fingers were skilled, his mouth is heaven on earth. The feeling of his tongue on me is a perfect storm, like a hurricane I want to be caught in forever.

He pushes me back down on the table, his palm on my lower belly, applying the perfect amount of pressure while his fingers tap my walls, and his tongue licks my center.

I see stars.

"You want my thick cock inside you, don't you, angel?" he taunts, and I moan through the laps around my clit and the consistent pounding of his hand in and out of my entrance. I've never felt anything like this before. I want to scream. "Tell me you fucking love it, Angelica. You like it when I suck on your clit. You're wilting like a dying flower, all because of me."

I can't manage to utter a single word as I meet his thrusts with my hips.

"That's it, baby. Let it go," he says against my clit, the heat of his words making the ripples of pleasure more intense. He strokes and caresses my g-spot relentlessly, while dirty talking and instructing me the whole way, the filthiness of his mouth driving me crazy.

"You taste so fucking sweet, *glykiá mou*."

"Grip my fingers with those tight walls."

"Your pussy is dripping for me, Angelica."

I completely forget we're in my best friend's house, at her engagement party, surrounded by hundreds of guests and staff right outside the door.

"Focus on my tongue licking you clean, like the dirty, little slut that you are."

The last words he says shoot a million firecrackers up my body, coupled with the pressure on just the right spot inside me, and my body jerks while his hand on my stomach holds me down. I feel like I'm going to explode, like a missile about to hit its target.

"Evan," I cry out, the sound strangled, and Evan keeps going, his tongue and fingers working me until I can't take the pressure anymore. I come violently, gushing everywhere, and it feels as if I'm a celestial body floating in space. My body releases all its tension, and I flatten on the table, heaving from the high of my orgasm. Evan slowly removes his fingers and plants kisses on the inside of my thighs.

He did it. Evan made me squirt.

He meets me at my mouth and kisses me. I feel like I'm going to sink into the deepest waters and never return for air. "Good fucking girl," he growls. The sleeves of his shirt are soaking wet, and his face looks indecent, the evidence of my orgasm all over his mouth and jaw. He's never looked so hot.

I want to touch him and make him feel good, too. I reach for his waist, eyeing the obvious bulge in his pants, but he grabs my hands, stopping me. "Go join the party before they notice you're missing."

I've never been with a man so focused on my pleasure that he would deny himself his. He helps me off the table, smooths my dress down, and fixes my hair. The act is simple, yet so intimate.

Every doubt, every question, every concern dissipates from my memory as I stare into the eyes of the man who has changed me forever. My stalker. My secret admirer. Guardian angel and devil.

I nod and start walking toward the door of the conservatory. Just as I'm reaching for the doorknob, Evan speaks.

"Angelica," he calls.

I rest my hand on the handle, waiting for him to continue.

"Don't you dare wash yourself. For the rest of the night, I want you to remember who you belong to."

"Never let go of that fiery sadness called desire." —Patti Smith

Evander

Straightening myself up, I roll my wet sleeves back down my arms and put my jacket on.

Angelica's scent is all over my shirt and fingers. I can't get enough of the pure feminine smell of her. She feels and tastes so fucking good, there's no way I'm washing my hands after this. My dick is hard as nails, so I do an up-tuck in my trousers, and head back out to the party.

As soon as I step into the cocktail area, everyone is being ushered inside the dining hall to start the party. My eyes quickly scan the room and land directly on Angelica, who is holding a champagne flute and animatedly talking to guests. She looks much happier than when I first saw her, and her shoulders are more relaxed. Her cheeks are flushed, and she has a cute, satiated look on her face. *All me, all mine.*

I'll strive to be the one to keep her satisfied forever, even if it kills me. I don't give a fuck if her father catches wind of our involvement. I dare him to try and stop me from taking her as mine. I'll gladly kill him or anyone else who intrudes. He deserves the wrath coming his way.

My eyes linger on her for a long moment. She finally turns around to follow the others into the next room. Her gaze crosses mine. She bows her head slightly and tucks a strand of hair behind her ear. Bringing my glass of *ouzo* up to my lips, I smile and take a small sip. *I've got you now, angel.*

Dion is in the crowd, too, having disappeared earlier. When I meet him at the bar, he looks agitated.

"What's gotten up your ass?" I ask him.

He scoffs and orders a stiff drink. "I saw Aria," he mutters, chugging the glass of liquor. "Another one," he asks the bartender. "When you went after Angelica, I kept my eyes on Gianis for a bit to make sure he didn't go after her, too. He eventually busied himself with other people, so I walked back toward the veranda to go out for a smoke. That's when I noticed someone standing in the far corner." He downs the second drink. "I couldn't see the person's face. All I could see was her figure. I knew it was Aria. She looked gorgeous from behind, with her long, blonde hair curled down her back. When she turned around and we locked eyes, she tried to run away. But I stopped her."

I'm eager for him to get to the point. "And then what happened?"

"I told her I wasn't going to let her marry him. I *can't* let her marry him, Evan."

He looks so defeated. I've never seen Dion this choked up about anything...or anyone.

"Dion, I know you. When you want something, you don't give up easily. I have no doubt you'll get the girl if you really want her."

"I really do, bro."

I nod at him and rest my hand on his shoulder, giving it a squeeze. We grab another drink. I have a feeling Dion is going to get drunk tonight. I just hope I won't have to be the one to babysit him.

The rest of the evening surprisingly goes by smoothly. When Peter and his goons show up, we ignore each other, keeping things civil for the sake of the party. The only time rivals aren't at war is when family is involved, and tonight, the party is full of innocent bystanders who don't deserve to be stuck in the crossfire. Jurian didn't show and that makes him lucky. If he were here, I would've waited until the end of the party and followed him until we were alone to torture him into giving me information, ultimately putting a bullet between his eyes. I'm going to end the fucker's life for trying to kill me and mine.

I occasionally peek at Angelica. She deserves an award for avoiding my gaze for so long. She's sitting at a table with her father, trying hard not to look my way. I grab my phone and shoot her a text.

Me: Look at me.

Her phone vibrates in her purse, and she grabs it, a small smile appearing on her lips when she sees that it's a message from me.

Angelica: No. I've seen enough of your face tonight and I'm trying not to attract attention.

She smirks at her phone and puts it face down on the table.

Me: Wrong. If I remember correctly, my face was buried between your thighs. You couldn't have seen much of it.

Her phone vibrates again, and she quickly grabs it off the table like it's a hot potato. Her eyes grow wide when she sees my message. She looks up at me, and I wink at her. She rolls her eyes at me.

Me: You're always such a good girl, except when you roll your eyes at me. I should punish you for that.

The phone is still in her hand when she receives my text. She squirms in her seat. I can see the redness of her cheeks from here. She glances over at her father next to her and angles her phone away from him.

Angelica: Leave me alone, Evan.

Me: Never.

I look at her as I put my phone down on the table. She shakes her head at my last text and bites her bottom lip. She's lucky we're in a room full of people. Otherwise, I would've stalked over to her, bent her over the table, lifted her dress, and smacked her ass until my hand was imprinted on her skin and her pussy leaked down her thighs. If she thinks she's getting away from me now, she's going to get a rude awakening.

The next day, I wake up to Dion sprawled out on my couch, fast asleep. The drunk bastard didn't even make it to the guest bedroom. He was so wasted last night that it was me, in fact, who had to babysit him. He could barely walk and was slurring his words for most of the night. I was surprised he didn't do anything embarrassing. Probably because he didn't want to ruin Aria's night, even though he wished it never happened.

I walk straight to the kitchen to make coffee. I had quite a few drinks last night, but I was sober enough by the end. As the coffee brews, I walk over to Dion and punch him in the gut. He lets out a loud groan and flips onto his side, clutching his stomach in agony.

"Wake up, *maláka*."

"*Ti sto diáolo???*" he swears. *What the fuck???*

"I need you to get the fuck out of my house so I can start my day," I bark.

"Always such great hospitality," he rasps. I laugh.

"Come on. You need to drink some water and coffee before you croak in my living room."

Dion reluctantly sits up and rubs his palms over his eyes. "At this moment, I'd rather die," he mumbles.

I hand him a cup of coffee and a bottle of water, and I go back to the kitchen to make breakfast. I think back to the engagement party. Angelica and I shared glances all night, but we didn't interact again after I sent her that last text. I watched her while she awkwardly made small talk with her father, chatted with family and friends, and danced with Aria. Gianis followed her around the whole night, his body not leaving her side once, except to let her go to the bathroom. The prick was tailing her around like a puppy. If I didn't know any better, I'd think he was a threat, but he knows better than to provoke me, especially after the altercation we had. Angelica didn't seem affected by him whatsoever either, so I relaxed and enjoyed the show.

Dion and I quietly eat breakfast next to each other, his head hanging low as he tries to avoid any form of light. I finish my food first, so I put my dishes in the sink. The clattering sound makes Dion wince and glare at me. I shrug and head to the bathroom to get ready. I didn't bother showering last night. If I'm being honest, I wasn't ready to wash Angelica's smell off me. I want her scent to be permanently etched on my skin like a tattoo.

And the only way for that to happen is to see her again.

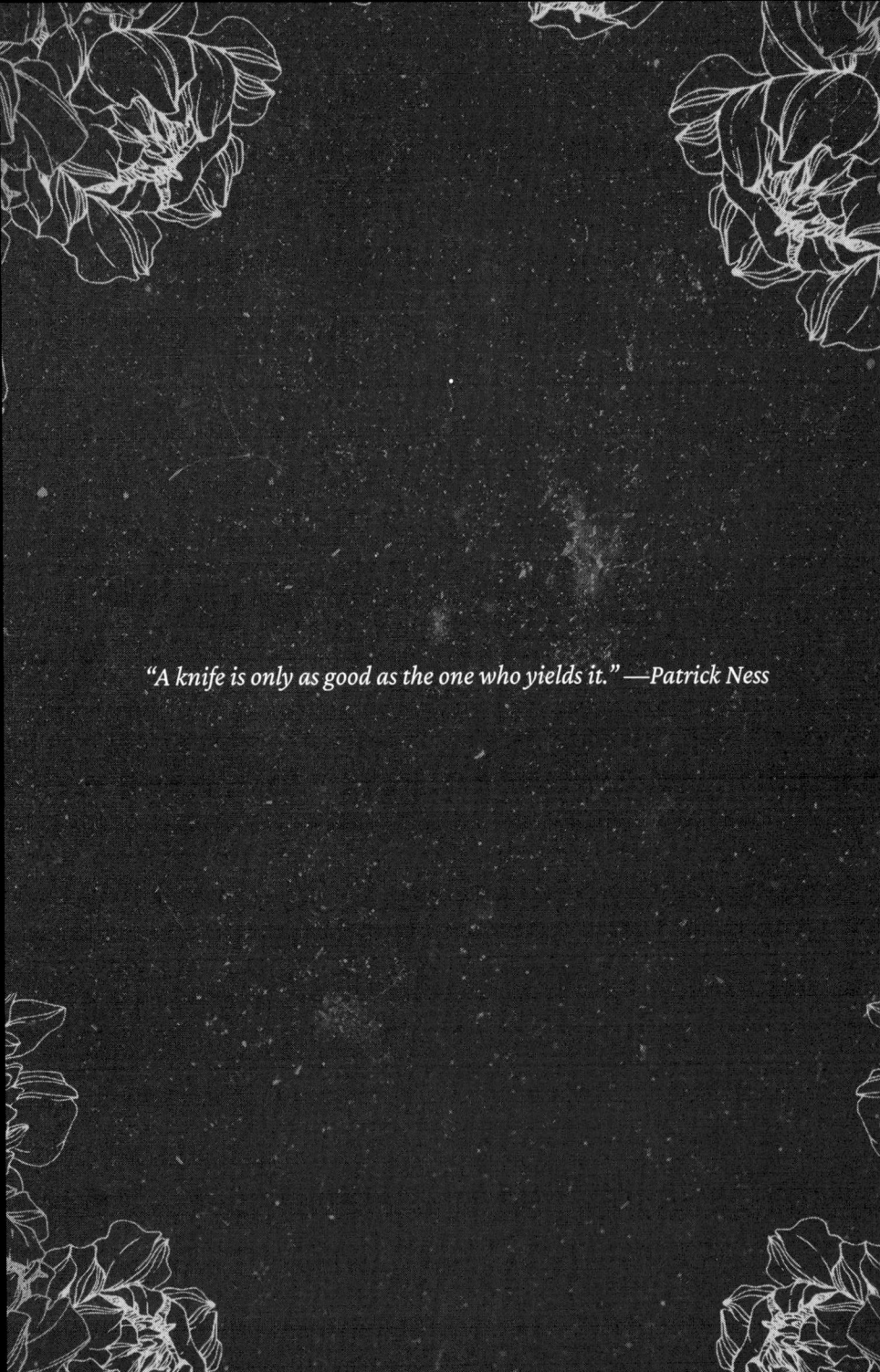

"A knife is only as good as the one who yields it." —Patrick Ness

Angelica

It's the morning after Aria's engagement party. It was late by the time the party wrapped up, so I stayed back and helped the staff clear things away, much to Aria's family's protests. Her parents are hosting a big brunch this morning, so I slept over to avoid the back and forth.

As usual, I wake up with Evan embedded in my mind, and what happened last night didn't help matters. I can still feel his tongue and fingers inside of me. A pool of heat settles between my legs at the thought. It's way too early to be feeling like this, but I can't get enough. Evan is slowly, but surely on his way to owning me in my entirety, and I can't even bring myself to be mad at it.

I get out of bed and wrap a robe over my nightgown. After quickly brushing my teeth in the adjoining bathroom, I leave the guest room to find Aria. I walk over to her bedroom across the hall and knock on the door. "Come in," she says, her voice muffled.

I crack the door open and slip inside her room only to find her laying face down in bed, still wearing her dress from last night. She turns around to face me, and it looks like she was painted on by a two-year-old.

"Oh my god. You look like a trainwreck!" I exclaim. She only groans in response.

I know that yesterday was hard for her to stomach. She had to fake a smile all night and pretend to be happy in front of friends, family, and strangers. She was miserable and couldn't wait for the night to end before it even began. She had a minor panic attack earlier in the day while getting ready, and I had to calm her down and promise that everything would be okay. I wish I could've stopped the engagement party from happening.

"You reek of booze, Ri. I didn't even see you drink anything other than a glass of champagne all night. When did you manage to get drunk?" I ask.

Her arm blindly reaches under her comforter as she fishes for something. She finally pulls out an empty twenty-six-ounce bottle of tequila.

My face twists in horror. "Please tell me you didn't drink that whole bottle yourself."

"Mmmmughhhh no, there was only half left when I found it at the bar," she manages to croak.

"Aria, that's still too much. You're hungover and your whole family is waiting to host your fiancé's family for brunch."

"I don't care anymore," she groans into her palms.

"Okay," I say, defeated. "Let's get you cleaned up and out of this dress before anyone sees you."

I help her out of bed and lead her into the bathroom so she can take a shower.

This is going to be a long morning.

Hours later, I'm back home and in the shower. I undo this morning's hairdo and remove all the bobby pins. I tilt my head back and let the warm water roll down my face and through my hair. I reach down to grab the coconut butter body wash. Dumping a generous amount of soap on a loofa, I start running it over my neck and shoulders. I expose my throat to the spray and the bubbles slide down my chest. The tingly feeling makes my skin flush, and the thought of Evan's hands gliding over my body instead of the suds creates an overwhelming feeling between my legs.

This sensation has been pooling in my stomach since this morning, and I'm aching to relieve it. I picture him standing at the door, watching me shower. I reach for the showerhead and bring it down to run the water over my breasts, moving it behind me to reach the backside, and all the way back to the front where I want it the most.

I aim the pounding spray on my center and jump at the pressure. I hold it over my clit long enough to get accustomed to the feeling and close my eyes as it starts to feel good. I continue picturing Evan's eyes blazing with heat, his jaw twitching at my every move. My orgasm starts building quickly. I move the shower head up and down, side to side, mimicking the movements of Evan's tongue on me the night before. Suddenly, it's too much to handle. I brace myself on the shower wall and I come hard, as hard as the pounding shower spray, my wetness mixing with the water running down my legs. My head falls back, and I press myself to the tile behind me, letting the water caress my body as I come down from the high. I needed that *so* badly.

Satisfied from my orgasm and comfortable in my lounge clothes, I tie up my wet hair. I'm ready to sit in front of the TV all evening, watching romantic movies with nothing but a bucket of popcorn. I put on Dirty Dancing and, while the opening credits roll, I dim the lights and place some candles around my living room to set the mood.

    This morning's brunch went smoother than I expected, but I'm drained. I had to be Aria's physical and emotional crutch the entire time. Her fiancé, albeit an outsider, was friendly and respectful. Hopefully he stays that way behind closed doors. I'm not sure how much Aria will be able to handle once they're married and living together. I'll be there every step of the way until then. I still haven't given up on finding a way out for her.

    I walk to the kitchen to grab my snacks when the doorbell rings. *Huh? I'm not expecting company today.*

    Setting the bottle of Perrier and popcorn on the coffee table in the living room, I rush to the door. Throwing all caution to the wind, I swing it open, expecting to see a kid selling scout cookies or a Jehovah's Witness, but my heart stops and my jaw drops at the sight of Evan, in all his glorious beauty, standing on my doorstep, carrying flowers and grocery bags.

    "Evan. What are you doing here? Have you given up on the whole being invisible part of stalking?" I ask teasingly.

    "Nice to see you, too, angel," he says deadpan, ignoring my attempt at a joke.

    I wasn't expecting him to show up, so I'm not dressed for company. I glance down at my clothes and my cheeks turn red. I'm wearing short-shorts and an oversized Antium U sweatshirt. I'm so embarrassed to be seen like this by him.

    "You are absolutely beautiful in your natural element, Angelica. Don't be ashamed. Any woman would kill to look like you right now," he says, sensing my insecurity. "Now, let me in before I drop all of these bags."

    I move out of the way. "Let me help you," I offer, grabbing the bouquet of peonies. "They smell amazing, thank you. I'll put them in water." My house is slowly becoming a garden.

There are peonies *everywhere*. But I can't complain. They bring life to an otherwise dull home.

As we pass the living room, Evan's gaze momentarily falls on the candles and the TV. I don't bother turning off the movie and continue down the hall. I sense Evan's eyes shift to my ass, and instead of feeling exposed, I'm flattered that he likes what he sees. He sets the bags down on the kitchen counter and looks around. He almost seems nervous and it's the cutest thing I've ever seen.

I smile. "I would give you a grand tour, but it's not like you haven't been here before," I say, my tone sarcastic.

"Keep making jokes and I'll sneak inside in the middle of the night and scare the shit out of you while you're sleeping," he responds casually.

"You wouldn't! That's just evil."

"I never said I wasn't," he says with a shrug of his shoulders. "You have yet to see to what extent. I am the devil, after all." He winks.

"I'll hide my pocketknife under my pillow and stab you with it," I reply with confidence.

"With that little thing you carry in your purse? That's foreplay for me, darling," he purrs.

Butterflies flutter in my stomach. There must be a chemical imbalance in my brain for my body to react this way. This man is deranged. Enough for me to want to run and hide. Instead, I'm drawn to him and his fucked up ways. He's a stalker. God knows what else he's involved in, and the longer it takes for me to figure it out, the more I ignore the red flags. I'm starting to not even see them anymore.

"What's all this?" I ask, pointing at the bags.

"I brought you dinner. I'm going to cook for you," he says proudly.

If I thought Evan couldn't get any more attractive, this

proves me wrong. I'm giddy at the mere thought of watching him cook in *my* kitchen. But all I want to do now is skip dinner and take him up to my bedroom. He has clearly turned me into a horny bitch.

"Grab one of the bottles of wine from the bag and help yourself," he tells me.

"This is too much, Evan. You didn't have to."

He walks around the island to me, and I suddenly feel blazing hot under my sweater. He palms the back of my neck firmly and tilts my head back to look up at him.

"I had to wash the smell of your pretty pussy off my body this morning," he says. I gulp and a little breathy sound escapes from me. He bends down, and my breathing stalls as he reaches my mouth. "I want to drench myself in your sweet aroma again."

He kisses me, but it's nothing like the one we shared yesterday. This kiss is delicate, savoring, and calculated. As if he's trying to keep some for later.

"I missed you and it's only been a few hours," he confesses, his lips still glued to mine. I melt in his arms.

"I missed you, too," I admit.

He lets go of me and starts unloading the bags. "Where are your knives?" he asks.

"In that holder," I say as I point to the counter behind him.

He reaches for the butcher knife and unwraps a large cut of beef. He finds a cutting board and sets it down, and I watch him as he grips the handle and starts slicing the meat with precision. He carves the steaks so effortlessly; I wonder how he became so experienced with handling a knife. I sit on one of my kitchen stools and observe him expertly maneuver his way around the kitchen.

"Like what you see, angel?" he asks, not taking his eyes off the meat, his fingers now tinged red.

My gaze moves from his side profile, down his muscular arms, to his veiny hands gripping the knife.

"You're very skilled," I reply, a little too raspy.

Evan looks at me and sets the butcher knife down. He quickly scrubs his fingers and wipes his hands clean with a rag, then grabs a boning knife from the rack. Instead of using it on the meat, he stands behind me and trails the pointy tip down the back of my neck, hard enough for me to feel a scratch.

"Does it turn you on?" he asks.

My chest expands heavily on every inhale, but I try to stay as still as possible. The blade against my smooth skin is frightening, but also extremely erotic. I've never experienced a danger so arousing.

"Yes," I admit with a mutter.

He lets out a deep and wicked laugh straight into my ear. "I knew you were a kinky girl, Angelica."

My breathing becomes louder, and I might soon combust from the pure eroticism of this moment. He grabs my ponytail and pulls on it hard enough to jerk my head back to his chest. He brings the knife to the side of my neck and applies pressure. "*Me kánis na kavlóno,*" he whispers. *You're making me hard.*

My back is pressed to his front, and I can feel his growing dick pushing against me.

"*Se thélo,*" I whimper. *I want you.* I rarely speak Greek. At this moment, I'm ready to do anything to get Evan to touch me.

"*Ti mou kánis ágele mou?*" he asks, his voice full of husk and lust. *What do you do to me, my angel?*

He flattens the knife against my neck and glides it over my throat, the sharp blade almost slicing me open, and he grunts as if he's frustrated. He pulls me up by my hair to make me stand and my eyes water from the pain.

"Get on the couch, now," he orders.

I hurry to comply and sit down, waiting for him to join me. Within seconds, he's right in front of me, and the tip of the knife is back at my throat.

"*Piáse to poulí mou,*" he demands. *Touch my cock.*

The request sends a wave of pleasure down to my core and the anticipation of touching him runs through me. I reach for his jeans and undo the belt buckle, followed by his button and zipper, careful not to move too much, still aware of the weapon at my neck. He inches his briefs down his hip. I follow the V down his abdominal muscles with my eyes. I want to lick it all the way down to the tip of his dick. My mouth waters at the thought of him in my mouth.

He presses the top of the knife deeper into my neck, and I spring out of my daze.

"Take it out," he barks.

I reach my hand into his boxers and grab onto his length. It's sizable. More than sizable, it's huge, thick, and warm in the palm of my hand. I free him and lick my lips as he nudges my mouth with the tip.

"Now, just like the little sex kitten that you are, you're going to let me fuck your delicious mouth until I come down your throat," he says, his voice sounding almost beastly. "If you slow down, I'll press the knife to your neck until I see blood, understood?"

I nod eagerly as a pool of wetness gathers in my underwear. I've never been this turned on in my life.

"Open," he orders.

I comply and he edges his dick into my mouth, allowing me to adjust to his size. When he reaches the back of my throat, I gag a little and he pulls out slowly.

"*Fuck,*" he groans. "Your mouth is perfect for me."

He starts thrusting in and out at a steady rhythm, making

the most delectable noises, and I can't help but moan in response.

"Such a good fucking girl, sucking my cock so well," he groans as he latches onto my hair with his free hand.

The feeling of the veins pulsing in his dick as they graze my lips, while he pushes to the back of my throat, combined with the taste of his precum on my tongue is driving me crazy. He amps up the speed and I struggle to breathe as he keeps deep-throating me vigorously. Tears are streaming down my face and my mouth is leaking saliva as he ruthlessly fucks my face.

"Tap on my thigh if it's too much," he grunts, as I try to pull my head away to catch some air. I hear Evan murmur. "Tsk, tsk, kitten. What did I say about slowing down?"

This isn't too much, and I don't want him to stop, but I just need to catch my breath. Deep down, I want him to hurt me. The adrenaline of having the knife so close to piercing my neck is turning me on like never before. I ignore his threat and stop sucking for a moment, causing Evan to hiss. He presses the knife harder. I feel a small puncture on my skin, and I gasp sharply around his dick. I feel a drop of blood trickle down the side of my neck. I shut my eyes, closing my mouth tighter on Evan, and I go back to sucking him with vigor.

"Is that what you wanted, angel? For me to draw blood?" he hisses through his teeth.

I nod, my eyes still closed as I suck and pull on him with my hand.

"Open your eyes, Angelica," he orders.

I open them and look up at him through the tears.

"You look like the most perfect, little slut sucking my dick. *Fuck*," he says, sounding almost in pain.

Evan's dick pulses in my throat as he slows his movements and spills into my mouth, his orgasm hitting him like a truck. I swallow his load before he pulls out of my mouth.

He throws the knife down on the coffee table and pushes me back on the couch. Burying his face into my neck, he inhales hard. He moves to the other side where the knife wounded me and licks the blood dripping down my neck. He growls and my body stiffens.

"Oh," I gasp.

He hums in appreciation and whispers, "Everything about you, including the blood traveling through your veins, is mine."

"Follow your inner moonlight, don't hide the madness."
—*Allen Ginsberg*

Evander

The taste of Angelica's blood on my tongue is heavenly.

Deep down, she's a freak just waiting to be discovered, and I'm more than happy to be the one to unleash her. I would kill any man who even thinks of doing the dirty things I have planned for her. I kiss her with the remnants of her blood still in my mouth and she moans into me, twirling her tongue around to taste the metallic flavor.

She is putty in my arms as I trail my hands up and down her body and kiss her mouth and neck. I yank her sweater over her head, exposing her perfect breasts, her nipples poking up and begging to be nibbled on. Her skin is warm as I place my lips all over her.

"Fucking beautiful," I grunt against her skin. "These are the most perfect tits I've ever seen."

I pull a nipple into my mouth and suck on it, catching her by surprise. Her back arches and she lets out a loud moan, goosebumps erupting all over her skin. I flip her onto her stomach.

"Undo your hair," I order as my hands travel down her back. When I get to her shorts, I slip them off her hips and down her legs, leaving her in a sexy little thong and exposing her entire delectable ass. I groan at the view and bend over to nibble on it as she frees her curls. They're still wet when she lets them down.

"It's too bad I didn't get to watch you shower," I say, grabbing onto the damp strands and wrapping them around my fist. I jerk her head back and her upper body slightly lifts off the couch. "Did you think of me while you were in there?" I ask into her ear.

Her voice is strained when she answers, "Yes, I did."

Picturing her naked and wet in the shower, combined with the way her ass is rubbing on my dick right now, makes me hard again. I start grinding my crotch onto her backside and she follows my movements, pushing her ass against me.

"Tell me." I shove the side of her face down onto the pillow and put my mouth against her ear. "Did you make yourself come?"

"Mhmm," she moans, and I huff. If I had shown up a tad earlier, I could've seen her bring herself to an orgasm for the second time. I would've had to rub one out while I watched. The image alone draws my hand to my cock.

I push her head down further into the cushion. Angelica looks like a delicate flower on the outside, but I'm not fooled by her soft exterior. She likes it rough, so that's how she's going to get it. I lift my hand up, and I slam it down on her ass cheek.

"This is for being a filthy, little slut." *Smack*. "And this is for rolling your eyes at me yesterday." *Smack*. Her body jerks on contact and she moans aloud. I raise my hand once again and give her another slap, my palmprint slowly leaving a mark on her soft skin with each hit. I spank Angelica over and over until she's a squirming and sobbing mess, begging me to fuck her.

"Evan, *please*," she cries.

I lift her ass so she's on her knees and reach under her

thong to slide my fingers through her slit. She's soaking. "You're so fucking wet, kitten. But I'm not done." I pull on her panties and let go, the fabric snapping down on her clit and making her flinch. I rub her throbbing ass cheek with my palm before I flip her onto her back and rip off her underwear. I spread her open, exposing her wet pussy, and I dip my head between her legs, dragging my nose up her thigh and sniffing her feminine scent that I'm getting to know all too well. My cock goes painfully hard at the sight of her, begging to be slipped right into her opening and impale her. I refuse to fuck her until I'm done playing. I grab the knife off the coffee table.

"Eyes on me, Angelica."

She looks up at me with her mesmerizing brown eyes, full of lust and desire, as I hover over her body, one hand resting near her head. Her chest is heaving. I cup her pussy with my free hand and rub circles over her clit with my thumb. Angelica instantly reacts to my touch and starts moving her hips to create more friction. She's met with a hard slap right on her clit and lets out a strangled cry.

"Not yet," I snarl.

I drag the knife alongside her face, down her neck and chest, around her breasts, poking her nipple with the sharp edge, and she flinches. She's breathing so heavily; I can see her chest movements clearly. I continue moving the blade down her stomach and leg, and I stop in between her thighs, near her throbbing cunt. I look up at her with a daring look and she lifts her head to look at the knife.

"Do it," she pants, knowing exactly what's on my mind.

"I want to taste you again," I say, and this time, I don't mean her pussy.

I push the knife into her upper thigh. Fear and pleasure are two sides of the same coin for some. And it's proving to be the case for Angelica. I can sense the indelible rush this dangerous situation gives her, the thrill-seeking in her shining through. Her response to this threat, albeit not real, is a sexual trigger for her. I'll be damned if I don't take advantage of it. The adrenaline coursing through my body at the thought of hurting her for pleasure immediately sends the blood straight to my dick.

"This is your femoral artery," I explain. "Depending on how it's severed, you could slip unconscious right away, or even die," I say, my voice low. Angelica shivers. "One slash would be enough. You wouldn't even be able to fight me."

I grip the handle of the knife so hard that my knuckles turn white. Angelica closes her eyes as she steadies her breathing. "Eyes."

Her lids fly open, and she stares at me with those doe eyes.

"Do it," she says again.

She's willing to risk her wellbeing and trust me with her life, and it's making me go feral. I could kill her in an instant and she still undeservingly has faith in me. *She's mine to protect.* There's nothing more attractive than trust, especially for a guy like me. The more time we spend together, the more I feel like I can unleash the unhinged sides of myself. I planned on putting on a show to get her to like me, but I never had to. My true self always feels welcome with her, and Angelica doesn't back down from anything, taking what I give her, no matter how much it pushes her boundaries.

I back away slightly and spread her legs wider. Her eyes never leave mine. I inch my way down her body and when I reach her pussy, I let out an exasperated sigh. "Fuck, Angelica. You have such a pretty cunt," I say as I split her folds open with my fingers. I spit on her, and she gasps. I flip the knife over in my hand and place the handle against her opening. She breathes out my name.

"This is mine to play with as I please, kitten," I tell her, the anticipation killing us both.

I slowly push the handle into her, and she inhales briskly, her mouth wide open. The finger grooves add an extra touch to the feel of the wooden grip. I take my time fucking Angelica with the knife as she watches the weapon go in and out of her opening. She seems surprised at the intrusion, but doesn't ask me to stop. Her face is a mix of confusion and intense arousal. She begins to moan, and the delicious sounds make this so much more exhilarating. The moans turn into little cries, she's close. But I won't let her come like this. I jerk the knife out and a huff of air comes out of her at the same time.

"*Fuck*. Such a good, little slut for me," I praise.

I pinch her thigh and make one small cut. She hisses from the pain but still doesn't tell me to stop.

"If you can't handle it anymore, say 'sunshine' and I'll stop."

I squeeze the skin around the gash and blood immediately emerges from it, thick and dark. Within an instant, my mouth is on the wound and I'm sucking on her thigh, swirling my tongue over the cut to draw the blood to the surface. Angelica whimpers and her hands move to my head to latch onto my hair. "More," she pleads.

I pop my mouth off her thigh, my lips stained red from her blood, and instinctively, I bring the knife back to her thigh and extend the cut, going a little deeper. Angelica lets out a long wail. Wanting to push her further, I make another slit and use my tongue to lick the streams of red trickling down her leg. She squirms when my saliva meets her cuts. I bring my fingers to her entrance and shove two digits inside her, causing her to cry out in pleasure. I work her pussy while I indulge in her blood. When her walls close in on my hand, I move my mouth to her clit. Angelica screams, her orgasm instantly rippling through her body. She's so spent by the end of it, she nearly passes out.

Still not over her climax, she mutters, "I want you inside me, please."

I've been waiting for this moment for so long, I can barely control myself.

"Once I take you, angel, there's no going back. Are you sure you want to do this?" I ask.

"Yes, *please*, Evan," she cries.

I grab my dick and tease her entrance, smacking her still sensitive clit with the tip. "I'm going in raw because there's no way I'm fucking you with anything between us. I'm clean."

She nods. "I'm clean and on birth control," she states. *Not for long.*

I move to stand in front of the couch and place her in a seated position, lifting her legs over my shoulders. I rub her opening with my dick to coat it with her juices and gradually inch my length inside, stretching out her pussy to fit me.

"Evan. I can't," she whimpers.

"Relax," I cut her off. "You're going to take me, Angelica."

She unclenches her walls and I push farther. When I'm buried to the hilt, I can't help but let out a groan. "*Fuuuuuck.*"

Fuck.

She's so fucking tight.

Her breathing is already labored. I can feel her insides pulsing on my dick.

"I'm not going to last long if you keep squeezing your pussy around me like that," I rasp out.

She lets out a sexy giggle and I start thrusting, fast. I couldn't slow down even if I wanted to.

"*Oh my god,*" she whimpers. "Evan, this—it's so *good.*"

"I know, kitten." *This woman will ruin me.*

Her moans keep getting louder as I penetrate deeper with

every thrust. With the sound of our bodies colliding and the slickness of her pussy, I'm on the verge of exploding. The blood is now everywhere. All over my pelvis, thighs, abdomen. It's all over Angelica and leaking onto the couch. But I don't give a fuck. The only thing on my mind is not coming prematurely. The sight of our bodies covered in blood, *her* blood, is so fucking sinful I can barely handle it. I need to pull out, so I don't finish too soon.

I flip her over and push her stomach onto the backrest. Her head dangles over the edge. She tries to get up, but I shove her back down to remind her who owns her. I slap her ass on the same spot I had spanked raw and she squeals. Her legs open wider, and I drop down to my knees to taste her again, sucking once on her clit, and her juices gush out.

"Always so fucking ready," I mutter.

I lick her from her slit up to her ass and she yelps in surprise. I smirk and continue licking circles around her tight asshole before dipping my tongue inside. I didn't think my dick could get any harder, but it turns to stone as my tongue keeps lapping over her. She can barely hold herself up as I introduce her to this new sensation. Her arms buckle, and she drops her weight onto the backrest of the couch.

"Such a little *poutána* for me. One day soon I'm going to claim this hole, too," I grumble.

I hold her down with a punishing grip before I slide deep into her pussy again. Her body goes rigid at the abrupt intrusion, and she moans so raspingly it makes my dick throb.

"Evan, it's too much," she whines.

I grab her hair and thrust even deeper, and she screams, reaching her hand back as if needing to brace herself. I lean into her until my chest is glued to her back and my mouth touches her ear. "I'm going to make you come so fucking hard you'll never be able to walk normally again. I'm going to ruin you for anyone else and make you my perfect, little slut."

She whimpers at my words, and I take that as motivation to keep fucking her into oblivion. I reach down between her legs to massage her clit. A thin coat of sweat covers our skin, only making it hotter.

"I'm so close, Evan. *I can't—*" she struggles to say.

"I know, angel. I can feel your tight pussy spasming around my cock. You take it so well," I growl.

If I don't end this soon, I might lose all sense of control. Her orgasm is close. I can feel it. I keep hitting the same spot at the same rhythm as I wait for her to explode.

"Come for me, baby. *Now*," I demand.

Angelica's pussy spasms and she cries, "*Evan*, I'm coming."

I wrap my hand around her neck without hesitation and press firmly. She instantly shatters underneath me. Her eyes close, and she stops breathing. I don't want her to faint, so I turn her head sideways and use my other hand to lightly tap her cheeks. A gurgled scream finally comes out of her mouth, making me explode, my cock bursting inside her. I slow my thrusts as her body continues shaking from her climax. I rub her back and kiss down her spine as she comes down from the high.

"*Dikiá mou*," I say. *Mine.*

After a couple minutes, I try to pull out of her, and she stops me. "No, stay," she pleads.

I lift her body while still buried inside her and lay us down on the couch in a spooning position. Her small frame fits perfectly in mine. I wrap my arms around her body, squeezing her tight against me, and her body relaxes even more. Even before I fucked her, I wanted to claim her, not only for my plan, but for *me*.

Now, it's clear as day that Angelica is mine to keep regardless of any situation we'll have to face. I'm ready to fight and kill to protect what we have. Because I love her. I'm *in love* with her.

I hope she'll feel the same when she inevitably finds out the truth.

"The truth will set you free. But not until it is finished with you."
—David Foster Wallace

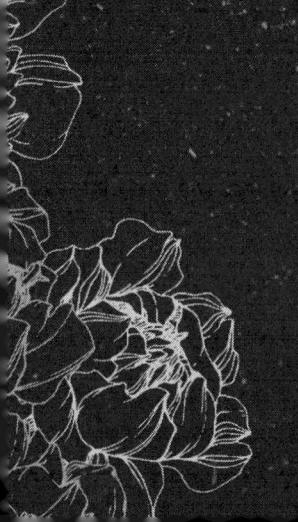

Angelica

*O*h, no.

My brain keeps telling me I'm an idiot for letting what just happened, happen. My body can't seem to listen. We just had sex, and as much as I want to deny that this won't change anything, it most definitely will. Evan is currently spooning me tightly and the feeling of his warm breath on my skin confirms I'm not going to want to let go of this moment anytime soon.

On cue, my stomach grumbles and I feel Evan's body start to shake behind me, his nose buried in my neck. He's laughing.

"I think someone's hungry," he says.

I blush in embarrassment and my cheeks go even redder when I spot the knife on the coffee table. It's almost unbelievable that I let him use it on me. I never thought I was a person with kinks, but seeing Evan handling that knife with such grace was enough for my legs to clench. Whatever *that* was between us needs to happen again. ASAP. What we did was taboo and so dangerous, but it was the best sex I've ever had. I've never come so hard in my life, let alone from penetration. His threat came to fruition because I can't feel my legs anymore. *I hope you're happy, Evan.*

Evan slides his dick out of me. When we get up, I groan in

protest. He hurries to the kitchen and comes back with a clean, wet rag to help clean me up. He didn't pull out, so there's no sticky cum for me to wipe off, but we're covered in blood. Evan kneels on the floor and carefully dabs the towel on my skin to remove the red stains.

"Stand up," he demands.

I get off the couch, and his face is now positioned exactly at the apex of my legs. Even though he was just buried deep inside of me, it feels different being exposed like this. He doesn't seem to notice my discomfort and instructs me to widen my stance.

"Now, don't move. I want to watch my seed leak out of you," he orders, a smirk appearing at the corner of his lips.

My hand flies over my mouth as I take in what he just said. My whole body feels like it's on fire and my face must be beet red. Slowly, I feel his cum trickle down my leg and I look down, mortified he's making me do this. He glides two fingers up my thighs to scoop his cum and keeps moving them up to my center before shoving the digits into my entrance. I gasp out loud, the feeling turning my insides into molten lava.

Evan growls. An actual *growl*. "This pussy is mine, Angelica. I want you to be full of my cum and pleading for more every time I see you. I don't want you to waste an ounce. Believe me when I say I will be putting a baby in you."

My response gets stuck in my throat and all I can do is nod. *A baby?* As much as the thought of bringing a child into this world worries me, it doesn't seem so scary with Evan. It excites me. He pushes me down on the couch, his fingers still inside me, and pulls them out once I'm sitting. The sight of him kneeling before me, sends butterflies to my stomach. I have no control over myself when he's around, so seeing him in a vulnerable position like this makes me feel superior for once, as if he's at *my* mercy.

"You like seeing me on my knees for you, kitten?" he asks, bringing his fingers up to my mouth and letting them rest on my bottom lip. I'm pretty sure he can read my mind at this point.

"Yes," I admit.

"How does that make you feel?" he asks as he nudges my lips open and shoves his fingers into my mouth. "Suck," he commands.

I do, tasting the mixture of my juices and the saltiness of his cum. His other hand grazes my legs. He could have me again, right now, and I'd be ready.

"Answer," he demands, slipping his fingers past my lips. "How does that make you feel?"

"Like I'm in control," I finally respond.

"You are a queen—*my queen*—and I will bow down to you until my last breath." I let in a little sharp inhale. I've never been worshiped like this, and it fills me with exhilaration and happiness. If I am his queen, he is my *king*.

He lifts my right leg, kissing his way up from my toes. Halfway up, he stops and says, "I am forever at your mercy, but when it comes to our relationship, I own you. But you own me just as much. Don't think of this as being oppressed. Think of it as me having your best interest in mind in every aspect of your life."

He resumes kissing up my thigh while he goes on. "I will never stop you from doing anything, going anywhere, or speaking to anyone," he says, finally reaching the top of my thigh.

He looks up at me, something like awe in his expression, like I'm the most perfect angel he's ever seen. "Unless it puts you in danger, or has a dick," he finishes.

Realizing what he just said, I gasp and smack his arm, indignant. He gets off the floor, chuckling hard. My brain wants to be annoyed at him, but I can't focus on anything other than the sound of his laugh and the bright smile on his face, and I grin back. I admit to not having seen him in many interactions with others, but I know for a fact that not a lot of people get to witness Evan happy. My heart swells at the thought of being that person for him, as much as he is for me. *He is my person.*

I'm terrified at the thought of where this will lead us. At the same time, I've only felt a sense of peace since Evan came into my life. What could go wrong?

After the best sex of my life, I had the best meal of my life.

After we took a shower, Evan got back to work in the kitchen and created a masterpiece. Not only is he good in bed, he's also a good cook. All I can picture is waking up to him every morning, the smell of fresh food reaching my nose and Evan greeting me with breakfast in bed.

We ate moussaka with Greek potatoes and salad, paired with the most delectable red wine. I don't know why we would ever eat out now that I've tasted his cooking.

We finish our meals and take the rest of the wine to the living room. Dirty Dancing finished a while ago, so I turn on Netflix to find something else to put on. Now that my relationship with Evan is clearly heading into 'serious' territory, I want to know more about him. I land on a new season of Top Chef, and let it play in the background.

I plead with myself not to, but the question slips out of my mouth before I get the chance to stop it. "So, what are we?" I ask nervously, toying with the hem of my sweater. *Who still asks that, stupid?*

Evan cocks his head and swirls his glass of wine, not seeming to notice my embarrassment from asking a question a fifteen-year-old would ask her first boyfriend.

"I thought we'd established that already," he responds.

Other than Evan calling me 'his' every chance he gets and declaring that he owns me, we haven't had an actual discussion about the nature of our relationship. I need clarity.

"I mean, kind of, but what is *this*?" I ask, gesturing between us. "I understand we belong to each other, but it's much more complicated than that."

"What's complicated, Angelica?" he asks. How am I supposed to bring him up to my father? How will he react when he finds out I'm a mob princess?

"For starters, we've embarked on a whirlwind romance without truly thinking ahead. We can't be in this bubble forever, Evan."

"I understand, but what are you worried about, exactly?"

I keep playing with the edge of my top some more, not meeting his gaze, and feeling even more nervous. Now is my chance to tell him the whole truth, so I brace myself for the impact of my words.

"I'm the daughter of a mafia boss. My father is the head of the Kouvalakis family," I blurt out.

I look at him and he stares back, not an ounce of emotion in his face. I'm worried I've already scared him off. After a moment, his face softens, and he puts down his wine glass to grab my hand.

"I know that already, Angelica. I don't care," he insists.

"What? How did you know?" I ask, shocked that he never brought it up.

He lifts one eyebrow and makes a face like *'are you serious right now?'*

The realization blurts out my mouth. "Right, you stalked me."

He smirks. "I told you I do my research, angel. I know your last name, and everyone in the city is aware of the families who run these streets. Do you really think I wouldn't have found out?"

He's got a point. I was aware he knew my full name, but it never clicked that he could associate it to my father. It's very clear what my family does, and Evan was my *stalker*. I shouldn't be surprised.

"Then, why didn't you say anything? I've been so worried that you'd want nothing to do with me if you found out." My voice ends in a whisper.

Not many people would willingly involve themselves with the mob if they can avoid it. It's dangerous, reckless, and so full of drama.

"I didn't think it was necessary to mention, especially if it's of no matter to me. All I care about is you." His eyes bore into me, unflinching. My heart stutters.

"You don't know my father, then," I state, my tone final.

"I know exactly who he is, Angelica. Trust me, he will not be a problem."

That sounds nice and all, but it doesn't fix my problems. The main one being my father. The second being that I don't know if I can fully trust Evan. My brain isn't wired to trust blindly. In my mind, it's guilty until proven innocent. He might not deserve this doubt, but I don't know any other way. I'm scared that my wariness will get in the way of what we have.

Who is he really? What business does he conduct with his uncle? What's his last name? Why have I never heard of him? Why do people want him dead? Why is he single and not married? So many unanswered questions. They make my mind go into overdrive. I can't bring any of this up to him. I just can't. It'll burst our bubble and potentially ruin what is now mine. *Him.* But in the end, there's still an obstacle.

"Tell me more about yourself, Evan. I feel like I'm being kept in the dark," I ask, trying for a light tone.

"What do you want to know, angel?" he answers absently, as if his mind has suddenly gone somewhere else.

"Your name. *Full* name. Where you grew up; where you went to school; who your uncle is. Will I be able to meet him?" I shoot and I catch a slight wince from him as he looks away. He hesitates for a few seconds before replying.

"My name is Evan Loukas. I grew up here, in Cebrene. My family lived in the old parts, where I went to school with Dion. Now, I live in the Heights," he answers stiffly.

Loukas? The name registers in my head, but I don't fully recognize it. It's not a prominent family name in the metropolis. I think back and a tragedy that happened when I was a kid comes to mind. A man and his wife were killed, and if I'm not mistaken, their last name was Loukas. I can't remember when, where, or how it happened, but it was the talk around town for a little while. I don't recall them having any children, but I was too young.

"What about your uncle?" I ask as I take a sip of wine.

Evan readjusts himself on the couch and clears his throat. "He's dead."

Shit. I wasn't expecting that. His parents, little sister, and uncle are deceased. Does he have any family left? "I'm sorry," I mumble. I feel terrible for bringing this up.

"It's okay, Angelica. It's not your fault," he says, squeezing my hand, and he gives me a soft smile.

I nervously gulp down some wine and decide it's better to

lay the topic to rest for now. Evan and I might still have some learning to do, but we have a lifetime for that.

Tomorrow, I'll go see my father and tell him about Evan, and not worry about the outcome. I've spent my whole life fearing him. I even left home to get away, but I'm not running anymore.

Part III
The Betrayal

"Betrayal is the only truth that sticks." —Arthur Miller

Angelica

Knowing what I've come here for today, a feeling of dread immediately washes over me as I walk through the door of my *baba*'s house. For the first time, I'll be standing up for myself, and I'm terrified. I've barely spoken to my father since the charity ball, but I know he's upset. I unexpectedly left Niko behind, and I've been avoiding Gianis. The latter won't bother my father as much, but I'm sure he's wondering about my behavior.

There are still extra guards stationed around the property. Eldora greets me with a quick hug and kiss, and hurries away to continue her housework. It's quiet, which is the usual around here. When I called this place home, it was often eerily silent, even with three people living in the house.

I catch a glimpse of my father sitting outside through the kitchen patio door, reading the newspaper, and drinking coffee. Although I can say I truly dislike this man, he's still my father and I somehow still hold the slightest amount of respect for him. He cared and provided for me when I was growing up. He showed me an abundant amount of love when I was a little girl, crying for my *mama*. I wish that image remained the only one of him I remembered. Sadly, that's not the case, and I've come to terms with it.

I try to visit him once a week to stay in his good graces, but our interactions only stretch so far. He asks me about my current pastimes, if I need money, and if I'm doing okay. I ask him about his health, his ventures, and whether he needs help with anything. I usually come over for lunch and stay for a couple of hours, until he has to get back to work or I get bored. But today is different. I'm here for a purpose, and as anxious as I am about the outcome, I put my big girl pants on this morning. I'm ready.

I join him on the patio and sit down. We remain in silence for a while. He keeps glancing at me, as if he has something to say but doesn't know how to. I've never seen my father so unsure about speaking up. I almost want to ask him what's on his mind, but I prefer to stay in the dark for as long as I can. We have never been good at communicating. When I was little, it was easy. I clung to him in the absence of my mother, and he acted like a dutiful father, tending to my every need. Even though we had a housekeeper and nannies, I never left his side. I loved him so much back then.

Things changed when I became a teenager. My mood fluctuated and I remember being so angry, but I didn't know why. There still seems to be a whole period of my life that's just blank. I have no memory of the lost time. But my father became cold toward me for some reason, barely able to look me in the eye. When I tried talking to him about what was going on, he claimed nothing was wrong, but things had changed. I noticed how cold he had grown. He was no longer the loving father I once knew. I spent many nights wondering what I'd done for him to behave that way. It hasn't been the same since.

The nightmares I had when I was younger started showing up again when I moved back to Cebrene a couple months ago. A reminder that I'm in Hell again. I still don't know if these dreams are real fragments of my memories, but they're always skewed and confusing. Images of women covered in long, conservative dresses hurrying groups of wide-eyed, little girls into spaces that look like classrooms. Children bunked in small rooms, clutching onto each other while the women came in to give punishments to the bratty ones. I never see myself in those dreams, but it always feels like I was there, watching and living everything with those girls.

My father finally speaks. "I was told you left Niko at the charity ball. Care to explain why?" he asks, with a judgmental tone. I only have one option: lie.

"I felt sick and had to leave unexpectedly. He offered to take me home, but I refused. I didn't want both of us to be missing at the table," I explain.

Baba nods, though he seems to doubt my answer. "How did you get home?"

Shit. Here's where I'll have to be careful. My father never asks questions blindly.

"I walked."

"You *walked*?" He narrows his eyes. At that same moment, I hear footsteps approaching and turn to see Gianis walking out of the kitchen to join us. *Yes, my saving grace.*

"*Yié mou*, sit. I was just about to talk to Angelica about something," my father says.

Gianis' face turns weary, but he complies and takes a seat between us at the round patio table. I don't get the chance to greet him when my father turns his attention back to me. "I heard about that boy you've been fucking like a little *poutána*," he hisses.

I almost spit out my coffee. "Wow," I choke out.

Fucking like a little whore. So much for not knowing how to approach the situation. My stomach twists at his harsh words and I'm too stunned to speak. Gianis' expression widens in shock and his nostrils flare as he stares at my father, hands clenched under the table, as if he wants to hit something.

But my *baba* doesn't even notice the shift in the air as he continues, his tone full of disgust. "Did you know that your *boyfriend* is the new Godfather of our rival family, Angelica? Evander is the *actual* Vasilakis heir. He is the nephew of the man I had killed weeks ago. I planned to take over his territory. Discovering that Evander is the successor has created an obstacle for us, but not one we couldn't handle. But now that you've been seen with him, you're going to fuck everything we've worked for," he spits.

I'm in utter shock. There's no way... *Evander Vasilakis?* I thought his name was Evan Loukas. I never knew his last name before last night, but I never once thought it would be Vasilakis. Everything starts piecing together and my heart sinks further and further. His dead uncle is Ignatius Vasilakis? His business is *mob* business. The club he owns is in Vasilakis territory. It was all under my nose and I chose to ignore it. His secrecy was because he was hiding his whole identity, knowing exactly which family I represented. His rival. I always knew he'd been withholding information from me, but I never thought it would be this destructive.

"First of all, it's none of your business whether I'm *fucking* him or not," I say, barely moving a muscle in my face. I'm never this blunt with my *baba*, but his comment sparked a fire under my ass. I'm about to eject out of my seat and land a punch right onto his face. "Second, how is that possible? I know the Vasilakis family, and he was never mentioned as the heir." My father had a long-standing battle with them, but never once was I made aware of Evan's—*Evander's*—existence.

I don't keep up with the ins and outs of the mob, but the Vasilakis family has been a thorn in my father's side for decades. As a young girl, I'd heard that Ignatius and my father were once allies, but something tore their friendship apart, and my father has been trying to destroy him ever since. I had no idea he'd had him *killed*. Regardless, it was always known Ignatius Vasilakis didn't have an heir, since he had no children of his own. His brother, who was the Godfather before him, was brutally murdered, alongside his wife and children.

"Surprise, *kóri mou*. It looks like your new boyfriend hasn't been honest with you."

How does he even know about Evan in the first place? I inwardly laugh at myself for even asking that question. How could I expect any less from my father? I came here expecting to have a grown-up conversation with a man who still treats me like a child. I should've known he would have his goons watching me. I give Gianis a glare, my anger pouring out. "Did you tell him?" I ask, my tone full of rage. I've never spoken to him like this. But he knew about Evan. Could he have impulsively told my father because he was jealous?

"No, Ang. It wasn't me," he replies, sounding distraught. I believe him. Gianis would never hurt me.

My father lets out a sharp laugh that doesn't reach his cold eyes. It gives me the chills. "My own daughter is betraying me for a man who lies to her. For *the Diávolos*. What have I done to deserve this disloyalty?"

How dare he say I am betraying him? After everything I've tolerated and looked past. This man is my father, but right now, he feels more like my enemy. I can't stop the fury bubbling inside of me. So much that I can't stop the next words from spilling out of my mouth.

"*Fuck you, baba*," I screech, my voice sounding raspy and high-pitched. "I've been nothing but a good daughter to you. An obedient one, at that. How dare you talk to me like I'm a piece of garbage and call me a little *whore*? I've never once gone against you, and you think I would betray you *on purpose*? You are as despicable of a man as you are a father," I spit, feeling sick with outrage and hurt.

What happens next, I never would've expected. My father gets out of his chair and slaps me right across the face. My head swings to the side from the brutal force of the hit, and I can taste metal in my mouth. I hear Gianis growl as he pushes out of his chair and slams his fists on the table, making our coffee mugs rattle.

"What the fuck, Peter?" He takes a moment to catch his breath. "Hitting your own daughter? I should kill you for putting your hands on her."

"Mind your own business and watch your mouth, boy. I could have your tongue cut out for threatening me. Don't meddle in things you don't understand," my father responds as he sits back down at the table, seemingly unbothered by what he just did. The heartlessness of this man still shocks me every time. My hand rises shakily to my burning cheek, and I cover it with my palm. Gianis kneels in front of me and yells out to Eldora to bring me an ice pack.

"Ang, look at me," he says. I face him and my eyes well with tears, but I refuse to let them fall. I will not allow my father to be the cause of anymore pain. The adrenaline that I felt in the moment starts to dissipate as the stinging in my cheek takes precedence. I can't hold back the tears any longer. Gianis tenderly cups my face with his hands and looks at me straight in the eyes, his expression apologetic, and wipes the falling tears away with his thumbs.

"I didn't tell him, I swear," he pleads, his voice barely audible. I nod.

I know if it had been anyone else, Gianis would've killed them on the spot. But he can't because of who my father is—the Kouvalakis Godfather of the Night, and his boss. We both know the ripple effect that would cause.

Eldora arrives with the ice pack, and Gianis gently rests it on my face, causing me to wince a little from the sting. My father puts down his newspaper and finally breaks his silence.

"You are to stop seeing him immediately, Angelica, or I will do the same to him as I did his uncle. Do you understand?" My father interrupts.

"Over my dead body," I seethe. I push myself off the chair, moving away from Gianis. He places the ice on the table, his eyes full of worry. He knows exactly where I'm going.

"If you think for one second that you can control me, tell me who to talk to, who to date, you are gravely mistaken," I spit. "I am no longer your concern. You are as dead to me as I am to you. Do *you* understand?"

I want to smash something, more specifically, his face, but my father does nothing. Doesn't say anything. Doesn't even look my way. "What happened all those years ago for you to hate me like this?" I cry out. "Why can't I remember? TELL ME!" I scream. "Why do I have nightmares? What aren't you telling me?" I've officially lost it as I start sobbing hysterically. My father keeps ignoring me and walks back into the house without responding.

"Angelica," Gianis says in a soothing voice as he stands to join me. He rests his palms on my cheeks again. "It's okay, *mikrí mou.*" *My little bird.*

My eyes grow wide. Gianis hasn't called me that since we were kids, when I would run around my backyard, pretending to have wings. I would fly into him and he'd fake an injury every time. That's when he started calling me his little bird. The nickname immediately fills me with a sense of peace and a slight twinge of sadness at how much things have changed. I wish I were that young again, with no cares in the world other than being with my best friends.

"What isn't he telling me, G? I can't take it anymore," I murmur.

He lets go of my face and runs his hands through his hair. "I don't know, Ang. I really don't know," he replies regretfully.

Breathless with anger, I turn to walk away, promising to myself to never step foot in this house again.

"Please, be careful," Gianis whispers right before I leave.

I force myself to smile. "I will, *Gianiaki*."

I hail an Uber to my father's property, and I wait for my ride outside the gate. I text Evan to let him know I'm on my way to see him. He's probably busy, so I don't bother waiting for his response before heading toward the nightclub. I have to talk to him right away and inform him of my father's threat. He needs to know what happened.

I don't want to believe what my *baba* told me. There's no way the Evan I know is my father's rival. He wouldn't lie to me, let alone keep this huge secret from me after everything we've been through and shared. I know there are things I don't know about him, but this would be big enough for a 'first date' mention, maximum second. A simple, "Hey, I'm Evander Vasilakis, by the way, the new Godfather of the Night. I'm technically your enemy, and your father wants me dead," would have sufficed. Surely, my father was just lying to get under my skin.

But if what my *baba* said is the truth, then why would Evan want to be with me, the daughter of the man who killed his uncle? My heart sinks. What if he was planning this all along? If he knew who I was from the start, there's no way he could truly like someone directly linked to the murder of a family member.

Was Evan playing pretend all along? What are his true intentions? I can't fathom this all being true. I want to vomit at the thought. *No.* Evan wouldn't do this to me, he wouldn't have lied like this. I reach for the elastic band around my wrist. I stretch it out wide and let it fling back onto my skin multiple times. One pain eliminates the other. I haven't had to resort to this in weeks, my mind too preoccupied in a beautiful nightmare with Evan.

My Uber ride pulls up and I hop into the backseat. Evan's office is only a 12-minute drive from here, but it feels like an eternity with the fate of our relationship looming in the air. As we approach the nightclub's entrance, I see Leon sitting on a chair smoking a cigarette. The car stops right in front of him, and he gives me a lazy smile as I step out.

"*Yiasou*, Leon. I'm here to see Evan. Is he inside?"

"Yes, he is, *noná*," he replies with a smile. *Godmother?* My brows knit in confusion, and he lets out a little laugh, not aware of the disorientation he just implanted in my brain. He clearly knows something I don't and I'm even more nervous to confront Evan now. I head inside, making my way through the empty nightclub. I approach Evan's office, and I stop when I hear murmurs from inside. Not wanting to interrupt his meeting, I tiptoe to the door to hear who's talking. I immediately recognize Dion's voice.

"*Afentiko*, I'm telling you this as a friend. Things are getting out of hand; she's going to find out sooner than later. She's at her father's house right now with Gianis. You gave her my last name, for god's sake!" He lets out an exasperated breath. "Sneaking around with her is only going to work for so long. Do you not think Peter already knows what's going on?"

Evan lets out a sigh, but Dion continues, "You have

completely derailed from the plan, and I understand, but don't lose sight of why we're doing this. Angelica is a means to an end. You can't have it both ways without dealing with the consequences."

A means to an end. Dion's last name. This new betrayal, sudden, yet inevitable, despite what my father said, feels like a blow to my system. I had convinced myself it couldn't be true. But I was too enamored with Evan to see the truth. To even *look* for the truth. I'd promised myself not to trust him so easily, but I let my guard down. Hearing Dion say those words triggers my primal fight reaction and a massive flood of adrenaline shoots through me, making me erupt right into Evan's office. The loud bang of the door against the wall surprises them, and they look at me with equal parts shock and confusion. Evan is sitting on the chair behind his desk, while Dion leans against the bookcase.

"Angel, I wasn't expecting you—"

I cut him off. "Why don't you tell me the truth, *Evander*? Who are you?" His face goes blank. The rage is burning in me like a blaze. I look him straight in the eyes, not backing down for one second. A moment passes before Evan's expression changes as his gaze moves across my face. I'd almost forgotten what my *baba* had done. I turn away from him as he stands up and circles around the desk toward me. He grabs the back of my neck and brings my eyes back to him, and my heart skips a beat from his touch. Even in our darkest moments, his touch can set my insides on fire.

"Who did this to you?" The words are a promise of agony to whoever inflicted this injury on me.

I jerk out of his hold and take a step back. "My father, after he called me a little *poutána* for fucking his NEMESIS!" I scream the last word as my face contorts with rage. Evan's expression matches mine. "This doesn't even matter now," I spit, pointing to the redness on my cheek and the gash on my lip. "I need to know the truth, Evander. I heard what Dion said to you, so don't try lying to me. Was any of this real?"

I glance at Dion, who has gone still as a statue, and I turn back to Evan. He doesn't even have to say anything. I can see the truth in his eyes. The sorrow, the fear, and the regret. I don't think I could even bear to hear the words from his mouth.

"Why?" The question comes out as a whimper. A tear breaks free, the rest following in an unbroken stream. "How...*how* could you do this to me?" I lift my hands to wipe my face. "You could've gotten what you wanted, Evander, if you'd just been honest," I scream at him, the tears flowing freely down my face now. "Couldn't you see I was falling for you? If you'd told me what happened, I would've understood. I could've helped you somehow. I would've done anything for you. I love you," I sob.

Evan winces as he hears those three words: I love you. Words I have never said to any other man until now. This was not the way I expected to profess my love to him. His expression is pained, and it looks as if he has just been stabbed in the gut. *Welcome to the club.*

"I guess I'm the idiot for going into this blindly. You were my *stalker*. I ignored all the signs. I might be crazier than you! I didn't even know your full name, for fuck's sake. I let you *fuck* me. Turns out, my father is right. I let you use me like a whore," I seethe, not caring that Dion is standing right next to me, his eyes moving back and forth between me and Evander.

My heart feels like it's broken in a million pieces. There's no way it can go back to what it was before. I let this man into my life, into my body, and into my heart. I allowed him to hold it, protect it, and he tore it apart. He betrayed me. I can barely see through my tears, but Evan is suddenly in front of me again. He grabs my arm and opens his mouth to speak, and I see red. I feel like I might spontaneously combust at any moment, as if someone set a slow and steady match beneath my center, deep in the pit of my stomach.

"Don't you fucking touch me, Evander," I yell, my voice coming out hoarse. I yank my arm back from his hold and storm out of his office, passing Sebastian and Gregory on my way out. Both of their faces are twisted in concern. *Great. They heard everything, too.*

Evan doesn't follow me out, and I don't know if that makes things better or worse. I hear a loud yell coming from the room and the sound of objects crashing to the ground. I try to wipe the overflowing tears off my face as I rush down the stairs. I can't breathe and I need air, now. I push the door open, and of course, it's raining. I look up into the sky and close my eyes, letting the rain fall on my face and mix with my tears. I'm in so much pain and I don't know where to go. I turn right and start walking. No, I start *running* down the street. I have no end in sight, but I keep going until I can't catch my breath and have to stop. I need to get as far away from here as possible.

I grab my phone out of my pocket. My hands are trembling, and I can barely see the screen with the rain falling so hard. I go through my recent calls, frantically looking for a specific contact, and I dial it. He picks up after two rings and I lose it at the sound of his voice, sinking down to my knees on the asphalt.

"Gianis, please..." I can barely get the words out through my hysterical cries. I hear rustling on the other side of the phone and then a car door slamming shut, the faint sound of the engine turning on.

"Send me your location and don't move. I'm coming," he says.

I hang up and send him my coordinates. I don't even know where I am, but I sit on the side of the road and wait.

Gianis pulls up within minutes and I'm shocked at how fast he got here. The car has barely come to a stop, and he is already outside, walking toward me. I try to get up, but I'm shuddering violently and can barely hold myself up. I don't know how long I ran for, but my legs are sore, and I'm so cold and wet from the rain. I spent the entire time snapping the band on my wrist so hard I had to switch sides. Both are bruised with blood blisters under my already sensitive skin. I turn my palms up and grimace from the stinging pain as the rain hits the broken skin. Gianis hurries to me and I jump into his arms, not caring that I'm wet and a complete mess. He feels me shaking and takes off his jacket to put it over my shoulders.

"Shhh, it's okay, *mikrí mou*, I've got you," he whispers into my hair and holds me tight. The feeling of familiarity surrounds my body. He rests his chin on the top of my head, and I let myself relax into his arms. The gentleness of his actions, mixed with the destructive feeling of heartbreak, causes me to sob uncontrollably into his chest, making his shirt wetter than the rain falling on us. He lifts his arm up and starts stroking my hair.

When I finally start to calm down, we disentangle and he leads me to his car, carefully easing me into the passenger seat. He cranks up the heat and moves off. He asks me what happened a couple times, but I can't muster up any words. I spend the drive looking out the window, focusing on the droplets of rain trailing down the glass. My breathing eventually slows, but tears keep forming in the corner of my eyes.

"Do you want me to come in?" he asks.

I shake my head. "I need to be alone."

"Angelica. I'll kill him. Just say the word. I never want to see you like this again," he says.

I can see the pain and the longing in his eyes as he looks at me and the waterworks begin again. This time it's a different type of heartbreak. The one I feel for Gianis. I'm crying because I love him, but not the love that he wants or deserves. Not the same love I feel for Evander. It breaks my heart because he is so deserving, but I can't give that to him. I unbuckle my seat belt, jump at his neck, and squeeze him hard. It takes him a few seconds to return the hug and he wraps his arms around my body.

"Thank you, G. I'll spare you the trouble, but your offer means the world to me, as do you."

He stays silent as I step out of the car. I haven't felt this much sorrow since my mother died, and even though this isn't comparable to the pain I felt after losing her, it's the closest thing to it that I've experienced in a very long time. This is the reason why I never let anyone get close to my heart. Not only did Evan betray me, but I also betrayed myself by allowing this to happen.

All the fantasies my mind has been creating about us being in a relationship are now null and void.

There is no playing house with the devil.

> "Honesty is very hard. The truth is often painful. But the freedom it can bring is worth the trying."
> —Fred Rogers

Evander

The last thing I should be doing right now is following her after what she found out, but I can't let her wander in the streets alone in the rain.

Leon wasn't at his post when she left, so I couldn't find out which way she went. I circle the area and finally find her standing in the street with another man. I stop the car far enough for them not to notice me and turn off the engine and headlights. It's getting dark, so I can't clearly see the identity of the person next to her, but I recognize the car. *Fucking Gianis.*

Angelica is in his arms, crying, and the intimate scene sends pangs of jealousy through my chest. The vicious kind of jealousy. *Fuck him.*

He's holding her and caressing her hair ever so gently, in the way that only a man in love would touch a woman. I want to chop off every single one of his fingers for laying them on her. He missed his chance with Angelica. She's *mine* now.

My irritation crackles, and I let out a strong guttural sound, punching my steering wheel hard. The fact that she called him when she needed comfort lights up something inside of me. I'm the person she should be calling when her world is falling apart, when she needs someone to pick up the pieces of her broken heart, not *him*. Not anyone else for that matter. This is on me. It's my fault. I should've known this would ruin her. Ruin us. I had no doubt she wouldn't react lightly to this news, but I hoped it wouldn't be this bad somehow, and that I could avoid it as long as possible.

My strong, yet soft, Angelica. A rose, beautiful and delicate, but she also has thorns. And like every beautiful thing in life, she comes with an arsenal of troubles that I am prepared to fight. There are many obstacles I have to face to be with her, but I would do anything to have her. Our families would never accept our union, but I couldn't give two fucks about them. If there's one thing the *Diávolos* isn't scared to do, it's eliminate all threats.

I only had one goal in mind before I met her, but everything changed when I got to know her, feel her, taste her, and *love her*. I knew everything would eventually come crashing down when she found out the truth. I just didn't expect it to come from her father.

Dion tried to warn me, but it was too late. I don't know how to fix this. I already wanted to kill Peter for what he did to my uncle. Now, I want to make him pay for putting his hands on Angelica and calling her a little whore. I don't give a shit if he is her father, he can rot in the lowest depths of Hell. I was immobilized by fury when I saw Angelica's injuries and heard the vicious words that he'd said to her. He didn't even bother telling her the truth about her childhood, only choosing to divulge the truth of my identity to get her to feel guilty and obey him.

Even after all the words she spat at me, '*I love you*' is all I can hear. It's been rooted in my mind ever since. Being loved by Angelica is exactly what I wanted. I should be happy. I have her right where I wanted her, but not for the same reasons I started out with. Now, I want her to love me because I love her. And I'll be damned if anything or anyone gets in the way of that.

I couldn't find the strength to say anything back to Angelica at that moment. I wanted to scream that I loved her back at the top of my lungs, but I couldn't. I don't deserve to be loved by her, especially now. But I will never accept a life without her. My angel. She came into my life and brought something I didn't know I was lacking. Happiness. Peace. She is not only the sun but the moon, and she came into my life to shine on me even in my darkest hours.

The pain in her voice when she asked me to tell her the truth will haunt me forever. I didn't even get the chance to explain the full story, because she saw everything in my eyes before I could even utter a word.

I couldn't hide the disgust I felt toward myself. The regret of stringing her along without being honest. The fear of her slipping away from me, without being able to stop her. Dion had come to me with a warning to be careful, as he knew we'd been seen. I had tasked him with making sure that no obstacles came in the way of the plan. Little did either of us know, I was the one obstructing its path.

Dion got word that one of Peter's men saw someone leaving Angelica's house. *That someone being me.* It didn't take long for them to dig further and realize I was Ignatius's nephew and the rightful Vasilakis heir. I can only imagine how livid her father was once he figured out that his daughter was involved with his rival. In different circumstances, I would say that my plan is working.

I've been living on borrowed time, and now it's all over.

The look of repulsion on Angelica's face was enough for me to want to fucking curl into myself. As much as I want to give her space, I can't bear to be apart from her any longer without telling her the whole truth. Knowing I'm the reason for her pain doesn't sit well with me. I can't let her go to sleep in that state. She deserves to know this wasn't her fault.

Dion saw the anguish on my face after I'd trashed my entire office and urged me to go after her, even if she refused to speak to me. It's not like I'm going to give her the option to ignore me, anyway.

I don't know where Gianis is taking her, but I know that Angelica would want to go home. I discreetly follow them all the way to her house and watch her get out of his car alone. Relief washes over me. If Gianis had gotten out of the car, too, he would have ended up with a bullet in his head, courtesy of me. Angelica would never forgive me for that, but I don't think I would've been able to control my impulses.

Gianis stays in her driveway for a few long moments, and I know he is debating whether to go after her. The longer he stays there, the more my frustration rises, and I have to hold myself back from walking over to his car and physically dragging him away myself. He's lucky that I'm sparing him right now.

I can't help but wonder if he feels anguish, too. The feeling of wanting what you can't have is something I'm experiencing all too well right now. I can sense Angelica slipping away from my grip more and more, every passing moment. I have to get to her. *Now.*

Gianis finally pulls out of her driveway, but I stay in the car for a couple more minutes to gather my thoughts. It's still raining and the sound of the drops on the car roof is soothing. I brace myself and head to Angelica's door and ring the doorbell. There's no response, so I start banging until I hear faint rustling from inside.

"Angelica, let me in. We have to talk," I yell over the loud noise of the downpour. Nothing. "Angel, I know you're in there. Open the door and let me explain." I hear a loud sigh through the door, but it remains closed. "I'm trying to be nice and allow you to let me in, but if you don't open this door now,

Angelica, I will break it down." This isn't going to be easy, but Angelica is a feisty, little angel only I can tame.

She fiddles with the lock, and I hear the slight creaking sound of the door opening. "I'm not your angel anymore," she replies, blandly, as she swings the door open. "If you weren't actually going to give me the choice to let you in or not, why didn't you just graciously unlock it, as you always do, instead of threatening me like a big, bad wolf?" she continues as she walks away.

She walks to the kitchen, while drying her hair with a towel. The quick glance I got of her face before she turned around showed puffy and bloodshot eyes, her face pink and blotchy from crying. She still looks so painstakingly beautiful. My heart twists inside my chest. I want to grab her, claim her lips, and tell her that I love her.

I slip my wet shoes off and follow her. The lights are dim, as if she doesn't want me, or anyone, to fully see her saddened face. We reach the island, and she grabs a bottle of whiskey from the cupboard and slides it across the counter to me with a glass.

I love her. Her perfect, pouty lips. The crease that appears between her brows when she's upset. The way my fingers tangle in her curly hair. I love her feisty spirit, her wild heart, and her little quirks. I love the rich color of her dark brown eyes, reminders of mountain terrain and nature; subtle, yet beautiful in every form.

Those words have been looming in my mind for what feels like an eternity. It takes me a minute to realize we've just been staring at each other. Her face isn't giving me many answers to what she's thinking, just a blank expression.

"Angelica, let me explain."

"I don't want to hear it, Evander. You betrayed me. Turns

out, hiding your identity is what you do best. What more is there to it?" she asks.

The careless front she's putting up is hard for me to accept. The walls I succeeded in bringing down are back up.

"Stop calling me Evander," is all that I manage to say. "That is not who I am to you."

Angelica laughs dryly and crosses her arms, tilting her head to the side. "*Who* are you to me, exactly, then? Enlighten me. I thought I knew you, but clearly, I don't."

"I am yours, Angelica. No matter the circumstance, I am yours and you are *mine*."

Angelica lets out a scoff. "*Yours*? The saddest thing about betrayal is that it always comes from those who truly care about us. But we're enemies, right? Given we're from rival families and all. You never actually *cared* about me," she says with a bite in her tone. My jaw tightens.

I pour myself a glass of whiskey, walk over to the dining table, and sit on a chair facing her. She leans against the kitchen island and watches me closely. Her hair clings to her neck, some of the curls sticking to her face. She's still wearing wet clothes and I want to rip them off, wrap myself around her, and take all the pain away. Instead, I sit and start talking.

"My uncle was the closest thing I had to a father. He raised me after my parents and little sister were murdered. He protected and took care of me. He kept my identity hidden so the people who executed my family wouldn't come back to kill me."

I start fidgeting with the glass to calm my nerves. Talking about my family's deaths is always hard.

"Whoever was responsible for their murder wanted the Vasilakis family extinct. If that person knew they had a son who had escaped and was still roaming the streets, they would've come for me. My uncle never told me who was behind it. He said not to worry about it, it had been taken care of, but he did everything in his power to keep me out of harm's way, just in case. He made sure to find the assailants and kill them before they could discover I was still alive. He cleaned up the crime scene and pretended that he'd found my body with the rest of my family. Ever since, I've been living in the shadows, only going by the name of the *Diávolos* in the streets."

Her eyes bulge out of her head at the mention of the nickname I've earned. I've referred to being the devil before, but I never called myself *the Diávolos* in front of her. I'm a household name in the streets, so she must've heard about the rumors. I put my head down in my palms and continue. "Ignatius knew that if anyone found out I was the heir to our family's legacy, they would want me dead." I still don't know the true reason why. Growing up, I tried questioning my uncle countless times about my past, but he never opened up. He claimed it was better for me not to know. Now that I think of it, I can't help but wonder if it had anything to do with the Sisterhood.

Angelica stares at me intently and sits up on the counter while I speak. Her expression is still one I can't read.

"I grew up under my uncle's watchful eye and he taught me everything I know. From being the man of the house to taking care of business. Everything he did was to prepare me for when he would be gone, but I never thought it would be so soon," I explain. "When I got the call from Dion that Ignatius had been killed, I could only think of one thing: revenge. I had my men investigate the murder, and we found out it was your father who gave the orders. I had no idea who you were at the time, but you were the perfect target as Peter's only daughter. I plotted to find you, make you fall in love with me, and use you to get back at your father. I wanted to kill him, Angelica, but I knew that if I directly responded to what he'd done to my uncle, I would be starting a war and putting my men and people at risk. There's so much going on in the background, a lot I needed to uncover, and I wouldn't have been content with just killing him and moving on."

I take a long breath and a few sips of my drink, Angelica still eyeing me silently. I want to climb into her brain and learn every single thought that is going through her mind at this very moment.

"You're actually the *Diávolos*?" she asks, and I can't tell if her question is out of curiosity or concern.

"Yes, that's what I am, angel. The devil is real. He doesn't have horns or a tail. He comes in the form of a man who was once innocent, untainted. I realized when I was a little boy, staring at my dead parents and sister, that hell was on earth. All the devils are here. From that day on, I felt no pain, and instead, became the one to inflict it, offering my enemies bargains they couldn't refuse with me, the *Diávolos*. I'm a very bad man, Angelica. I initially planned on using you to kill your father, not caring about your feelings or the consequences."

Angelica winces at my confession and I visibly see her try to swallow down her tears. Her voice cracks when she speaks, "You kill people. For a living."

I smirk at her remark, though I feel anything but amused right now. "Yes, among other things."

"What did you do to the man from the club, Evander?"

"I killed him," I reply bluntly.

She inhales a sharp breath. "Why? He was innocent! It was my fault he got caught up in that situation," she says, growing frantic.

"He touched what's mine, Angelica. You might've been the one to initiate it, but his fate was sealed. He was at the wrong place, at the wrong time," I explain, without an ounce of regret. I don't give a fuck if he was innocent. He put his filthy hands on my girl.

"You're sick," she spits with a trembling voice. "How could you kill so mercilessly?" Her breath hitches as a realization dawns on her. It takes everything in me not to go to her and take her in my arms. "Niko," she sobs. "What did you do to him?"

I can't say the words, knowing she won't take the truth lightly. Niko has been a presence in her life for as long as Gianis has. He's her ex, too. The only way to get rid of him was to kill him.

"Answer me!" Angelica shouts as she starts to panic. She paces around the kitchen, her breathing loud and shallow. I see her reaching for her wrists. That damn habit she has of hurting herself. *Not on my watch.* I get off the chair and stalk over to her. She notices me approaching her and backs up into the kitchen counter. *Is she fucking scared of me now?*

"Get away from me, Evander," she warns, but I ignore her. She turns around to walk out of the room, but I grab onto her wrist and yank her to my chest. I hug her tightly against me and she squirms in my arms. She's crying profusely. "Let me go. Please," she begs through her sobs.

"I won't let you hurt yourself, Angelica. Not in front of me, not ever. I'm going to hold you until you calm down, and then you're going to tell me why you started self-harming."

She doesn't give up trying to escape, so I squeeze her tighter. I don't know if this will help, but touch always helped me when I was having one of my episodes. Pressure on the skin sends a signal of safety to the autonomic nervous system. That's what my psychotherapist had told my uncle when I was a kid.

Angelica finally stops moving, but she still can't seem to ease her breathing.

"He's dead?" she asks in a shaky voice, but it sounds more like a statement. I don't answer.

A whimper escapes her lips. "Niko," she mumbles. "How could you? He was important to me."

"He was in the way."

"Of what, Evander?" she barks.

"Of us, Angelica. I know your dad has been planning on marrying you two. I know your history with Niko. He would've wanted it. I'm surprised Gianis didn't get to him before I did."

When she hears Gianis's name come out of my mouth, she flinches. "Don't you dare touch a hair on his head, or I will kill you myself. I swear to god," she seethes. I actually believe her.

"You have nothing to worry about, my angel. Gianis and I have an understanding."

She doesn't bother asking me about said arrangement, which I appreciate. She doesn't need to know the things that were said between him and me. If I'm being honest, our altercation was a pure dick measuring contest. It would've been faster to just pull out our cocks and a ruler.

She's still twisting in my arms, but I don't let her go. "Do you still want to kill my *baba*?"

"Yes, I do. I wouldn't be able to go on knowing the person responsible for my uncle's death is still breathing and free. Your father is up to something. I have to stop him before it's too late." She stops moving and I hug her tighter. I debate how to tell her how I feel. "Believe me when I say my plan to use you and exploit your feelings went straight down the drain once I laid eyes on you. I didn't know it at the time, but I never stood a chance," I say, quieter. "This was meant to happen so I could find you and make you mine."

Angelica's head tilts forward and I feel teardrops on my forearms wrapped around her waist.

"I didn't intend to fall for you, Angelica, but I did. You will always be my lifelong affliction, the cause of my distress. You are everything I never knew I wanted." I slowly turn her around to face me. Her eyes meet mine as I reach for her shaking hands. "I can't think properly when you are around. I can't bear to be away from you, my body and soul ache for you, whether you are near or far." I fight the urge to take her mouth in mine and taste the saltiness of her tears on my tongue. All I want to do is hold her in my arms and let the torrent of her tears soak through my shirt. I lift our linked hands and rest them on my chest, letting her feel the racing beat of my heart pulsating under our fingertips. "See what you fucking do to me?"

Angelica's fingers clench around my hand. I can see the torment in her eyes as she struggles with whether to be mad or to give in to her feelings, give in to me. I put my forehead against hers and we close our eyes. I can hear her trying to hold on to her pride with every shallow breath. I open my eyes. "Angelica, look at me."

"I can't," she rasps.

I run my fingers through her hair, moving the strands that are still stuck to her face, and she finally opens her eyes. Our gazes meet and I stare deeply into the darkness of her pupils, our heads still connected. I lean in, slowly, giving her the chance to stop me, and I feel the heat of her breath on my lips. My heart skips a beat. Hoping it can calm the silent war within her mind, I wait for her breathing to slow down, and I kiss her, our lips tentatively searching, tender and hesitant. It's a kiss filled with regret, vulnerability, and pain. Angelica tenses at first, but relaxes at the feel of my tongue tracing her lips, pleading to be let in. She opens her mouth, and our tongues meet. My hand digs into her nape, slightly bringing her head closer to me to deepen the kiss. She pulls away, gasping for air.

"Evan, I–I can't do this," she whispers. "How could I ever forgive you?" Her voice is pained.

Something fierce unleashes inside of me. I refuse to let her think she can dismiss me.

"Do you truly believe you could ever get rid of me?" I ask as I take a step back, not letting her drop my gaze. Testing her.

"You don't own me, Evan," she spits out.

"You're going to see soon enough that I can get anything I want."

I pull my handgun out of the waistband of my pants and cock it. Angelica stares at it and a look of shock crosses her face. I grab her hand and place the handle into her palm. Her entire body freezes.

"Evan, what's going on—"

I cut her off before she can finish the sentence. "*Forgive me*," I pull her closer and lift her hand with the revolver to my throat, my mouth a mere inch away from hers, "or fucking *kill me*, Angelica. Because I won't be able to live in a world where you hate me."

Her breathing is labored as she looks me deep in the eyes. She's still holding the gun up against my throat. The fear in her eyes mirrors mine as she realizes she could never live without me either. But for a moment, I know she debates shooting me. I don't blame her. She pushes the barrel of the gun deeper under my jaw, and I'd be lying if that didn't wake my cock up out of its slumber. Within an instant, her lips crash onto mine and I meet her eager tongue with an equal amount of anger and passion. The weapon is still up against my neck.

I grab both sides of her face and pull her away from my mouth. "Fuck, Angelica. I never want to be the cause of your tears ever again. Good tears only. But, god, you're beautiful like this."

I kiss her deeply again and she moans into my mouth. I lift her onto the counter, push her legs apart, and nestle my way in-between them, grabbing her by the waist and bringing her closer to me. Her pussy radiates heat. I can sense her need. I ease back out of the kiss, keeping myself close to her face. "Tell me, *moró mou*, if I were to disappear from your life, would you still think about me when you're all alone? Would you still touch yourself at the thought of me?"

Angelica sucks on her bottom lip. "Yes."

The response goes straight to my cock. "Good." I cup her jaw and run my thumb across her mouth. "Put the gun down if you're not going to use it." She sets it on the kitchen counter.

I need her to worship me as much as I worship her. I don't care that I don't deserve her. I want her bound to me. I'll end the life of anyone who tries to take her away from me. Angelica has been mine since the day I first saw her, even if she didn't know it. "You belong to *me*, Angelica."

I grip her ass and grind my dick between her legs, and she whimpers. Her breasts are pressed against my chest, and I can feel every inch of her body. I let out a sound of frustration that there is still a layer of clothing between us. Her legs wrap around my waist, and I bury my face into her neck, nipping at the sensitive spot under her ear, tracing the curve of her throat with my tongue. She tilts her head to the side to give me more space, inviting me to continue. I plant kisses all over her skin and she moans. A shiver shoots down my spine from the beautiful sound. I bite down on her shoulder, causing her body to spasm in pleasure and pain.

I put my lips to her ear. "I think I know what you need, my angel," I whisper softly. "A good tongue-fucking."

My words steal the breath from her lungs and her legs start to shake in anticipation. I slide her body closer to the edge of the kitchen counter and spread her legs wider. I move her skirt up her thighs. Her plump pussy is exposed through her thong, now a darker shade of pink from her wetness. "Fuck, Angelica. If you keep wearing skirts, you'll be my undoing."

I put my fingers on her throbbing clit and her body immediately moves as she starts working her hips into my hand. "Eager, aren't you, kitten?" I tease. "Keep rubbing your pussy against me." She obeys and I feel her clit throb every time she presses into my hand. "Good girl."

"Evan." My name rolls off her sweet tongue in a moan.

Fuck. My gaze stays locked on hers as I start lightly rubbing her clit over her thong. "I'm going to put my face between your legs and lick every inch of your pussy until you come all over my mouth."

I keep moving my hand. She's so fucking wet. I *have* to taste her. "Then, I'm going to fuck you with my tongue, and when you're close to coming once more, I'll slide my fingers into your beautiful, sweet pussy and kiss you until you explode."

A noise escapes her lips and I catch it with my mouth, finding her thong with my hand and lowering it down her round ass. She lifts her hips to allow me to take it off, and I throw it to the side. I slowly break away from her lips and trail kisses all the way down her chest until I reach the top of her breasts. She's not wearing a bra. *Perfect.* Her nipples are hard and poking out of her damp top. I find one with my teeth and bite it over her shirt, causing her to wince. I smirk and run my thumb over it to soothe the ache. I grab onto her top and drag it down, releasing her breast. I don't waste a second before taking it into my mouth, sucking on her nipple as she moans. The sounds she makes are getting me so fucking hard that my erection is almost painful. I unclasp my belt and unzip my jeans, reaching into my boxers to free my cock. Angelica's eyes fly wide open as she watches me stroke the length.

"See how fucking hard you make me, Angelica?" I take her hand and replace mine with hers. "Keep stroking it while I kiss you," I order. She does. Her touch feels so fucking good.

I dig my fingers into the flesh of her ass to lift her hips. She lets go of my cock and places her hands on the counter, bracing herself for what's to come. I watch her. Analyzing her breathing full of need, demanding a release. I drop to my knees and nestle myself in between her thighs. I plant kisses all around, purposely avoiding her clit, teasing her so much that she lets out a cry of desperation. "Be patient, kitten."

I trace her folds with my tongue and the anticipation almost becomes too much for me to handle, ironically. I can't wait another second to taste her. I swing her legs over my shoulders and spread her open. "Hold on, baby." I dip my head down and use my flattened tongue to lick all the way from her opening to her clit.

"Oh, god," she cries out.

"Fuck. You taste good," I groan against her wet pussy.

Angelica's head flies back and she lets out another moan, grabbing onto my hair and pulling on it as she meets my tongue's movements with her hips. I take her clit in my mouth and suck on it with the perfect amount of pull and her legs close around my head. Her moans are driving me crazy, and all I want to do is slip my dick inside her. But I have to take care of her first, show her how much she means to me. Then, and only then, will I allow myself to take her with my cock. I keep sucking on her clit while making circles with my tongue until I can tell she's close.

"Come for me, Angelica," I demand, "I want to hear you. Loud and clear."

That's all it takes for her release to build and her legs to start shaking. She works her pussy against my mouth, and I feel her throbbing under my tongue, her clit swelling more and more with every stroke. She comes wildly all over my mouth and lets out a series of moans I know will be embedded in my mind forever. I hold my tongue there for a moment, waiting for the thrashing of her hips to stop.

"You taste so fucking good, *moró mou*," I say as I lift myself off the floor.

"Kiss me, Evan," she says breathlessly.

"Right now, you could get anything you want, angel." Not just right now. I'll give her anything she wants, always. I kiss her and she wraps her arms around my neck. "I'm not done with you yet," I say in-between kisses.

"More?"

"I'm greedy."

I lift her off the kitchen counter and take her to the couch, not breaking our kiss until I've laid her down on her back. I make my way down her body again. This time, I tongue-fuck her until she reaches the edge. Just as she nears her climax, I stick my fingers inside of her and kiss her into oblivion, while she pulsates around the digits. I want to do it over and over again. I meet her lazy eyes and she looks so serene. The power this woman has over me is nothing I've experienced before.

She consumes my entire existence and I never want to let her go, even if it kills me.

"To love is to lose control." —Paulo Coelho

Angelica

I open my eyes, and I'm greeted by Evan's bare chest. *A sexy, manly, steel wall.*

I feel...good. But *this*, this can't keep happening.

As much as I want to hate Evan for what he did, my body isn't cooperating and it's frustrating as hell. I'm angry at myself for letting him in my house when I vowed not to talk to him. Not this soon. I need time to process what happened. The last few months of my life have been a whirlwind and I just found out it was all a lie. But instead, I'm staring at Evan's sculpted chest after having two mind-blowing orgasms. My thoughts are interrupted by his voice.

"Welcome back." He plants a kiss on my forehead.

"Oh, did I fall asleep?" I ask shyly. "I'm sorry."

"Don't apologize, my angel. You needed it."

"How long was I out for?" I rub my eyes.

"Not long. Maybe twenty minutes."

I feel his warm breath in my hair and it sends shivers down my body. I bury my face into his chest, and I get a whiff of his scent. *I can't get enough.* All I can think about right now is Evan's tongue all over me and it sends a tingling straight to my stomach, settling into a weight between my legs. I look down and see his arm wrapped around my waist, our legs intertwined. How we both fit onto the couch with his six-foot-three muscular frame is beyond me. I shouldn't even be cuddled up with him like this. A mere few hours have passed since I found out he lied to me, and I'm already lying with him. *I want to kick myself.*

"Hey...talk to me," Evan says, snapping me out of a daze again.

I want to say everything and nothing at the same time. I always get lost in his eyes and the look he's giving me at this moment isn't helping. I lower my head.

"Angelica. Say *something.*" Evan runs a hand through his hair, and I hear him release a breath of frustration. "You've barely said a word since I got here."

"What do you want me to say, Evander?" I sigh.

I'm so conflicted. On one hand, I never want to speak to him again, and on the other, I want to give us a chance. After basically being forced to listen to his side of the story, I learned of his true intentions and how things supposedly changed once he met me. But he hasn't apologized, yet. Although I still can't forgive him, I understand where he was coming from. Losing someone you love leaves a hole in your heart, and Evan lost four important people in his life. I can't imagine how much grief he must be feeling. If I found out who was truly responsible for my mother's death, I would probably plot my revenge, too. But it doesn't excuse what he did to me.

"I thought I told you not to call me 'Evander' anymore," he says.

I frown at him. "But that's your actual name."

"To everyone else, not you," he replies, sternly. I roll my eyes. I wiggle out of his hold and he lets me go. I get off the couch and retrieve my underwear off the kitchen floor.

When I get back to the living room, he's sitting up and his

gaze goes to my wrists. "Tell me about that," he says, pointing to them. I hesitate.

"It's nothing."

"It can't be, Angelica. You hurt yourself," he retorts.

I decide to be honest, not wanting to follow in his footsteps and continue the chain of lies. "It started when I was around twelve years old. My *baba's* cronies would come in and out of the house regularly. It was just after my mom died and I always felt so unsafe. One day, a creepy man who'd come to see my father scared me. I ran to my room and had my first anxiety attack. I didn't know how else to take the pain away, so I began to use the elastic band as a way to cope. Our housekeeper, Eldora, tried to talk to my father about my troubles, but he wouldn't listen. So, here we are." I take a large inhale and puff out the air.

Evan's face turns red, his eyes darken. "Peter is not going to get away with this. How could he let his daughter suffer?"

"I was no longer his child at that point. Something had shifted between us, and I never knew why. One day he was a doting parent, the next he acted like he was disgusted by me. He wouldn't talk to me. I grew up thinking he hated me, until I started hating him back. I'd have nightmares or flashes of memories about being stuck in a strange place, and anytime I brought them up to him, he'd just dismiss me."

Evan's face goes white as a ghost's. "Tell me more about those flashbacks," he demands.

I don't have it in me to say anything more. I need to remove myself from this situation. "I'm going to take a shower," I say as I walk through the hallway toward the stairs.

"We aren't done talking."

"Well, *I'm* done talking, Evander."

"The fuck you are, Angelica."

He's angry, but I don't care. He can't just come here,

demand forgiveness, and expect me to give it to him, as if he deserves it. Things have already gone too far.

I walk into the bathroom after grabbing a change of clothes, and I hear Evan's heavy steps marching up the stairs. He barges in, his fists clenched. *Déjà vu.*

"Do not deny me, Angelica."

"How many times do I have to tell you? You don't own me," I growl in frustration. "How dare you come here and demand things of me like you didn't fuck everything up?" My anger suddenly springs back to life as I start shouting at him. "Get off your high horse, Evander, self-entitlement is not cute." I step closer to him. "You are delusional if you think you deserve my forgiveness. I don't care who or what you are. Everything that happened between us in these past months means nothing now," I spit out, hurt and fury mixing together.

Evan looks at me, dumbstruck, and I see the moment rage overtakes him. His jaw muscles clench and I take a step back, fearing what he's about to do. His eyes darken further. It's as if he's entering fight or flight mode, and definitely leaning toward fight. *Shit.* I recognize this behavior from the masquerade ball. I bet if his anger goes too far, he'll lose all self-awareness and do something irrational. I scream his name, anticipating what he's going to do, but I'm too late. He lunges, and for a split second, I think he's about to pounce at me, but he swings his arm behind me and hits the bathroom mirror, punching right through it and causing the glass to crack under his knuckles.

My hands fly to my mouth, but a sob manages to slip through, and I move out of the way.

His fist is still against the mirror and he's looking down at the sink, bracing himself on the counter with his other arm as he tries to control his breathing. *He's blacking out, shit.* I rush to Evan's side. Hopefully, if I touch him, he'll calm down. As I near him, I see blood dripping from his knuckles down the glass, pooling on the counter.

"Evan! Oh, my god," I cry out in panic. There is so much blood. "Why would you do something so reckless? Look at your hand!" I exclaim. I hurry to the linen closet and grab a towel. I run back to the bathroom and Evan is now shaking and has his eyes closed. I softly place a hand on his arm, but he flinches away from my touch. "Evan, snap out of it. You're hurt. Please," I beg him.

He doesn't move, so I place my hand on the side of his face and caress his cheek. I sense him slowly coming back to reality. After a while, he lets out a sigh and licks his dry lips before speaking.

"Angelica, I'm so sorry. I wasn't going to hurt you. I—"

"I know, Evan," I interject. "I know you would never physically hurt me."

Evan is a bad man, a murderer, but I'm confident he would never lay a finger on me. He is my protector, my safe place. And right now, he needs me.

He lets out a breath as relief washes over him.

"We're not done talking about your sense of entitlement, but I'll allow a break to take care of you before you bleed to death."

Evan finally lifts his head and turns to me, showing a hint of a smile. I gently wrap his injured knuckles with a small towel and lead him to my bed.

"Sit here and wait for me. Don't get blood anywhere." I give him a stern look and point my finger at him. He laughs softly, but it doesn't reach his eyes.

A couple minutes later, I come back to the bedroom with a first aid kit and kneel in front of him to tend to his injury. I used to do this with Gianis when he started training as a fighter and would come to my house full of cuts and bruises. It only got worse when he became my father's enforcer. Stab wounds, gunshot wounds. You name it, I saw it. So, injuries like these don't affect me as much.

"You're a stupid, stupid man for doing this." I sigh.

After cleaning most of the blood on his hand and making sure no shards of glass were stuck in his cuts, I apply some ointment to his knuckles and wrap his hand with a bandage. Evan just watches me.

When I'm finished, he breaks his silence. "I'm sorry for lying to you, Angelica, and for dragging it on, even after I started caring for you. I'm sorry for playing with your emotions and betraying your trust. I'm sorry about everything."

He looks so vulnerable, sitting at the edge of my bed. I nod, urging him to keep talking.

"As soon as I realized my feelings for you were genuine, I drove myself crazy trying to figure out a way to still do right by my uncle without hurting you. You have to believe me, Angelica."

"I want to believe you, Evan. But you hurt me," I say as I get off the floor.

Everything comes rushing back. My father's insults, the slap, Evan's betrayal, Gianis comforting me. Hot tears stream down my cheeks. I squeeze my lids shut in the hopes of stopping them. Evan pinches my chin and lifts my head up to his eyes, sparkling with hope.

Hope is the only thing that can get us through this dark time.

"If you need me to get on my knees and beg, I will."

Before I get the chance to respond, he lowers to the carpeted floor and kneels in front of me. He stares at me intently, his gaze piercing my soul. A tingly sensation runs down my body and I'm suddenly aching for him. We sit there, unmoving, looking at each other. I knew Evan was a dangerous man, involved in dangerous things, but I never expected him to be a *Godfather*. *What does this mean for us?*

Even if I decide to forgive him, we come from rival families who hate each other. The Vasilakis family would never accept me as one of them, and my father would probably kill me if I told him I was going to keep dating his literal enemy. I promised myself I would never fall for a mafia man and risk ending up like my mother. *Dead.*

I still struggle with tearing myself away from the mob world, and forgiving Evan is just going to suck me right back in. Reality hits me, and I'm reminded of Evan's plan. Can I truly be with someone who wants to kill my father? As much as I dislike him and what he represents, he's still my blood. He's family. My father's voice pops into my head and the sting his insults caused is still there. The harsh way he spoke to me is something I will never forget. I'm so overwhelmed right now. I don't know who to be more frustrated with.

Evan lets go of my chin and I shake my head on my descent back to earth. I didn't realize I was having a full-blown internal conversation with myself.

"Angelica. I'm going to need you to talk to me. Tell me what's in that beautiful head of yours."

I feel a flutter in my chest. I absolutely hate how much of an effect this man has on me. *I must stay focused.*

"I have nothing to say to you, Evander." I decide to finally go take a shower, but Evan shifts to his feet and grabs my wrist, stopping me dead in my tracks. "What the—" I look down at his hand gripping my arm and I attempt to jerk it away. "Let go of me."

"Not until you talk to me," he says with a warning look.

"Make me," I seethe as I try to free myself to no avail. *He's so damn strong.*

"Don't make me fuck the words out of your mouth, Angelica."

"I dare you," I spit.

"Don't underestimate me, sweetheart. My dick is my best asset."

I scoff. He looks so proud of himself for that comment. *Douche.*

"I love a good challenge, and you need to be taught a lesson for denying me." His voice turns low and dangerous. He's not going to back down.

"I wouldn't touch you with a ten-foot pole." *Who does he think he is?*

"That's not how you felt earlier when I was face-deep in your pussy, fucking you with my tongue."

I freeze in place. "*Me aidiázeis.*" *You disgust me.*

Evan tugs on my wrist and my body crashes into his chest. He grabs my shoulders and turns me around in one swift movement, placing my back to his front as he takes both of my wrists in one hand, binding them together like a handcuff, and secures them behind me and against his stomach. I try to fight him, but his strength is overwhelming. There's no way out. He takes his other hand and puts it on my throat, pulling my head back so that it's resting on his shoulder.

As much as I try to ignore my feelings, they overpower me, and I seem to cave every time. My body reacts to Evan's touch and words, even when I don't want it to. He truly possesses me. I can't let that distract me.

"Say that again, angel. It sounded good."

Evan's hold on my neck is squeezing the air out of me, but I manage to speak. "Go fuck yourself," I croak.

"I'd rather you do it," he retorts. "Even when you hate me, I can smell your arousal from a mile away, *agápi mou.*" He brings his lips to my ear. "I don't disgust you, Angelica. It's the complete opposite. I know you want my cock, and I'll give it to you, but..." He tightens his hold on my wrists, and I let out a little cry. "Only if you admit that you and I are endgame. I don't give a fuck if you want to stay mad at me for days, months, or even years. I'll deal with it and earn your forgiveness. But never forget you belong to me and that every inch of you is *mine*."

My wrists hurt from his grip, and he has me in the most uncomfortable position, but I can't help but melt into his hold at his whispered words.

"Your body, mind, and soul are mine. I've ruined you for anyone else. I'll kill anyone who gets in between us, Angelica. If I can't have you," he brushes my ear with his lips and nibbles on my earlobe, "no one else can."

I'm weak. Mentally because I can't think straight when he is around, and physically because he literally has me in a choke hold.

"Do you understand, Angelica?"

My knees buckle and I swallow hard. "Yes."

I want to be angry and thrash out at him, push him away, but I can't. I love him. I want him to claim me. Take me and leave his imprint on me. It doesn't mean I forgive him. He'll have to work for that. Any other words literally get stuck in my throat when he lets go of my wrists and turns me back around to face him. He looks down at me, his big body hovering over my small frame, and brushes the back of his uninjured hand down the side of my face. He's eyeing me like he wants to devour his prey and my whole insides tingle in anticipation. Right now, in this room, Evan has all the power. And not just here, but everywhere he goes. His presence commands attention that is almost impossible to ignore.

He runs his tongue across his teeth and sits back down on the bed. "Come here," he orders.

I take a couple steps, until I'm standing between his legs and he slips his hand under my skirt, digging his fingers into my ass. The tension grows and my clit swells. All I want to do is grind on his leg to ease the ache. He leans forward and untucks my shirt from the skirt, kissing my stomach all the way up to my breasts, and leaving a trail of butterflies that flutter up to my chest. I throw my head back and let out a quiet moan, and at that very moment, he lifts my shirt over my breasts and sucks one of my nipples into his mouth, pulling out a cry from me. I feel his hand trail from my ass to my center and he spreads my folds, gliding a finger over my wetness.

"Fuck. Is this all for me, angel?" he asks, his lips still covering my nipple.

My body feels like it's on fire, my entire core pulsating with need every time his lips touch my skin. A desperate noise escapes my mouth and Evan shoves two fingers into my entrance. I suck in a deep breath. He grins at my reaction. I crave more, so I move my hips against his hand, creating the friction I need and intensifying the feeling. Evan takes his fingers out and I almost protest. He gets up and buries his face in my neck and makes a sound of satisfaction that turns me on even more.

"You feel and taste like paradise, Angelica."

He kisses his way to my lips, and I eagerly open my mouth to meet his tongue. At this point, I would hump his arm if it meant I could get my release. I'm so turned on, I can barely function. Evan turns us around and lowers my back onto the bed without breaking our kiss. His body floats over mine before he gently brings his hips down and presses his erection between my legs. His dick is bulging out of his jeans. I need him inside of me.

"Evan, I want you," I say in a breathy moan.

"You don't *want* me. You *need* me," he says as he takes off my shirt.

I'm completely naked under him and I try to fight the urge to cover myself. Evan sees my arms start to lift and stops me right away.

"What did I tell you about hiding from me, kitten?" Evan stares down at me, our breathing heavy and full of urgency. I bite on my bottom lip. Being with him feels so *right*, even though I know it's wrong. I shouldn't want him right now, but I do. Without a second thought, I unbutton his pants. I reach into his jeans and grip his dick. I don't think I'll ever get over how big he is. My body becomes restless under him. How much longer until I can feel him inside of me? I start getting frustrated, which seems to amuse him.

"Use your words, Angelica. Tell me what you want."

"I want—*need*—you inside of me. *Please.*" The last word is barely audible.

Pushing his pants down, he takes the tip of his shaft and glides it over my clit, teasing my entrance. I shudder. *I can't take it, anymore.*

"Evan, *please*. Fuck me. *Now.*"

His eyes are filled with a desperate hunger. "I just wanted to hear you beg."

I wrap my legs around his waist as he slowly inches his length inside of me. I close my eyes and squirm with pleasure and pain, his girth barely fitting.

"You're so fucking tight, Angelica. You were made for me."

My arms swing to his neck and he lowers himself down on me.

"Keep your eyes open and look at me while I'm inside you." He pushes all the way in, hard, and I cry out loudly, the sound quickly turning into a moan. But I keep my eyes fixed on him.

"Good girl," he praises.

His thrusts quicken and I meet them with my hips. He tries to withdraw, but my legs stay hooked around him. I won't allow him to move away. I clutch his cock with my vagina for extra emphasis. *Pussy power.*

He growls. "Fuck, Angelica. You're going to fucking make me come already."

I smile, fully aware of the effect I'm having on him as I rock back and forth. Evan pulls my legs from around his waist and pushes them toward my chest, giving himself more leeway and changing the angle. He hooks one leg over his shoulder and moves even closer.

"I think it's time I teach you that lesson." He grins wickedly as he places my arms up above my head, securing my wrists with his large hand, his other on my neck. Then, he pounds into me, repeatedly, until my hips can't keep up with his movements. Each thrust goes deeper and sends ripples of pleasure throughout my body. My eyes threaten to roll back. I feel every inch of him and any sense of control I had quickly dissipates. The pressure from his hand wrapped around my neck makes my eyes water.

Evan's molten eyes meet mine. "These are the only tears I ever want to see rolling down your cheeks, Angelica." He grunts and unhooks my leg from his shoulder and lets go of my wrists. "Hold on to the headboard," he commands.

I grab onto the railings, my spine curves to meet him, and he plunges back into me with so much force I shake from every thrust, air forcefully leaving my lungs every time. My moans get louder and louder, and that only seems to make Evan wilder. I can feel my orgasm nearing and my breathing turns erratic.

He places a hand on my lower stomach and presses down gently. *Holy. Shit.*

This is a feeling like no other. I can't contain my desperation. His thumb lands on my clit and he circles it. A cry of pleasure escapes my mouth. I'm so close.

"*Pes to ónoma mou*, Angelica." *Say my name*, he says with eagerness. "Say my name when you come."

Right then and there, I lose it. My orgasm rolls out of me like ripples of thunder as Evan rams into me with a hard and steady pace. "Evan!" I scream, my body twitching under him as the knot of pleasure explodes, sweeping through me while I come. I'm gushing, soaking both us and the sheets. This is the *best* sex I've ever had.

I let go of the headboard and grab the back of Evan's neck, lowering his face to mine, and I kiss him deeply as the last waves of pleasure go through me. He doesn't stop the pace and a moment later, I feel his cock pulsating inside of me as he reaches his climax, only slowing down when his orgasm reaches the end. We stay intertwined, our bodies glued together, not wanting this moment to be over. He lowers his face into my neck, and I listen to our hearts beat in unison.

"You can run but you can't hide." —*Emily Giffin*

Evander

The screeching sound of tires on the pavement alerts the guards of my arrival when I pull up to the Kouvalakis estate. I expected to be questioned at the gate, but it opened as soon as my car approached. I didn't waste any time before rushing to the door.

I jump out of my blacked-out Aston Martin, having chosen this car for the mere speed of it, and I leave the engine running as I take the front steps two at a time. The blood coursing through my veins feels like lava about to erupt. I don't even care if the guards flanking the property open fire on me.

I woke up to an empty house, Angelica nowhere to be found. I cursed at myself for letting her escape my hold. I'm usually a light sleeper, but I fell into the depths of a slumber only the demons in my dreams could wake me from. But I didn't dream of them last night because *she* was next to me. I expected her to still be upset when she woke up, the emotions and adrenaline of the night before having dissipated. But I didn't think she'd run away. Regardless of the night of love making and pleas of forgiveness, I knew she would still be angry at me in the morning. I was prepared to do anything to make her believe my intentions are no longer cruel. That I love her enough to feel like this life with her is worthwhile. Trust is the best proof of love, and I'm ready to earn hers again, no matter how long it takes.

I searched for Angelica, hoping that she was simply in the bathroom taking a shower, downstairs making breakfast, or outside drinking coffee. But she was gone. I ran back upstairs to her bedroom to get my phone. I have access to her front door feed on my phone, but I needed to see where she went. I called Dion and barked at him to send me the footage of the cameras around her house and on her street. I hung up and slammed the device down on the bed. I couldn't stop running my fingers through my hair while I waited impatiently for the videos. The ping jostled me out of my panicked daze. I pressed play on the first file. It was footage from a few hours before, around five a.m., and it showed Angelica creeping out of her front door with a duffle bag, not bothering to lock it behind her before hurrying down the street. *What the fuck is she doing?*

I clicked on the next video and it showed her running down the road toward a car. The images were black and white, and grainy, so it was hard to see, but she hopped into the passenger side. The car did a U-turn and sped away. I'd quickly memorized the license plate number and texted Dion to search for the owner of the vehicle. Several long minutes later, I received a reply. I wasn't even surprised. Of course, she'd call him to come save her. *As if she needed saving in the first place.*

I make it up the stairs of Angelica's childhood home and start pounding on the door with my fist. It swings open and I immediately grab Gianis' collar, lifting him off the ground slightly. He pushes me away and I stumble back. My face is laced with a ferocity I've never felt.

"*Poutánas yos.*" *Son of a bitch*, he seethes as he walks right up to me. "How dare you show your face here? I should fucking kill you."

I don't flinch and tilt my head to the side. "I'd like to see you try," I reply, almost playfully. "I didn't come here for you, *Gianis*. Where the fuck is she?"

Gianis throws his head back and laughs. "You're on enemy territory, Evander. I could do what I please to you. You're lucky Peter isn't here." I couldn't care less if he was, I would've taken the risk to find out where she is.

"Again, I'd like to see you try." Each word comes out laced with more venom than the last.

"After what you did to Angelica, I should slit your throat right here," Gianis spits.

If he tries to kill me, I'll have to fight back. I don't trust myself not to do something I can't take back.

"*Skáse*. What happened between Angelica and I is none of your fucking concern," I seethe, taking a step closer to Gianis' face.

"It makes it my concern if it involves her," he retorts, and pushes me away, right on the previously injured flesh of my shoulder. Motherfucker. I press my lips together to hide my reaction to the pain. I can almost see the flames bursting around our heads as we face off for the woman we both love.

I grab his finger and squeeze, slowly twisting his hand to the side, and Gianis winces. "Where. The. Fuck. Is. She? And don't fucking make me ask you again."

The car that Angelica hopped in was Gianis'.

She left me in the early hours of the morning, with the only other man she trusts, and my soul and ego can't handle the fact that for the second time in less than 48 hours, she's called *him* to rescue her. I'm so fucking angry, I don't know what to do with myself. My hands are begging to be put to use, and Gianis' face is the target. I understand she has things to process and needs time to heal, but I was supposed to be there for her every step of the way.

"Fuck you, Evander. I don't have to tell you a thing. I will always protect her, especially from pieces of shit like you," he hisses out.

"She was never yours," I say, my tone laced with contempt.

"*Tha sou spáso to kefáli sta dio.*" *I will break your head open.* Gianis pushes me back with all his strength and I swing back. He pulls out a shank from the arsenal of weapons he carries on him and I expose my own in return. I cock my gun and aim it right at his face. If he wants to duke it out, I'm fucking ready.

"Tell me where you took her or I will kill you. You will never see her again."

"If I die, you die. I'll go peacefully, knowing she won't be hurt by you again," Gianis responds, determination in his eyes.

The guards who were keeping a distance are now slowly moving toward us, their guns cocked and pointed at me, ready to shoot on command. I put my glock down, away from Gianis' face, and take a step back.

"If it weren't for how much Angelica cares about you, I wouldn't hesitate to take your life, forfeiting mine in return," I say.

"I could say the same exact thing, Evander. She's the only thing keeping us both alive. So, get the fuck away from here and never come back. She's not here, anyway."

The soldiers withdraw their weapons and make room for me to leave. I walk backwards toward my car and hop in, driving away as soon as I shut the door. I let out a loud growl as I pound my fist on the steering wheel more times than I can count. My anger is uncontrollable, and I think of how stupid I was to let her slip away from me. Her father's house wouldn't have been the first place she'd go, but I knew Gianis would be there. I didn't give a fuck if Peter had been the one to answer the door. He wouldn't have been safe from my wrath, either. Gianis was expecting my arrival, probably aware of the situation and that I'd come looking for her. Angelica must have told him what happened.

I park my car in the underground parking lot of Saintville, but instead of going upstairs to my penthouse, I head outside. I start to sprint, trying to rid myself of the anger, anxiety, and fear that she's gone for good. This is the second time Angelica has run away from home, but this time, she will be hunted down.

You can hide from the devil, but he will always find you.

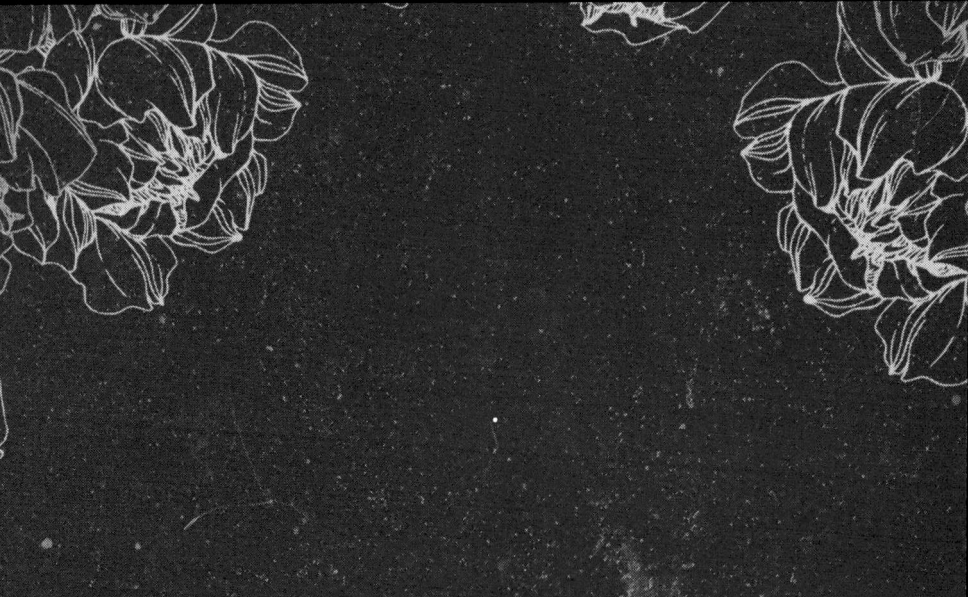

"And in the end all I learned was how to be strong alone."
—*Unknown*

Angelica

I don't know how I got the doorman to let me in, but it seems my charm still works. He must have recognized me from the countless nights I spent here during my time in university. I greeted him with a flirty smile, and he didn't think twice before letting me in.

I climb up four floors, drag my feet to apartment 404, and lift my knuckles up to knock on the door. Before I get the chance, I hear two faint female voices talking animatedly through the wall and I lower my hand to listen. I smile at what I know is happening on the other side. I hear rustling close to the entrance seconds before the door unlocks and swings open. I stagger back.

Amanda stares at me bewildered, the garbage bag she's holding falls from her hand. Nicole hears the light thud and approaches her from behind, asking, "What happened? It looks like you've seen a…" she sees me just as she's finishing her sentence, "ghost."

"Oh my god, ANGIE!" Nicole screams. "I can't believe it's really you!" She brings me in for a hug and Amanda snaps out of her stupor and joins in on our embrace. I hug them back tightly, tears forming in my eyes. I've missed them so much. I haven't spoken to them in months. Not since I moved back to Cebrene.

"We've been worried sick! You stopped replying to our messages. Where have you been?" Amanda asks.

My face contorts with guilt. I feel terrible for cutting them out the way I did. I was too worried after what happened with Hendrick to keep in contact with them, in case I put them in danger.

"Yeah! We thought you'd been kidnapped or something. We almost filed a police report, until Amanda remembered that we have each other's locations and saw you were actually back in Cebrene." *About that...*

"I'm sorry for leaving so abruptly. I didn't really have a choice." I let out a long sigh and lay my bag down on the floor, letting my shoulders hump forward. I'm so tired and mentally drained. I just want to curl up on the couch and cry for hours.

Nicole grabs my belongings and helps me inside. "Sit, we were just making breakfast. I'll make you a coffee. It looks like you haven't slept in ages, girl," she says.

I chuckle softly as I scoot my bum up on one of the stools in the kitchen. The tightness in my chest loosens up the tiniest amount as familiarity invades my senses. I used to sit here almost daily with the girls and Daniel, without a worry in the world. I thought life was good, but my four years of freedom ended so quickly.

I have some explaining to do, but where do I start? The last time I saw them, a couple months ago, I thought my whole life was figured out. It might not seem like a long time, but we used to see each other regularly and talk every day. What I've been through in that short timeframe is enough to write a novel.

Nikki hands me a mug and Amanda sits next to me on the

other chair. "We don't have to talk yet if you're not ready," she says.

"I'm so sorry for leaving you guys in the dark," I say as I slump onto the counter. "When I had to leave, I didn't have time to explain. I didn't really know *how* to explain. Now, I appear out of the blue, expecting you to accept me with open arms, when I've been such a shitty friend."

"Are you fucking kidding me, Angie? We've been best friends for four years. Do you think we would stop caring about you because you disappeared for a little while? If anything, we're upset that you couldn't tell us what was wrong and allow us to help you," Nicole explains. "All we care about is that you're alive. Anything else doesn't matter," she continues.

"Yeah, we, including Danny, are here for you no matter what," Amanda adds.

I don't deserve them. It saddens me to think I was taken away from my friends when they were the only people keeping me sane. I'll never forgive my father for stealing every single good thing in my life. He's been the cause of so much pain, but it all seems so little now, after what I found out about Evander. I feel defeated. I shouldn't have run, but I couldn't stomach waking up to him and facing what he had admitted. I'm tired of being used as a pawn. First, it was my father, now him. All of this has brought up more memories I don't understand from the parts of my life that are missing or unexplained. My dreams are getting more and more realistic and dark.

Evan and I fell asleep in each other's arms last night. A nightmare woke me up early in the morning, but he didn't flinch at my sudden awakening. My nightgown was soaked, and I was breathing hard as I came back to reality.

I'd dreamt that I was in the car with my father. He kept glancing at me through the rear-view mirror, beads of sweat rolling down his forehead as we passed tree after tree. We'd been driving through the middle of nowhere for what seemed like hours. Every time I asked him where we were going, he answered that it was a special place where I would be taken care of. He couldn't shake the visible worry off his face as he tried to tell me all the wonderful things about this location.

"There are many girls there, most of them your age, so you will make new friends," he says.

"But I don't want new friends. I already have Aria and Gianis," I argue.

"I know, kóri mou, and they will still be there when you get back," he explains.

My heart starts beating fast. How long is he leaving me there for? "I want to stay with you, baba. I don't wanna go!" I cry.

He reaches his arm back and pats my knee. "I'll be back for you before you know it, agápi mou," he says, his voice full of sorrow. Why was he taking me to this place if he was sad about leaving me?

We neared a building surrounded by tall trees, secluded from any form of human life, and baba helped me out of the car while I cried. I latched onto his leg when a woman wearing a head covering approached us. I closed my eyes tightly, wishing it was all a bad dream.

The woman tore me away from my father and I kicked and screamed, but he just turned away and got back in the car, not even looking back before driving away.

I'd woken up suddenly with air stuck in my throat. I felt sick to my stomach, so I rushed out of bed and locked myself in the bathroom, hurling my guts into the toilet. Whatever dream that was couldn't have been a mere fragment of my imagination. It had to be real. I knew I needed to get out of there right away. I rinsed my mouth, brushed my teeth, and tiptoed out of the bathroom to check if Evan was still asleep. He hadn't budged and I could hear his steady breathing.

I didn't want to tell him I was leaving. He would've never let me go.

I grabbed a bag from my closet and stuffed clothes into it. After quietly making my way downstairs, I called Gianis and he answered after three rings. I don't know how I did it, but I managed to escape without Evan even waking up and had Gianis drive me to the train station. I told him what had happened and made him promise not to tell Evan where I was going. He was apprehensive, but he agreed.

"Don't do anything stupid," I said to him as I exited his car.

"Same goes to you, *mikrí mou*. Call me if you need me," he replied with a sad smile.

I headed into the station and bought a one-way ticket to Antium City for the second time in my life. It was a risk to go back to the place where I got kidnapped only weeks ago, but anywhere is better than Cebrene. I turned off my phone, not bothering to let anyone else know where I was going. Aria will throw a fit, but I know Gianis will take care of her until I come back. *If I do.*

When I arrived in the Big A, I decided there was only one place I could go. Now, here I am, in Nicole and Amanda's shared apartment, drinking coffee and getting ready to spill the beans on the shitshow that is my life.

I take a deep breath and tell them everything. From who I truly am—daughter of a mob boss—to what brought me back to them today. I explain how I grew up with parents, who once loved each other but fell apart over the years. How my mother's death was ruled an accident, when I believe foul play was involved. How there's a part of my life after her loss that I can't remember but has haunted me ever since. How the relationship with my father became strained over the years, causing him to punish me for just trying to be my own person. That I ran away from home at eighteen to come to The Big A and start a new life, wanting to forget the one I came from. And, finally, how I was forced to go back to the Metropolis of Cebrene after I was kidnapped the night of our graduation celebration, which led me straight into the arms of the devil.

Nicole and Amanda stare at me, their expressions stunned. I let out a nervous laugh in anticipation of their reactions.

"Holy shit, Angelica. Your life sounds like a movie," Amanda says, letting out a whistle.

"I can't believe we've been friends with a fucking *mafia princess* this whole time," Nicole squeals.

I flick her on the nose and laugh. Of course, that's what she would focus on.

"It's nothing special," I tell her. "Trust me, I wish I wasn't."

"Speak for yourself, bitch. I'm bored as fuck and in dire need of some entertainment. At least let me live vicariously through you," she says, her voice laced with awe.

"You're deranged, Nikki. Who would willingly want to be in the mafia?" I ask, laughing at her ridiculousness.

"I do. Switch places?"

Amanda chimes in. "Don't you have enough excitement with your boy, Danny? It's already full of drama, just how you like it." I turn to her, and we high-five, laughing at Nicole's expense.

"I hate you both," Nikki says.

"So, what about this guy, Evander? What's going to happen now?" Amanda wonders.

I don't know the answer to that. I have so much on my mind, I can't even imagine accepting this as my new reality. The thoughts of my past and what my future will hold are overwhelming. Will Evan still be in it? Will he kill my father? What would I be expected to do as the sole heir to the family business? Do I want to live the rest of my life in hell with the devil?

I shrug, not having an answer to her question.

"Do you love him?" Nicole asks.

"Yes," I respond without hesitation.

"Then, everything will work itself out. You can stay here as long as you want," she concludes. *I hope so.* I don't know how long I'm going to stay, but I need time to make sense of everything.

We spend the rest of the day vegging in the apartment and, eventually, the girls summon Daniel to come keep us company, too. Nicole called him to tell him I was in town, and my ears practically shattered when he screamed on the speaker. "I'm coming over right now!" he yelled.

The doorbell rings about an hour later, and Daniel immediately picks me up and spins me around.

"I missed you too, D-bag," I tease. He suddenly drops me, and my ass hits the floor. "Ow!"

"That's for calling me a douche," Daniel says proudly.

"That's what you are, so I don't know why you're so surprised," Nicole intervenes, rolling her eyes.

"Roll your eyes at me one more time and see what I stick up your ass to make you permanently cross-eyed," Daniel retorts with a smirk. Nicole crosses her arms and glares at him, spitting darts out of her eyeballs.

"I see you both haven't missed a beat since I've been gone," I interject.

"You have no idea. It's gotten worse since you left. Turns out, I can't tame these beasts on my own," Amanda says, a sigh escaping her mouth as she shakes her head.

We spend the evening eating so much popcorn that my clothes will probably still smell like butter in a week. By the end of the night, we're all ready for bed, and I beg Daniel to stay over. The girls have a guest bedroom with a double bed. I don't feel like sleeping alone tonight.

My thoughts go to Nikki and wonder if she would be okay with Danny staying over. Amanda couldn't care less, but I wanted to make sure Nicole would be fine with it, considering their history. I don't know what has been going on between them since I've been gone, so I don't want to cross any boundaries. When I ask her, she grunts out a *yes* and walks into the bathroom without adding anything else, in typical Nikki fashion.

A little over a week later, I'm still in Antium, trying hard to distract myself from what happened with Evan. But the shock and hurt haven't lessened, and my nightmares still plague me at night. I've tried to come up with a plan of action, ways to cope, and how to deal with the new information I learned, but it's to no avail. What bothers me the most is figuring out the holes still present in my childhood memories.

I wake up in a tangled web of limbs and an arm splayed across my stomach. Daniel is lying on his back, his body twisted to the side, and his mouth wide open, letting out little snores. I giggle as I remove his arm and stretch my body. After updating him on my life's adventures the first day I got back, he's stayed over every night. He refuses to let me sleep alone. I've tried to reason with him. I could sleep with Amanda or Nicole, but he put his foot down. *Stubborn ass.* I know he missed me, but I think it's just an excuse to be closer to Nikki. I told her to take him away from me and she laughed in my face, claiming he's my problem now. *Bitch.*

I get out of bed and leave Daniel there as I sneak out to go to the bathroom. It's late enough in the morning that the girls could be awake, but early enough to be left alone to ponder my thoughts a bit longer.

After relieving myself, I make my way to the kitchen and sit at the island while I wait for the coffee to brew. I reach into one of the cupboards and pull out my pink Antium U mug. It's been several weeks since my disappearance, and the girls haven't forgotten about me. All the little items I'd left around their place are still here, and my heart swells at the thought.

I spot my phone in the far corner of the dining room, resting in a trinket bowl. I stare at it for a moment and debate turning it on. I haven't checked it since I got here. I needed time to just *be*. And it was much needed. The girls and I caught up, went to our favorite restaurants, took a walk in Hasting Park, and went shopping. I missed being normal. But a small part of me worries I've been too reckless. What if someone finds out I'm back and tries to take me again? I'm not sure I'd be so lucky the second time around.

I grab it off the mantle and press the power button. The screen lights up with hundreds of notifications. I scroll through them and see many missed texts from Evan freaking out, the messages getting angrier as the days went on. But they suddenly stopped two days ago. A prickly sensation races up my spine. I have a bad feeling about this. I keep scrolling and see that Aria reached out, asking about my whereabouts, and Gianis informed me that Evan paid him a visit. *Shit.*

I finish my coffee just as Nikki walks out of her room. She rubs her eyes sleepily, while making her way to the kitchen counter to pour herself a cup.

"How did you sleep, babe?" she asks.

"Pretty well, given the 'situation' still sprawled out on the bed," I say with a teasing smile. She snorts.

Nikki walks over to me and wraps her arms around my shoulders, and I lean my head on her side. Amanda strolls out of her bedroom minutes later and joins us for breakfast, while Danny still sleeps his life away. As we're cutting veggies to make omelets, we hear a loud bang on the front door. We all jump in unison. Amanda lets out a squeak, almost dropping the carton of eggs in her hands, and Nikki clutches her chest. The knife I was using to cut the tomatoes flies out of my grasp and onto the floor.

My heart almost comes out of my mouth as we all stare at each other. Danny hears the commotion and comes stumbling out of the room in his boxers. "What the hell is going on?" he asks, his face still riddled with sleep marks.

The person at the front door continues to bang on it. Daniel cracks it open, careful to hide us from the person's view.

"Can I help you?" he asks the stranger, his voice sounding half asleep, half weary.

"I need to speak to her. Now," the man responds, his tone full of ice and fire.

The color drains from my face as I recognize the voice. Nicole and Amanda stare at me in disbelief, instantly understanding who it is.

He found me.

"You're everywhere except right here and it hurts." —*Rupi Kaur*

Evander

Someone better fucking open this door before I break it down. My skin is hot from the fury I can't keep at bay. I've barely slept a minute since Angelica ran away nine days ago. Now that I'm finally here, I can't wait another minute to see her. I'm not sure whether to yell at her for leaving me high and dry or devour her mouth because of how much I've missed her. A part of me left with her that morning, and I need it back. I need *her* back.

I pound on the door relentlessly, not caring if anyone is asleep. I might be an asshole for giving them such a rude awakening, but my beautiful angel left with no explanation, and there's no way I'm letting her get away with it. It wasn't that difficult to find her, but even a week without her was too long. She turned off her phone, but never removed the SIM card, so I was able to get one of my hackers to track it. A day later, I was right next to him as he broke into the device and got her location. I could've left right that minute and come to Antium, but I decided to give her some space. I might be possessive and controlling, but I'm not a total piece of shit. *Okay, I am. But I sometimes choose to have common sense.*

I knew she couldn't have been driving because she doesn't have her license, and Gianis wouldn't have let her leave with a stranger. So, she either got on a plane or a train. I asked my guy to go through her bank records and he found a transaction at the train station. *Bingo.* Angelica wasn't trying too hard to stay hidden. Men like me get what they want, and what I want is for Angelica to come back home to me, or I'm going to raise hell. Patience comes easily for me, and I'm willing to give her all the time in the world to come to terms with her new reality, but I'm not willing to forfeit her presence.

There's commotion on the other side and the sound of something clattering on the floor. I bang on the door again and, finally, the lock clicks and it wedges open.

"Can I help you?" the man asks.

I can't contain the look of utter shock on my face. The guy standing at the entrance is boxer-clad and shirtless. *And fucking dead.*

"I need to speak to her. Now," I seethe, rage boiling in my veins.

I hear nothing but silence from inside the apartment. But I know she's here.

"Angelica," I call out, unnervingly calm. "I know you're in there. Don't make me cave your friend's face in to get by."

The guy looks at me and raises a brow, daring me to try.

"I don't know who you are, buddy, but I'd watch your mouth if I were you. She doesn't have to see you if she doesn't want to," he replies brazenly.

Wow. This guy has balls. He clearly doesn't know who I am. I could easily blow his brains out in less than thirty seconds and he's putting up a fight. This must be her friend, Daniel. *But why the fuck is he almost naked?*

"Where is she?" I try to peek behind him to get a look at who's inside. I shove the door and it bounces off his foot as he holds it in place. Without thinking, I grab him by the neck and he chokes on his breath.

"Open the fucking door, Daniel. I know you care about her, but I need to get in, and I wouldn't want to *accidentally* hurt you." I over-enunciate my words to make sure he understands exactly how far I'm willing to go to get my woman back.

"Danny!!!" Angelica yells from the other side. *I knew she was in there.* "Evander, let him go! Now! Put him down. You're hurting him!" she screams.

Finally, I have her attention. I set Daniel down and he clutches his throat as he catches his breath. "Fuck you, man. What is wrong with you?" he seethes.

I square my shoulders. "I told you to get the fuck out of the way and you didn't listen."

"It's okay. I got it," I hear Angelica whisper from behind him.

He turns his attention to her and murmurs, "Are you sure? You don't have to do anything you don't want to."

Angelica's hand pokes out beside him and grabs onto the door. "Yes, I'm sure." She looks at her girlfriends and nods, a silent confirmation that she's okay. Daniel backs away, eyeing me like a tiger, and they all retreat to the bedroom. Angelica is now standing in front of me at the entrance. My heart beats loudly in my chest. Gorgeous isn't enough of a word to describe this woman's beauty, even though her lips are swollen from biting them, a nervous tick of hers I recently started noticing, and she has bags under her eyes, making her look tired. I just want to hold her against me and merge her soul with mine. It hurts to see her like this, but I deserve this pain. I inflicted it on myself by betraying her.

There is a story behind her eyes. Her face is etched with worry and twisted with grief.

"Come home," I demand, my voice warmer than before.

"No."

I place my hand on the door to push it open, but she blocks me from coming in.

"Let me in, Angelica," I order, growing impatient.

"No," she repeats.

"Angelica," I say, breathing in deeply. "I'm going to give you ten seconds to move away from the door or I'm barging in."

Her eyes blink, her body rooted in its place as her mind processes my threat.

"*Se misó,*" *I hate you,* she hisses.

She walks backward into the apartment, and I follow, walking her straight to the couch. Once her legs reach it, she flops down and I bend over her, putting my arms on the backrest at each side of her head. I inch my face closer, until the tip of my nose touches hers and my lips tickle her mouth.

"Is that how you really feel, *ágele mou?*" I ask.

"I wish I never met you," she spits.

I bring one of my hands to my chest, feigning offense as I clutch my shirt to my heart.

"Ouch. You hurt me, sweetheart," I tease. It only makes her angrier. I don't know why I'm being a dick right now, but it seems to be my go-to coping mechanism. Hurt whoever hurts you.

Angelica attempts to shove me away, but I'm an immovable brick wall in front of her. She snarls, frustrated that she can't escape the cage I've created around her.

"You know what, you're right. I don't hate you. I hate myself for loving you," she admits. That hits me somewhere in the chest. I almost believe her. I somehow convinced her to fall in love with me, but keeping the truth hidden was not in my favor.

"*Angeloúdi mou,*" I say, softly, as I caress her cheek. "I've failed you, and I'm deeply sorry. I never meant to hurt you. I made a mistake by keeping everything from you," I continue as I kneel in front of her and intertwine our fingers together. "I'm not perfect, but you make me want to be a better man. Let me be better for you. Give me the chance to prove I am worthy."

Angelica closes her eyes, and when she reopens them, tears fall down her face. I kiss the side of her cheek and catch a droplet, tasting the saltiness of the liquid. I use my thumb to wipe the wetness away.

"*Ísai i psichí mou*," I tell her. *You are my soul.*

She sniffles and her eyes soften a bit, and her body seems to relax.

"I need you, Angelica."

She surprises me and grabs my face, bringing our lips together in a tender kiss. I press my mouth harder onto hers to savor her. I've missed her so much it hurts. She lets go just as suddenly and pulls away. Her breathing is fast.

"Evan, *se agapó*." *I love you.*

My heartbeat jolts. I smile. "And I love you, angel. Come home. Marry me and live with me, away from your father. I'll protect you."

Angelica shakes her head, and my heart sinks a little. "I love you, but I can't trust you, Evan. I need time. I need to be away from all *that*. From Cebrene, my *baba*, Gianis, the mob, and from you. I left without saying goodbye because I'm a coward and knew that if I spoke to you first, I would stay. I can't be around you if I want to heal. I need to do this on my own. Please understand," she pleads.

I narrow my eyes and look deep into hers to see any signs of bluffing. I don't. She's being truthful, and the least I can do is give her space, but I don't want to.

"I know this will be hard to do," she acknowledges. "But in order for me to forgive you, I need this."

"I'm not going anywhere, Angelica. I'll give you time, but

I'm going to stay in the city until you decide to come home with me."

Angelica's head tilts to the side and lines form between her eyebrows. "You're staying in Antium City?" she asks.

"Yes. Dion and Xander will manage things for me while I'm gone. As long as it takes," I confirm.

She opens her mouth several times before forming the words. "What if I stay here for months? Where are you going to live?" she asks, her voice full of confusion.

"Don't worry about me, angel. I often do business with my counterparts in Anzio, so I have an apartment here. Like I said, I'm willing to wait. Take all the time you need, but I'll be right here."

She nods. I feel like I just cut out my heart and handed it to her on a silver platter. I know she'll come back to me; she has to. But I'm worried she'll start to believe we're no good together. We are. She is the perfect potion created to heal my soul. I cup her face, give her a gentle kiss on the lips, and she doesn't push me away. What I'm about to tell her next will change the course of her life. All my hard work investigating my uncle's murder and her father's plans has all come down to this.

"Before I go, there's one more thing you need to know," I say.

"Everyone is like a moon, and has a dark side which he never shows to anybody." —Mark Twain

Angelica

A heaviness settles in my chest at the thought of finding out another truth. I have no idea what it could be, but I'm not ready for it. I glance around the room, refusing to make eye contact with Evan, and I wrap my arms around myself. "What is it?" I ask him, nervously.

"Do you know what 'The Sisterhood' is?"

I've never heard of 'The Sisterhood,' but my body tenses at the mention of it. The name triggers a response in me that I don't understand, and I freeze. I think back to conversations I've overheard from my father, but I don't remember that name. It sounds somewhat familiar, but I can't put my finger on why.

I shake my head. "No. What is it?" I ask with a sigh.

Evan sits next to me. He rests his elbows on his knees and joins his hands together, taking a moment to gather his thoughts before he continues.

"In my search to find out why your father murdered Ignatius, I went over some interesting documents found in my uncle's office and laptop mentioning an organization called 'The Sisterhood,'" he explains. "With the help of my men and team of hackers, I looked into the name on the dark web. We found details of an establishment, where they hold young girls and reform them into child brides and sexual slaves for the rich. The sisters are responsible for overseeing the children's education and subject the insubordinate girls to harsh, physical punishment."

I flinch at this news. I stare at Evan in disbelief that something this terrible exists. The world is a scary and evil place. I'm aware that horrible things happen right under our noses, but this sounds completely totalitarian and archaic.

"I dug further and came across a forum, where its users were discussing young girls. Someone with the username '2young4you' leaked records of all the children that were ever admitted into the establishment," Evan continues, his jaw clenching in anger. "I'm still trying to figure out how my uncle was involved, but it's a starting point," he adds.

"Okay, but what does this have to do with me?"

"I have reason to believe you were sent there as a child, Angelica. There was a name on the list dating back fifteen years. Hera Kouvalakis. Eight years old. It would've been right after your mom passed away," he replies, cautiously, as if afraid to spook me.

I tune everything out as my heart starts to beat hard, the pounding going straight to my head, the ringing in my ears deafening. It's too much. I jump off the couch, grip my hair, and scream. An earth-shattering scream. I have the vague awareness of Danny and the girls bursting out of their rooms, but I pay them no mind. I can't. My body feels like it's being electrocuted. Immediately, visions from the years of my childhood I'd blacked out flash through my mind, and I'm overwhelmed. Everyone is shouting at me in the room, but the sounds are faint, as if my head is submerged under water. I wish I were actually drowning right now.

"Angelica," someone calls, but the voice is muffled. "Angelica," Evan says again, and he grabs me by the arms and shakes me to get my attention. But I can't focus on anything other than the images appearing before my eyes.

My most recent nightmare now makes more sense as memories of my father dropping me off at a secluded place start to surface. The sound of my cries echo in my ears, begging him not to leave me. The voices of those little girls screaming as they were punished by women wearing head coverings.

"He took me to that place," I murmur, my whole body shaking in shock and disbelief. "I remember it now."

I allow Evan to take my hands in his and he pulls me against him. He puts his nose in my hair, inhaling deeply. It somehow calms me, triggering me to take a deep breath.

"I recall going, but I don't remember anything else," I say, my voice cracking. "What did they do to me? Why would my father take me there?"

"I don't know, *angeloúdi mou*, but rest assured, I'm going to do everything in my power to find out. And I'm going to kill anyone who ever hurt you with my bare hands," he seethes.

Tears start falling and I sob in Evan's chest. Daniel, Nicole, and Amanda stay at a distance. For a moment, I forgot they were even here. Right now, all I can focus on is the warmth and safety of Evan's arms. I burrow deeper into his chest and he squeezes me. "I've got this. I've got you," he whispers against my hair.

Even though I love him so much it hurts, I hate him an equal amount. It might not make sense, but it feels like ever since he barged into my life, my entire world started to crumble. Everything I've ever known and understood doesn't make sense anymore. All my relationships are questionable. Do Aria and Gianis know I was sent there? Does Eldora? If she did, she's been lying to me my whole life. I can't stomach any of that right now. And my father. Why would he send me somewhere so terrible, when our relationship was doing so well at the time? I can't make sense of any of this.

"Your father is up to something, Angelica, and I will stop him. Xander is following a lead and came to me with more information yesterday. He showed me the records of the sisters who worked there..." Evan hesitates, visibly distraught by what he's about to say next.

I inhale a deep breath and hold it in, hoping the lack of oxygen can somewhat appease the agonizing pain I feel in my entire body, and I brace myself for the impact of his words.

"Your mother's name was on the list, Angelica. She was a nun at 'The Sisterhood.'"

Epilogue

Two months later

Evander

"Look to your right, *afentiko*," the voice crackles through my earpiece. I swipe my palms over my black cargo pants and readjust the black balaclava over my face. I fucking hate wearing these things, and even though I'm away from anyone's eye shot, Dion insisted I be extra careful. Given who we're targeting, he's not wrong. But I'd never tell him that. *Cocky motherfucker.*

I glance to my right. *X marks the spot.* I look through the scope of my Remington rifle. I see my target clearly. This moment is life-altering. Not only because I'm about to kill a man, but also because I know I will feel an inch of peace once I do. I wipe away the beads of sweat that have gathered above my brows. I don't know if it's hot in here, or if it's just me, but I'm nearing the point of suffocation.

The past six weeks have been stressful, to say the least. I've been on autopilot, buried in my work, trying not to think about Angelica and how much I miss her. We haven't spoken since I last saw her and it's eating at me, as if parasites live freely in my body. It's a disgusting feeling, but I'm dealing with the consequences of my actions. Again, if Dion heard me, he'd say, "I told you so."

I'm set up on a rooftop, looking down at the entrance of the adjacent building. A group of men just exited the front doors.

"Range?" I ask.

"Six-hundred yards," Dion responds. "He's moving. You got him?"

I rearrange my bipod legs and stabilize the rifle at the top of it. It's windy as fuck. I'm hoping I'll be able to defeat the shifting winds. I reach for the handheld wind anemometer in the pocket of my vest. Dion is acting as my spotter, but he's not close enough to track the wind accurately. I calculate the windage and adjust my shot accordingly. I need to make sure the bullet is accurately calibrated to avoid it going adrift. I have one shot, one opportunity.

I take a deep breath, wrap my hand around the sling, nice and tight, and drop to my knees. A calmness pours over me.

"Yeah, I got him." I pull the trigger. The bullet whooshes straight into the enemy's head.

"Man down," Dion states.

Bullets start to ricochet as the group of men try to figure out where the shot came from. I let my body sink to the ground. Jurian is dead.

Peter is next.

Six months later

Angelica

My eyes fly up over my laptop, and I glare at the person standing right in front of me, disrupting my beautiful view of Hasting Park. I let out a sound of frustration. "Do you mind, D-bag?"

"You've been such a pleasure to be around for the past six months, Ang. I'm *so* glad to have you back," Daniel says sweetly.

We're at a small cafe in the Park on a Friday afternoon. I've been coming here almost every day. I don't know if I can confidently say I've moved back to Antium, but I've been here for half a year already, and I'm not sure whether I'll ever return to Cebrene. I like it here, it's calm.

I always sit at the same two-person table, right against the window, overlooking the main path that's surrounded by large American Elm trees. I've been writing. Not necessarily a novel, but my story, my thoughts, my memories. You could call it a memoir of some sort. I don't want to publish it, but my therapist says journaling can help. You know, to remember everything I've been through so I can work through it. I'm getting better and my memories are getting clearer, but I'm still in a state of avoidance. I'm not scared to face the demons inside me, but I'm terrified to face the ones who live *outside*.

I haven't spoken to my *baba* since running away. It's kind of giving me *déjà vu*. But the day will come, and I will be ready.

Evander has been a constant shadow, reminiscent of the time he used to stalk me. The only difference is that this time, I know he's the one in the darkness. For the first two months, he left me alone. I never saw him, he didn't make his presence clear, and we never interacted. But something shifted and he began to make *appearances*. I'd catch glimpses of him outside of my apartment, the coffee shop, the gym. We still haven't spoken, though. It kills me inside, but I know it's for the best. I still love him. I don't think I'll ever stop. He's the blood that runs in my veins, my lifeline.

I look over to Danny, who has now taken the second chair at my table. "You wouldn't be here if you weren't happy I was around," I state with confidence, and he scoffs.

"Whatever. Still writing that autobiography of yours?" he asks.

I roll my eyes. "Yes."

My friends have been supportive of my project. Even Aria and Gianis are involved. They're the only two people from home that I've been in contact with. We've had many discussions about our childhood, but there's still a lot to unpack.

"Good," he responds, sounding sincere, and we grin at each other.

Daniel pulls out a book from his bag and reads next to me while I type away.

Hours later, we decide to leave. My stomach has been growling for the past hour. Daniel wants to head home, but I need to grab food first. "I'll meet you at your place," I shout as he crosses the street to catch the train. He gives me a salute before disappearing in the station.

I walk down the secluded path in Hasting Park. It's not dark yet, but the immense trees with full leaves obstruct the little sun left. It's a bit windy, so I close my sweater and hug myself to warm up. Not many people use this trail, but I've come here enough times to know it ends at the corner of Duylumus and Fortify Street, where my favorite taco shop is located. Just the thought of food makes my stomach clench. I haven't eaten since this morning.

As I walk, I sense a presence behind me. My initial response is to freeze, but if anyone is following me, I wouldn't want them to think I'm scared. *Fear is nothing but a state of mind*, I repeat internally. I take a quick breath in and force myself to keep going and not turn around. I slightly increase the speed of my steps. I can see the streetlight at the end of the path from where I stand.

But the feeling of being followed persists. I glance around using my peripherals, but there's no one in sight. I want to grab my phone, but looking down is the worst thing I could do right now.

My mind begins to reel. What if someone is out to kidnap me like last time? Could Hendrick have heard I was back in town? I wonder if he's still trying to get to my father. It wouldn't be smart to take me a second time, but mobsters are unpredictable.

I reach into my pocket, anyway, and quickly pull out my phone. It's 6:56 p.m. The sun is setting by the minute. Soon, it will be dark. I should hurry and get out of the park, but instead, I decide to mess with whoever is following me and make a sharp turn into the trees. It's definitely not smart of me to derail from the path, but I need to do *something*.

I hear footsteps getting louder and my heartbeat increases tenfold.

I turn around and back into a tree. I sling my backpack forward, pull out my glock and cock it, pointing it in front of me. I've started carrying a handgun instead of a knife. "Whoever you are, it's best if you leave me alone," I try to say in a steady voice. My mind goes to Evan; I wish he were here. I'm not sure to what extent he's been keeping an eye on me, but now would be a good time to show himself.

No one responds to my threat, and I no longer hear any footfalls. I let out a sigh of relief. Maybe I scared the person away by taking out my gun. *Or maybe no one is actually following you and you've become too paranoid.*

As I'm about to put the weapon in the waistband of my pants, someone puts their arm around my neck from the back and pins me to the tree. My breath gets stolen and I choke. I attempt to aim my gun behind me, but it gets snatched out of my grip. "Leave me alone. When I get out of this hold, I'm going to kill you," I croak. I'm angry. I'm tired of people trying to hurt me. Haven't I suffered enough?

"Not if I kill you first," the stranger responds and my body immediately reacts to the voice.

A man appears from behind the tree. He's wearing a black balaclava, but there's no mistaking those hazel eyes. They pierce through my soul, just as they've done many times before. I start shaking. In fear? Anticipation? I'm confused, but my heart rate continues to increase, my chest visibly expanding with every shallow breath.

He pulls a rope out from his pocket and ties it around me and the tree. Then, he takes the rest and ties my wrists together. I'm now fully bound to the trunk, and I can't move. I squirm against the restraint, but I know it won't do anything except hurt me. My wrists will be the last to feel pain, though. The skin there is used to friction.

My assailant rips my sweater open and shoves my shirt down from the collar, exposing my breasts to the cool air, and my nipples harden right away. He grunts loudly and slaps them both, eliciting a moan out of me. I can't help it. He always knows how to bring out these reactions from me.

He pinches each pebbled bud between his fingers and twists them lightly. I hiss.

"Fuck. These tits are fucking beautiful," his low voice rasps out as he lowers his mouth to my right breast. He captures my nipple between his teeth and pulls. A pool of wetness gathers between my legs. I wiggle a bit more against the rope. I'm starting to get uncomfortable now.

"You're not going anywhere, Angelica," he whispers against my ear and goosebumps erupt all over my body.

"Open your legs," he commands, but I don't listen. I never do at first.

He takes my gun from his waistband and points it at my chest. Small whimpers escape my mouth. I never know what he'll do when he visits me.

He puts his foot between mine and shoves my legs apart, keeping his eyes on me. His pupils are dilated.

"Always disobeying me. We'll see how much longer you'll last," he taunts.

He moves the gun up my neck, throat, and chin, letting it trail against my skin. He reaches my lips. "Part them." I open my mouth.

He pulls the gun away from my face slightly. "Lick it," he orders. My lips are trembling, but I obey and let my tongue slide across the metal of the weapon. It tastes bitter and cold. I want to spit out the nasty flavor. My face twists in disgust, but I don't stop until he tells me to.

When I least expect it, he shoves the glock in my mouth and my eyes automatically swell with tears.

"Now, now, kitten. Don't cry. I'm going to make you feel good," he promises. He always does, but to get to that point, he always has to break me first. I'm starting to crumble already. I sniff and try to stop the sobs from coming out, but I can't. Saliva trickles down my chin, and my nose starts to run. I'm a mess and he loves it. He shoves the firearm in and out of my mouth a few times, and I squeeze my eyes shut. The gun is cocked, so he could easily pull the trigger and end my life.

When he's satisfied, he jerks the handgun away and drops my pants below my hips, exposing my thong. "Always so wet and ready for me," he growls. "No matter what I take, you always give. Even if not willingly, you always end up folding in the end, my angel," he says.

He pushes my underwear aside and I widen my stance. *I'm sick.*

I don't look down. I won't. I know what he's about to do and I can't stop it.

I feel the cold metal against my folds for a second, but it's replaced by his fingers. He shoves two digits up my entrance and starts beckoning, my knees buckle, and I moan. After a couple minutes, he removes his hand and rubs my wetness all over my clit as he circles it with his thumb.

He brings it to my mouth. "Suck on my finger. If you need to bite down, do it. Understood?" He instructs and I nod. I'm still crying but he doesn't care. This is part of the fun for him.

I feel the cold metal again, but this time, it's pushed against my opening, and I let out a sob around his thumb. I slowly bite down on it while he works the gun up my entrance.

"Good fucking girl," he praises as I take what he's giving me. I'm soaking wet, I always am. He's the only one who brings out this side of me, and as much as I don't understand this carnal urge, it makes sense for us.

He fucks me with the cocked gun until I'm a withering mess and my orgasm rips through me like a volcano. He removes his thumb out of my mouth and it's riddled with bite marks and some blood. He uses the same finger to wipe the tears off my face, leaving streaks of crimson on my cheeks. When he finally pulls the glock out of me, he gets down on his knees and eats me out like a starved man. He runs laps around my clit with his tongue, grunting in satisfaction every time I make a sound of pleasure. He places his mouth around my center and sucks on my clit until I come again, this time even more violently, as if the first one only aided and abetted the second.

He lifts himself off the ground. "You did so good, *moró mou*," he says gently. He always gets soft at the end of these encounters. He caresses my face and I nestle my cheek into his palm.

He undoes the knots and releases me from the tree. My body slumps forward, but he catches me.

He holds me until I'm able to catch my breath. We've never

done anything this intense before. Usually, he sneaks into my room, follows me into the gym changing room, or corners me in the underground parking lot of my building.

He takes his mask off, and I look Evan in the eyes. He stares at me a moment longer before kissing me tenderly. I kiss him back.

We haven't had an actual conversation in six months. These are the only interactions we've had.

"Go," he says, and I gather myself to leave. I step back out on the path and look back. Evan watches me. I continue the walk until I reach Duylumus Street. I'm suddenly not hungry anymore, but I'll order the tacos, anyway. People pass me on the street, and I feel dirty. No one knows I've just been fucked by a loaded gun. The worst part is that I liked it.

Evander is one of the demons I'm not ready to face. We both know it.

But he'll take anything he can get.

And I'll give him anything I can.

Author's Note

To read the continuation of Evander and Angelica's story, stay tuned for part two of *The Diávolos*. Book two in the *Godfathers of the Night* series will hopefully be out later this year.

More suspense, dirty secrets, and kinkiness to come...

Acknowledgements

I don't even know where to start. I feel like I'm accepting an award and haven't prepared a speech!

This book is a labor of love. My interest in reading started long ago, when I'd created my own book club for like-minded friends who enjoyed reading, too. It didn't last very long, but it was impactful enough to make me want to write. Many years later, I found my love for reading again, and my will to write came along shortly after. Then, *The Diávolos* was born. However, it wasn't called that at first. It was something like "Eyes on me" or "Give me your Eyes." Thank god I changed the title, LOL! I've worked so hard on this story, and I hope my perseverance and dedication shone through. Writing a book is hard as shit! I did it, and I'm proud, but I couldn't have succeeded without an army of people around me.

To my Alpha readers and real-life besties, Amanda and Nikki, thank you. You both were my starting point, when this story was merely a thought. I had to show you both how much you meant to me by writing you into the book. I hope I did you both justice! Amanda, *ma jolie amie*, thank you for your countless Google searches for Greek names! If it weren't for you, Evander, Angelica, and every other character in the book would be nameless, haha! You did so much more than that, though, and I'm forever grateful. I'm so happy we got closer throughout this journey. Nikki, *bb*, my bestest friend, I would've quit a long time ago if you weren't there to call me out on my bullshit. You are my rock! You took my ideas and ran with them, always making things better and spicier! You are the best hype woman anyone could ever ask for, and I thank god for putting you in my path a year ago. Special S/O to Chris for tolerating our nonsense. I can't wait to sit on your couch, pants-less, on top of a nice, fuzzy blanket, eating sandwiches. See you soon!

To my Beta readers, Dani, Sarah, and Andrea. Thank you, thank you, thank you. You made me see things I hadn't noticed, add important details that were missing, and weren't afraid to let me know when shit just didn't make sense, LOL! I was so nervous having people read my work for the first time, but you all made me feel so comfortable. Andrea, thank you for sending me all your reactions. Girl, if there's anyone who knows how to make me feel good about my story, it's you! I still have the image you created of yourself and Evan as Tom Holland and Zendaya. Sarah, your 'no bullshit' approach was exactly what I needed. You elevated my story with your amazing insight, and I'll be forever grateful that you accepted to read my book. I'll send you the biggest monster peen ever as a reward! Danielle, *ma chérie*, you are the best of both worlds. You were a hardass, but knew how to soften the blows, haha! Our 'friendship+' means the world to me! This was the beginning of our come-up and the start of our co-writing journey together. This means forever!

To my wonderful friend and editor, Jennifer. M'love, what would I have done without you? You are dedicated, talented, and a genius! Thank you for putting so much energy into this story and taking all the time to perfect it. You took *The Diávolos*, turned it upside down, and made it a thousand times better. I owe the success of this book to you! I trust you wholeheartedly, and I can't wait to keep working together on my future projects AKA creep on each other in the doc *wink wink.*

Stevi, your proofreading eye is like no other! I'm so happy to have met you and so blessed to have had the opportunity to work with you on my book. You are so kind and such a pleasure! I can't wait to keep working with you in the future.

An honorable mention to my designer and formatter, Melissa. You took my vision for my cover and nailed it! Thank you so much. I already know the cover for book two is going to be amazing. And Katya, you marketing whiz! I truly appreciate your help and I'm thankful for you. You're good at what you do and you're a great friend, too!

Bookstagram. Oh, booksta...you changed my life. I met some of my bestest friends because of you and a handful of amazing people who will hopefully always be a part of my life. Jessica, Shantelle, Amanda, Jasmine, Cierra, Liz, Jackie, Max, Yasmine, Brooke. These are only a few. If I didn't mention you, don't hate me! I have the memory of a goldfish. Just know that if you've supported me, I will never take it for granted! Thank you!

To my hubby, thank you for putting up with my 382,733 ventures throughout the years. You've always supported me and never doubted me for a second, regardless of how big or small my ideas were. I finally found my calling, and I'm so grateful to have you by my side. You've always told me, "You miss 100% of the shots you don't take." Look, I did it!!! You countlessly offered to help me, even though I always said no. Turns out, you're not that useless after all, LOL! *Hebak toz.*

To my family and friends who have supported me throughout this journey, thank you! I appreciate you.

To everyone who will give me a chance and read my stories, thank you! I hope I make you all proud.

Printed in Great Britain
by Amazon